I0586719

LOVE IS A BEACH

# DARCY
# COMES
# FIRST
# FOR A CHANGE

*Lilliana*
ANDERSON

INTERNATIONALLY BESTSELLING AUSTRALIAN AUTHOR

# DARCY COMES FIRST (FOR A CHANGE)

LOVE IS A BEACH

LILLIANA ANDERSON

Ebook & Print Edition

Copyright © 2019 by Lilliana Anderson

All rights reserved.

No part of this book may be reproduced in any form or by any electronic or mechanical means, including information storage and retrieval systems, without written permission from the author, except for the use of brief quotations in a book review.

Cover design by *Ember Designs*

Editing by *Making Manuscripts*

 Created with Vellum

*To Lochie, my real life Archer.*

# FOREWORD

Darcy and Leo's story started from a tiny idea I had many years ago where a newly single mother met her new man via her son tackling him to the ground. That tiny sliver of information stayed in my ideas folder until it grew into something more tangible thanks to the many stories my mother-in-law would tell me about her beachside lifestyle and the characters she met along the way.

Nana was born out of those stories, just as Archer was born from my own eight-year-old son (I actually recorded our conversations to get Archer's voice right.) So there's a lot of reality in these pages. I think there's a slice of my reality in every book I write. I tend to mix it all in with the crazy, fun, emotional fiction that you're coming to expect from me. And I hope this one is funnier than most.

I laughed *a lot* in this book.

It also took me longer to write because it's almost twice as long as my regular books are. But it doesn't *feel* like a long book. It's an easy read that will have you reflecting on your own life, or that of someone you know, with the knowledge that everything gets better, and there's joy everywhere you look. You just have to choose to see it.

Anyway, I'll quit rambling there and let you read. I hope you finish this book with a massive smile on your face and happy tears in your eyes. And then I hope you force everyone you know to read it as well, because we all need a Nana, and a Leo in our lives.

DARCY

"It's great news for the Field family, Kevin. You're in remission." The doctor smiles brightly as Kevin's mouth falls open.

My hand flies to my mouth as I gasp, my entire body flooding with relief-filled endorphins. "Thank God!"

"Wow." Kevin shakes his head, shock evident on his pale face. Remission is the word we've been hoping for during the months of radiation therapy. Now it's here. The fight was worth it, and my husband will live. He'll live, and our children get to grow up with their dad healthy and alive. *Thank. God.*

Eight months we've fought this, with Kevin undergoing treatment for testicular cancer while I tried to hold everything together on the home front, maintaining normalcy as much as I could. We haven't told a soul about his diagnosis—not even our kids—preferring to fight this quietly for the sake of everyone's sanity. Kevin hadn't wanted anyone treating him differently, and we'd both agreed that worrying the kids was unnecessary. The knowledge would have sent our teenage daughter into a hormonal woe-filled tailspin, and our eight-year-old would have wanted to film the entire process for his YouTube channel as a 'Try Not to Cry' video. Let's not go into the drama either of our parents would have caused. No. It was best we kept this to ourselves, especially since Kevin is cured now and everything will be OK.

*We're going to be OK.*

This may be the understatement of the year, but I don't think I realised what toll this process has taken on me personally. I've been so busy making sure Kevin was comfortable and the kids were looked after that I haven't stopped and thought about myself—how frayed my nerves have become, how tired and tense my body is. Suddenly, I can breathe again, the weight I've carried on my shoulders is finally gone. *I have my husband back. I'm not fighting alone anymore.*

Tears fill my eyes as I reach across the ruler width of space between our chairs and touch Kevin's arm. "Remission," I whisper, smiling so hard it hurts my cheeks.

Kevin blinks. "Wow."

AS WE LEAVE THE HOSPITAL, excitement bubbles out of my chest in the form of words, detailing the ways we should celebrate.

"Champagne," I say, looping my arm through his. "And not the sparkling wine kind, *real* champagne from France. And dinner. Actually, anything you want, just name it. We'll get Mum to keep the kids and make a night of it because, *remission*, Kev. Can you *believe* it?"

"I want a divorce, Darcy."

"What?" The words hit me like Miley Cyrus swinging in on her wrecking ball. Boom, right in the chest. We stop walking and face each other.

"I..." He looks at the concrete floor in the parking garage like the words he needs are written down there. I look too. Nothing but our feet and years' worth of dirt and scuff marks. He meets my eyes again. His faded blue ones look pained, his dark unruly brows arching down. "Dar." He takes my hand. "You had to know this was coming."

I snatch my hand back. "No." I say it so loud that it echoes. "I didn't know that at all." *I can't breathe.* "Why?"

"Because I almost died. Now I want to live."

"What the hell have we been doing these last twenty years? Spinning in circles?"

"Dar." He looks at me in that horrible pitiful way that only those knowingly breaking your heart can accomplish. "We got married so young—"

"So what? We have children, Kevin. A *life*!" Hysteria coats my words. I'm not sure if I'm going to laugh, scream or cry, but something is coming. I can't stand here and be understanding when my husband—the man I've spent twenty years of my life with, the man I just nursed through eight months of cancer treatment—tells me that he doesn't want me anymore.

"I know this sounds selfish. But I feel like I've been waiting all this time for my life to start. It's always, 'wait until the house is paid off,' 'wait until the kids have grown up,' 'wait until you get that next promotion,' or 'until you retire.'"

"I can't believe this," I mutter, my eyes wide.

"I don't want to wait until I'm retired. I want to live now, experience a different life *now*."

"So, let's experience the world together. You know, we could pull the kids from school and travel anywhere in the world if that's what you want. Sell everything and just go. We could do that. You don't have to leave us to change your life."

He gets that pitying look on his face again.

My stomach recoils. *Oh...oh dear...* "Unless..." I take a step back, choosing my words carefully. "It's not the world you want to experience, is it?"

He shakes his head.

"I see. It's other women?"

"Dar." He reaches for me but I dodge him.

"No. Don't 'Dar' me. We have a life, Kevin. A *good* life. And you're throwing it all away because cancer made you realise you didn't fuck enough in your youth?" I rake my hands through my hair then start to laugh. It's a mad laugh, one of those laughs that doesn't belong in the situation. But it's all so ridiculous. Too ridiculous. *Is this even real?*

Just to make sure, I pinch myself on the arm. "Ow."

"Did you just pinch yourself?"

I'm not laughing anymore. Tears fill my eyes as I stand across from my husband and realise I don't actually know him anymore. Twenty years, two children, a home, friends. Does he really not want what we built together?

Or is it...just me he doesn't want? Surely he'd never walk away from his kids. *How long has he felt this way?*

"Well," I say, blowing out my breath, trying to calm down so I'm not a public crying mess. I want to argue with him, to fight for us, because I have no idea where this came from. No inkling he wanted to leave. If he'd said something sooner, we could have worked through this...this...whatever it is. But if there is one thing I've learnt from the twenty years I've spent by this man's side, it's that there's no changing his mind. Once he's decided something, that's it for him. Standing before me, he's chosen to leave. He's chosen to leave our marriage, our home. *Forever.* "I guess we need to apply for this...divorce of yours then."

He presses his brow together, ever so slightly. "I still love you, Dar. I just...we want different things."

Pressing my lips together, I give him the fakest, bravest smile I have in my arsenal. "Yeah, I'm getting that." I wipe my hands over my face and swallow my raging emotions so deep I'll probably get an ulcer. "Let's just...go home, I guess. We need to figure out what—*how* —to tell the kids."

He scrapes his teeth over his bottom lip as he stuffs his hands in his pockets. "About that..."

## TWO

DARCY

"Breathe."

The paper bag is so loud, I can barely hear my sister's encouraging words. Well, encouraging is probably the wrong word to use. *Instructional* might be better, because she's basically making sure I don't die from lack of oxygen.

Kevin did not return from the hospital with me. He didn't come home to pack his things or say goodbye to his children. Seems he's been planning his escape from what I've always considered a happy marriage for quite some time. He didn't want anything from his 'old life', said he wanted to 'start fresh' with someone new. *That* was the precise moment I started screeching out a string of expletives that probably sounded like a train whistle. He shrugged, said he really was sorry and walked away, leaving me to deal with the fallout of his...his...monumentally cowardly escape from reality. That's the best way I can think to describe what just went down.

"I...don't...know...what...to...doooo," I whine between

my gasping pants. The words are muffled inside the bag, but somehow, Jo hears me and lifts the hand she's using to rub my back to push my blonde hair out of my eyes.

"Fuck him," she says as she secures it behind my ear. "Let him go. If he can't see what an amazing woman you are, what an amazing wife and mother you've been all these years, then he can go and get fucked by a donkey." Jo is tougher than me. When we were kids, and the neighbourhood kids teased us over our father's drunken singing (he was terrible and hiccupped half the words) I'd get upset and burst into tears, but she'd give them an earful before threatening to knock their teeth down their throat. It didn't take long before they learned that you didn't mess with a Sullivan and get away with it.

"A donkey?" I sniffle, lowering the paper bag.

"Yeah, 'cause then he'll really be a donkey's arse."

I can't help but laugh at that one. My sister is always excellent in a crisis.

"You, Darcy, are better than anything Kevin has ever offered you. You know that, right?" She's also never really liked my husband. Possibly because she's always been my first call whenever things go wrong between us. Every big fight, every frustrated moment was heard by my sister's understanding ear. She's always felt that Kevin wasn't good enough for me, called him lazy, selfish and controlling on more than one occasion. She absolutely hated that Kevin never let me work, even after Archer went to school. He said that the kids needed me home. While he always made sure I had enough of an allowance to pay for the things I needed and was fine with me running an Etsy store for 'pocket money', Jo still felt I needed physical and financial freedom of my own. But that's just the tip of her iceberg of problems with Kevin. To her credit, she's always been candid in her advice despite her feelings. We don't have a lot of secrets, Jo and I. Which of course means she's also the only person I've told about Kevin's illness—I know, I know, I wasn't supposed to have told *anyone*. But she's my sister and I tell her *everything*. I needed *someone* to vent to, and I knew the information would never go any further.

Jo peers into my eyes with her identical blues, her mouth set in a straight line. "You are going to be *fine,* Darcy Sullivan. Do you hear me?"

"It's still Field. I'm not divorced yet."

She shrugs. "You'll always be a Sullivan to me."

As I calm slightly, I catch the time changing to two o'clock on the microwave clock. "Oh God, what am I going to say to the kids?" They're still at school and I need to get my story straight before three o'clock rolls around.

"Just tell them the truth."

"The truth?" I have to close my eyes and force myself to swallow the lump in my throat. "It will break them."

"It won't. They're tougher than you think."

The truth. I can do that.

"A HOLIDAY?" Archer's eyes go wide as he spoons Coco Pops into his mouth.

"Yes. I thought we might go to the beach, visit your great-grandmother. She has a lovely place right across from the water in Bayside." I think when Jo said 'truth' my mind heard 'deflect'. It's my tried and true way of dealing. Run away and pretend nothing is happening. It's like the cancer diagnosis all over again: if I just keep acting normal, maybe nobody will notice that everything has changed...

"The *beach*." Somehow his bright blue eyes get even bigger. "First it's breakfast for dinner and now we get to go to the *beach*." In the eyes of an eight-year-old, it's like a second Christmas. "Hell yes."

"Language, young man," I admonish, although I'm smiling too. His enthusiasm is infectious, and I feel a stab in my heart as I wonder how Kevin could leave this without so much as a goodbye. Archer is such a funny, happy-go-lucky kid. All he needs is love and a little attention and he's golden. I can't recall the amount of times I've spotted him trying to learn about paintball and computers just so he'd have something to talk to his father about. He was so *good*. And I can't wrap my head around the desire to walk away from that. "We can pack our bags and leave right away if you like."

"Yes," he yells, shoving his chair backwards and rushing for his bedroom. "I'm only packing bathers."

"And underwear. You need underwear." I smile and place a single Cornflake on my tongue, crunching the slightly sweet morsel as I meet Abigail's assessing eyes. Abigail. I feel that Kevin's leaving is going to hurt her the most. At fourteen, she's old enough to have noticed that something has been going on of late. She's her father's daughter, the child he got along with the most. I've often found them sitting at the table, long after dinner chatting about her friends at school. To her, learning he's gone is going to be the moment she loses her trust in men. As that stabbing sensation fills my heart once more, I know I want to delay that moment as long as possible.

Maybe it's selfish of me. I don't know. But as much as I know I should just tell my children that Kevin got sick, got better then left, I can't bring myself to say those words. So, I'm trying to do something fun instead. And getting out of this house—this giant box of memories—is the most fun thing I can think of right now. And we need fun. Some good memories to fill in the space between now and the reality of our situation, before I'm forced to hurt them with the ugly truth.

"What's *really* going on?" Abby asks, one heavily lined eye narrowing as she tries to read my thoughts.

As mist coats my eyes, I start clearing the table so I don't have to make eye contact while I lie. "Nothing is going on, sweetheart. Your father got called away last-minute for this work thing"—I told them he was at an IT conference in Vegas—"and I thought it'd be fun for us to do something last-minute too."

That eye gets even smaller. "What about school?"

I tuck boxes of cereal under my arm as I balance bowls and milk in both my hands. "You can take a couple of weeks off. It's year nine. Nothing you can't easily catch up on." I shoot her a bright smile, keeping my voice breezy as I drop absolutely everything into the sink. "It'll be fun."

She looks between me and the sink where the milk bottle has lost its lid and white liquid is glugging out, coating cardboard. "Something isn't right with you."

"Everything is perfect," I say, my tone a touch too high as I keep that smile plastered on my face. I move closer to her and place my hands on her shoulders, guiding her out of the kitchen towards the stairs. "Just go and pack. We haven't seen Nana in years. This'll be an adventure."

"I have a maths test."

"I'll write you a note."

"And an English CAT."

"Abby, please. Just go with me on this." I plead with my eyes, hoping she'll drop it.

She rolls her eyes. "Fine. But if I have to repeat year nine because you've had some weird mental breakdown, I'm getting emancipated."

"Sounds amazing," I say with a smile as I give her a gentle push towards her room. All I can do is smile and pretend. I can't face reality. "Be ready in twenty minutes."

## THREE

## DARCY

"There aren't any lights on," Abigail points out as I trip up a step on the way to my grandmother's ground-floor apartment. I feel like a teenager again, sneaking up here at night with Jo, whispering and giggling because we'd been drinking cheap beer with boys while sitting on the rocky groynes. I can hear the crashing of waves on those rocks, the power of the ocean telling me everything is going to be OK. I close my eyes and take a deep breath. *This feels like I'm coming home.*

"It's OK," I say in a whisper, reaching out for Archer's hand, helping him onto the wooden deck.

"Does she even know we're coming?" Abby asks, standing at the open gate but not venturing any farther inside. She hasn't been here since she was Archer's age, so it's understandable she feels like a trespasser. And Archer wouldn't remember this place at all, he was a toddler during that last visit. It's been so long since I've smelled this air and anticipated the exceptional company that is my grandmother. Too long. And at the end of the day, that's my fault. Kevin never liked Nana and her quirky outspoken ways, so somewhere along the way, I stopped fighting for my right to visit her and settled for phone calls and letters instead, coupled with the occasional hug and conversation at an extended family gathering. Even that communication has been few and far between. I haven't been a good granddaughter at all.

"I have an open invitation," I whisper back. Which is true. Every time I've spoken to or seen Nana she's said, "Come and stay with me. Any time you want. My door is always open." As much as I know I should have called before driving three hours in the dark, I didn't have the mental capacity to explain the reason why. Showing up unannounced at ten o'clock at night, bags in hand, means she'll take us in now and ask questions later. I need a quiet moment to breathe, to work out what the hell I'm supposed to do next. *"You'll figure something out, Dar. You always do."* Those were the words Kevin used when I asked the same question of him earlier today. I'll figure something out. Ugh. *Dump it all on Darcy; she'll sort it out and I'll get off scot-free like the manchild I've always been.* Bastard. He obviously doesn't give a shit about the predicament he's put me in. But that is typical Kevin—he's always thought of himself first. It is the one thing I've always hated about his personality, how whatever he wanted was so much more important than everything and everyone else. There were some days when I wished I had that Moving Pictures song, *What About Me* on a recorder so I could press play instead of arguing with him. I mean, once he decided that he wanted to go to a paintball tournament that took place at the same time as his daughter's birthday. Her thirteenth. Who does that kind of thing? And still, she thought he walked on water. Man, I was *livid* that day.

Frowning slightly, I force my mind back to the matter at hand, ushering both children up onto the decking so I can close Nana's gate and get us inside.

God, it's so easy to focus on the shittiest parts of a person when you're angry at them. And after twenty years of marriage, there are plenty of times he's been a less-than-stellar human being. But, he was my human being, and despite his faults, I had still loved him through it all. I guess the hard realisation in this moment, is that he obviously didn't love me. Not enough to stay, anyway.

"Is there a doorbell?" Archer asks when I don't move again. He drops my hand and walks up to the large glass sliding door, pressing his face against it.

"At the front door there is," I reply, clearing my thoughts once again. "This one is kind of like the back door at our place."

"Does she leave it open like we do?" He grips the handles and pulls them apart with a dramatic flick of his arms. They slide open effortlessly, almost silently.

"I guess she does." I return his infectious smile and pull the billowy curtains to the side so we can all step through. Abby still hasn't moved. "It's fine," I assure her. "Nana is always asking me to bring you here for a holiday. She'll be ecstatic to see us. I promise."

With her patent-pending teenage eye-roll, she clomps across the deck, muttering something about breaking and entering and police sirens. I smile because my fourteen-year-old daughter is so straight-laced I often wonder how she's mine. But then I remember how straight-laced I've become in recent years. I used to be carefree and ready for mischief. But I let that fall away and replaced it with responsibility and organisation. You know, I could probably write a step-by-step guide on leaving behind your misspent youth to become the textbook version of the perfect wife. Sure, my current abandoned status could affect sales numbers, but it could be worth a shot. After all, I'm going to need some sort of income now. I can't imagine it's going to be easy getting child support after the way Kevin left, and I don't want to rely on him, anyway. I'm too angry to need him for anything.

In the silent darkness of the living room, both Archer and Abby stand unmoving, bags in hand, waiting for me to tell them what to do next.

"You know she's going to wake up in the morning and have a heart attack when she finds us here," Abby says in a harsh whisper while I close the sliding door.

"You are so dramatic. Wait here. Sit on the couch or something, I'll go and wake her to let her know we're here. No heart attacks needed."

"She's old, Mum. Be gentle."

It's my turn to roll my eyes. Nana, known as Esme Aubrey Sullivan to her friends, is the most active eighty-three-year-old on the face of the planet. Her entire life has been one big adventurous celebration. Her only son—my father—was exactly the same, except his gregariousness had been channelled into a life of excess, which became his downfall when complications from Type 2 diabetes took his life at fifty-two. Nana, on the opposite end of the scale, is healthy as a horse. A hippy at heart, she was a vegan before it became popular with the Facebook spruikers of today. A nuclear bomb could go off and Nana would survive, claiming her crystals and daily echinacea tea was the reason behind it. She's something, my nana. And I love her dearly—even though my mother did her best to discredit her by calling her a 'kook' and a 'crackpot' while we were growing up, I always thought she was fabulous.

Turning for the short hallway that leads to the bedrooms, I freeze and catch my breath as a rather sleepy-looking man comes sauntering out, giving his nether region a bit of a scratch—his *naked, rather wrinkly, nether region.*

*Crap.*

Throwing a look over my shoulder to where my children are supposed to be sitting, I find them standing with wide-eyed looks as the older gentleman staggers to the refrigerator and opens the door, filling the room with enough light to clearly highlight his, er...

"Look at his saggy old man balls," Archer yells, just as Abby starts screaming hysterically.

*Oh God.*

Everything goes a bit crazy—well, *crazier*—from here.

Freaked out, the man stands so fast I actually hear the moment his back cricks. Then he clutches at it, howling in pain as he turns away from the fridge to grab for the bench, giving us an unfettered view of his old-man package as it swings from side to side, a stretched-out memory of his youth, hanging far closer to his knees than a dick and balls has the right to be. People go on and on about combatting saggy breasts with supportive bras, but

I'm thinking there needs to be a movement highlighting the need to secure one's balls. Gravity is not kind to those things, and for some reason, I can't stop staring as the whole package horrifyingly dangles and sways hypnotically. Abby's screams get louder, snapping me from my trance, and now she's also covering her eyes with her hands and whirling around, possessed. *Jesus.*

Archer, being the unflappable kid he is, pulls his iPhone from his pocket and holds it up. "Even his pubes are white," he yells, delighted. I'm pretty sure he's filming.

"Archer. Put that down," I command, marching over to him and snatching the phone from his grip. "Abigail, stop your screaming for heaven's sake. The neighbours will think you're being murdered."

"Good, my life *is over*," she argues, cupping a hand at the side of her face so she can look at me without seeing the naked groaning man. She'll be scarred for life after this. "I'll never be able to look at a penis now."

Well, there's an upside to everything. "Excellent. That will save your father and I a whole lot of worry," I say instinctively, a stutter hitting me in the chest as I realise that *I'm* the only one with that worry now. Kevin is gone. He left without saying goodbye or caring how upset and adrift we'd all become. It's just me and the kids, and—

The lights flick on. "What in heavens..." Nana appears amongst the fray, a flowing blue kimono wrapped around her strong and slender body, giving off the impression she's floating as she moves towards her injured friend and takes in the unfolding scene.

"I'm so sorry, Nana. I should have called," I start, suddenly feeling so out of line and so out of place. "I wasn't thinking." Actually, all I've been doing is thinking. But my thoughts are so random and frantic that I'm not even sure which way is up right now. Coming here was more of an instinct than a decision, because Nana has always been the person to whom I flee. The one person who never failed to catch me.

Nana waves my apology away. "Pish," she says. "The more the merrier, I always say. Although, George here might be thinking otherwise." She laughs, her eyes sparkling with mischief while she enquires over her friend's injury. Her amusement makes my nerves settle a little. This was the right call. Just being near her makes life feel better. Nana makes everything better. She always has.

"I'm OK," her friend—George—pants in his gruff voice. "Just got a fright is all."

"Why don't you go and put some pants on?" Nana suggests. "I'll be in soon."

He nods and toddles off, his left hand cupping his manhood as his right clutches at his back, his stark white butt cheeks wrinkling at the fold with each step. Archer giggles. He thinks this is the most entertaining night of his life.

"Is it safe to open my eyes now?" Abby asks.

Nana chuckles. "Yes, dear. The coast is clear. Although I'm not sure what all the commotion was about. It was just a naked body. We all have them, you know."

"Not like that," Archer yells, his volume seeming caught at only one level.

"Archer," I hiss while Nana smiles.

"Well, yes, yours is a little different to his, isn't it? Gravity gets us all in the end I'm afraid. But, as long as your bits still work no sense hiding them, right?"

"Oh my God," Abby groans, covering her face.

Suddenly, I'm smiling, and Nana is standing in front of me, holding out her arms. "I'm so happy you're finally here, my beautiful Darcy."

"Nana." I fall into her embrace, feeling small again as she gives me a tight squeeze that tells me she knows I'm hurting and that she's here no matter what. Despite my mother's dislike for her mother-in-law (an issue that only intensified in the years following Dad's and her divorce) my love for Nana is unending. In a family of high-achieving, logic-driven women, Nana has been the only one who I felt understood my 'outside of the box' thinking—something I never lost with all of my responsibilities. I could organise the crap out of a family schedule, but I'd create that schedule using a chalkboard on the ceiling so it was always within view without taking up too much space.

Looking back, I think I had the best of both worlds growing up. While my mother pushed routine and goal setting, Nana encouraged spontaneity and exploration. "Fly wherever the wind takes you," she used to say. She was fun and enchanting, and I swore I'd be exactly like her when I grew up. But then, I grew up, and somewhere along the way, my mother's lessons grabbed hold and didn't let go until I was just like everyone else. Well, on the outside, anyway.

## FOUR

"Want to talk about it?"

It's now closer to twelve. The children are asleep in the spare room, and Nana and I are out on the deck, looking at the moon-lit sea and drinking some sort of tea she says will give me clarity.

"Kevin and I went to the hospital today," I tell her, pressing my lips together because I don't want to cry. I'm too hurt to cry. "He's been battling cancer."

"Oh my." She places a hand against her chest.

"He's OK. He's in remission now—which is what we were at the hospital for. They told us today that his tests came back cancer free. Exciting, right?"

She nods, but she's not showing any further emotion. In true Nana style, she knows we haven't come to the punchline yet.

"I wanted to go out and celebrate." I wipe a hand across my nose, sniffing. "But Kevin, well, *he* suggested a divorce instead. Said we got married too young and he wants different *experiences*. Can you believe that? He survives cancer and the first thing he does is dump his wife and kids for some woman he met through a friend. Which friend, I don't know."

"He was cheating on you?"

I shake my head. "He says he didn't, that he was waiting for the right moment to tell me. But, I don't know." I touch my fingers to my forehead and rub back and forth. "I keep trying to piece all of this together, find clues, you know? But it's all a jumble up here. We had our troubles like all married couples do, but I didn't think...I just didn't expect *this*." It sounds like a cliché, I know. But I'm truly blindsided. Perhaps I shouldn't be— we were far from perfect people—but I did think we'd gotten to a stage in our relationship where we'd fought every fight there was to fight, that we'd gone through the worst and come through it as a stronger unit. I thought we'd grow old together.

"How did the children take it?"

I shift my gaze to meet hers, concerned and wise. "They don't know. They didn't even know about the cancer. I couldn't tell them. I don't want to explode their world."

She nods, understanding.

"I told them he's gone away for work, so we're taking a holiday of our own. I needed to get out of there. I know this is running away, but I'm so angry." I hold my hand out to show her the quiver of my fingers. "I couldn't stand to be anywhere near anything that reminds me of him."

"Well then, I think you came to the right place." She reaches out and takes my hand and holds it for a few moments. A warming comfort spreads up my arm and envelops my chest, allowing me to take a deep, sobering breath. "You'll find new strength here." She releases me then relaxes back into her chair, her body weight causing the wicker to creak in the quiet night.

"I just need some time. Time to wrap my head around this and figure out what I'm going to do next. I feel like I'm adrift and tumbling, and my chest, it hurts."

"Of course it does, my sweet, trusting girl. You take all the time you need. You and the kids are welcome here, and I'm so pleased you came."

"I'm sorry it isn't under better circumstances." My voice wobbles as my eyes fill with the tears I've been trying so hard to keep in. They spill out and race down my cheeks, falling from my jaw and splashing against my chest. When I wipe at them, the torrent is barely interrupted. I cover my face. "I'm sorry, Nana. I'm such a mess."

"Oh, pish." She wraps me in her warm embrace. "This is what family is for, dear girl. Let someone else take care of you for a change. You grieve, you cry, you scream. Do whatever it is you need to do to feel right again. I'll take care of everything else. Don't you worry about a single thing."

"Nana," I cry, hugging her back, clinging to her as I sob against her shoulder. She just said everything I needed to hear. Everything I needed to feel loved. In the midst of my turmoil, I know I made the right choice in coming here. *This* place is where I'll heal.

IT TAKES three days before I'm fit to leave the confines of the fold-out bed in Nana's craft room. We tell the kids I have the flu and they visit me sporadically, bringing with them soup and bread rolls. Archer regales me with stories about his adventures with Nana, and Abby asks if I'm sure it's just the flu. When I assure her I'll be fine, she expresses a desire to make some friends her own age, kids she's been seeing at the beach across the street. I tell her that's fine as long as we know where she is and when she leaves happy, I have a rare moment where I smile and consider myself ready to face the world.

But then I remember why we're here and the tears come again.

So. Many. Tears.

They seem unending until I wake up on that fourth morning to the smell of porridge and the sounds of laughter. Even Abby is laughing. Nana simply cannot be disliked. Suddenly life feels bearable again. The sun is still shining, life is continuing, and the tears are just... gone. Like my tear ducts have finally dried up and the cloudiness in my mind has cleared. No more time for self-pity. Kevin left. That's the cold-hard fact that I have to face, and lying in this bed isn't going to change that. It's time to accept my new reality of the abandoned wife—

*Blergh.* That sounds awful. I don't want to call myself that. How about I focus on the other side of this unfortunate coin and call myself a 'newly single mother' instead? It might soften the mental blow a little.

Although, *single?* I certainly don't feel comfortable with *that* adjective just yet. Maybe a newly *solo* parent. Yes. I think that works best. Darcy Field: Solo Parent;

Writer of lists; Keeper of schedules. Yes. That suits me. I'm going with that. The new me is born.

Pushing up from the bed, I wonder if the new me has had an altercation with a Mack truck. Everything aches and my face feels all puffy. When I shuffle into the bathroom, the new me looks back with craggy hair, red-rimmed eyes, and a chapped nose.

"You are one sexy list maker, Darcy Field," I tell myself, my voice all croaky and hoarse. Running the shower, I do all the things one is supposed to do when scrubbing away a three-day self-loathing binge. I wash and condition my hair, scrub my skin raw, shave my shavables, and brush my teeth. When I emerge, all warm and smooth-skinned, I wrap myself in a fluffy purple towel before the new me encounters her first problem.

"Er, Nana," I call out, talking through the cracked door.

She comes almost immediately. "Is everything all right, dear? Feeling better?"

"I am. But, ah, this is quite embarrassing actually: I seem to have forgotten my clothes."

She frowns. "Your clothes? Are they in the bedroom? No one will care if you walk from here to there in a towel, sweetheart."

"Ha, I wish that were the case. No. I mean, I don't have any clothes at all. I didn't pack any."

"Oh, dear. Well, just wait there and I'll get you something. Then if you like, you can join us in the kitchen for breakfast. I made porridge."

"Thank you, Nana. I'm starving actually." I haven't had real food since the day Kevin left.

She grins and touches the flat of her palm to my cheek. "I'm happy to see you up and about, my love."

"Thank you for letting me wallow, Nana," I whisper.

In response she smiles and nods. "I'll get you those clothes."

Once I'm dressed in a borrowed kimono, I head into the kitchen area, finding Nana helping Archer as he happily sprinkles dried fruit over his bowl of cooked oats. "Not too much, dear. It'll be too sweet."

"I like sweet," Archer replies, tongue poking out in concentration. Then he spots me and his face brightens. "Mummy!" He jumps up and runs towards me, colliding against me full force, holding me so tight that I miss him even though he's standing right here. I never want this level of affection to end, but it will. He'll grow up, and this age will be but a moment in my memory. Sigh. Childhood is too short.

As if on cue, Abby breezes past me without stopping. "Nice dress," she says, shooting me a smile over her shoulder as she takes a seat at the breakfast table. *Well, that's something I guess.* She already has a tan, and her hair is textured from the salty air. I feel like Rip Van Winkle waking up covered in vines. Life kept going without me, without Kevin. *Stand up and live, Darcy. Join in. You've already missed enough.*

Bending to kiss Archer on the top of his head, I take a breath and give myself a secret smile. *I'm going to get through this.* Day one of a new life begins with a cuddle and a family breakfast.

I take my seat at the table. "Well, this is nice, isn't it?" I say, inhaling the vanilla-scented oats as Nana places a bowl in front of me. It warms my heart seeing my kids warm so quickly to Nana. I feel like they've missed out on so much time with her, time I really cherished as a kid. I unintentionally robbed them of that by not pushing for more time here. I could have brought them here alone since Kevin didn't want to come along. I didn't try hard enough.

I'm glad they have the chance to get to know her better now, and I also vow to make visits to Nana's a regular thing in the future.

"There's no milk." Abby scowls and lets the porridge drip from her spoon, her mouth turned downwards.

"There's rice milk," Nana says with a smile.

"That's not milk. It's opaque water," Abby counters. What was I saying about how nice this moment was?

"Rice milk is still milk," I reply. "It works just fine." Reluctantly, she pours some in her bowl, looking like I'm making her eat fried crickets or something. But it's nice to see that while my own world seems shattered, theirs is still whole. That was the point in coming here.

Pushing away from the table, I pick up one of Nana's handmade ceramic mugs and carry it over to the kettle to make myself a cup of tea. "Want one?" I ask Nana. She shakes her head.

"No, thank you, dear."

"I didn't even know you could milk rice," Archer says, his face scrunched up in thought while he mixes the fruit and porridge. "Do they even have titties?"

"Archer," I gasp.

Of course, Nana just laughs it off and explains that rice milk is made by soaking grains of rice in water.

Archer is fascinated by the process, but disappointed there are no milking teats on a 'rice plant' (his term).

While they chat, I make my tea. There's an entire drawer dedicated to it, and I pick a simple Earl Grey blend, spooning it into a tea strainer before I drop it in my mug.

"You're so patient with him," I say as I sit at the table, my mug warming my hands.

Nana smiles and pushes the dried blueberries my way, obviously remembering they were my favourite as a child. "I'm old. All I have left is time."

"Well, I'm going to the beach," Abby announces, pushing her barely eaten breakfast away.

"Are you asking or telling me?" I give her my *stern mother* look as she sighs and drops a hip.

"Is it OK if I hang out at the beach today?"

"Of course. Just wear sunscreen and keep your phone with you."

With another sigh, she saunters off, her bare feet slapping on the white tiled floor as she heads for the bedroom she's sharing with Archer to change.

"It's a hard age," Nana says, her keen eyes taking in the exchange. "Caught between a kid and an adult. You know, she's been making friends with some other kids her age. They seem to get along quite well. And you can see them from the deck if you need to. Perhaps giving her at least the illusion of freedom could help."

"You don't think she should ask permission to go out?"

Nana shrugs. "Did you when you stayed here?"

I down the rest of my tea. "It was a different time then."

"I think you'll find that times haven't changed that much. People just talk about the crappy things more." She gives me a knowing look then picks up my empty mug and looks inside.

"Are the tea leaves telling you something?" I ask as she turns the mug around and studies them.

"I haven't the foggiest. I just like trying to make shapes out of them. Like clouds. See, that kind of looks like a lion doing ballet, don't you think?" She shows the mug to me and all I see is a dark mess, but Archer is on top of it, peering in and adding, "He's on roller skates."

I smile and eat my porridge, enjoying the moment. I honestly don't remember the last time I felt this *light*. The last eight months with Kevin's treatment were so full of anxiety and activity that I felt like I was constantly spinning plates, panicked one would fall. And as much as Kevin leaving was a dick move, I actually feel...better now. Sitting here watching my grandmother and my son giggle over tea leaves, it hits me that I don't have to worry about him anymore. That constant thought about what Kevin needed and what Kevin thought or felt is no longer required by me. I don't even have to *do* anything for him anymore. And I'll tell you this, that thought just made me feel a fuckload better. I still hate that he left, hate that he ran from his kids, but if that means I never have to wash another item of his clothing, never listen to him moan about the kids being too unruly, I'll take it.

I'll take it.

## FIVE

## DARCY

"I had a dream that this was all a dream. I hadn't come running here in the middle of the night the way I did, and Kevin didn't leave." Nana and I sit on a bench at the beach and watch Archer search for shells in the sand. "I was at home and everything was normal. Even the cancer was a dream. And I was angry because I was folding laundry and he was playing some game on his computer, chatting to someone on his headset like he couldn't see me working right beside him."

"Sounds like a nightmare to me. Didn't he do his share around the house?" Nana is using a Japanese paper fan to create her own breeze even though the ocean's wind keeps whipping at our hair and clothes.

"Not really. He always said that he made the money so I ran the house. He was a traditionalist."

She scoffs. "Last I heard, women had the right to vote and everything these days. No need to live like it's the fifties. Did you ever have time to play computer games?"

"With the kids' school and activities, the housework

and errands? No way. I was lucky if I had time to read a book a month."

"But Archer is at school now. Surely you had time to yourself during the day?"

"I'm on the school council and I help out with reading groups and the canteen at Archer's school. At Abby's school, I help run the uniform shop. Then there's weekend sports and errands. I'd have dry cleaning and post office visits...Kevin would only eat meat that was brought that day, same as bread. So, I shopped every day."

"Oh my. I didn't realise you were his personal assistant. Where was your time for you?"

I stopped for a moment. "I don't know. I took a little here and there. I like making and decorating journals. So I'd do that to relax, but I also sold them on Etsy because Kevin didn't like the clutter they created. I like to keep busy."

"And you were married for what? Twenty years? You could have murdered someone and been released in the same amount of time. And they give you time to read and laze about in prison."

"Oh God, Nana. It really wasn't that bad."

"Sounds like abject servitude to me. I divorced at least two of my husbands for less."

I shrug. "He *did* work a lot. And he mowed the lawns, took the rubbish out. Stuff like that."

"Well then, let's give him a medal, shall we? Two whole household duties. What a man." She flings her hands out dramatically.

I laugh. "I know things weren't perfect between us,

Nana. I mean, they were far from it. But I always thought things would be different when the children were older. I'd get the chance to work and Kevin could work a little less and we'd spend more time together, be a little more equal, you know?"

"Oh, sweet girl, men *never* change. You're adorable to think that, but from what I saw and heard over the years and with what you're telling me just now, he had you right where he wanted you—firmly under his thumb. Frankly, I think you're far better off without him. Kick your shackles off and be free."

I take a deep lungful of air then let it out in a whoosh. "If I'm honest, I do *feel* better without him. I mean, now that the shock of it has worn off and I'm analysing everything, I feel...lighter. Does that sound horrible?"

"No, darling. It sounds exactly right. I don't think you realised what an oppressive force that man was in your life."

I sigh. "You sound like Jo."

"We can't both be wrong."

"I don't think he was oppressive per se. He was just... ugh, needy. God, I'm making him sound horrible because I'm angry, but he wasn't always bad. I mean, he worked hard; late nights, intense conferences. It's why I could sell this trip to the kids so easily. He gets called away for conferences all the time. And I wasn't ignorant to his faults. I just wanted us to work, and I was willing to push aside all that petty fighting about housework and whatnot. We both came from broken families and we always swore to each other that we'd never split. I stood by that promise because as much as I didn't like him sometimes, I never hated him enough to separate him from his children. And now, look"—I lift a hand to indicate Archer —"our kids will grow up without a father, all because he couldn't keep a promise. I hate that he gave up on us, Nana. And I hate that there was zero warning. It's like our marriage was a balloon he grew tired of holding, so he stuck a pin in it, and now we're all..." I blow a raspberry, my tongue between my lips as I wave my arms around like an octopus.

Nana chuckles before growing serious again, thoughtful. "Did you ever wonder if maybe those business trips and late nights at work were signs of an affair?"

I suck in my breath because no, I hadn't thought that. I'd always trusted that he was as invested in our relationship, our family, as I was. Were there niggles of doubt occasionally? Of course. But I trusted him. He'd always said cheaters were cowards, so I trusted him to choose us always. What a fool I was.

When I go to speak, I have to clear my throat to keep my voice from wobbling. "I don't know what to think anymore, Nana. I'm quite lost to be honest. I'm in this strange limbo where I was married and suddenly I'm separated, and I'm trying to find a way to be OK with that. Thinking about Kevin cheating when he was always adamant he never would... It won't help me."

"Oh dear. I've upset you."

"No, Nana, you haven't. I just...I just want to focus on what's in front of me. The kids, a new direction. What ifs will just make me crazy."

Nodding sagely, she pats my hand. "You're definitely in a bit of a tailspin, but I think I know what you need. I'll take you to Betsy. Remember her? She's my oldest friend and the biggest busybody in town, knows everything about everyone. She says it's because she reads the cards, but I know she's just an eavesdropping gossip." I smile because I do remember Betsy. She and Nana have always been as thick as thieves. From memory, they met on the first day of school way back when and haven't been out of touch since.

"How's Betsy's gossip going to help me sort my life out?"

"It wont. She'll read your cards though."

"I thought you said she isn't any good at reading cards."

"I didn't say that. She's excellent. But she's also a gossip. Don't tell her anything you don't want her to know."

"Won't she see everything in the cards?"

"Pish. She just deals them. She doesn't know what they mean."

"I am so very confused right now."

"Of course you are. But the cards will give you focus so you can make decisions about your future. You'll see." She smiles and nods, scanning the length of the beach and taking in the array of characters littered along the sand, soaking up the sun, swimming in the sea. "Speaking of new focus." She folds her fan up and lifts her chin, indicating a figure running towards us along the shoreline: black shorts, shirt off, heartrate monitor strapped about his tanned chest. I don't give him much more than a cursory glance, but he does look somewhat familiar. I'm not sure why.

"Looks like he's really into his fitness."

"That's not the kind of focus I'm talking about, dear. You've been with the same man for twenty years and now you're free. Look at him properly. Surely your ovaries hurt just looking at him. A fine specimen of man if ever I saw one. Leo is his name. Used to play rugby for Australia, but he's retired now. Does radio and a bit of sports commentary on the telly during footy season and has some furniture business on the side. But don't let that bore you, the eye candy is supreme, wouldn't you say? At forty-five, the man certainly hasn't let himself go."

"Good-looking or not, I can't even think about men right now, Nana. I *just* broke up with Kevin." *Actually, I was just dumped by Kevin.*

"All the more reason. And you don't think in these situations, dear. You look. You *feel*. You know they say the best way to get over a person is to get under someone else. I don't know who came up with that pearl of wisdom, but they were right on the money with it. You have to clear away those sexual ghosts."

"Sexual ghosts?" I roll my eyes and focus on watching Archer sift sand through his fingers.

"The memory of the last time you had sex. If it's with a person who conjures up a bad memory, you need to clear that away with a good one. And don't you think a man with a body like that would be amazing in bed?"

"I don't know. Maybe he's always had it easy and never had to try?"

"No way. He moves too well, carries himself with pure confidence. There's no bravado there. Which you'd notice if you took a look by the way." She purses her lips in my direction.

"Fine, Nana, I'll look at your candy." With a reluctant sigh, I turn my attention to this Leo character and try to appreciate him for the 'specimen' Nana thinks he is. I don't need to look for long.

*Wow.*

Dark hair, slick from hard work. Glistening skin, tan and taut, stretched against the most perfect six-pack I've ever seen outside a magazine. He even has that V thing that makes my insides do a little flippy cartwheel that steals my breath and makes me go, "Oh."

"Exactly. Doesn't matter how old you get, a body like that doesn't go unnoticed." Nana lifts her hand like she's about to call him over.

"What are you doing?"

"I'm calling him over. A bit of a flirt is good for the soul, dear." She grins and calls out, "Yoo-hoo, Leo," while she flicks open her fan and flutters it at him like she's performing some Victorian era courtship ritual.

My eyes go wide in horror. I am so not OK with him coming over. He's too beautiful and I'm a mess. Looking at men from a distance is one thing but calling them over and engaging in conversation when I'm, *oh God*...when I'm *wearing one of Nana's kimonos.* Which wouldn't be a problem if Nana wasn't also wearing a kimono. *We're sitting here in matching outfits.* Kill me now.

And now he's running towards us. Great.

And he's smiling. Eyes moving from Nana to me. She's wearing a pink kimono, mine is blue. We look like the fairies in *Sleeping Beauty* fought over colouring us and neither of them won.

*And* now he's smiling even more.

Fantastic. He thinks I'm a joke.

"Hey, Esme," he says as he gets close, eyes meeting mine with an overly amused smile. "Hi. I don't think we've—"

"JOHN CENA!"

I see my son diving through the air but I don't realise what's going on until it's too late. "Archer, no."

*Oof.*

*Oh shit.* My hands cover my mouth as Leo goes flying sideways, taken out by a tackling eight-year-old practising his WWE moves.

"Da da der dah," Archer sings, holding his fists triumphantly in the air. I rush to where Leo is lying in the sand, gripping his knee and groaning.

"Are you OK?"

"My knee. I think I tore something." I help him sit while crouching beside him.

"Oh God. I'm so sorry. He's..." I try to search for the right word as I inspect Leo's sore knee. "Rambunctious." I glare at Archer who's suddenly looking very sheepish.

"I didn't mean to hurt him," Archer swears, his voice high, distressed. One harsh word and he's going to burst into tears.

Leo nods and waves a hand. "It's OK, kid. This knee's been playing up for years."

"It doesn't look dislocated or anything," I say, prodding it lightly and watching for his reaction. "But it is starting to swell."

"Can you stand, Leo?" Nana asks, taking Archer by the hand and holding him safely beside her. "Darcy here studied osteopathy at university. You can come to my apartment, ice that leg, and she can take a proper look at you."

"An osteo?" he asks, grunting as he lets me help him up. He has the most magnificent eyes. I'm not sure if they're green or light brown or both.

"It was the plan. But I didn't even get past the first year. Became a mum instead. But I can definitely ice it and help you strap it if needed."

"I'm game."

Helping him walk the short way across the street to Nana's apartment building, I settle him on one of the outdoor chairs then go inside for ice. Nana is walking back slowly with Archer by her side. They're talking and I'm wondering what's being said while I place the bag of ice on the table and shift another chair over to elevate Leo's leg.

"I'm Leo," he says, holding out his hand while I'm standing with his foot tucked under my arm, placing cushions beneath it.

"Oh, I'm sorry. We haven't properly met, have we?" I drop his foot. "I'm Darcy." He winces in pain as his foot slips past the cushions and bangs against the chair. "Oh no. I'm sorry, I'm so sorry." *Can this get any worse?* "I'm not normally this clumsy. Here." I pick up the bag of ice, my movement hasty as I try to recover. But instead of handing it to him, I toss it and he doesn't catch it. It sails past his long legs and lands on his lap, clocking him right in the cojones.

"Fuck." He groans and doubles over, jerking back again when his knee objects to the forward movement.

"Oh my God. Oh my God." I'm muttering and trying my best to somehow right a situation that just seems to be getting worse and worse. Then the tears come. I don't even want them but here they are anyway, leaking out of my eyes and making me look crazy and hormonal. "I'm sorry," I say sniffing. "I don't know what's wrong with me today."

"It's OK. I'll live." He's still kind of groaning through the pain as he meets my eyes and gives me a wan smile. I catch a note of sympathy there. And that just makes the eye leaking even worse.

"Bloody hell." I turn away and wipe at my eyes with the backs of my hands.

Leo wraps a large hand around my left wrist and looks up at me with concerned eyes. "Are you all right, Darcy?"

You know when you're upset, and someone—especially someone who has no real reason to be kind—asks you if you're OK then you say you're fine but you start crying just because you were asked? Well, that's what this is like. One hint that someone sees I'm struggling and I'm a blubbering mess.

"I..." I can't get any more than that out before my throat tightens up.

"How's the patient?" Nana sing-songs, pulling open the gate.

Leo gives my wrist a light squeeze before he releases me and turns his attention to Nana. "Nothing a restraining order can't fix." He looks at me and winks, offering me a half-smile as he places the bag of ice on his knee. And he's gorgeous, so the whole comment and accompanying action is completely adorable. I know it's a joke, but I'm not myself, you see. So, I don't react like my usual sane self by laughing along and seeing the funny side of the clumsy 'help' I've given him. Nope, that doesn't happen at all. What *does* happen is far more embarrassing: I *burst* into full blown tears. And not your regular quiet sobs either. No, they're great big heaving, wailing sobs that make me look unstable.

Unable to stop, I do the only thing I can. I run inside the apartment and lock myself in the bathroom. I'm not coming back out until Leo is gone. Or until I get really hungry...or until someone else needs to use the bathroom...or maybe when hell freezes over. I don't know. I'll play it by ear...

## SIX

## LEO

A door slams somewhere inside the apartment, causing us all to jolt slightly from the sound. It isn't the first time I've sent a woman running in tears, but it is the first time I wasn't an arsehole before it happened.

Or was I?

I quickly run through the few words Darcy and I actually said to each other, and decide that no, I wasn't an arsehole...this time.

"Seems like you two really hit it off," Esme says, an amused glint in her eye as she takes a seat beside me.

"I hear I'm an acquired taste."

"Aren't we all?"

"Is she okay? Should we check on her or something?" I ask, adjusting the ice so it's balancing properly on my knee. She was dressed as Esme's younger twin, and like her grandmother, Darcy is a good-looking woman. Although, judging by the way she ran off crying, she might also be crazy. Which would make sense, I tend to be attracted to women with problems bigger than my ability to fix them. I went to a therapist once who called it a superman complex. Whatever that means…

"Don't all women run from you screaming?" Esme's smiling and I can tell she's just joking, so I take no offence. The woman has the heart and humour of a twenty-year-old inside an eighty-something body. She won't tell me her exact age, but since I live next door to her, she's told me enough stories about her youth that I've done the maths and narrowed it down to a decade. In this whole complex of apartments, she's definitely my favourite person. A lot of the older women are just busy-bodies, but Esme is a lot of fun. I have a lot of time for her.

"Nana, is Mummy okay?" the little boy who tackled me asks, tugging on Esme's sleeve while he stares at me with big blue eyes that match his mother's.

Esme cups his heart-shaped face between both of her palms. He's a cute kid. When he isn't attempting to dislocate knee joints. "She's just fine, Archer. Tired from too much sun, so I think we should leave her to get some rest. Why don't you go and have a look in the freezer? I think there might be some Icy Poles in there."

His eyes light up and he runs off, brown hair bouncing, his mother's distress already forgotten, but then he stops suddenly and turns back around, biting at his bottom lip as he takes a squint-eyed look at my propped leg. "I'm sorry I hurt you, Leo," he says.

"It's OK, mate, I know you didn't mean it."

Satisfied with my response, he smiles and resumes his run for the freezer. Kids that age are so easy. So different from the moody teenagers they become.

"Seriously though, is Darcy all right?" I ask Esme, keeping my voice low so the little John Cena fan can't hear me.

Esme nods. "She will be. She's just had a rough few days, nothing a bit of rest and reprioritising can't fix."

"She's the granddaughter you keep talking about, right? The one with the husband who won't let her visit?" I didn't get a good look at them side by side to see a family resemblance. Darcy has light blonde hair with big blue, sad puppy-dog eyes. While Esme has almost metallic grey hair with sharp dark eyes that take in everything around her. They have different energies too. Something I've only started noticing since Esme opened my eyes (well, senses) to them. We have some very interesting conversations.

"Not anymore, the husband is out of the picture now." She says that part real low then holds a finger against her lips so I know that information is secret.

"No wonder she's upset."

"Oh, he was awful, Leo. Jo kept me abreast of the situation over the years, and I really don't understand why she stayed. But that's neither here nor there I guess. The point is, she's here now and I feel like I have my girl back." Esme smiles, looking like she's revisiting a fond memory. "She's my favourite if I'm honest."

"I never would have guessed." I smile. She loves telling me stories about her granddaughters, Darcy in particular. I get the impression she'd have liked a daughter, but she only had the one son and stopped having children there. I'm not sure why.

"My son didn't do a lot of good in his life, but he gave me granddaughters so I'm grateful for that."

"You don't talk about him much."

"He passed a few years ago. Complications from alcoholism."

Oh shit. "I'm sorry to hear that. I didn't realise."

"How could you? As you said I don't talk about him. Our relationship was...complicated. When he married, he chose the woman who hated everything outside the norm. A very straight-laced judgemental woman. When they divorced, everything became even more compli-cated. He went a little wild and I could never get through to him. I think that perhaps we were too similar and too different at the same time. Does that make sense?"

"Oddly, Yes."

She reaches over and gives my forearm a squeeze. "Of course it makes sense to you, dear. You and I are kindred spirits."

It sounds ridiculous and cheesy but I have to agree. "You know you're my favourite person, Esme."

"Don't let Arthur hear you say that. He's the jealous type, you know."

"Arthur? I thought I saw George down here the other night?" She nods and I can't help but laugh. "How many have you got on the go this time, Ez?"

"Four." She giggles like a girl and I shake my head.

"Building yourself a harem, hey? Good for you."

"What can I say? I have a lot of love to give." Esme is the most gregarious of the senior citizens in our building. The single and widowed men (and a lot of the married men) all think she's the sun and the moon. It's odd to observe, because younger men wouldn't be as willing to share a woman's time the way they are. But somehow it works, and they all walk out of Esme's apartment the next morning whistling with a little more bounce in their step.

"Although, I do think I should drop it to three."

"Uh-oh. Your list has had a casualty?"

"Not that kind of casualty. I just think Arthur and I need a break. He's from upstairs—I think you met him at last year's Christmas party—and he wants things to become a little more serious between us. Doesn't like sharing with the rest of them."

"And you aren't interested in settling down with only one guy?"

"Oh no," she says, crossing her legs and smoothing her long dress over them. "At my age, serious is the last thing I want. I've been married three times, all ended in divorce within the first couple of years, which I took as the universe's way of telling me to remain a single free spirit. Nothing ties me down. Except the sea of course, I will always be connected right here to this spot." She takes a deep lungful of air, serenity softening her features. "Did I ever tell you that the house I grew up in *and* raised my son in was also here?"

"Right here?" I point downward. I haven't heard this story.

She nods. "They knocked it down to build this complex. I was one of the first to buy off the plan."

"Wow." I sit back, knitting my brows together. "You sold your family home to make way for the apartment building?" I'm not sure I could do something like that.

"Seven other families and I did. I'm the only one who

stayed. The rest took the money and ran, I don't know where."

"Did you *want* to sell your house?"

"Not at first. I decided that keeping this view to myself was selfish"—she gestures to the expanse of beach and ocean to our side—"so I sold along with everyone else, allowing this project to go through. I've met so many wonderful people because of that decision. I have no regrets. A life shared is a life well lived, don't you agree?"

"Says the woman who says no to commitment." I smile. I love her brand of wisdom. Primarily because she reminds me a lot of my late mother. She also lived an unconventional life. She was fiercely independent, never married, refused to rely on anyone else to provide for her. When she fell pregnant with me at forty-one, she'd been around the world twice already. While she didn't exactly plan on having children, when she learned of my existence, she trusted that The Fates had stepped in to show her a greater plan for her life. And she was honestly the best kind of mother I could ever imagine having. She supported me through every important moment in my life—my rugby career, my marriage, *my son*...my divorce. She was always there, always ready to cheer me on or listen when I needed to talk, and she was so wise and worldly. I didn't always appreciate that when she was around, but now that she's gone, I realise how much I miss her words and guidance. Sometimes I feel like she talks to me through Esme. But that's probably really weird and something I'd never say out loud, so don't tell anyone, OK?

Esme waves a hand in the air, the light reflecting off

her quartz ring. "I don't say no to commitment, dear boy. I say no to monogamy, to boredom, to *sameness*. I can't live my life on loop, as there's far too much to do."

I nod slowly. She's so right. Every time I have a conversation with Esme, I leave her apartment feeling like my mind has expanded. I've realised that in life you need to be more than just book-smart. You need to be life-smart too. When my mother was alive, I was too caught up in myself to let her wisdom fully sink in. But now that I'm older, more mature, I listen to Esme spout similar theories, and her words connect dots from my past and spark understanding in my present. Most of my life was about football: training, playing, then commentating, reporting. I've had 'a life'—my mother would have called it a *big life*—but most of it felt like running on a treadmill —so much effort that didn't really get me anywhere. Each day was focused on football, football, football. Until it wasn't anymore. I'm not sorry that it's gone. And I'm not sorry all the hard work paid off financially. I have no real regrets over the way I conducted myself during those years. I always gave it my best and I've made life-long friendships, meeting and succeeding goals beyond what I thought possible. But I am glad that I'm not living in that loop anymore.

"I get where you're coming from, Ez. But I can't say I agree with you on the monogamy thing. I don't think I could share a woman I cared about."

"You do strike me as a one-woman guy," she says with a smile.

"I am. And I like it that way. But I do agree with you

over living a varied life. It's a little soul sucking to keep repeating the same old routine day in day out."

She turns a little in her seat, folding her arms across her middle. "If you could change two things about your life what would they be?"

"Only two?" I say, giving it a bit of thought. "I think the first thing I'd do is quit running." I laugh a little as I lift the ice pack from my knee, which is looking considerably swollen. It's not dislocated, but I'm pretty sure I've torn something. In truth, I probably should have quit running a long time ago and chosen something with less impact on my joints. Years of football have not been kind to my body.

"And the second?"

I look inside to where her great-grandson, Archer is devouring a lemon Icy Pole, kicking his feet that hang over the edge of a chair while he sits at the table, watching some superhero cartoon on the TV. He seems so innocent and carefree. I feel a sense of longing in my heart just watching him. "I'd force my ex to let me spend more time with my son. There is only one year left where I can legally request to spend time with him. After that, I don't know what's going to happen. I think I'll lose him."

Esme gives me an approving nod and places her hand on my arm. "Would you like some pot, dear? It'll help with the throb in your knee. You know I don't believe in taking pills. Natural is always best."

"Sure, Ez," I say with a smile, and before long, I'm getting high with my eighty-year-old neighbour in the middle of the day. And it's not the first time, either.

## SEVEN

DARCY

With a pot of pumpkin curry that Nana insisted I deliver, I cross the hall and knock on Leo's door. After yesterday, I feel I owe him some sort of an explanation, or at least an apology for the damage my son did to his knee. He opens the door with a forearm crutch looped around his left arm.

"Oh God. It's even worse than I thought," I moan, noting how he's keeping all his weight off that damaged knee.

He smiles, and boy, does my stomach flip. "It's nice to see you too, Darcy."

"I brought you pumpkin curry," I say in a rush, holding it up and wanting so badly to just thrust it into his arms and dive back inside Nana's apartment. I'm not currently equipped with the ability to converse with attractive men.

"How about you bring it in?" He lifts the crutch a touch, showing me that he's not capable of carrying the large pot himself.

"Oh! Of course." See? I'm acting a bit stupid. How does one be alone with a man who isn't their husband or family member? It's been so long since I've had to deal with any of this. "Where do you want it?"

"In the fridge will work," he says, standing aside to let me through. Self-conscious of the fact he's directly behind me, I walk up the short hall that leads from his front door to the rest of the apartment. The layout is a mirror copy of Nana's with an open-plan kitchen dining, and a second hall that leads to the bedrooms and bathrooms.

"Your kitchen is on the same wall as our kitchen," I point out once I clear space for the curry in the fridge. It isn't hard, because Leo doesn't have a hell of a lot in there. Beer, water, milk, cheese, some workout drink, and random fruits and vegetables. Everything looks fresh and I'm pleased there aren't any science experiments in there like there would be if Kevin was left to his own devices.

*Oh.*

I step back and close the fridge door, frowning as I catch myself in the thought, angry because I don't want to think about Kevin anymore. I've just spent three days in bed crying over the man, and frankly, he doesn't deserve the space in my thoughts anymore. But how does a person do that? Shut someone out of their thoughts after twenty years? I'm finding it especially hard since Nana suggested that his overtime and last-minute conferences and client meetings were just a cover. God, what if they were? I said I didn't want to think about it, but the seed is planted and now, it's *all* I can think about, because did he? Did he lie about work so he could shack up with other women behind my back? I suppose it would explain the decline in our sex life in recent years. I'd put it down to maturity and a naturally decreasing libido, and when he discovered the lump, I figured the radiation made him not want sex at all. Was I wrong in thinking that way? Too understanding? Because now, standing on the other side of this, I'm thinking that perhaps I really should have seen this coming, perhaps he was cheating on me all along. Had his insistence that he hated cheaters been utter bullshit? A ruse to cause me to never doubt him? I mean, he *has* jumped straight into some new life with a woman he *met* while we were together. Was he cheating on me with her? Using me as his nursemaid while she fulfilled his other needs?

I'm already banging my head on the stainless steel door before I realise what I'm doing.

"Whoa there." Leo's hands wrap around my upper arms and he steers me away from the door, hobbling a little as he guides me sideways so I'm standing with my back against the bench and Leo is balanced on one leg in front of me.

"How do you know if someone is cheating on you?" I blurt, unable to keep the concern in any longer.

His eyebrows shoot up and he scrubs a hand across his jaw.

"I'm sorry. I shouldn't have asked that." My face is all scrunched up and I keep my head down. *I'm losing my mind. What am I doing saying this stuff to a stranger?* "I should just go. I'm not fit for human company."

"No. It's fine, er...I suppose it's in the missing time. When they say they're going somewhere but the timing doesn't really fit. That's how it was with my ex, anyway. She'd say she was out shopping or at an appointment, but she'd get home too late then blame the traffic. I don't know. She always had answers, but there was just something off about them." *A woman cheated on this? Holy shit.* What hope is there for someone like me then?

"Like, getting told on a Thursday you were needed for a team building weekend or forgetting there was a paintball tournament on the morning you had to leave?"

He tilts his head a little. "Maybe. Heading straight for the shower the moment they walk in the door is another."

"Oh God." *The air con wasn't working in the car, so I'm all sweaty. I'm going to jump in the shower.* I close my eyes as my stomach twists, and I drop my head back, hitting it against the cabinet door.

"Hey, hey," he cajoles, wrapping his hand around the back of my head to stop the destruction of brain cells. "Don't beat yourself up over this. I didn't know either. I found out when I stopped by a sick teammate's place to drop the new training schedule off and found her car there. It was only after that I could look back and see the signs."

"How long were you married?" *Is it wrong that I'm enjoying the way his fingers are making soothing motions in my hair?*

"Four years."

"Do you think it was happening the whole time?"

"Maybe." Shifting his hand to the side of my face, he pushes my hair back and inspects my forehead. "I think it's my turn to get some ice for you."

"Only if you throw it at me then run away crying," I say, attempting a joke.

"I'm not promising anything, but I'll try." He smiles and releases my hair, placing his hand on the bench at my side. "Especially if we're going to keep dragging up shitty memories."

"I'm sorry." I feel like I'm always apologising to this guy. "You don't even know me and I'm dumping all my shit on you and asking personal questions. Just...forget this ever happened, OK?"

"It's OK. It happens all the time." He smiles warmly, and I spot a hint of a dimple.

"Women frequently come in here and bang their head against your cupboards?"

He laughs. "No. People ask personal questions."

"Oh. Of course, because you played rugby?"

He looks at me with a slightly narrowed eye and a curious quirk to his mouth. "You didn't know about my wife already?"

"No. I don't really make a habit out of googling football players. And I don't read gossip magazines, so..."

He lifts a hand and rubs the back of his neck. "That's good to know."

Now it's my turn to narrow my eye at him. "But you knew about my husband, didn't you?"

A sheepishness coats the smile he produces. "Esme might have mentioned the split. I wasn't aware of the circumstances though."

"I'm not even sure of the circumstances. He walked out and I'm left trying to find a reason."

He bows his head slightly and catches my eye. "Sometimes people just don't know what they have."

A slight pang hits me in the chest. Somehow, this man I barely know has managed to say something I dearly needed to hear. Years of feeling under appreciated and overlooked as a 'homemaker' has left me feeling undervalued. His words, simple as they are, provide me with a sense of worth. I was a good wife to Kevin. I know I was. He's the one who ruined things.

"Thank you," I say, smiling slightly, and he shrugs as if it's no big deal.

"She talks about you a lot actually. Esme. All good things. I get the feeling you're somewhat of a favourite."

"Well, she's the best person I know. Coming here...I didn't really give it much thought. I knew I had to come."

"She's missed seeing you."

"I know. And I've missed her too. It was just...hard before. But I'll be sure to visit more often."

"That'll make her happy. Give us a chance to get to know each other too."

I laugh. "You actually want that after my head-beating display?"

"Well, Ez thinks you're cool, and I happen to think she's a pretty good judge of character."

"Ez, huh? I guess that means you talk often?"

He bounces a shoulder. "She's my neighbour. I don't have some weird old lady fetish or anything."

I bark out a laugh. "I wasn't suggesting—" Closing my eyes, I shake my head. "I simply meant that you probably know more about me than I know about you. That must be an interesting change for you."

He folds his arms across his chest and nods appreciatively. "It is. It's refreshing."

I'm a little on the back foot, unsure how to feel about his prior knowledge, or even his friendship with my grandmother. I feel this need to question him about what he knows and how close they really are, analyse every detail. But then I realise that I'm probably a little jealous because he's been here with her and I've been, well, living the wrong life with the wrong man. I guess his friendship with Nana works in my favour. He's been given the version of me Nana sees, the one where I'm still young and carefree, so full of potential, and I decide that's refreshing for me too. He doesn't know me as Darcy and Kevin. He only knows of me as Esme's grand-daughter and I'm OK with that.

"Want to wipe this whole slate clean and try again?" he asks suddenly.

"Try what?" I risk meeting his greeny-brown eyes and find them studying my face. He's standing quite close. *Oh, he smells nice.* Like soap and warm skin. I'm a little dizzy.

"I'm Leo," he says, holding out his hand for me to shake. "I live next door to your nan."

For a moment I hesitate, but the kindness and sincerity in his eyes sees me slipping my small hand into his large one. "Darcy," I practically whisper, a small smile playing on my lips. "I'm staying with her for a couple of weeks."

"It's nice to meet you, Darcy."

"Nice to meet you too, Leo." I'm blushing because

he's close and we're still holding hands and this feels really intimate.

"OK," he says, smiling as he shifts back a little. "Now that's sorted, how would you like your ice? On your forehead or inside a drink?"

I bite my lip. "Definitely inside a drink."

OVER THE NEXT TWO WEEKS, I stop by Leo's daily to check on him. I figure it's my duty since my kid is the reason he's hurt, and Nana keeps cooking things for him, so it's no real trouble. He invites me in each time and we have a drink together and talk. It's maybe forty-five minutes out of my day, but I find myself looking forward to what us mums call 'grown-up time'. I learn that he has a son a little older than Abigail, and that after his marriage ended badly, he hasn't had a serious relationship. Although, he *was* married to a model—who is now an actress on Neighbours, a popular Aussie soap— so, I guess it's kind of hard to top that. I felt so out of my depth when I learnt that. Something about hearing the word 'model' makes the rest of us girls feel like a wilting rose, or worse, one of those poor unfortunate souls from *The Little Mermaid* who couldn't pay the Sea Witch back in time. Yikes. But, the information does help me relax around him. It tells me that not only is he out of my league, but that even if he wasn't, I wouldn't have to worry. He's in the same position as me, the left-behind and wounded, now a little guarded. It cancels out that possibility of male/female tension between us and means I can focus on being myself around him, which is something I haven't had the luxury of doing for a very long time. Just Darcy. It has a nice ring to it, don't you think?

The night before I'm due to go back home, Nana decides to take Archer and Abigail out to dinner and a movie as a farewell treat. She's been a godsend while we've been here, looking after us all while I've licked my wounds and gathered my strength. The kids have had a ball, and I feel somewhat ready to face my life again, however that will look from this point forward.

So, they're out and I'm sitting alone on the deck, enjoying a glass of wine and a few more hours of peace. I haven't forgotten that I still need to break the news of Kevin's abandonment to the kids, but for now, I'm enjoying the pause on my life before I have to press play again.

The smokey scent of BBQing beef floats past my nose and my stomach growls, suddenly craving whatever's cooking. Nana's vegan, so I haven't had meat since we got here. Not that I mind, as Nana is a fantastic cook. She could make eating stones appetising. But I do miss my beef, and like a cartoon character following a scent trail, I rise from my seat, sniffing the air.

"Oh my God, that smells amazing," I say as I place my hands on the railing and lean over so I can see around the privacy screen that separates Leo's deck from Nana's.

He's standing over a smoking BBQ, turning a couple of steaks and smiling at me. He gets about without the need of a crutch now, only needs a brace on his bad knee for support. "If I knew the scent of cooking meat would lure you over here, I would have tried it out sooner."

"I see. This is a ploy to get me to come over?"

He finishes with the meat and shuts the lid on his Weber. "Of course. I've got the steak and salad. You've got the wine, and from the commotion I heard earlier, you're the only one home."

"I feel thoroughly spied on right now."

"Pitfalls of apartment living." He shrugs as he moves closer and leans on the railing right next to me. "Get over here," he says, inclining his head towards his apartment.

With a grin that takes over my face, I bite my lip then grab the open bottle of wine, handing it to him before I collect mine plus a second glass and head around to him.

"You've made an excellent decision, Darce. I'm told I cook a mean salad."

"What about your steaks?" I ask as he opens the gate for me. He takes the wine glasses from my hands and pulls a face.

"Edible at best."

"Shame I'm not here longer, I could teach you how to make them so tender they melt in your mouth."

"I'm drooling just thinking about it," he says, setting the glasses on the outdoor table before disappearing inside and coming out with a bowl of salad and two plates with cutlery.

"Wow. You really did plan this."

"I had a little nudging from Esme. She told me you'd be eating on your own tonight, so I thought we could eat together since it'll be our last chance to hang out. You didn't mention you were leaving earlier." He tops off my glass of wine and hands it to me before filling his own.

"Well, my job here is done. You can walk, and I don't

think you're planning on suing for damages, so..." I take a sip to hide my grin.

He laughs as he takes a seat across from me. "This has been about buttering me up? The whole friendship thing was a fake."

I laugh in return and run my free hand through my hair. "You sound put out, Leo."

"I am. Who else is going to walk in here and beat their head against my refrigerator and talk to me every day?"

"You had friends before I came along. I'm sure you're looking forward to getting your life back. Between me and Archer, you probably feel like you don't get a moment to yourself." Archer has become adept at climbing around the privacy screen like a monkey. I've found him following Leo around, talking incessantly more often than not.

"Archer's a good kid," he says with a smile. "Did you know that slugs have four noses?"

I laugh. "I did not. He told you that?"

"Sure did. Turns out, elephants are the only animal that can't jump."

"See, I did know that one. Archer loves his weird and wonderful facts. Did he tell you the fascinating thing about koala fingerprints?"

"No. But I'm on the edge of my seat here."

I lean forward like I'm about to let him in on a big secret. "Well, seems they're so similar to humans that they've been suspected for committing crimes."

He sits back in mock horror. "I knew there was something insidious behind those little black eyes."

"It's always the cute ones you've got to keep an eye on."

With the conversation flowing, that first glass of wine goes down pretty easy, as does half of the second.

"I'm going to miss it here." Pressing my lips together, I look out to the ocean and take a lungful of air. "It's so much more peaceful than the suburbs. Life feels better here, you know?"

He nods. "I do."

The scent of charcoal touches my nostrils, reminding me why I came over here. "I think the steak might be a little on the well-done side."

"Oh shit." He jumps up and lifts the lid of his BBQ. Smoke billows everywhere and when he pulls out the steaks, they make a clinking sound against the plate. Meetings my eyes, he gives me a small shrug and a shamefaced grin. "I hope you like pizza."

## EIGHT

## DARCY

Leo clears away the pizza boxes, while I carry our plates into the kitchen. "You really do cook a great salad," I say, placing the dishes in the sink.

He laughs and leans against the bench, arms folded across his chest. "I warned you. I need help."

"I'll write it all out for you before I leave."

"I'd prefer it if you came back and showed me." He meets my eyes and his darken just a touch, creating this intensity that causes tension to build inside my chest. It's been so long since I've looked at another man and felt this way that I'm out of practice and not sure how to respond. But I'm fairly sure I'm reading interest in his eyes. Which doesn't make sense because he's out of my league, right? We're just friends. He knows my husband left *me* to find a *better life*. And Leo dates models and TV personalities and I'm...well, I'm not either of those things. I'm a suburban housewife—correction, I'm a suburban house*mum*. Retired rugby players who defy the aging process by becoming better looking at forty-five than they were at twenty are *not* supposed to look at suburban housemums this way. And when I say 'this way' I mean the way that men look at a woman when they're asking about something innocent, but between the lines they're really asking for sex.

*Wait. Does Leo want to have sex with me?*

I risk lifting my focus from the side of his face to direct eye contact, and yes, yes that's exactly what I think Leo wants.

*Holy fuck.* But I can't. I'm *married*—well, no, I'm *separated*. And Kevin is likely off somewhere doing God knows what with whomever he pleases, so it's not as if I'm not *allowed* to have sex. No one is stopping me. It's just...oh my God, is this actually happening?

I shift my gaze to the tip of his nose. It's easier to look at someone when you're feeling a little thrown if you focus on some other facial feature.

"I, uh, I don't know when I'm coming back," I say. My mind's running like a fat little hamster on a wheel.

"You're leaving for good?" His expression changes and he looks a little hurt, maybe just disappointed. "I thought—"

"I know." The only thing I *do know* in this moment is that I'm ruining this. I'm throwing up walls without actually considering this could be real—that Leo Murphy, Australian rugby royalty, could actually be interested in little old me. I'll probably do what I do best and run away instead. It seems to work quite well for me these days. "I'll have to get the kids properly settled after I tell them...well, you know what I have to tell them. We've got a bit of adjusting to do before we can come back again."

"I get it." He nods, and I know from our previous conversations that he really does get that I need to focus on my kids, but that doesn't stop his expression from visibly closing off.

We stand there awkwardly for a moment then I lift a hand and point towards his front door "I should probably go." Leo lifts his brow but doesn't move. "OK. Thanks for dinner. And, um, thanks for everything else."

"My pleasure," he says.

"Was it? Really?" I ask, studying him a little closer, because I feel like I'm leaving and I'm messing this up. Like, if I don't find out what's behind this tension right now, it'll haunt me for the rest of time. And when I do finally bring the kids back to see Nana, he'll have moved on to the next pretty little thing and there really will be nothing here. I'm rambling, I know. But I've been drinking, and time is ticking, and a thousand other things...

A smile quirks one side of his mouth. "Yes, Darcy. You are a pleasure to be around."

"I am? I really don't get that sense from most people. I often feel like I'm annoying and in the way."

"You really aren't." He's smiling fully now.

"Are you sure? Because you seem a little annoyed, and I don't want to leave with you being annoyed with me."

His expression shifts again, softening this time, and he relaxes his stance, unfolding his arms and holding a hand out to me. "Come here for a second."

I look from his hand to his face. "Why?"

He laughs. "Humour me, Darcy. I want to try something."

Slipping my hand into his, I step a little closer. "Try what?"

With a gentle tug of my hand, he pulls me towards him and kisses me.

My eyes go wide with surprise, and I register that his are filled with mirth, but when he wraps one of his hands around the side of my neck, the energy of the moment changes and suddenly I'm melting against him, hands on his broad chest, a sigh against his lips. His thumb moves against my cheek, his fingers tangle in my hair, and his mouth takes control of mine, tongue probing gently as it pushes inside. Then as quickly as it started, it stops and he's pulling back and looking into my eyes. "Just as I thought."

"What?" That totally came out as a breathy whisper.

"You taste like pizza," he says, his tongue snaking out to lick his lips.

I was expecting something a little romantic like, "Just as I thought, you're an amazing kisser." Well, hopefully better than *that*. I'm shit at all this romance stuff, but you know what I mean. I thought he'd make a comment about my lips being soft or the intensity of the moment. Not that I taste like pizza. Still, his response does get a laugh out of me.

"So cheesy," I joke, giving his chest a playful shove as I roll my eyes. "Now I'm really going."

I step out of his embrace, a huge smile on my face because a kiss from a hot guy, no matter what your age, is a smile-inducing thing.

"Don't stay away too long." *What the hell am I doing walking away?*

I get about two steps before I turn back to him. "Actually, I think I want to try something too."

He grins as I close the distance between us and wrap my arms around his neck, our mouths colliding in hungry passion. His hands go to my waist then up my back and down to my arse, all the while crushing me against his strong body in a possessive hold.

"Wow," I gasp, my fingers tangling in his hair as we come up for breath.

"Is that what you were hoping for?" His fingers press firmly into my arse cheeks.

I nod. "I think we should maybe test it one more time."

"Just to make sure," he whispers in agreement as he tightens his hold around me, caging me with his arms.

I nod again and then his mouth is back on mine and his hands are roaming and our bodies are so close I can feel his growing need. It startles me as much as it spurs me forward, moaning in his arms, fingers twisting into his shirt and his hair as I kiss him harder, needing him closer.

The gut-wrenching hurt and confusion I've been feeling drifts away the more we kiss, replaced with a carnal desire that might just be a Band-Aid to my pain. But in this moment, it feels like all that matters. I want to lose myself to this feeling and think about it later. For once in my life, I want to forget about what I *should* do. For one moment, I want to feel free.

"I think I need to see your bedroom," I gasp, pulling his shirt free from his jeans and pushing it up his chest.

"Are you sure?" he asks while I'm lifting my arms so he can pull my shirt up over my head.

"Yes." I pull at my bottom lip with my teeth as I look up at him. "There's something else I want to try."

"Jumping on my bed?" He grins as his heated gaze roams over my body. I'm in my bra and a pair of capris. There's no lace on my bra. I wasn't expecting something like this. It's just a basic beige mum bra, and instead of feeling self-conscious when he unhooks me, I'm glad to have that thing off my body. His eyes drink me in like I'm some delectable treat.

"Something like that." I laugh a little as my fingers work at his fly. We're kissing and laughing bumping and knocking our way down the hall to the main bedroom. His mouth and his hands are roaming, and I'm moaning and thinking I might combust if we don't do this soon. It's obviously been far too long for me. Far too long and—*no, I don't want to go there.* Not now, not while this beautiful man's hands and mouth are on my body. *Focus on the moment, Darcy.*

We fall on the bed in a tangle, laughing when something sounds like maybe it broke beneath us. Then we're shucking our pants and getting naked as fast as we can, touching and kissing the entire time. We're caught up in this frenzy because if we take even a moment to pause and consider what we're doing, we might think better of it and decide it's a terrible idea. Which it probably is, but I can't let my mind go there. I need this. I need this moment where I feel wanted. I need to chase away those *sexual ghosts* as Nana put it.

"I want you inside me *now*," I gasp as he sucks lightly against my neck.

"And I want inside, believe me, I do. But, I'm thinking—"

I press my body against his length, rolling my hips. "Don't think, Leo. Feel."

"Are you sure about this?" Leo asks as he pulls a condom from his side drawer.

"Positive," I say, leaning up on my elbows, watching as he rolls it down his hard length. It's the first moment we stop since we started, and we're panting and feeling a little crazy. A minute ago we were just friends saying goodbye and now we're in his bed, and I'm staring at a rather impressively sized cock. "I want this." *I need this.*

Bringing his mouth to mine, he kisses me as he positions himself at my entrance and pushes inside. I moan because it's wonderful to feel so full, and my eyes roll back as my fingers press into his skin. I wrap my legs around his waist, pulling him deeper and deeper, so close to release. But then I notice he's taking his weight more on one side, favouring his good leg.

"Your knee," I gasp while my body sparks and crackles like a livewire.

"I'm OK." He leans down and sucks my nipple into his mouth and I just about yip from pleasure.

"No. Roll over," I tell him. "I don't want you to get hurt."

"As you wish," he says, wrapping an arm around my waist then rolling so I'm flipped on top. We laugh through the sudden shift, bringing our mouths together a moment before our bodies start moving again.

"There we go," I say, brushing my lips against his as I rock my hips over him. Oh my lord, he feels so incredibly good. Closing my eyes, I place my hands on his chest, loving the firm bulge of his pecs beneath my palms. I take him all, grinding at his base as I let my head hang back, my longish hair brushing against my shoulder blades, every nerve ignited, ready for what comes next.

And that's when things get a little wild. Well, wild for me, anyway.

I press up on my knees and slide back down his shaft, moaning from the sensation. My God, I've missed this. He's a great fit, so it feels amazing, and taking control only allows me to take him in on the perfect angle, hitting me in that special spot for optimum pleasure.

"Holy fuck this feels good," I pant.

"You're telling me."

Blame it on the wine. Blame it on my recently broken heart. But I have zero inhibitions. I call out my pleasure, tell him how fucking sexy I think he is while I dig my nails into his chest then lean down and kiss him, biting his lip (and possibly drawing blood) at one point. Then I lean back, placing my hands behind me to alter the angle, which opens me up enough that he uses his thumb to rub against my clit, sending me over the edge in a howling gasping mess that has me...

*Oh God.* I'm not sure I can relay this accurately because I really don't know what comes over me at this point. I grab a hold of my breasts and shove them up so high that I can lick my own nipple as I come. I suck the damn thing into my mouth and swirl my tongue around it and I completely lose myself in the pleasure of it. In the moment, it feels like that hottest thing I've ever done, but when the orgasmic shudders subside and reality sets in, it turns out I'm just a forty-year-old woman sitting on top of her Nan's next-door neighbour, holding her tits up about her neck and looking foolish. I feel absolutely ridiculous.

"Wow," Leo gasps, placing his hands on my thighs, running his fingers up and down. "That was—"

"I should go." I frown and release my tits. They bounce twice, well, it's not a bounce exactly, more a double tug as gravity takes them back to where it's dragged them over the years. Then I place my hands on his chest and rock my body to the side, climbing off him. His dick causes a popping sound as it leaves my body and it's anything but dainty.

*I need to go. I need to go. I need to go.*

"Darcy, you don't have to leave. In fact, I'd like it if you stayed."

I'm up already and shaking my head, picking up my underwear and pants and pulling them on while trying to rake my hands through my hair to straighten it out. "The kids will be back soon. I need to be there for them. Where's my bra?"

"The hall," he says as he pulls the sheet across his waist and sits up, watching me carefully.

"The hall. Of course. Thanks," I say, breathless, confused, conflicted. The sex was...amazing. But my instincts are telling me to get out, to run away. This is crazy. I'm not ready to be in another man's bed. I was just dumped for heaven's sake. *What was I even thinking?*

I don't know what to do, so I turn away and head down the hall. Just being out of Leo's bedroom and collecting my clothes feels better than lying next to a man —who is not my husband—in post-coital glow. It's possible I'm freaking out a little. This is so out of character for me.

"Darce?"

I don't want to go back in there. I want to skulk away, drive back home, then only ever visit Nana on the days when I'm sure Leo won't be home. But since I'm no coward—or maybe I am and I'm just a glutton for punishment—I poke my head back through the door as I pull my shirt over my head. "Yeah?"

"Are we OK?"

Giving him a bright smile, I tuck my shirt into my capris (which is another thing I never do) and nod. "Yeah, Leo. We're fine. Great, actually. I just...I...ah."

"You have to go," he supplies.

And suddenly, I stop rushing and realise how awful I'm being. "I do. And I'm sorry, Leo. Really I am."

He gives me one of those accepting, understanding nods. "It's OK, Darcy. I get it."

"Thank you," I say in a relieved rush. He really is a great guy. And maybe, *maybe* when I get over my current embarrassment, I'll be able to be in the same room as him again. Perhaps in a month or two? But when my brain decides to throw up the image of the whole nipple-sucking moment, I close my eyes and wince, changing my assessment to maybe ten years or never. I can't see myself getting over this one quickly. "So yeah. I'm going to go now. Thank you for dinner and the, uh..." I wave my hand at the bed.

"The sex?" he offers, his brow raised, but at least he's smiling now.

It reduces the tension in the room, and I laugh a little.

It's high-pitched and uncomfortable. "Yeah. The sex was great. You're really good at it, by the way." I give him a thumbs up. *A thumbs up.*

Kill me now.

He chuckles at my awkwardness. "So are you."

"Thanks. So, uh, I guess I'll be seeing you."

He nods. "Goodbye, Darcy." It sounds so final when he says it like that. I get all tight in my chest.

"OK. Goodbye, Leo." I hesitate for about half a second then get the hell out of there as fast as I possibly can, trying not to freak out and start banging my head on his refrigerator before I make it to the front door.

I just had sex with another man. A new man. A man who isn't my husband. And while logically, I know that's fine for me to do, I'm still a little messed up by the reality of it. When I said 'I do' at my wedding, I meant every-thing that came with it. And now, those vows, *all those years*...they mean nothing. This break-up is really happening. My marriage is over. I'm officially a statistic. And while I understood it was over before now, it's only just fully sinking in.

## NINE

## LEO

Dropping my head against the pillow, I cover my face with my hands. *Fuck.*

That wasn't what I was expecting.

I wanted to kiss her, yeah. She was talking like she might never come back, and for the first time in many years, I didn't want the connection I had with someone to be momentary. Ever since Tash and I divorced, I've kept my relationships casual and physical. It isn't that I was afraid of letting someone into my life again, I simply didn't want to. One long-term relationship and a divorce was about as much as this guy could handle, thank you very much. In the beginning, the idea of juggling rugby, fighting to see my son and keeping a functional relationship going on top of that felt like more trouble than it was worth. I trained, I played, I spent time with Niall and when the need arose, there was always a girl ready and willing.

Did I whore around for a while after my divorce? Hell yeah, I did. I think any guy in my position would.

But like all things, those meaningless encounters lost their attraction and I opted for casual relationships instead. Even when I hit my late thirties and football was over, I still wasn't willing to bring another woman into my life. Niall and I were growing further apart, Tash was being more difficult than ever, and my mother had taken ill. I didn't have time for myself let alone someone else. I kept things simple and honest, and when that didn't work anymore, I said goodbye and moved on. Somewhere along the line, I stopped those kinds of encounters too. And before I could decide what I wanted next, Darcy showed up.

Clumsy, crazy (the good kind) and quick to laugh, her visits quickly became the best part of my days. Esme had often spoken of her like she was some ethereal being, sent into the world to allow everyone around her to bathe in her light. These conversations often came about after an evening spent sharing a joint, and I always thought Ez was just letting the happy-making endorphins colour her words. Darcy sounded too good to be true. A free spirit who loved hard and exhibited unwavering loyalty; did such a person even exist outside of fiction? I didn't believe it for a second, but it sure sounded good.

Now that I've met her—the real-life messy version of her—I want more. While she isn't some ethereal being, she definitely does have this light inside her. It's dim at the moment, damaged by the shit her husband has put her through, but I can see it, lighting up her eyes, making her a pleasure to be around. She makes me feel good again, makes me want to believe that she is the woman Esme said she was. The more time I spent with her, the more I could see the truth in it. She stood by a man who I feel has used and abused his situation, taken advantage of her kindness, and placed bruises all over her heart with his mishandling. She's a treasure, and if I'm one hundred percent honest with myself, I kissed her because I wanted to give her a reason to return. Maybe it's that superman complex I'm told I have, but I want to show her how a man is supposed to treat a woman like her.

Now I probably sound like the crazy one.

With a sigh, I get up from the bed and head into the bathroom, my knee offering a little resistance as I get it moving again.

Is it egotistical of me to think a kiss could lure her back? Maybe. But I like her. Even if Esme had never told me a single thing about her, I'd still like her. She's funny, she speaks her mind, and she doesn't try to be someone she's not. She doesn't give a shit about my rugby career, didn't hint that she might be interested in my money. She just treated me like any other person and that's something I haven't had for a long time. So yeah, I kissed her because I wanted her to keep thinking about me enough to come back.

"And now you've gone and fucked things up," I grumble as I drop the condom in the bin. All those years of casual flings have obviously taught me zero restraint, and she may never come back because we were stupid and fell into bed way too soon. At best, I just made myself a rebound fuck. At worst, we've ruined what friendship we had with maybe fifteen minutes of sex. It was good sex —great sex—but it was too soon, way too soon. I should have been stronger and told her that we needed to wait.

I'm a fucking idiot who should have listened to my head more than my dick. Those things always get you in trouble.

Blowing the air out between my lips, I turn on the shower, hoping the cool spray will get my head on straight.

She felt so unbelievably fucking good in my arms, pressed against my body, writhing and whimpering. Great, I'm getting hard just thinking about it—the way she took control, riding me and playing with her tits... wow. Just, wow. I can see that moment living in the mental spank bank for a while.

Wow.

I turn the heat down to nothing, letting the ice-cold water shock my system and force some sense into this damn head of mine.

That look on her face when we finished: instant regret. It's enough to have me thumping my own head against the wall.

I fucked up.

I let her down.

We should have waited.

*God, I'm going to miss her.*

## TEN

## DARCY

I suppose when I *really* think about it, I knew Kevin wasn't happy. He'd always been somewhat of a 'sad sack'. Not that he was clinically depressed. No, not at all. It was just that he rarely found happiness in any given situation. I often joked that he was the Eeyore of the family because he always looked at what was missing instead of what was there. Through most of our relationship, I was the perpetual family cheerleader—*Oh look, Abigail is dancing to the Wiggles; Archer can catch a ball while hopping on one foot; look how beautiful the sky is tonight; isn't life wonderful?*—I could sigh with happiness, and point, and pep everything up until I was blue in the face and it would barely muster a nod of enthusiasm.

Up until now, I'd thought it was the way he was. I mean, some people simply couldn't see the bright side of life. But it didn't mean they were *unhappy*. Just unenthusiastic. Like Daria in that show...well, it's also called *Daria*; she had a single monotonous tone and acted as though she hated everything, but she was still happy in her own way, putting the world down and overanalysing things was her jam. I honestly thought Kevin was like that. After all, we are the MTV generation, known for our cynicism and ironic take on life. We *invented* self-deprecation. I thought he was *normal.* I thought *we* were normal—the yin and the yang, the light and the dark. I thought that was part of why we'd worked for so long... And now, well, I feel dumb. I've obviously been living in a bubble, refusing to see what was right in front of me, because why? Because I didn't want to fail.

I hate failing.

When I was studying year eleven maths, I failed a class test and was mortified. I begged and begged my teacher to let me re-sit it, and he refused point-blank, saying it wouldn't be fair to the rest of the class and I'd have to work harder next time. Well, I did work harder. I studied my arse off for that class and ended up being one of his best students. From that moment on, whenever something wasn't working for me, I doubled down and pushed harder, and my marriage was no exception. If I noticed Kevin pulling away, playing a little hard for Team Kevin, I pulled out those pom poms until he was waving the flag for Team Family again.

Of course, he'd been less happy over these past months. No amount of cheerleading from me was going to change that. But it was expected, wasn't it? I mean, he had *cancer.* Anyone would be down in the dumps over that. It was *understandable.* So of course, I saw his unwillingness to talk, to be touched, or be affectionate as a symptom of his illness, not a herald of the end of our relationship. I convinced myself that I was being a good wife by taking care of his immediate needs and giving him the space he needed to get well.

I didn't think the amount of space he needed was all of it. Or that the space he *wanted* was actually occupied by someone else. *I might hate him.*

But now I know, I can see that he was right: I should have seen this coming. The signs were there all along, but I hadn't wanted to see them. I'd made excuses and pretended they weren't there. I had lived in denial, convincing myself we were happy when he obviously wasn't happy at all. I feel stupid. I feel naïve. I feel thrown away, cast aside. He moved on the moment he walked away from me—probably before—and I didn't seem to have a problem falling into bed with another man either. So now we're over, the sexual ghosts chased away. Kevin and Darcy are no more. Kaput. Just like that.

Since that day in the parking garage, I've done a lot of soul-searching and self-discovery. And I've discovered I'm a bit of a wanton ho. Before you scoff and say, puh-lease, you should hear me out on this one. I came here messed up over one man, and I'm leaving messed up over another. If that isn't a ho-like turnover, then I don't know what is.

I never should have let things go as far as they did with Leo. I know I have no one to blame but myself. Leo was more than gentlemanly, asking if I was sure, and I was animal-like in my insistence that yes, I wanted to rip each other's clothes off and bump uglies in unencumbered frenzy.

What must he think of me?

Every time I remember the way I behaved, the way I

grabbed myself...*oh lord*...my stomach twists with embarrassment and I want to hide under a blanket and never come out. *Thank God, I'm going home today.* I don't think I could face him again, knowing he saw what he saw last night. *Ugh. Kill me now.*

I know that to most, my actions probably aren't a big deal, but to me, that is *not* how I behave in the bedroom. I mean, I'm not a limp fish, and I'm not a missionary only girl, I'm just...I'm *normal.* I don't howl and talk dirty and bite and suck my own...ugh...you know what I did. I am so far out of my comfort zone, which is crazy. I came here because Nana *is* my comfort zone. I used to come here when I was Abby's age to escape my overbearing mother. Back then, it felt like Nana was the only person on the planet who understood me. I'd run into her welcoming arms, stay a few hours and sometimes a few days to listen to her wise and understanding words or spend time partaking in whatever spiritual pursuit she was involved in at that time. I always loved her brand of crazy. Once I came here and she and three friends had formed a witches' coven, complete with a cauldron, the purpose of which (see what I did there) was to put a hex on a cheating soon-to-be ex-husband. Whether it worked or not, I have no clue, although, the thought *has* crossed my mind to get them to reconvene and try again on my behalf. But that's not the point; *my point* is that there's always something fantastic going on with Nana. The life she leads is one of total and utter distraction. It's why hers was the first and only place I considered running to. It's the perfect place to escape myself, because I realise now that I've become a lot more like my mother than I ever thought I was. What a sobering thought.

"Why don't you stay longer?" Nana suggests as she sits on the end of my bed and watches me fold clothes into Archer's backpack. He literally packed nothing but his bathers and underwear, and I frown and try to untangle a John Cena action figure from a pair of Spiderman undies. I don't even know how he did this.

"To be honest with you, returning to the house is the last thing I want to do. But the kids have to finish up with school; Abby's already missed her final exams. I've already been on the phone with her school getting everything rescheduled before school breaks for Christmas. I simply can't keep them here any longer. Not to mention the fact that Archer and I don't have any clothes." I've been washing and wearing the same things over and over so I didn't have to repeat the kimono twinning incident again.

"You can get more clothes." Nana shrugs and reaches for the tangled toy and undies I'm holding, expertly extracting the action figure.

"I really can't, Nana. The kids have two weeks left of school and it's going to be the first Christmas without Kevin. I have to find a way to get through that and still keep it fun for the kids."

"All the more reason to come back. Have Christmas here. The kids can spend the day on the beach and we can invite your sister. Maybe even your mother. I always do a big all-day party. They won't even think about Kevin."

"I don't know, Nana." *Would they want that? Would*

*it be good to have a Christmas here so it's different from what they're used to? From what they're missing?* I don't know... "I just feel like I have to go back there and face my life, get the kids back into a routine..."

"Oh pish. Life doesn't have to be about the chains that bind us, Darcy. It's about realising that we put those chains there ourselves. We have the key to unlock and shake them away whenever we want."

"So, you're saying I should just throw my hands up in the air and do whatever I feel like doing?"

She smiles and nods once. "Wouldn't we all be happier if we started doing what we wanted instead of what we should?"

"That's a very tempting idea, but as much as I love you and I love it here, I really need to go. I can't stay."

She narrows her eyes and studies me for a moment. "Did something happen between you and Leo last night?"

My cheeks go bright red, and even though I answer no, she doesn't believe me.

"Oh my, you slept with him." She claps her hands together and beams with pride. "Well done, my beautiful girl. Well done. How was he?"

The heat of embarrassment burns its way up my neck. "It doesn't mean anything. It just...it *happened.*" I take the toy and the underwear from her and throw them in the bag.

"Oh dear. Was he terrible in bed? I really thought he'd know what he was doing, what with the way he carries himself; you don't get that with men who are just subpar between the sheets. True confidence comes when a man knows he has the ability to make a woman scream and beg for more. And I was so sure he had that in him. How incredibly disappointing. But that's the trouble with good-looking men, I suppose." She lets out a sigh as she shakes her head.

"What? No. He wasn't terrible at all."

"He was just OK? That's almost as bad as being terrible in my opinion. If he didn't get you off, dear, I'm going to have to have to talk to him. This just won't do."

"Nana!"

"Don't worry, I'll be tactful about it."

"Tactful as a sledgehammer, I'm sure."

"Well, I won't have any male friend of mine being an average lover. I expect better for you."

"Oh my God, you don't need to talk to him. I'm not going to give you a blow-by-blow—which I'm sure you want—but I assure you, he was more capable and"—I clear my throat and check the doorway to make sure no children are hovering around—"he got me off just fine."

Her eyes light up and she grins from ear to ear. "I knew it. He's got the right kind of hips on him." She even claps, so pleased her original assessment was right.

I pull the zip closed on Archer's bag. "Can we drop this topic please? It doesn't matter what kind of hips he has, because I won't be seeing them—*him*—again."

"Heavens, why? If I were you, I'd at least add a man like that to my roster. You see the abs on him? Didn't get bodies like that much in my day. The men around my age have little ET bellies; remember that funny little alien in the movie? It's not very sexy. But you take what you can get when you're old as dust. As long as their maypole works and they give as good as they get I'm a happy lady."

Does anyone else have an eighty-something grandmother who talks this openly about her sex life? No? So, it's just me then.

"I'm glad you're well satisfied, Nana." It's the most diplomatic response I can come up with. I'm still a little scarred from seeing her friend, George's 'maypole' on our arrival.

She sits back and waves a dismissive hand. "Who's ever really satisfied? We always need more. Which brings me back to you: why don't you want to see Leo again?"

"Because I live three hours away. Because I *just* split with my husband. I'm not you, Nana. I can't jump from bed to bed without consequence. I'm not looking to add another man into my life right now."

With a slow intake of air, she presses her lips together and straightens her spine. "I think I might make some of those oat and raisin cookies the children like. For the drive home."

"Nana," I call out as she walks from the room. "I didn't mean..." But she's already gone, and I feel like shit. Nana has been nothing but good to me my entire life. *Why the hell did I say that?*

## ELEVEN

DARCY

Pulling up outside the red brick house in Bairnsdale feels like a knife in my gut. I've called this place home since before Abby was born. I thought this was the dream—married, a nice house, and a couple of kids who can handle being in the same room with you. My happiness resided within those walls, and now I'm not sure where it is, or whether I'll ever get it back. Or even if it was happiness to begin with. When I look at this house through my recently opened eyes, all I see are the false truths I let myself believe. I see the memory of a woman who bent and shifted, constantly altering herself to fit some unattainable ideal. I wonder now at what point I decided to bend and keep bending. I wanted a career in osteopathy. I wanted my own practice... I had goals. But I gave them all up, became the stay-at-home wife and mother he wanted me to be. I did *everything* that man asked of me. And I didn't ask for much in return. I gave him *everything*, and he left me with *nothing*. I've no credentials, no work history, no way of paying my half of the mortgage. I'll end up living with my mother, and she'll take over and squash down the light in my children too. They'll end up like me, forced into a box, a fucking shell of a human trying to please everyone while forgetting herself. I don't want that for them. I don't want that.

And now I'm hyperventilating. Great. Just fantastic. I haven't even gotten out of the car yet.

"Are you OK, Mum?" Abby asks beside me, her young face filled with concern.

I nod. *Calm the fuck down, Darcy. Your kids need you.* "I'm fine, sweetheart. Just tired from the drive."

And I'm angry.

The more I think about my life with Kevin, the more of a fool I feel for sticking it out as long as I did. He was barely even a participant. I'd been this whirlwind of activity, fabricating this image of happy perfection before me. I was holding too tight, trying too hard. I know that now. But it doesn't make me feel any better. It just makes me feel used because I'm not even sure he wanted the life we built. He was simply...there, getting me to do everything while pleasing himself. *Ugh.* I feel blind and stupid, and angry, angry, *angry*.

*Why the hell did he stay so long if he was so bloody unhappy?*

*Why didn't I notice and end things myself?*

*Why did he get to leave me?*

*Why did he get to leave us?*

"Are you going to turn the car off, Mum?" Abby asks while I stare at the house, lost in thought.

"I was going to put it in the garage," I respond absent-mindedly.

"Isn't Dad's car in there?"

"No. He isn't back yet."

"When is he back?"

Archer leans between the seats. "Can I press the button to open the door?"

"I don't know," I say, answering Abby.

Archer takes it as an answer to him and sits back with a humph.

I still don't move.

*How the hell did I let myself get here?*

In the beginning, things were great between Kevin and me. They always are though, aren't they? We kind of fell together during our first year at university, we got along and the sex was good, so that was that. Moving in together was out of necessity more than desire—his lease ended, and my roommate was moving out. Getting married was a mutual decision—we'd been at dinner with friends and they'd asked when we were going to tie the knot. Kevin looked at me, shrugged and said, "September?" I smiled and said, "September." And three months later we were just that, married.

It had all seemed so simple with him in the early years. No big fights, no dramatic teething problems that our couple friends seemed to experience. We walked step by step through life doing what needed to be done to keep going, hurdle after hurdle. Slowly, the arguments came but it was never anything relationship ending. Perhaps due to my upbringing, I was always quick to apologise and put things right. He was quick to accept my apologies and tell me how I could do better. They say you choose your partners to mirror the parent you struggled with most because you become comfortable in that conflict. I've often wondered if I chose Kevin because he was a softer version of my mother, and I felt safe knowing how to navigate that kind of personality.

I know I keep focusing on the negatives of our relationship, so I probably seem like a complete doormat where Kevin is concerned. But there were good times. There were lots of good times. And there was comfort too. I did feel content with him, and I felt cared about (not for, he wasn't that kind of person) and I think that's why I stayed, and why I thought we were forever. My mother always said that no one was perfect and at least he wasn't an alcoholic or a drug abuser, and I counted myself lucky because of that. *He could have been worse...*

"Why are we still sitting here?" Archer asks. "Can we go inside?"

"Soon," I say.

One thing I'll never regret about my time with Kevin are the children. They were something we'd spoken about but hadn't planned. And even though Kevin rarely showed his feelings, he'd been ecstatic when we welcomed Abigail into the world, and he'd doted quite heavily on her as she grew. I was the one who suggested a second child. With Abigail at school, I missed having a little person following me around all day and grew rather clucky. I'd always wanted two kids, but Kevin had concerns about our ability to provide for them. When he received a promotion at work, I practically begged for that second baby. It felt like he was giving me a wonderful gift when he finally agreed, and he was happy when Archer was born too. Just not the way he was with

Abby. I put it down to a second-time dad thing. But I think it was more than that. I think he resented the time and attention having another baby took away from him. Because it was around that time he took up paintball and started spending weekends away at tournaments.

But now I'm thinking that there were no tournaments. And that the bruising on his body wasn't from paint bullets. I think they were hickeys. I think that's when he started cheating on me.

*I feel so stupid now.*

"Aunty Jo just pulled up," Abigail points out, looking up from her phone. "Were we waiting for her? Is that why we kept sitting here?" Glancing her way, I notice a picture she's taken of herself, a filter inserting dog ears into her brown hair and widening her blue eyes. She is growing up to be beautiful, so beautiful. It hurts my heart knowing that I have to cause her pain when I explain what Kevin has done. *He's such a fucking coward for leaving this to me.*

"Yeah," I say with a wan smile. "We were waiting for Jo."

"Yay, Jo-jo," Archer calls out, unclipping his seatbelt and jumping out of the car.

"You coming?" Abby asks, unclipping her own belt.

"In a minute," I say, handing her the house keys. "You go inside with Jo while I put the car away and get our things."

"You might want to open the garage door to make that happen," she says. "Just a tip." Then she hits the button and I have a momentary freak out when I wonder if Kevin's car *is* still there. But there's only vacant space.

While I expected there'd be a time where he changed his mind and came to collect his things, something about knowing he was in the house without my knowledge sits uncomfortably in my gut. *What did he take?*

"Thanks, honey," I whisper as she opens the door.

"Are you OK? You're being kinda weird."

"I'm absolutely fine. I'll put the car in the garage and come right in."

Abigail gets out slowly, giving me that look she gives when she knows I'm not giving her the whole story. It's a look I'm very accustomed to, because Abigail always thinks I'm keeping things from her. She loves to remind me that she isn't a child anymore and can handle grown-up things. But then she has a meltdown because the bottom of her hair is flicking in the wrong direction and she needs to wear it up instead of leaving it out like she wanted. Call me crazy, but I want to protect her from the big bad grown-up world as long as possible. For a few more moments anyway.

Knowing Kevin's been here, I park the car then pull out my phone, powering it up for the first time in two weeks. I wait as the Apple symbol lights up the centre of the screen before a picture of the four of us in front of a campervan pops up on my lock screen.

I take a moment to look at us all. Kevin and I are sitting on a fold-out chair, holding up our drinks and smiling while Abigail and Archer pull faces behind us. It was taken a little over two years ago when everything seemed a little less strained, more innocent. Archer was a cheeky little six-year-old and Abby was only twelve. High school hadn't turned her into a sarcastic beast then. And

Kevin was still going through the motions of daily life, pretending he wanted to be a part of us.

Despite our troubles, he'd frequently told me that he loved me and praised me to anyone who'd listen, telling them I was the heart and soul of the family. While he didn't often direct his praise *at* me, I thought he was happy with me.

*Was he lying? Even then?*

Staring at the photo, our faces suddenly disappear as notifications pop up. Texts from Jo asking where I am. Texts from my message service telling me I have unheard voicemails. Coles wants me to know their big catalogue sale is about to begin, and my dictionary wants me to know the word of the day. It's 'phatic', if you're interested. It means 'denoting speech used to express or create an atmosphere of shared feelings, goodwill, or sociability rather than to impart information: *phatic communion'*.

The rest of my notifications continue to populate my screen. But not one of them is a message, a missed call, or a voicemail from Kevin. No *phatic* declarations telling me he was wrong, that he wants to come back to me and the kids. Nothing. Not even a 'how are you? How are the kids?' or an 'I'm coming over to get my things.' *Fuck.*

*Bang, bang, bang.* The window rattles from Jo's rapping knuckles, scaring the crap out of me.

"Jo," I yell as my phone slips from my fingers, drops between my knees and slides somewhere near the foot pedals. I lean forward trying to catch it, instead hitting my face against the steering wheel and setting off the horn. *Hoooonk.* I sit back and rub my face. "That was your fault." I scowl at my sister through the closed window. She's laughing, her bleach-blonde hair bouncing at her shoulders, quivering along with her mirth.

Careful to avoid the steering wheel, I retrieve my phone from beneath the brake pedal and open the car door a little too quickly so Jo has to jump out of the way. Then I stand and place my hands on my hips. "Kevin's been in the house."

"I know," she says, her eyes widening as she mirrors my hands-on-hips stance. "If you checked your phone occasionally, you'd know exactly what's been going on since you left. I've been coming every day to keep an eye on things."

"I'm sorry. I was with Nana. I needed to get away."

"I know, I've been keeping tabs on you."

"She's been giving you updates?"

"Yeah, I call her every day. We talk about you all the time."

"Is that why my ears keep burning?"

She laughs a little. "Take it as a compliment, sis. You're obviously a very interesting person."

"I doubt it." I roll my eyes in response. "What's been happening here that you needed to keep an eye on?"

"I brought wine," Jo says. "You'll want wine."

"Oh my God. What did he do?" Now I'm *really* worried.

"Let's just say you'll be wanting to get drunk and burn anything he left behind once we're through."

"What? Tell me what he did?"

"Come inside, Darce. He's a user. Always has been, always will be. He only ever wanted you for what you could give him. He was never going to play fair."

I ball my fists at my side, the pitch of my voice rising. "Tell me."

"I was really hoping to tell you this after we'd had a few glasses of wine—"

"Jo, *please.*"

"OK." She places her hands on either side of my shoulders and looks into my eyes. "Darcy...I think you've lost the house."

## TWELVE

"Holy fucking hell." I stare at the pile of paperwork covering my bed: multiple credit card statements, details of bank accounts I wasn't aware of, and here's the kicker: notices of default on our mortgage and the bank demanding repayment on loans taken out in my name. *How did he even manage that?*

"I wasn't snooping," Jo says. "Well, I was actually. But it was for a good cause. I had a feeling he was up to shit behind your back, and well, I found all this in a shoebox in the garage. I think he came looking for it too, because when I got here and his car was gone, he'd made a bit of a mess in there. I cleaned it up though. Cleaned up that cereal castle in your kitchen sink too."

Covering my mouth at the same time as I grab for her hand, needing the moral support, I shake my head from side to side, disbelieving. "How could he do this?" I didn't think we owned credit cards. We'd agreed that if we couldn't afford to pay for something, we didn't get it. The only exceptions to that rule were the mortgage and the cars. My car seems to be the only thing I still own, mind you. "How could he ruin us? How could I not *notice* he was ruining us?" I'm shaking. I feel sick. I can barely stand.

"He was your husband and you trusted him with the family finances. None of this is your fault, Darcy. Even I never saw this coming, and you know I never liked the guy."

"But it is my fault," I snap, grabbing a handful of the papers and holding them in my fist. "This is me being complacent." I grab another handful and hold it between us. "This is me being too stupid to pay attention."

"Darcy." Jo looks at me, her eyes full of worry, laced with pity. "We'll figure this out."

"What's to figure out? I'm broke, I'm useless, and I'm alone. Twenty years of my life, wasted." I throw the papers in the air.

"Love is a bitch," Jo says knowingly.

Archer pushes the door open at that exact moment, his eyes travelling upward while white paper dances side to side before landing on the floor and back on the bed. "Mummy?"

"Love is a beach," Jo corrects quickly. "I mean, I love the beach. That's what I said. No swearing here."

"I know what the B word is, Jo-Jo." Archer walks straight over to me and wraps his arms around my middle.

I wipe a hand over my face before holding him back. "What is it, sweetheart?" I smile, keeping my face and expression as calm as possible.

"Why are you throwing paper in here?"

"Because it's fun." Releasing him, I scoop some up in my hands and hold it out. "You want to give it a try?"

A little smirk curves his mouth as he shrugs. "Sure."

I hand him the pile, and he crouches low before throwing them up, releasing them with a jump, his hands held above his head as they flutter back down like butterflies. "You're right," he says, crouching down to scoop them up again. "This is great."

He throws them up again, squealing with delight as Abigail opens the door and frowns at what her mature fourteen-year-old-no-time-for-childish-games mind probably sees as crazy. (And maybe it is. I'm not the best judge of sanity at this point.) "You never said when Dad would be back," she says, her eyes scanning the scene before her, taking in the papers and the mess.

"About that," Jo says, grabbing for overdue notices when she looks my way and sees that I'm staring at Abby and smiling manically.

"What's going on?" Abby's eyes get all narrow and suspicious.

"Darcy?" Everyone is looking at me, expecting me to explain. "Want to tell them where their father is?" Jo hides the papers behind her back.

*I can't.*

"Oh yeah." I shake my head, waving a hand in the air as though everything is fine and my whole world isn't imploding right now. "Your dad... He...um... he isn't finished with his conference yet." Jo's shoulders slump as she shoots eyeball daggers at me. I try to shoot sympathy lasers from my eyeballs, but I don't think she's having it. I turn my attention to the children. "In fact, he'll be gone until the new year. He wants us to go back to Nana's to spend Christmas. She's already planning a big party for it. You're invited too," I say to Jo. "And Mum."

"Mum going to Nana's for Christmas?" she scoffs. "That's a laugh. Never gonna happen."

"I'm not going either," Abby snaps. "Tell Dad he has to come home."

"Yaas queen!" Archer cheers, ignoring everyone else. "Christmas at the beach." He waves his hand in the air like he's praising the Lord.

One out of three ain't so bad.

"No arguments, Abigail. You'll finish up with school and then we're heading back to Bayside."

"What about what I want? I have a life, you know." Abby's pitch rises to a shriek with each word. She's looking at me like I just set her favourite pair of shoes on fire then threw all of her make-up on top. She pulls out her phone and holds it like a weapon. "I'm calling Dad. This is crap." Shit. I really didn't think this part through.

"Abigail," I call out as she stomps off, looking to my sister for help.

"Don't look at me," she says. "You're the one telling all the porky pies."

Tearing out of my bedroom, I chase after Abby, needing to stop her. What happens when she calls Kevin and he answers? What happens when he fills her in on his plans and breaks her heart too? Nope, nope, nope. He doesn't get to do that, not this close to Christmas.

"Abigail." I burst into her room.

"This is weird, Dad." Crap. "I don't understand why your conference is happening over Christmas."

I rush for her, fully prepared to wrestle the phone from her hand when I hear, "Just call back, OK? We haven't seen you in two weeks." And I stop, straightening up so I don't look like a mad woman as she hangs up and looks my way. "Voicemail. It didn't even ring." God, he's an arse. I know I was trying to *stop* the conversation, but still, how can he do this to his daughter?

"Maybe they don't have service where he is." My heart is beating so hard right now and I'm not sure if I can keep this up, keep covering for him. I need to be honest here.

"How have you been talking to him?" She looks up at me with young, innocent eyes that trust. She trusts that her dad is busy with work and not off dipping his sausage in a new pot of sauce. *Living.*

Not that I can talk.

Ugh.

Sitting next to her on the bed, I place my arm around her shoulders and hug her to me, breathing in her familiar scent and remembering happy times while I destroy her concept of life as she knows it. *God, I hate this.* "We need to talk, honey."

"About?"

"Your dad," I say.

"What about him?"

"He's um, he's not at a conference."

Her brow tightens and her eyes start shining. It's like she knows what I'm about to say. "Where is he?"

A massive lump lodges in my throat, and it takes a bit for me to swallow it down to speak. "He left us. Moved out."

Water creeps into her eyes. "Does that mean you're getting a divorce?"

"Yes. I think so. I'm so sorry, honey."

"Why?"

"Because your father..." I stop myself before I give the details, remembering how Leo had mentioned that his relationship with his son was strained because he took his mother's side. I don't want to be the wedge between my children and their dad. There may come a day very soon where he realises what a colossal arse he's being and decides to pick up the phone and call them. I want them to be grateful when that happens, because kids need their dad too. "He just needs some time on his own for a while."

"So, he's coming back?"

I lift my hand and tuck her hair behind her ear, my fingers brushing her cheek. "I don't think so, sweetie. But maybe he'll come see you."

She flinches away from my touch. "What do you mean you don't think so? How could you let him leave? Did you even *ask* him to stay?"

"Of course, I did. I..." I shake my head. How do I explain this to her without making Kevin look like the enemy? I can't tell her that I practically begged and it didn't make a lick of difference. If I tell her he left us for another woman, it'll crush her. So, what do I say? "He needs time on his own." That's the best I can come up with.

"Call him!" Tears stream down her face and I realise I'm crying too. "Call him and tell him to come back. Tell him I need him."

"It's OK," I say, wrapping her in my arms and stroking her hair like I did when she was little. She shakes against me. I hate Kevin for doing this. It would be so easy to throw him under the bus right now, but that's not who I am. And I think that makes me hate him even more.

"Please, Mummy."

How do I say no to that? "I'll call him, honey." Not that I think he'll pick up. But... "It'll be OK. I'll call him."

## THIRTEEN

## LEO

"Tash." There's exasperation with a dash of warning in my tone.

"Leo," she responds, her voice childish and condescending. Even over the phone, I can tell she's pulling faces at me, rolling her eyes.

"I haven't had Niall during the Christmas holidays for the last two years. The ocean air will do him good, get him out of that dungeon you created for him."

"It's a man cave."

"It's a room under your house that doesn't get sunlight; it's a dungeon."

She scoffs. "I suppose you think he should be outside playing football or something. He's seventeen, Leo. He has his own life now."

"I know. But this is the last Christmas before he turns eighteen." The last Christmas before the custody arrangement ends. If I can't get through to him, he may choose to never see me again. I have to try. "Tash. Please."

"I can't make him want to spend time with you," she retorts.

I press my lips together, fighting back a sigh as I press the fingers of my free hand against my closed eyes. "Can you at least ask him? *Please*."

When Tash and I signed our divorce papers, I was still playing professional rugby. The time I spent on the road and my international travel schedule meant that the judge sided with her in our custody case. She got him full-time, and I got him every other weekend and every other holiday. It wasn't enough. I reopened custody proceedings when I retired, but Tash is a decent actress, and she really likes taking my money, so the arrangement didn't change much. Now I'm left begging for time and paying through the nose every time I want it.

"I'll give you ten grand," I say, pushing my fingers against my eyes. *This is so fucked up.*

There's a pause before, "Make it twelve and I'll think about it." The line goes dead.

I groan—I drop my phone on the couch, put my hands over my face, and let out a long, frustrated groan. Fuck. After all this time, why the hell does she keep using him against me? I swear I've spent the last thirteen years with my balls held firmly in her vice-like grip while she's called the shots and poisoned my son against me. She twists every situation so I'm the bad guy and she's the poor abandoned woman who wouldn't hurt a fly. Hate is a word I rarely use, but I'll use it where my ex is concerned. Narcissist also comes to mind too, but I feel that's used a little too loosely nowadays.

There have been times where I've wanted to give up

the fight and let her have what she wants, which is me out of the picture. At first, she hated me because I wouldn't forgive her affair, and then it morphed into this wild need to crush me. Google my name and you'll find a bunch of unpleasant allegations about me, all unfounded and only published inside gossip magazines. But once that shit is out there, it sticks, and I've been forced to defend myself in the court of public opinion more than a few times. But again, I wouldn't let her win. I worked too damn hard to let her affect my career with her pettiness, and when she couldn't mess with my career, she messed with my relationship with my son. And I still won't go away. I'm not going to let her ruin me. I'm not going to let her destroy what sliver of a connection I have with my own kid. I believe that if I get a good solid block of time with him, I can turn things around, get him to see that I'm not the evil arsehole his mother paints me as. And if I'm lucky, when he turns eighteen next October and finishes school, he'll choose to come visit me himself.

I don't know. Maybe that's just a pipe dream. But I have to give it a good go. Otherwise she wins and all these years of fighting will have been for nothing. *Fuck, I hate this.*

Dropping my hands, I move to the fridge and grab a beer, tapping off the cap before heading out to the deck, needing some fresh air to clear out the buzzing in my brain. I stand at the railing, sucking down my beer while I stare at the calm ocean. *Serenity.*

This view was my sole reason for buying this place. Being near the ocean centres me. When I was a much younger man, I was prone to angry outbursts. I took a lot of what I had in life for granted. That included my marriage and my family. While I never cheated, I wasn't a good husband to Tash. I fell prey to the same cockiness that a lot of footballers succumbed to—believing my own shit. When enough people tell you how awesome you are, it ends up going to your head. Add to that a hefty salary and media attention, and you have yourself a recipe for the most arrogant pricks on the planet.

Not that Tash was some paragon of virtue. She had her issues too, and at the end of the day, we never should have married each other. She chose me because she wanted to be a WAG and I was her ticket to achieving that goal. She liked the money. She liked the way people treated her and the doors being my wife opened for her.

I married her because I was an arsehole who thought landing the hot model most guys could only beat off over was the epitome of 'making it'. Then we added a kid to the mix and, well, you see where that got us.

"I could never be upset with you... My home is your home, sweetheart. You know that. When do you need to be out?"

Turning my head to the side, I find Esme sitting in the dark on her deck. She's talking on the phone and... she's *vaping*?

"The end of December? What in heavens? Was he ever going to tell you?"

I sniff the air, the unmistakable earthy musk filling my nose. I move to where our decks join and lean over my railing so I can see her past the privacy screen. She spots me right away and we exchange a smile.

"Just do whatever you need to wrap things up on

your side. I'll clear out the other two rooms and you can stay as long as you need." She gives me a look that means she's asking if I'll help with that. I nod like I'm saying 'of course' then she says, "It's no trouble at all, dear girl," as she rises from her seat and offers me the device.

I take it and inhale, letting the smoke fill my lungs before holding it in. It doesn't take long before my mind is light with synthesised happiness.

"It's good stuff," I say, the smoke escaping as I hand the vape back to her.

She shrugs and takes another pull as she listens to her caller then offers it to me again. I refuse. I don't mind a drag, but I've never been one to get baked at every opportunity.

With a shrug, she blows out the smoke and gestures for me to come to her side of the deck. Of course, I oblige the request.

Normally, I climb around the screen like a kid, but with my knee still strapped from my fall, I take the long way, grabbing a couple of extra beers while I'm at it. Conversation is better at night with a drink in hand.

She's finished with her caller when I get to her and I hand her an opened bottle, which she lifts in thanks as I sit.

"That was Darcy," she says, nodding at the phone that's face down on the table. "She and the kids are going to be staying here for a while."

"A while?" I lift my brow. I'd be lying if I said she didn't cross my mind more than once today. Primarily because I'm still kicking myself for jumping into bed with her. I want the chance to redeem myself, show her I'm interested in *her*. The sex part—if it happens again—is a bonus.

"That husband of hers is a piece of work." Esme shakes her head. "He's cleaned them out. Lost the house and left her with a mountain of debt she can't possibly pay."

"That motherf—" I stop myself before I say the whole word. But seriously, who the fuck does that to his wife and kids? It's bad enough he left, but what fucking arse-hole leaves his wife with intentional debt and without a roof over her head? His kids...

"No. I think you're right to say it. He definitely is a motherfucker. They'll be here a few days before Christmas, so we've a couple of weeks to get those rooms cleared out. The kids need to finish off the school year and Darcy needs to organise storage of whatever personal belongings the bank isn't claiming. What an absolute nightmare. Someone needs to make that man pay for this."

"If the courts don't get him, I will." I clench my fist and my knuckles pop. I don't tend to go around hitting people, but some circumstances call for busted faces and broken bones.

"Oh, that's very sweet of you, dear." She pats my closed fist. "But it won't be necessary. I'll put a vex on him, make it so his junk won't work anymore. Testicular cancer will be the least of his worries."

"He left without warning too, didn't he?" Darcy didn't give me many specific details during our chats but what I did know made my blood boil. I wasn't an awesome husband, not by any stretch of the imagination, but one thing I did do right was remain faithful. From the sound of things, Darcy's husband was running around behind her back and left her to go and experience new pussy without hiding it anymore. Her words, not mine. I don't know the guy personally, but I'm pretty sure my old violent streak will struggle to stay dormant if we ever come face to face. In my book, you don't step out on your woman. Ever. If you want to sow your seeds, have the decency to break it off so you're single first. The cheating culture was the one major thing I hated about rugby.

"Walked out the day they discovered he was cancer free. Has nothing but farts for brains that man," Esme says, and I try not to laugh—I obviously have the humour of an eight-year-old—because she's dead serious right now. I wipe a hand over my face to keep it even as she picks up her vape then titches when she realises it's empty. "Who leaves a twenty-year marriage without saying goodbye to his kids?" She's shaking her head, picking up her beer and lifting it to her lips.

"Arseholes," I state.

"Exactly." She drinks her beer and sits silently for a moment, her glassy eyes looking past me as she works her lips back and forth. I hate seeing such hopelessness in her eyes. "I shouldn't even be speaking to you about this. It's not my story to tell."

"I won't repeat anything."

She pats my hand again. "I know you won't. But, still, Darcy is about to move out here with the kids. She's still processing—hasn't even told Archer yet."

"Does her daughter know?" I barely met Abigail in the two and a half weeks they were here, but she seemed like your typical teen: angry at the world, trying to find her place in it.

Esme nods. "Didn't take it well, apparently. And Darcy isn't great with confrontation, so she's trying to find the right time to tell Archer. We're all sworn to secrecy."

"My lips are sealed," I assure her, nodding with my brows knitted because I don't think there will ever be a right time. Archer is a smart kid, so he'll pick up that something is going on.

"Thank you."

"Darcy isn't hoping he'll come back, is she?" The thought and the question jump into my head at the same time.

"Kevin?"

I nod, and Esme smiles like she knows more than she should.

"I don't think she could stand to be in the same room with him. She just... She has a very gentle heart and I think she's hoping he'll at least speak to his kids to explain why he left."

"I can understand that."

"Can you? I don't understand it at all. Rip the Band-Aid off, I say. Expose him for the selfish bastard he's always been. If he doesn't want that amazing woman and those gorgeous kids then he shouldn't be spared a fleeting thought, because I'm sure someone"—she pauses and looks at me—"will be happy to be the kind of man she needs." She sits back in her seat and waves a hand. "But I'm harsh and impatient, and Darcy is kind and loyal. It's why that man could take advantage of her all those years.

She always sees the best in people. I don't need to tell you how worried I've always been for her." She often spoke of Darcy as though she were a bird with her wings clipped. "Her sister is just like their mother, barrels through life like a big wrecking ball, going after what she wants, never taking shit from anyone. But Darcy was always a dreamer, always a hoper. I don't think I've ever told you, but once she brought home this awful stray dog who bit everyone that came close to him, including her. Everyone agreed that he was dangerous and needed to go to the pound. But not Darcy, she put so much love on that animal, that it loved her with every bit of his little doggy heart. He still hated everyone else, but Darcy was special. I suppose she always thought she could do the same thing with humans, why she married a man who was quite harsh. She always thought love could fix things." She touches her fingers to her lips as she stares off, thinking.

Knowing this wanker manipulated Darcy really pisses me off. From what I can tell, she's the whole package. She's intelligent, beautiful, kind, thoughtful, sexy... although I don't know if she believes that about herself. To even consider that he belittled Darcy fucks with my brain. Over the years, I've seen plenty of players manipulate their women, some of them even took things physical, and I hope to God that wasn't the case here.

"Was he cruel to her?"

She inhales like she's surprised I'm sitting here. "Not physically. But mentally, yes, he treated her as less than himself. Was always very controlling and used love as a weapon. One of those men who *seems* like a nice man, but won't let his wife have any other interests besides taking care of him."

"Doesn't sound like love to me."

"No. It doesn't, does it? I think he loved that she loved him, if that makes sense." She sighs then frowns at her now-empty beer bottle. "I need to shut up." She smiles and meets my eyes. "Booze and dope are making me chatty."

"Why don't you tell me about your craft group then?" I figure a change in subject will keep both of us from feeling guilty about airing someone else's dirty laundry. But in a way, it's good to get a bit more background information since I can't seem to get Darcy out of my head. She's been through a lot, so I'll have to be patient, which isn't going to be a problem for me. When I'm this interested in a woman, I tend to see that interest through to the bitter end. I'd rather go down fighting than not fight at all, so I won't pretend that I'm not pretty fucking excited that Darcy's coming back so soon. She only left this morning, and I already miss our daily chats. Not that I struggle for company—I've got plenty of friends to call on and plenty to do work wise—but Darcy very quickly became my favourite part of the day. The next two weeks are going to pass slowly. I wish I had her mobile number so we could talk. But then, she's got enough on her plate right now. I still can't believe that bastard cleaned her out.

"Craft group. You don't want to hear about a bunch of old ladies getting drunk and gasbagging, do you?"

I grin. "Of course I do. Surely you've been up to some kind of shenanigans lately." Esme's 'craft group' is comprised of four other women in the complex who like to mix cocktails more than they like to do craft. They get a few drinks into them and get into all kinds of trouble. Some involving the cops, but we don't talk about those times...

"In that case, have I got a story for you. See, we took up quilling, which is when you wind up strips of card to make pretty pictures. Carla showed up with the supplies thinking we were supposed to be crocheting." She pauses to giggle, which makes me smile. "Anyway, we were drinking whiskey sours and crocheting with Carla, and you won't believe what she had us making. Willy warmers." She throws her head back and cackles so hard her shoulders bounce.

"Willy what?"

"Willy warmers." She wipes a stray tear from her eye. "They're little penis pockets."

"What?" Now I'm laughing.

"Look it up on your phone."

I do as she says and find these strange-looking socks that cover your dick and your balls and tie with a string around your waist. Why a bloke would ever want one is beyond me. "Did she know that's what they were?" I ask, holding up my phone only for Esme to lose it, laughing so hard that the sound becomes a wheeze.

She shakes her head. "She thought they were children's toys. They were animal designs—chickens, elephants, snakes—and it wasn't until we put them all together and looked properly that we realised that it was shaped like a dick and balls."

I have tears and my stomach hurts from laughing.

"She said she found the pattern on Pinterest when she was searching for animal pouches. Was going to give them to her grandkids to keep their canteen money in." Her laughter becomes a squawk and I can barely breathe.

"Oh my God, imagine you hadn't realised."

"I know."

I wipe away my tears, now running down my cheeks. "What will you do with them now?"

"Oh, that's easy. We're making more to sell at the Bayside Hospital fete at the end of March."

"The hospital is happy for you to do that?"

"Oh no. We're saying they're coin pouches. We want to see how long we can get away with it for."

"You ladies are evil." I shake my head, still laughing as I wipe at my cheeks.

"We're crafty, actually. You should come. It'll be hilarious. You'll be the only one in on the joke."

## FOURTEEN

## DARCY

"I'm probably too old to be asking this, but I have a grave concern about spending Christmas at Nana's," Archer says in his usual thirty-year-old scholarly way. He's taking a pause in the marathon Roblox session he's been having on his iPad from the back seat of the car since we left Bairnsdale. All I want to say is thank God for portable Wi-Fi. That is quite literally the best invention of the twenty-first century and makes long road trips a breeze for parents. (Unless the Wi-Fi won't connect, of course.)

"What's that, mate?" I glance at him via the rear-view mirror and he's got his mouth all twisted and his nose crinkled up in thought.

"Well, it's just that we always have Christmas in the same house and I'm worried that Santa won't know where to go," he admits, mumbling that last bit as his eyes dart towards Abigail.

"Oh my God, Archer," she shoots over her shoulder. "You are *not* that naïve."

"If you don't believe you don't receive," he yells back, and suddenly our peaceful car trip is a yelling match.

"Enough, enough," I say to them both. "Abigail, quit harassing your brother, and Archer, don't yell at your sister. Of course Santa will know where you are, you needn't worry."

"Yeah, because it'll be Mum and Nana doing the gifts," Abby mutters under her breath. I shoot her a wide-eyed look that says, 'shut your mouth' and she just rolls her eyes and looks away.

"How does that song go?" I ask, giving Archer a flash of a smile as I glance back at him before returning my eyes to the road. *"He sees you when you're sleeping. He knows when you're awake."*

"Stalker." Abby coughs out the word, which I ignore.

"That means that no matter where you are in the world, Santa keeps an eye on you. And on Christmas morning, your presents will be under the tree and your stocking will be full and it'll be just like it normally is."

"But at the beach," he chirps. It's been the source of his excitement the entire time we were packing up our belongings. I say belongings, because the bank will be selling our furniture too. Kevin really did a number on our finances and I'm going to need a good lawyer to sort this all out. God only knows how I'll afford one.

"And without Dad," Abigail adds and then we all go quiet. I can't fight about this with her again. She's gotten to the point where she thinks I'm purposely keeping her from seeing or speaking to Kevin. But at least she hasn't been nasty enough to spill the beans to Archer. He'll still get the illusion of a nuclear family for a while longer.

Thankfully he hasn't really asked much about his father, but then, he's never known a time when Kevin didn't go away on his 'trips'. Archer's been the least of my worries, which I'm grateful for, because with Abby so snappy and the head-spinning legalities of an impending bankruptcy, I don't think I can handle another peep of negativity. I'm barely holding on as it is.

One day, when I've recovered from this hideous time in my life, I'll get the chance to let my sister know how truly grateful I am for the help she's been over the last couple of weeks. Even though she hasn't always agreed on the way I've handled things, she's been by my side, doing everything she can while providing me with wine like it's water. I wouldn't be as together as I am right now if I didn't have her support. I'd probably be in an alcoholic stupor, wailing on the bathroom floor using toilet paper as tissues. The poor kids would be beside themselves. So, yeah. Lots to thank Jo for.

"Well." I clear my throat. "I'm sure your father will have a wonderful Christmas, wherever he is, just like we'll have a wonderful Christmas at Nana's." I give myself a nod of approval for not calling him any foul names. I was angry at Kevin in the beginning; for abandoning us, for running off without manning up and facing the consequences of the life he left behind. But anger seems too small a thing now. Then, I had a house, and I *thought* I had savings to rely on until I could find some sort of work. Now, I quite literally want to kill him. I'm not angry anymore. I'm murderous. He's taken absolutely everything from me: accommodation, finances, possessions, stability, and I'm pretty sure he took my dignity too, and without the resources to fund a good attorney, I've no idea how I'm supposed to figure this out and recover any of it. I fucking hate, hate, hate him *so much* for this. I wouldn't piss on the man if he was on fire. There's a massive difference between being unhappy and moving on than leaving the person who's walked alongside you for twenty years destitute. Thank god I had a separate personal account for my Etsy earnings, it's all I have left.

"Isn't he in Vegas?" Archer asks.

"What, honey?"

"Dad. Isn't he in Vegas? Is it winter there?"

"Ah, yes," I reply. "America has opposite seasons to Australia."

"Will he see snow?"

"No, mate. Las Vegas is desert. I don't think it snows there."

"Oh. That sucks."

"Not if you like the warm weather," I say, catching the angry pouting glare shot my way from Abby. I should probably admit that I haven't told either of the children about our current homelessness. When we were packing up our things, I told them it was because the fumigators were coming in and we didn't want the poison on anything that couldn't be washed. I know it seems awful, I'm lying to them again, but after the way Abby reacted over Kevin leaving, I've decided to stick a pin in all bad news until the new year. Then I can break it to them that they need to change schools and Nana can hold my hand when Abby flies into a tailspin, and Archer does whatever he's going to do when he realises his life isn't the same anymore. I fucking hate the position I'm in. I just keep thinking if I can get through each day then I'm one day closer to being all right again.

Did I mention how much I hate Kevin?

"YOU KNOW," Nana says, standing in the doorway of the kids' room. "I'm going to get my carpenter friend to come over and build you both a bunk bed."

"Bunk bed." Archer claps and jumps in excitement. Abigail looks like she wants to be anywhere but here. She's been like this ever since we arrived a little over a week ago. Every day that goes by, she talks to me a little less. It's gotten worse since Christmas, when the day passed and he didn't call. Worse still on New Year's, when she hoped and hoped for a message at midnight but ended up with nothing. *Fuckwit.* It breaks my heart. And I don't know how to help her through this without making it worse.

Nana says she's just processing the break-up in her own way, and that I need to give her space. But I don't know if that's a great idea since I gave Kevin space and he cleaned us out and left. Space just creates distance in my opinion. I hate that I'm seen as the villain. But I still have to keep the communication lines open for that moment when she finally stops blaming me and just *needs* me. I have to be ready when she is.

And I know I keep saying this, but I fucking hate Kevin for what he's doing to our family. Hate, hate, hate,

*hate.* I feel like my brain is on fire with the amount of rage I have directed at that man.

Nana pulls out her phone and starts tapping on the screen, her eyes squinting. "I saw a picture on Pinterest of a bunk bed that reaches right up to the roof and cuts the room in two. That way you each get your own side and Abby gets some much-needed privacy. What do you think?" Nana holds out her phone so both Abby and Archer can see.

Abby sits up, placing her own phone face down on her foldout bed. "That's how you want us to live?"

"Better than the cots you're on now," Nana says. "We don't have a huge amount of space to work with, but there's a wall on one side of each bed that acts as a privacy screen. It'll feel like you have your own room."

"So, this is it, is it? We just give up and live here now?" Abigail folds her arms and glares at me.

"For now," I say, trying to stay calm so I don't start shaking her to find some sort of sense. She should be thanking Nana for wanting to do something so special for them.

"Why can't we just go back home? Christmas is over. So is New Year's. And Dad should be back soon, right?" Her eyes challenge me, that mouth of hers so tight it resembles a cat's bum. "I want to go home."

"You know why we can't go back home," I say, my eyes darting between her and Archer. He's listening with rapt attention. He loves it here, but I'm guessing he wouldn't mind returning to familiar surroundings either. I really need to sit down and explain this to them, but it's New Year's day, and they were both up late last night watching the fireworks from the beach. They're tired today, and it's obvious that Abigail is emotional. I think it'll be best if we wait another day or two before I drop the bomb.

"We can't go back because it's getting fumigated."

"And painted," I blurt, like I need a new excuse for delaying things.

She rolls her eyes and stomps out of the room. "Fucking bullshit excuses," she mutters.

My mouth drops open and I'm about to yell out to her, ground her or *something*, but Nana touches me on the arm and says, "Fighting with her will only drive a wedge between you. Give her time." And I close my mouth again. I suppose we all have to deal with this in our own way. Still, I don't like my fourteen-year-old daughter throwing tantrums and swearing in front of her little brother.

"I think the bunk is a really cool idea," Archer says from the edge of his bed, where he's been sitting quietly, twisting the leg on his John Cena figure around and around and around.

"Thank you, Archer," Nana says, sliding her phone back into a hidden pocket in her kimono.

"Is Abigail right though, Mum?"

"About what?" I really hope he isn't going to mention the bullshit excuses part. My son has a cheeky streak and an excellent poker face.

"That we're living here now?"

Pressing my lips together, I exchange glances with Nana. "For a little longer, yeah."

"Until Dad gets back?"

I nod. "Yeah." The word comes out as a bit of a whisper. How do I tell him the truth? I'm not ready to break his heart too. I couldn't stand it if he starts to hate me the way Abby does.

He smiles, runs over and hugs me before he announces he's going to play. And suddenly, that tiny gesture from my beautiful boy makes me feel about a thousand times better.

"I guess he likes it here," Nana says with an amused smile pulling at her lips.

"Thank God. I don't think I could take two angry children right now."

"I understand why, but you'll need to tell them both the truth sooner or later. School goes back first week of February. You only have four weeks."

"I know. I'll tell them. I just... I need to deal with the fallout on my end first. Once I know where we stand financially, then I can break it to the kids."

She touches me lightly on the cheek, pressing her lips into a smile before announcing she's going to put the kettle on.

I blow out my breath and take a seat on Abigail's bed, my hand hitting her discarded phone. When I hit her home button, I tell myself it's not because I want to snoop. It's because that's what you do when you pick up a phone, right? It's like a habit. And because my thumbprint is registered on both of my children's phones, of course it unlocks fully. Once again, I tell myself I'm not snooping. But the iMessage app is open and I happen to *see* it unintentionally. Message after message to Kevin:

**where r u?**

**Plz come home**
**Mums taking us 2 nanas.**
**It's xmas. Why aren't u here?**
**Where are you?**
**Happy New Year!**
**I miss u, daddy. Please call.**

Over and over again she's sent these messages, and not once has Kevin replied. I don't know this man, anymore. One who cares so little about his own flesh and blood. It's agonising to witness, and as I slip the phone back where I found it, I have to fight back my tears. My little girl is hurt and angry, and there's nothing I can do to fix it. She needs her dad.

"God damn you, Kevin," I mutter under my breath.

## FIFTEEN

## DARCY

"What is this?" I ask later that night. The kids are in bed and Nana and I are partaking in a glass of wine out on the deck, and suddenly a group of women come walking down the footpath chanting. They're wearing dark cloaks and holding candles, and they stop right in front of Nana and me. I feel like I'm in that scene in *Indiana Jones and the Temple of Doom* where they pull the guy's heart from his chest. I place my hand on my throat and recoil.

"This is your cleansing ritual," Nana says, her eyes gleaming as she opens the gate and lets the women in.

"My what?" I'm basically crouched on the chair like a mouse is on the floor as the women take their places. It's dark, and they all have hoods on, their candles held in front of them. I can barely make out their faces, but I think I met a few of them during Nana's Christmas party. I'm also positive I spot Betsy under one of them. I lower my feet back to the ground, figuring I'm safe since these are Nana's friends. Seems they're performing a throw-back to their coven days.

"Out with the old, make way for the new," they chant over and over.

"The new?" I laugh and pick up my wine glass, taking a hefty drink since there is obviously a whole show to see. "Is this because it's a new year now?"

Nana picks up a bundle of twigs she must have had stashed in the garden bed then lights the end of it with a BBQ lighter, waving it around and joining in with the chant as smoke billows out.

I cough and wave a hand in front of my face. "Is that sage? Great. OK."

Three of the women set down their candles and pull a long ribbon from their sleeves, each handing me one end to hold.

"What is this?" I ask, but I'm getting no answers. They just keep chanting and passing the ribbons between them, braiding them together.

The final lady pulls out a massive set of dressmaking scissors, and suddenly I'm not sure if sitting here is such a great idea.

"You need to cut ties with him, dear," Nana explains.

Now I get it.

"Close your eyes and picture your relationship with Kevin," she coaches. "Imagine this cord is the invisible string that connects your heart to his. When you're ready, pick up the scissors and repeat after me."

A smile plays on my lips, but I do as she says, closing my eyes and picturing Kevin's and my togetherness. I recall a lot of the small things, holding hands at the cinema, debating over world events, sharing a bottle of wine, bringing our children into the world. I see one of his rare smiles, a private moment of tenderness. And I also see the cold, hard glare of anger, the look of indifference when he lacked empathy. I see the sneaking and the scheming, and then I don't want to see any more. I want it over.

Keeping my mind focused, I picture that the braided ribbon runs through the streets and finds its way into his hands. I see his face, watch his lips move, forming the words 'I want a divorce'. Unlike that day in the parking garage, they don't hurt me anymore. In fact, I'm relieved when he says it.

I pick up the scissors.

"I cleanse my heart of Kevin Field," Nana starts, and I repeat her word for word.

"By cutting this cord, I cut him from my life and let him go. I ask the universe to fill my heart with healing light to make way for my future. May the mother guide me on the right path."

Then I cut the cord, and the ladies set it alight with their candles and drop it into the silver bowl that decorates the middle of the table. Nana waves the sage around a little more, then the women all say, 'Love and light," then snuff their candles with their thumb and forefinger.

The moment they finish, they fling off their cloaks and hang them over the backs of the chairs.

"Got anything to drink, Esme?" one of them asks. She has white hair, wire-framed glasses and a slash of red lipstick across her wilted mouth. "I'm a bit parched after all that chanting."

"Lots of wine in the fridge. You know I'm never lacking refreshments."

"That's why we love her," another lady with dyed red hair says as she sits across from me. Helen, I think her name is. "She keeps us all fed and sedated." She smiles and her eyes practically disappear. I'd put her in her late seventies, but I could be wrong.

"It's nice to see you again, Helen." I reach across the table and touch her hand, saying hello to Betsy, the lady next to her, while I do. She's always reminded me a lot of Sophia in *Golden Girls* with her small stature and large glasses.

"You think your nana has something a little harder than wine in there?" Betsy asks. "I haven't had a drink all year."

That one gets a lot of laughs and eye-rolls. "That's a dad joke if ever I heard one," another lady says. Carla. I met her last night at the beach. She was with her grown children and grandkids, and the best way I can describe her is 'beige'. From her oversized cardigan to her glasses and hair. She's monotone. "I have to tell you, we don't normally practise witchcraft. We prefer regular craft— the paper and glue kind—but we made an exception for you. Esme has told us all about you, and we feel like you're part of the family."

"Oh. Well, I'm honoured," I say with a smile, lifting my glass as one is set in front of her. I'm fairly sure I'm going to need a lot of wine to get through tonight. Doing something symbolic like cutting ribbon feels oddly free-ing. It almost gives me the confidence to start moving forward. I can't do anything to legally end my marriage for another eleven months, but I can sever ties emotionally. Then I can set myself free. So, that's a start.

"And this here is Martha," Nana says, setting bottles of wine on the table as the lady with the lipstick takes her seat, placing a bowl of nuts between us all.

"I hear you've attracted the attention of our favourite rugby player," Martha says, smiling wide, a smudge of red coating her incisor. I war with whether I should tell her or leave her be while trying to control the heat in my cheeks over the mention of Leo in our conversation. It hasn't been easy since we returned, knowing he's right next door and avoiding him like the plague. It's not that I don't want to see him, it's more that I can't face him. I feel so foolish over the way I left things that I'm not sure I can look him in the eye. I actually almost ran into him on the street on Christmas Eve, and I freaked out to the point where I ducked behind a telegraph pole to avoid being seen. Then I had terrible anxiety, thinking he might stop by Nana's on Christmas Day, but it turned out he was spending the day elsewhere with his son. And that just made me feel stupid, because of course he has his own life outside of being Nana's neighbour. I don't know what I was thinking.

However, that didn't stop my eyes from scanning the crowd and drifting to observe his quiet apartment on New Year's Eve. He was nowhere to be seen, and I'm conflicted as to whether I'm glad or disappointed by that. It's like I don't want to see him and I do want to see him at the same time. And that's a strange place for me to be. I mean, how do you even behave towards a man when you licked your own tits after clawing at his chest? There's no handbook on dealing with the aftermath of sexual embarrassment in social settings, so I don't really have a step-by-step on how to do this. But I know I can't avoid him forever. The man lives next door.

"So, uh…is that what this ritual was about?" I ask, my gaze landing on Nana. "Leo?"

She shakes her head. "No, darling. The cleansing was all for you, to get rid of the bad energy of he who shall no longer be named. The girls have heard the rumours is all."

"Rumours?"

Martha sits forward. "Oh yes, you're the talk of the complex, a pretty single mother spending time with our most eligible bachelor. Everyone in the building knows something happened between you two."

My mouth falls open. "I'm sorry? They, um…they know what exactly?"

"That's all we have," Helen adds. "We asked Esme for the juicy details. But she's so tight-lipped."

"That's why we're coming straight to the source," Carla puts in, resting her chin on her hand.

"I, uh, I don't know what to tell you," I start, rubbing the back of my neck as I pick up my wine glass. I hide behind it like it's a shield. "I suppose Leo and I are friends at best. I was helping him with his sore knee and then I went home. That's where it ends." And I won't talk to them about him when I can't even manage to speak to the man himself.

Martha pouts and pushes her coarse white hair from her eyes. "You at least like him though, right? A man like that doesn't come along every day."

"And we're all too old to chase him. So, it'd really help us to live vicariously through you," Carla adds, her voice as mousey as her looks.

"And they'd be so great together," Helen says.

Lots of nodding and ah-huh-ing happens around the table.

"There is nothing going on between me and Leo," I insist. "He's way out of my league, so don't even go there."

"Oh pish," Nana says. "You're never out of any man's league, my girl."

I roll my eyes a little and sigh, shaking my head as I wave the sounds of agreement away.

"I think you should go for it," Betsy says. "He needs a good woman in his life. And you're an excellent woman."

"No. I don't think..." I hold my hand up, my head spinning from all the voices and the prodding.

"All right, ladies. That's enough," Nana says over the top of everyone. "Darcy can find her own man in her own time. She doesn't need us pushing her into anything."

"Thank you, Nana," I say, grateful she came to my rescue.

"Although," she goes on, leaning in close. "If I was your age and single, he'd be the first horse I'd choose to break in my new saddle."

"What does that even mean?" I say, frowning while everyone else cackles with laughter.

## SIXTEEN

## LEO

*Friends at best.*

I honestly wasn't eavesdropping, I just happened to arrive home a few moments before. The apartment felt a bit stuffy, so I opened the deck door to let the breeze in. It also carried the rather loud conversation happening next door. And since my name was mentioned, I listened.

Sue me.

I know Darcy is avoiding me. She's been here for over a week and while we've both been busy with the holidays —I spent an uncomfortable day with Tash and her family in the Toorak home we once shared at Christmas then Niall and I spent New Year's Eve in the city alone—it's as if she's pretending I don't exist. *Friends at best.* What am I supposed to do with that?

To be honest, I've never faced this kind of a conundrum with a woman I've been interested in. It may sound conceited, but normally, I smile, flirt a little, then she's in my bed until she's not anymore. They don't tend to sleep with me then hide behind telegraph poles just so they don't have to speak to me. This is new.

I guess I could back off completely and wait until she comes to me. But that's not how I operate. When I want something, I go for it. Maybe it's the competitive sportsperson in me, I don't know, but I've never been good at sitting back and waiting. I need an active role in pursuing my goals.

Shit. That sounds terrible. Darcy isn't a *goal*. But she is a want, a desire. For whatever the reason, Darcy is the first woman I've met in a very long time who ticks all the right boxes, and I feel as though I won't be able to move on until we explore whatever our connection is. Maybe it turns out that I really like the idea of her, and all we're meant to be is friends and neighbours, but maybe, just maybe, there's something more for us. Something with substance.

I sound like a sap, don't I? My advanced years are mellowing me out big time. You never would have caught me talking like this in my twenties, or even my thirties. But my forties, well, they're a different story. Maybe this is my mid-life crisis, or maybe I'm just finally growing up and realising that there needs to be more to a relationship than lust. I'm looking for my best friend and lover all wrapped up in one.

See what I mean? I'm sappy as fuck. I don't know what's going on with me. I don't normally act like this.

Anyway, Darcy has been back in Bayside for nine, maybe ten days, and she doesn't want to see me if the telephone pole incident is anything to go by. It was a ridiculous move. She's a full-grown woman and a telegraph pole can barely hide a child. And Archer was with her so he was excited and called out to me. I'm not a dick, so I said hi back, but I kept it all brief since Darcy was hissing at him to come stand by her. My ego took a major hit. Was she hiding because she didn't want to see me? Was it because she hadn't washed her hair or something? I know women worry about that stuff. Or is she so regretful over having sex that she can't stand to look at me anymore?

I'm going crazy trying to figure this shit out.

Later that day, I found Archer's most prized possession, his John Cena action figure, on my side of the deck. It had a little note rolled up, tucked under its plastic arm. *'I'm not allowed to play on your side anymore. Here's John Cena so you don't miss me.'* I thought that was fucking cute. Cute, and a little sad. Despite being a bit gung-ho, he's a good kid, and I never minded it when he climbed over to my deck and talked my ear off. I bought him a brand-new John Cena doll and left a note with that saying, *'Thanks, kid. This one's so you don't miss me.'* I don't even care if that's weird.

So, I'm planning on having a conversation with Darcy. I've given her space over the holidays to focus on her kids and get used to the idea of me living close by. But it's time for us to have a chat and clear the air. And I'm not going into this without a plan. She's in a bad place right now and the last thing she needs is me chasing after her. I need to take a big step back and prove to her that

I'm here as a friend more than anything. She'll need time to heal after the shit her husband put her through. It's going to be hard not to touch her, but I think that's the best play—show her I'm here, and be the guy she needs when she needs me. *Keep my damn hands to myself.* I can do that. I'm sure I can.

## SEVENTEEN

DARCY

"John Cena and me have the same birthday." Archer's voice travels down the hall. I lie in bed, staring at a ceiling that's painted to look like Van Gough's The Starry Night. This ceiling wasn't even painted when we came here the first time. Nana is always redesigning and rearranging things. She says boredom is the murderer of free spirits. *I wonder how she managed this in only two weeks?* It's quite wonderful.

Although, I think I've spent more time staring at this thing overnight than I've spent sleeping of late. I've examined the intricate brushstrokes as if the answers to all life's questions might be within them. They're not. But it helps pass the time. I'm not used to sleeping alone yet. I wonder if I ever will be. Twenty years of sharing a bed with another person is a comfort you don't easily forget, no matter how angry you are. The presence of a warm body, even the familiar snores, it's like a security blanket I'll never get back, and I do admit I miss that.

"The same birthday. Wow. What do you think you like most about John Cena?" *Wait. I know that voice.*

"I just told you. We have the same birthday."

The man chuckles. *Is that?* "You don't think any of his wrestling moves are cool?"

*Oh my God. It is.*

Curiosity draws me from my room. I creep down the hall, standing out of sight as I listen to Archer talk. I want to confirm who it is, but it's also rare that a mother gets to listen to her child converse with another adult. They're always so different when they know Mum is around and listening.

"I don't really know any of his wrestling moves," Archer says, in his matter-of-fact manner. "Mum says the WWE is too violent for a kid my age."

"You're only eight, right?" I peek around the corner and my suspicions are confirmed, Archer is talking to Leo. My heart starts galloping in my chest. *What is he doing here?*

"Yeah. But I'm a mature eight, you know? I'm more of a ten or a twelve in my head."

"I'm not sure that's much better to be honest." I can hear the smile in Leo's voice.

Leaning against the wall, one arm folded across my middle, I press the thumb of my other hand against my lips, trying to keep quiet as I listen and try to decide how I'm supposed to be around Leo again. Do I hide here and wait till he goes? Or do I bite the bullet and walk out there like everything is normal?

"Whatever, man," Archer says, his voice taking on this quality that tells me he's acting tough now. "I don't think I get enough credit for how grown-up I really am. I know heaps of stuff. Stuff they don't even teach in school."

"Really? Like what?"

"For starters, I know that there are so many stars in the sky that you can't even count them in your lifetime."

There's a pause and I imagine Leo is lifting his eyebrows or nodding, something most adults do when listening to kids.

"I also know that it takes so long for the light to reach Earth that a lot of the stars we look at are already dead."

"Really?"

"Yeah," he says. "Dead like your dreams."

*Oh God.* I cover my mouth with my hand, trying not to laugh. He's so cheeky.

"I guess you're right there." Leo laughs out loud, a hearty sound that's nice to listen to. A sudden pang hits me in the chest as I realise that I've missed our afternoon drinks and chats. We had a good thing going before I messed it all up by getting freaky on him.

"I know other stuff too," Archer continues.

"Yeah?"

"Yep. I know that my dad isn't coming back." *Oh my God. What?*

My heart stops beating.

*He knows. How?* Did Abigail tell him?

"That's gotta suck," Leo says, not giving anything away.

"It does. And it doesn't. He never liked it when I made noise, and I like making noise so it's more fun when he isn't around. Nana said she'll teach me to play the ukulele. It means 'jumping flea'. Did you know that?" My knees wobble and my stomach drops. I didn't know he felt that way about Kevin. *I'm his mother. I should have known this.* Swallowing hard, I press my hand against my chest.

"Ukulele means jumping flea? No. I didn't know that at all. I wonder why they called it that."

"I don't know that part. I can't know everything, Leo. Sometimes you're gonna have to look things up yourself." I smile again, biting my lip, because I'm also trying not to cry. I'm a bit of an emotional mess here. Meanwhile, my eight-year-old is out there being an absolute champion about me uprooting his life with little explanation. My fourteen-year-old daughter is the angry one. Between the three of us, we seem to have the five stages of grief covered.

"OK, Archie, I'll do that." Archie? They're doing nicknames? "You're a very smart kid, you know."

"It's good of you to notice, Leo. But, I do have one more question for you."

"Shoot."

"Do you like nuts?" What? *Oh no. Not this joke.*

"Sure, I like nuts," Leo replies, unsuspecting. *Oh no. Oh no.*

I jump out of my hiding place just in time to see Archer grabbing himself on the crotch and yelling, "Then how do you like deez nuts?"

"Archer," I yell, as he runs off giggling and disappears outside where I can see Nana working in her herb garden. "I'm so sorry about that, Leo. I—" Oh. He's even better looking than I remember.

Leo's grinning broadly, his shoulders shaking from laughter as he sits at the counter, coffee in hand, wearing a red checked shirt, cotton drill work pants, and lace-up boots. Even dressed as a lumberjack, he's beautiful without trying. I think he's even more gorgeous than he was at the beginning of his rugby career—I should know, I've googled him a lot lately. I focused on his pictures since the rest was mainly football and nasty divorce stuff, that I didn't need in my head, so I've become somewhat an expert on his face over the years. This one is definitely my favourite. I really like his laughter lines and the tiny bit of grey that shows through in his stubble. It's hot.

"It's good to see you, Darcy," he says, turning that mega-watt smile on me, causing something in my stomach to flip about. *This isn't good.* I'm reacting like a teen girl when the cool guy notices me. My cheeks feel really hot.

I force myself to remember I'm a grown woman, who, if my life was chronicled on Google images like Leo's, wouldn't fair so hot in the ageing game. I've had to put a hell of a lot of work into looking semi decent ever since I hit my thirties. Having children and sacrificing sleep gave me dark shadows under my eyes for days, an arse that sags if I don't work out for five minutes, and don't even get me started on the random hairs that sprout from my chin. Men always seem to age better than women. I don't think it's fair since we're the ones who need our youth more; chasing kids is *not* easy.

"How have you been?" I want to keep our conversation as light as possible, otherwise I'm likely to start picturing him naked. *Shit. Too late. I see it.* And if I close my eyes it's worse.

*Boy, it's getting really warm in here.*

"I'm good. Just here to measure up the room for the bunks. Esme said you knew about it."

"The bunks? You're her carpenter friend?"

He reaches for the tape measure on his belt, pulling the tape out and letting it go again as a demonstration.

"You're a carpenter?" I'm struggling to believe this.

"Sure am, certified and everything."

"I thought you did commentating, or something?"

"In the winter, yeah. But I don't enjoy being idle for the rest of the year, so I take a few odd jobs to keep me busy. I do a fair bit of restoration work."

"I still can't wrap my head around you being a carpenter."

He laughs a little. "I was raised by a single mother who believed in backup plans. Football can't be forever, she always said, so I also learned a trade as well."

"Wow, your mum sounds like a smart woman."

"She really was."

"Was?"

He nods. "Passed a few years back."

I scrunch my nose a little and lean against the door frame, my fingers playing mindlessly with the ribbon on my sleep shorts. "My dad passed a few years ago too. Stroke."

"Cancer for me. Lung."

"I'm sorry you went through that."

"I'm sorry you lost your dad."

We take a moment, silent, eyes locked. Then I pull up one side of my mouth and break contact.

"Well, I should probably get dressed and let you get back to work," I say, thumbing over my shoulder.

His eyes drop from mine, taking a moment to travel downward before they flick back up. "Don't hurry on my account."

I look down, realising I'm standing here in a camisole and frilly boxers set. They're more like *really* short shorts that show off a lot of leg, and the silky camisole isn't hiding much either. Plus, it's all pink silk and white lace, far too girly for a forty-year-old woman to be wearing with my saggy boobs and spider veins.

"Oh crap." I clap my hands over myself and reverse back into the hallway, spinning around so fast that I trip, fall forward, and land on my hands and knees, my hair falling in my face. I scramble to get back up, my feet skidding comically on the floor, squeaking against the tiles and making a right noise.

"Need some help there?"

"Ahhh..."

Hands, warm and strong, grip my waist to steady me and help me back up. They remind me what it's like to be touched by him, and every nerve inside me starts dancing about excitedly, my mind throwing up images of our one and only coupling. *It's so incredibly hot in here.* Needing to break the connection of his hands on my skin, I stand too fast, crick my back and yelp with pain.

"Oh God. Oh God."

"Whoa there," Leo says, his fingers digging a little deeper into my flesh. I close my eyes, my face burning so hot that I'm sure I'm bright red.

"I'm OK," I force out, trying not to lean back against

him and let out a tiny moan, because well, that would be inappropriate when my daughter is still asleep in the room only a few feet away from us.

"Are you sure? I feel like you're gonna land like a sack of potatoes if I let go."

"I promise I'll be fine," I say, my voice merely breath. "I need to get Abby up anyway, otherwise you won't be able to do your job."

"OK," he whispers, releasing me slowly and stepping back. "Come and see me later?"

His greenish eyes lock with mine and I don't know whether to refuse or nod. But I don't get the chance to do either when Abigail shuffles out of the bedroom. "Mum? What are you doing?"

I spin around to face her, wide eyes. "I'm uh, this is Leo. He's measuring your room for the bed," I explain in a rush.

"I know who Leo is, Mum." She looks me up and down the way Leo did, but her version is horrified. I'm feeling practically naked right now. "Where are your clothes?"

"I'm going to get them now," I say, pointing to my room then basically power-walking my way there. I lock myself in and drop my head against the closed door. I am so fucked up right now. My marriage has ended, my daughter hates me, my son is happy his dad is gone, and I'm making eyes at the neighbour I've already fallen into bed with. Does it get much more complicated than that?

## EIGHTEEN

## DARCY

Tucking Archer into bed that night, I take the opportunity to talk to him about what I overheard him saying to Leo. He's been so busy tagging along with Nana all day (something I loved doing as a kid) that I haven't been able to sit down with him until now. He never complains about being bored here.

"Do you want to talk to me about your dad? I heard you tell Leo this morning that you don't think he's coming back."

He rubs the back of his hand across his nose. "I'm right, aren't I?"

"How would you feel if you were?"

He shrugs. "I dunno. It's always more fun when he's away because he only likes it when I sit and be quiet. He doesn't like doing cool things I want like bowling or swimming. It's only stuff he wants to do and most the time that's just playing on his computer."

"I'm sorry you feel this way, honey. I didn't realise."

His lips twist from side to side as he plays with the

gold band that still adorns my finger. *I guess I can take that off now.* "I still want to see him sometimes. But I'm OK if he doesn't live with us anymore." That strikes me as a huge admission from a little boy, and I wonder how long he's been harbouring that level of resentment towards his dad.

With my mouth tight, I look at him for a long moment; his light brown hair, shiny from his bath; his golden skin, tan from the sun. The gaps either side of his bottom teeth remind me he's still so young, but the words out of his mouth, and those big blue, *wise* eyes, tell me that perhaps I *have* been underestimating him. He's more grown-up than I want him to be. He sees the shittiness in this world and takes it in his stride. And that makes me sad. He's only eight. He shouldn't feel the weight of these things.

"What makes you so sure he's not coming back?"

"I can just tell."

I run my fingers through his soft hair, pushing it back from his forehead. "How can you tell, buddy?"

"Because your eyes are sad. You keep smiling and telling us everything is good. But your eyes are really, really sad."

"I see." I take a big, sobering breath, struggling not to let my sad eyes leak sad tears. "I'm sorry I didn't tell you sooner." My words come out as a whisper, coated in emotion.

He shrugs. "It's OK. Grown-ups never tell kids things. We're used to figuring it out for ourselves."

I laugh a little at that. "Is that right?"

"Yeah. Like how I had to figure out that the tooth fairy is really you."

My head pulls back of its own accord. "You don't believe in magic anymore?" If he doesn't, I think I'm going to cry.

"I do. The Easter bunny and Santa Claus are the real deal, but the tooth fairy is a big ole fake."

A smile plays on my lips. *Thank God.* "What makes you so sure the tooth fairy isn't real?"

"I woke up when you put the coin under my pillow the last time."

"I see. What makes you so sure I wasn't just checking to see how much you got?"

"Because you have more money than me. What would you want with two dollars when you have money in the bank?" *Not any more...*

Running the backs of my fingers along his cheeks, I bop him on the nose with my index finger. "You're far too smart for me."

"I know," he says, so sure of himself. He rubs his eyes, his fists so big yet still so small. I'm revisited by flashbacks of him as a baby, rubbing at his eyes and griping until I swaddled him tight and sung him a lullaby. Those days went by too fast.

"I should probably let you get some sleep, hey?"

"Is Abby coming to bed soon?" he asks, mouth opening wide with a yawn he can't stop.

"Maybe in an hour or two."

"She still thinks Dad is coming back and we're going home," he informs me.

"I know," I whisper. "She just wants everything to go back to normal, I think."

"Normal is boring." He sounds just like Nana. "I like it better here, anyway. There's always stuff to do. Will we go to school here now too?"

No sense in hiding that truth anymore. "Yes. With your father gone, we can't keep the house." I'm keeping the entirety of our financial ruin to myself. As smart as Archer is, I don't think it's right to involve him in my money woes.

"Because you don't have a job?"

"Yeah. But I'll find one and then we'll start fresh on our own again."

"I want to stay here with Nana."

"I think we'll be here for a while," I whisper, pulling his blanket a little higher up his chest.

"That's good. I'm excited about the bunk bed."

"Maybe Abby will like it too." As I take a deep breath, I can feel how full my heart has become from talking to him. He's such a special boy, and I'll do every-thing in my power to keep him happy and carefree too. No light squashing needed.

"Yeah. But she won't tell you that. She's too grumpy."

With a chuckle, I tickle him. "No picking on your sister."

He giggles and wriggles, sighing when I stop my assault. "What is she doing, anyway?"

"She's talking to her friends." Abby is on the deck in a group video chat with her friends back home, keeping her voice low so none of us can hear the conversation. But it doesn't take a genius to know she's complaining about me for bringing her back here. Not only does she think I'm keeping her from her father, she's also suffering from a serious case of FOMO (fear of missing out). Her friends are hanging out and planning sleepovers and whatever else teen girls like to do, and she's not there and a part of it all.

"Is she talking to her new friends or her old friends?"

"She has new friends?"

He nods. "She was windsurfing with some kids today. Me and Nana saw her with a boy. She was smiling lots."

"A boy?" Abby with a boy? She's always been so adamant that she was too busy with school for boys.

"There were girls there too. But a boy was showing her how to use the board with the sail on it. She kept falling off, but she was laughing, so Nana said we shouldn't bother her."

"That was a nice thing to do. Did Nana say if she knows the boy Abby was windsurfing with?" Windsurfing. Abby has never shown any interest in board sports before, either. I feel so out of touch with my kids right now. I always thought I knew them, that I could pre-empt their wants and needs, be the kind of mum who was involved. Seems I've become anything but. My life feels like a total sham now. I don't know anything or anyone. I don't even think I know myself.

"Mummy?" For all of his grown-up words, he can't let go of calling me Mummy.

"Yeah, hon?"

"Does Abby know we're changing schools?"

"Not yet. I thought I'd try and talk to her when she's in a better mood."

He chuckles as he rolls over, pulling his blanket up to his neck. "That might be never."

"She'll come around eventually."

"I hope so for your sake," he says, closing his eyes. "Night, Mummy."

"Sweet dreams, Archer."

Leaning down to press a kiss to his plump cheek, I flick off the lamp, leaving him with only the soft glow of his dinosaur nightlight to keep him company. Within seconds his breathing evens out, and I pause in the doorway, completely in awe over this little kid who seems to be raising himself. Thank God, because I'm obviously doing a terrible job on my own.

## NINETEEN

## LEO

"Where have you been all day?" I ask as Niall stomps up onto the deck and heads straight inside to the kitchen, tracking sand inside with each step.

I open my mouth to comment, but press my lips back together instead, watching as he pulls open the fridge and takes out a Pepsi Max, popping the ring, and gulping down a long thirsty drink. Then he pulls out the ham, mayonnaise and mustard and starts making himself a sandwich.

"Your dinner is in the microwave. That fried chicken you like."

"This is fine," he says, shoving his sandwich into his mouth then heading for his room without another word. I look at the mess he's left on the kitchen counter and grit my teeth, placing my hands against the marble benchtop and doing my best not to react. He's doing this on purpose, pissed because I insisted he be here until school goes back next month.

"You'll have to talk to me eventually," I call out, my

statement being met with the slamming of his door. *Excellent.*

I mutter under my breath as I tidy up his mess and dump his uneaten dinner in the bin. I paid a small ransom to Tash so she'd back down and let Niall stay here for the summer school holidays. He was fine when he thought it was just between Christmas and New Year's, but when he realised it was all of January too, he decided I was once again public enemy number one. You'd think I was the devil with the way he's been glaring at me. My instinct is to yell and lay down the law, but I know that's not going to get me anywhere because Tash has had years to poison his mind. If I'd been a deadbeat rugby-playing manwhore with a bunch of illegitimate kids all over the place, I would understand it. But when we were married, I always spent as much time as I could with Niall, especially in the off-season, which was a pretty large chunk of the year. I know he was only little, but doesn't he remember something of those times? There's photo evidence and everything. I'm bitter things are where they are, but manipulation is something Tash does well, so the best thing I can do is be patient and *show him* I care. That I'm not the bastard his mother paints me as. But it's hard feeling so out of control where your own flesh and blood is concerned.

Time is ticking. I have less than a month to get through to him. He's seventeen now, this time next year, he'll be an adult, there'll be no court orders enforcing my right to see him. Once he turns eighteen I'll have no hope and Tash will have won. Another entitled arsehole will be released into the world, and I'll be disowned by my own son. *She'd love that.* Although one thing I'm looking forward to is getting my balls back. No more child support means no more extortionate bribes to enforce my right to see my son. No way. Soon, I'll be done forking out money to help fund her lavish lifestyle. She can find some other schmuck to take advantage of instead. Once he's eighteen, if Niall needs financial help from me while he still studies, he'll have to speak to me in full sentences and ask himself. I'm not dealing with Tash anymore.

Sweeping the sand out onto the wooden deck, I push it through the small slots between the planks then hose it all away, watering my garden while I'm at it. It's one thing you get used to living alone—this whole tidying up thing. I like order, and my mother always taught me to clean up after myself, so I don't see it as a big deal. My son, on the other hand, probably hasn't picked up a broom in his life. Neither has his mother, really. She's always had 'people' to do those things for her.

And do I want Niall to be a self-centred arsehole for the rest of his life? *No.* And that fucks with me because I want him to be respectable—*respected*—so he's a decent human being with goals and aspirations. He's got it in him. I see it in those rare moments when he forgets to have a chip on his shoulder, like when he carried bags of groceries home for Esme last week. I spotted them walking along the footpath together talking like he actually has a good head on his shoulders. I just wish he used it more often. I wish Tash would quit letting him do whatever the hell he wants. He needs boundaries in his life.

Wiping my hand over my face, I let out a groan,

pushing away my shitty thoughts. There's no point in being sour. My ex-wife is my ex-wife and there's nothing I can do to change the way she is. Standing here lamenting it will only drive me crazy, like beating my head against a brick wall.

As I set my broom down, the distinct smell of weed wafts my way and I know that Esme is out on her deck, puffing away the way she does, not giving a shit about the legalities of what she's doing. I'm fairly sure the local cops turn a blind eye to an old woman sparking up, anyway. She isn't hurting anyone.

"Smells good, Esme," I say, leaning on my railing and poking my head past the privacy screen. I'm surprised when I find myself looking at a startled Darcy. "Don't run away." I give her a friendly smile. "I'm not going to dob you in to anyone."

She's frantically waving smoke away as it pours out of her mouth and nose, coughing a little. "My back is hurting and Nana doesn't keep painkillers in the house."

"She likes to be all natural, your nan."

Darcy smiles and looks at the joint in her hand. "She does." The weed must be mellowing her, because this is the longest I've been able to look at her without her turning tail and running in the opposite direction. It's a bit of a relief, because I've really missed her and our chats. And I'm trying to be a gentleman and not focus on my desire to get her in my bed again, but that would make me a liar. I fucking want her. I want to watch her writhe and moan again. I can't stop thinking about it.

"Got a hit in that thing for me?" I gesture to the joint

and she smiles, high as a kite before getting up and approaching me.

"It's all yours," she says. "I'm not so used to this stuff anymore." She gestures at her head, her fingers doing a little bit of spinning action. *God, she's adorable.*

I hold the joint between my lips and flick the lighter, pulling the hot smoke into my lungs. "I really need to give this shit up," I say. "But a puff here and there is good for the soul. So, Esme says, anyway."

"That's what she said to me too." She giggles and leans forward on the railing, the wind pushing back her light hair as she breathes in deep. *Fuck, she's beautiful.* It almost hurts to look at her and want her this much. "The air smells even better when you're high."

I laugh. "Everything is better when you're high."

A slow giggle bursts from her lips, and I notice how pretty her smile is. I'm so used to seeing her serious or stressed that it's nice seeing this relaxed side of her. Even though it took a magical leaf to make that happen.

"You're right. And I'm so happy right now. I can't even feel my back—or my toes—and I'm pretty sure I don't have a single problem anymore."

I take another inhale and offer the joint back to her. "This must be pretty powerful stuff."

She waves it away. "I'm just a lightweight, I think." Leaning with one arm along the railing and the other holding up her head, she grins at me while she studies my face. "Is your knee hurting any more?"

I glance down to where it's strapped up, wrapped in a support brace that I've had to wear on and off depending on how hard I push myself fitness-wise.

"Not really."

"I'm sorry I've been avoiding you," she says, leaning forward a little, her fingers raking through her hair.

"It's OK."

"No. It's not. I've just... I've had so much going on in my head and my life is a huge mess. I don't know what I'm supposed to do with myself, let alone with my kids. I don't think I can add you into the mix too." She pinches her brow together.

"I get it, Darce. I really do. You're forgetting I've been through a shitty divorce. I'm not here to pressure you or add any stress. I'm happy to be your friend, or even the guy you smoke a joint with on occasion." She laughs at that. "It doesn't have to be more than it is, okay?"

"And what about"—she keeps a grip on the railing and she leans back touch, hesitating a little before continuing—"what happened before I left?"

I take a deep breath and squint a little. "I'm not gonna lie. That part was a lot of fun and I wouldn't say no to a repeat performance, but I also understand it's maybe a little too soon for you."

"You wouldn't be pissed if I just wanted to go back to being friends?"

"That would make me a really shitty person if I was, wouldn't it?"

She lowers her head a little, eyes locked on mine in a discerning stare. "That's not answering my question, Leo." She's swaying a little, and it's hard to take her seriously. She really is a lightweight. Her pupils are huge. She's smashed.

"No, Darcy. I wouldn't be pissed at all. We both kind of...lost control that day."

"Oh God." She covers her face with her hands and groans. "Don't remind me. I could just die of embarrassment every time I think about what I did."

"Embarrassment?" I've had a lot of comments about my prowess in the bedroom, but embarrassing has never been one of them. Call me proud, but they've been mostly positive comments. I like to think I know what I'm doing.

"The whole"—she grabs her boobs and lifts them up, while she rolls her eyes—"thing."

I can't help but let my eyes drift down. "I thought that part was hot."

She meets my eyes and her cheeks go bright red. "No, it wasn't. It was over the top and that is so not how I normally behave in the bedroom." *Pity.* "I guess I lost control like I was having a breakdown or something and you got a front-row seat." She's rolling her eyes again.

"Since we're being candid, if it makes you feel any better, that moment has featured pretty heavily in my fantasies of late."

"It has?" She seems pretty shocked by that revelation.

I bounce a shoulder. "Like I said, it was hot. You have absolutely nothing to be embarrassed about from my point of view. Sometimes it's good to be out of control. It lets you live in the moment. Besides the timing of things, I wouldn't change anything about what we did that day."

"It came out of the blue, didn't it?"

"It did and it didn't. I was pretty into you from the get-go."

She laughs. "In those few moments before Archer took you out?"

I shake my head. "Nah. I saw you out here a few nights before. I'd gone for a walk because I couldn't sleep, and when I came back you were sitting out here alone, staring out at the sea, so lost in thought you didn't even notice me walk right past."

"That was probably the day Kevin left. I think I was shell-shocked."

"Well, I thought you were beautiful."

Her fingers touch her lips, hiding her smile. "Well, I think you're beautiful too," she says after a moment. "I'm surprised you don't have all the women around here tackling you when you run along the beach. It's quite a sight, you with your shirt off and all."

Now I'm smiling. *She thinks I'm beautiful too.* I lean in a little closer. "I don't want any other women tackling me, Darcy. I want you. I won't pretend I don't. But I understand that you need time before you can handle having a new man in your life. Just give the word, OK? Until then, we can keep this as friends. Does that work for you?"

She blows out a heavy breath then presses her teeth into her bottom lip. "I don't understand why you want me."

"I want you because you're real."

Her hand floats up and she presses her fingers against her forehead. "I'm so high right now, and it's really hard for me to remember why we should only be friends. Because you"—she blows out her breath so it makes a high-pitched 'who' sound—"are *so hot.* But I know, I *know* that only being friends is for the best. For a while, anyway. My daughter, Abigail, isn't taking the separation well at all. She's been desperately trying to get in contact with her father and the *arsehole* won't even return a single text. You'd think that would make her angry at him but no, she's taking all of her anger out on *me*. She's holding out hope that everything will go back to normal and we can all go home. And that's just not going to happen. I still haven't told her she has to go to school here too because she's going to implode or screech so loud it'll make my ears bleed. We are not coping, Leo. Not at all."

So much information came in such a short burst of time that I'm not sure how to hold my face. Firstly—and this is the point I'm happiest about—she seems as into me as I'm into her. Secondly, she's having trouble with her daughter, something I can more than empathise with. I'm caught between wanting to fist-pump the air and nod in understanding. In the end I go with, "Can't be easy on you," because that literally covers everything she just said.

She lets out another steady breath. "It feels impossible. Everything about my life feels so complicated right now. I have no qualifications for anything. Kevin didn't think I needed a university degree once I became a mother, and when he left, he took most of our money. Ruined my credit. Lost the house. I'm drowning here, and I don't even know where to start. I mean, I know I need a job, but what am I supposed to do with no work history that will also provide for me and the kids?"

She's stumbling over her words like her tongue is too thick for her mouth. I finish the rest of the joint and bury the butt in my garden with the toe of my shoe, listening while she talks without pause. All I can think is that she's amazing. She really is lost and overwhelmed, and not once has she belittled her husband even though he fucking ran off and buried them financially. I always vowed not to speak out about Tash, but even I would have struggled to keep quiet if she'd succeeded in ruining my career and left me in a position of nothing. This woman before me deserves a crown. I wish I could pull her into my arms and tell her everything is going to be OK. Because it will. I'll make sure of it.

"I'm *forty*," she laments, while I stand here falling for her even harder. She's stronger than she knows. "I can't go back to school and start again. I'll be retirement age before I even start a career. And I can't live here for the rest of my life and sponge off Nana. She'd let me, you know? She's so generous like that, but I'm not one to take advantage. Have you ever had that, Leo? Someone taking advantage of your kind nature? It sounds contrite when I say it out loud, but I give and I give and I give. And really, I just want the people around me to be happy. But no one is trying to make me happy. Do you ever get that? That the only person in this world who actually cares about you is yourself?" She pauses and stares at me for a moment, but before I can answer, she gasps and puts her hand over her mouth. "Oh, that sounds so horrible. I have Nana, and she cares about everyone. And I have my kids; they care. I sound so selfish. I mean, it's not like I'm the only woman who's ever had her husband survive cancer only to leave her the moment he finds out he'll live. I don't *know* anybody who went through the same thing, but with all the billions of people on this planet, surely one other person went through the same thing." She laughs, but the pitch has changed. I'm reeling, because I can't quite wrap my head around that last part.

"Are you saying that you helped your husband through cancer treatment then he left as soon as he was given the all clear?" Have I mentioned the desire to punch this guy in the face before? Because now I wouldn't mind breaking his legs too.

She nods, pressing her lips together like she's feeling ill. "It's the first thing he said when we got out of the oncologist's office. I was talking about celebrating his remission and he told me he wanted a divorce." She frowns. *What a fucking arse.* "I think I need a drink. Do you have a drink?"

"You know I do." I hold out my hand, and without even hesitating, she takes it. But then she just looks confused.

"Why am I holding your hand?"

I laugh. "So you can climb over to my side of the deck. It's where the drinks are. Your side has dope and my side has alcohol."

"Oh, I get it." Gripping my hand a little tighter, she climbs around the privacy screen, quite nimble for someone who was complaining of a sore back. I shift a hand to her hips, steadying her as her bare feet hit the decking.

She sucks in her breath, and all I want to do is lean in, taste those full lips...

"All right?" I ask.

"Yeah. I just miss this," she says.

"This?" I frown, not sure what she means *and* not wanting to jump to conclusions.

She tightens her hand, still in mine, then nods towards my other hand at her hip. "Dancing." She smiles then shakes her head. "I know that's not what we're doing, but it reminds me of dancing. It's been so, so long."

"Did you dance much with your husband?"

"Oh, God, no. He hated it. It's funny, I always dreamed as a girl that I'd get married and we'd be one of those couples who do the dishes together and dance to the radio." She relaxes her grip and steps back. "Silly when I think of it now."

I catch her back up again and lift my hand so that she spins beneath it, releasing a small giggle. "There's nothing silly about wanting someone to spend time with you." I pull her back towards me and we sway to the sound of the ocean, the haze of our minds making it easy to slip back into familiarity. She feels so good in my arms.

"That's all I wanted," she whispers, looking up at me. "Companionship, someone who cared about me, loved me as I was. Marriage was very different to what I imagined it was going to be."

"Perhaps that's because you were married to the wrong person."

"Maybe," she muses, her eyes searching mine. "What did you think marriage would be like?"

"I don't know, but it definitely wasn't what I got."

"When did you decide you were through?" The weed has definitely taken away all of her filters, because we only skated around this topic previously.

I smile, enjoying this strange and personal conversation we're having. "The day I found out she was cheating on me. I packed a bag and left then and there."

"Did you want to take your son?"

"I did. But I was still in training, still touring. The courts thought he'd be better off with his mum. I got weekends and holidays when I wasn't working."

"Did you miss him?"

"Every day. Tash has made it very difficult for me to keep seeing him."

"But you keep fighting for him anyway." She smiles. "You're a good man, Leo Murphy."

Then she rests her head on my chest and I smile too, because this feels profoundly right. Her body against mine, the scent of her shampoo in my nose. I brush my mouth, featherlight against the top of her head and hum the tune of a song I don't know the name of, enjoying every moment we remain like this. When I finish, she sighs and lifts her head. "I think I'd like that drink now," she says, pulling her hand away from my touch, making me realise that just being friends with her is going to be an incredibly difficult feat. *Who am I kidding?* I already knew I didn't just want to be friends with this woman. But if that's all she's got for now, I'll man up like the lucky bastard I am and take it.

Lucky I'm a patient guy.

## TWENTY

I wake up with a headache and a stiff neck. No doubt the dry throat is from sleeping with my mouth open. On the couch. *Ugh. I haven't fallen asleep sitting up since the kids were babies.*

With a groan, I lean to the side. My memory's fuzzy, but I'm pretty sure I got high, climbed over to Leo's, danced to no music then got drunk, during which, I unloaded *all* of my problems onto him. Must have been a riot for him—not.

*I need water.*

Trying to stand and stay asleep at the same time, I wriggle from the couch, knocking into something hard on my left side. I open my eyes with a start. This feels a hell of a lot like another body. My fully open eyes confirm what my hands feel: Leo is sound asleep next to me, his arm draped over the back of his comfy leather couch, body slumped to the side, soft snores coming along with his breath. There's even a nice shadow of stubble coating his cheeks and chin. *Would it be weird if I touched it?* I'm going with a yes on that one. Still, it's very sweet seeing such a big brawny guy looking all soft from sleep. Although I should probably stop watching Leo sleep and focus a little more on the fact I'm not even in the right apartment. "Fuck." I pat my hands over my chest, thankful when I find I'm fully clothed. At least I didn't get freaky with him again.

"Language, young lady," a new voice says behind me. Startled, I spin around, one hand doing a quick swipe over my face to clear away any drool and smooth over my hair.

"What the?"

Sitting at the dining table eating cereal is a young guy who I'm assuming is Leo's seventeen-year-old son. He has the same dark hair and hazel eyes as his father, but his skin is lacking the deep tan that goes hand in hand with a life by the sea. In fact, it's a little sunburnt.

"I'd give you my name, lady, but I don't reckon he'll keep you around long. No offence, but you're not his usual type."

I open my mouth, not sure what to say or if the current scene is even worth an explanation, but before I can even form a complete thought, I notice the time on the microwave in the kitchen and jump up from the couch.

"It's eight fifteen."

"Oh, he picked a clever one this time," the kid says, giving me a little clap. "Well done. It *is* eight fifteen."

I shoot him an unimpressed look. "I need to go."

"The old folk's home doesn't know you're out?"

Pursing my lips together, I decide I have enough

issues with my own teenager, and leave that one alone. I really need to find my shoes so I can get back to Nana's. The kids will be up by now, and they'll be wondering where I am.

*Shit.*

"Where the hell are my shoes?" I do a full circle before I remember and slap my hand against my forehead. "Oh God, I wasn't even wearing any."

"I take back the part about you being smart."

I roll my eyes and head for the sliding door. "Tell Leo thanks and that I had to go, will you?"

He responds by yelling, "Hey Leo, your latest conquest says thanks for the peen."

I want to bang my head against the double-glazed glass. *Peen? What the... Ohhhh.* "We didn't..." I stammer, walking backwards for a couple of steps as Leo sits up and rubs his eyes, looking as confused as I felt when I first woke.

"Darcy?" Leo turns and finds me trying to make my escape.

"Your latest is trying to do the walk of shame," the kid tells him through a mouthful of cereal.

"I'mnotbutthanksforthechat. Andthedrinks. Gottago bye." I say each word so quickly that they all run into each other. I pretty much take off in a puff of smoke.

I have no idea how I managed to climb around the privacy screen last night, so I take the long way around to Nana's deck, speed-walking because the concrete isn't being very kind to the soles of my feet.

"Darcy," Leo calls after me, but I move faster, pushing in through the sliding door and closing it tight so attractive ex-football stars can no longer be heard. *What the hell is wrong with me?* I have responsibilities. I can't go getting drunk and falling asleep on my—incredibly sexy—neighbour's couch.

I place a hand on my face and let out my breath. It's like I can't handle being a human anymore.

"Good morning," Nana chirps, grinning at me knowingly as she places bowls of Bircher muesli on the table in front of the kids. "Hungry?"

"Morning, Mummy," Archer sing-songs, diving a silver spoon into the fruity concoction in front of him.

Abigail frowns as she looks me up and down. "Where have you been?"

"I...uh..." I look to Nana for assistance.

"She went for an early morning walk," she says, rescuing me, because my hungover mind cannot come up with a feasible excuse right now.

*Thank you,* I mouth. She winks in response then prepares a bowl for me too, setting a cup of strong tea to the side of it. The nourishment is just what I need after too much beer and...bourbon, I think? I can't even remember. It was a giant drunken pity party.

"What are your plans today?" I ask Abby when my brain feels a little less raw.

She shrugs.

"I hear you've made yourself some new friends. Parasailing was it?" I frown, trying to remember.

Abby rolls her eyes. "Windsurfing, Mum. And maybe I'll tell you about my social life when you explain what's going on with Dad."

I am far too hungover for this.

"Your mother is doing the best she can right now, Abigail. I suggest you give her a little credit. She's not the one who left you all," Nana says, her lips tight, her voice surprisingly calm.

Abigail's mouth drops open like she can't believe anyone would dare take my side.

"Yeah," Archer chimes in. "Give Mum a break. If Dad wanted to talk to us he'd answer one of your fifty million text messages." He holds her phone up and scrolls through the messages to demonstrate.

Abigail practically launches herself across the table. "You little arsehole. Give that back."

"Both of you stop it this instant," I yell, my voice ringing in my ears to get over the din of their shrieking while they chase each other around the apartment. Abigail manages to fake Archer out and snatch her phone out of his hands, and I realise he also has his own phone and is filming the whole thing for his YouTube channel, no doubt.

"Wait for it," he says, turning the camera on himself.

*"What did you do?"* Abigail looks like her head is about to explode.

Archer giggles. "I sent Snapchats of you sleeping to everyone on your friends list."

Oh crap.

Abigail screeches, a high-pitched sound that I'm surprised isn't shattering the glass, then she launches herself at Archer, and the next thing I know, they're rolling around on the ground, pulling hair.

"That's enough. That's enough. That's enough," I yell, trying to break them apart. I succeed only slightly, holding them both by the back of their shirts while they continue swiping at each other. We're all red-faced and yelling.

Then we aren't. We're drenched with ice-cold water that Nana throws over the top of us. "You act like animals. I treat you like animals," she bellows.

"Nana," Abigail gasps.

Archer laughs. "Epic." He shuts the camera off on his phone.

"I can't even begin to tell you how disappointed I am in you two right now," I say, snatching the phones from the both of them. "You'll get these back when you learn to behave. Home by five, and drop the attitude." I point a finger at Abigail then shift my glare to Archer. "And apologise to your sister for messing with her phone."

"Sorry," he mutters.

"You will be grounded for the rest of the holidays if you are so much as a second late," I direct at Abigail. "And same goes for you if I so much as suspect you pulled any pranks at the holiday club today. Got it?"

"Yes, Mum," they both mumble.

"Now apologise to Nana."

"Sorry, Nana."

Nana nods graciously. "Why don't you go get cleaned up? Then we can start the day over."

Skulking off, one heads for the bathroom while the other goes into their room. Nana pulls me aside and looks at me with a twinkle in her eye. "I'm dying to know where you were last night." She waggles her eyebrows.

I can't help but laugh. "You'd think you were in high school still."

She shrugs. "In my day, most of us girls didn't make it that far."

"You would have loved it. Everyone loves talking about everyone else's business. Especially if it has something to do with dating."

Her eyes light up. "Oh, is that what you and Leo were doing last night? Were you on a date?"

With a laugh, I shake my head. "No. We were honestly just talking. Nothing else."

"Until eight o'clock in the morning?"

"We fell asleep on the couch."

"With your clothes still on?" She looks disappointed.

"Yes. Talking generally requires clothes."

She waves her hand in the air and starts clearing away breakfast dishes. "The best type of talking happens without them. It's called pillow talk and it's beautiful and soul bearing."

"Speaking of clothes, I'm drenched," I say, deciding to change the subject.

"Yes. Sorry about that. You were collateral damage."

I wipe a hand over my wet arm. "No. It's me who should be saying sorry. They acted like mongrels and they know better."

"Trying times," she says, shrugging the whole thing off in her unique way. "Why don't you get changed yourself while I clean up this mess? You can use the en-suite bathroom. Use the spa bath if you like, and take a moment to de-stress."

This woman has a way of taking a bad situation and turning it on its head. I want to be her when I grow up.

"Thanks, Nana. For everything. I don't know where I'd be without you."

She kisses her fingers and salutes me like we're in *The Hunger Games*, and I walk away chuckling to myself, wondering where in the world she comes up with this stuff.

## TWENTY-ONE

## DARCY

"I'm spending the afternoon with the girls," Nana informs me the following Wednesday while she and I move around the kitchen clearing up. "You're welcome to join us if you like. Martha is bringing the ingredients for slippery nipples. And Carla is bringing supplies for our craft project."

"Cocktails and crafts?" I can't not smile over this.

"Mostly cocktails, but we give the craft thing a good go. We're continuing our crochet project this week."

"Cocktails and crochet? Sounds interesting. I have to take Abigail to get her school uniform sorted, but if I'm back in time, I'll be happy to join in." Unsurprisingly, I'm not expecting this outing with Abigail to go well. She reacted as expected to the news about going to school in Bayside, with a total screaming meltdown. In fact, she broadcast her hatred of me and this place all over social media, and the entire township of Bayside probably heard about it too. She didn't agree quietly.

"Oh, yes. You'll need a drink or two after that. And a

good giggle. Just wait until you see the little pouches we're making. We have plans to set up a stall at the Bayside Hospital fete that's happening at the end of March. So we're gathering stock for our product line now." She lifts her brow and gets all coy.

"What exactly are you making?" My eyes narrow on their own.

"We'll see how long it takes you to figure it out." She smirks then looks to the hallway as Archer emerges, ready for another day at holiday club. It's been great for him because he's already met a couple of kids who will be going to his new school. He's been so easy-going during this big shift in lifestyle and location.

"How do you make your nipples slippery, Nana?" he asks, his brow knitted as he ponders such a thing. "Do you use butter?"

"A slippery nipple is a drink for grown-ups," I explain.

"Oh, like wine."

"Yeah, like wine."

"Did you know that wine with a picture of an animal on the label is called critter wine?" he asks, and I'm suddenly imagining him in a tweed suit, sitting by a fire with a cat in his lap. The mental image makes me smile.

"Where'd you learn that?"

"I dunno." He licks his lips, spins around and finishes it with a ninja kick. "Are we going soon?" he asks Nana.

"As soon as you have your shoes on," she says.

Archer runs into the hall, then a loud bang and raised voices startle us from outside.

"Get back here, Niall," Leo booms.

Nana and I look at each other with raised eyebrows.

"That doesn't sound good," I say. Poor Leo. He's trying so hard to have a relationship with his son, and his son wants none of it. I often see him at the beach, hanging out with all the other teenagers who don't like being around their parents over the holidays. Abigail included. At least she's making friends, I tell myself when I watch her from the deck. Seems she's willing to smile and laugh with anyone. As long as they aren't me.

Looking out the glass door, we spot Leo's son walking down the footpath, his middle finger held high in the air. Leo follows him out, but seems to think better of giving chase, his tense shoulders slumping before turns back to the building. He catches my gaze through the glass, and I shrug before giving him a sympathetic smile. He does the same in return before he shakes his head and seems to do a full body sigh. I feel so bad for him. I want to hug him. But that's not what friends do.

Maybe it should be...

"That boy's mother has a lot to answer for," Nana mutters, shaking her head.

"So I hear." Since my accidental sleepover at Leo's place last week, we've had a few conversations through the privacy screen between the decks. It's been like a confessional where we talk out our frustrations over belligerent teenagers. I've discovered that his ex is a real piece of work. Kind of makes me glad Kevin is out of the picture. Life is hard enough without a tug of war over the children. "I don't understand what ruining your child's relationship with their father is supposed to accomplish."

"It's about control, I think. She wants Leo suffering. The lies she's told." She shakes her head and titches. "If the courts were any good, they would have seen right through her."

"Are you talking about all those allegations she made about him in that TV Soap magazine? I didn't think any of that went to court." Tash had accused Leo of financial and psychological abuse in an interview not long after their divorce. There wasn't a shred of evidence and Leo was open and cooperative when those accusations sparked a brief follow-up by police. The matter was dropped as soon it was raised, and Leo refused to be interviewed over the matter or say a bad word about his ex-wife, going on record to say he has always provided a more than comfortable life for her and was 'deeply hurt their relationship has come to this'. Two months later, an article came out accusing Leo of cheating and fathering a love-child with 'an unnamed fan'. More unsubstantiated lies.

"He told you about those?"

I nod. "And I saw them online. I didn't read them until recently, but the picture she painted doesn't sound like the Leo we know." The thing that struck me most about them was the timing. It was as if they were designed to keep her name in the spotlight until her celebrity was at a level she could leverage. When she landed a role in *Neighbours*, her complaints about Leo stopped. Funny that.

"Not at all. That Tash is the kind of woman who gives the rest of us a bad name."

"I hope I never meet her."

"Oh, you will. Just keep an eye out for the flying monkeys, they'll herald her arrival."

"She's *that* bad?"

Nana pats me on the arm. "My dear, she's worse." I *really* don't want to meet her. I'm not even dating Leo and I'm scared. *God, what would she do to me if I was?* A cold chill runs down my spine at the thought.

I may have to start hiding behind telegraph poles again.

## TWENTY-TWO

## DARCY

"I have about a thousand different balls of wool and all those metal thingies in different sizes," Carla says, pulling items out of a large knitting basket. She's all beige again, and I wonder if she owns any other coloured clothes.

Nana's always had eclectic taste in friends. During my lifetime, I've seen many faces come and go. Only Betsy seems to stay. I once asked Nana why the members of her group changed, and she said it was because they got too boring for her.

"I was worried that maybe they died," I said to that.

"Oh yes, some did. Dead is probably as boring as a person can get, you know."

"What about Betsy? She's the only one I see time and time again."

"Well, for one, she wouldn't go away even if I wanted her to, and second, she's always got a good story to tell. So, she stays."

These cocktails and craft afternoons, I'm told,

happen once a fortnight. From what Nana tells me, the women all live in the building, and they take turns hosting. Today, it's Nana's turn, which means she provides the nibbles, but the other ladies bring the drinks and craft supplies.

It's been a gaggle of giggles from the moment the first guest arrived. These women are all aged between seventy and ninety, and they're so full of energy that they're making me feel old. I'm exhausted just watching them. Granted, I was exhausted the moment I walked in the door. We had to get Abigail's uniform on back order and she went into meltdown mode, saying it was a sign from the gods that moving here was a terrible idea. She even suggested going to live with my mother so she could continue going to her regular school. I'm not sure if she realises that option would actually be a punishment and not a reward.

"Catch it," Helen yells, as a ball of wool goes skimming across the table and onto the floor. I scoop it up before it rolls past my foot.

"Good work." Carla beams as I place it with the others. "Now, I think we need some music in here."

The apartment seems to explode with activity, and no one really has any real idea what they're doing. Martha and Betsy are lining shot glasses along the edge of the kitchen counter, trying to get the layering right on their Slippery Nipples. Every time one of the drinks doesn't work out, they down it and start again. By my count, they've each had four shots. And since there's Sambuca in those things, they're both teetering a little and splashing more liquid on the bench than they're getting in the glasses. There's a lot of 'whoops' and 'oh well' followed by laughter coming from them.

At the table, Helen and Nana are holding pages of a pattern at arm's length as they squint at the dark writing and discuss which balls of wool they'll need to use. Carla stands at the television with the remote in her hand, trying to find a decent music compilation on YouTube.

"Want some help?" I offer, holding my hand out for the remote. She hands it to me and scratches just behind her ear, pulling some of her beige hair free from its tortoise shell clip.

"It's so much easier when you can cast it from your iPad," she says.

I smile. "I love how good at technology you all are."

"Well, you either learn it or you get left behind, don't you? And there's so much great stuff on that Internet. I really like having the video going with my music."

"There sure is." I find a compilation of show tunes pulled from movies like *Singing in the Rain* and *How to Marry a Millionaire*, and since Carla approves, it goes on the big screen.

"Oh, looks like we're ready to go," Nana cheers, grabbing bowls of nuts and vegetables and some hummus she whipped up before her friends arrived.

Martha and Betsy carry over trays laden with prepared Slippery Nipples, wobbling a little as they set them between us.

"Every time you mess up and have to unloop a row, you have to take a drink," Betsy says, pointing a crooked finger at the pattern where some woman is making a rooster-shaped mitten-looking thing. It seems fairly easy, but after a few shots, it'll be impossible.

All I can think is that I can't pick Archer up from holiday club swaying on my feet. "What if we don't drink?"

"Then you have to drink two." Carla cackles, picking one up and drinking it before anyone has started. I can see myself having to carry her upstairs to her apartment before long.

"A couple won't hurt," Nana tells me with a wink as she hands me a shot glass. "Bottoms up."

I hold the glass near my mouth, the strong scent of aniseed hitting me in the nose. Taking a deep breath, I knock the shot back and groan as it burns away at my throat. The ladies all cheer for me, and I'm starting to feel like Alice at the Mad Hatter's tea party. Soon we'll be running around the table to switch seats.

We're halfway through our first rooster (I'm proud to say I haven't needed to drink yet, unlike Betsy and Martha) when there's a knock at the front door.

"Come in," Nana yells, not bothering to get up and check who it is.

"What if it's a serial killer?" I ask, shocked she'd let anyone in unknown.

All the women burst out laughing as if I just said the funniest thing.

"Honey," Martha slurs. "Anyone knocking on that door is already in the building. It's probably Helen's husband looking for food or something. Man can't feed himself."

"Whoa, craft club is in session," Leo says, his voice

booming over the din. He nods hello to everyone and gives me a secret smile, one that's much more intimate than the one he gives everyone else. When the other ladies turn my way, I focus on the neck of my rooster as I crochet the final round and connect the whole thing up in preparation for making the beak and waddles. That's when I see it. "Why am I crocheting a dick glove?"

The women practically fall off their seats, roaring with laughter.

"Still working on your willy warmers, I see." Leo holds back his laugh but not his smile.

"Willy warmers?" I look around the room. "That's what they're called? Why are we even making these?"

Nana is trying to answer but she's laughing too hard to form words, so Leo explains. "They're going to sell them at the hospital fete as coin purses. They want to watch the reactions as people realise what they are, and I guess laugh at the people who unwittingly buy them."

I look from Leo to Nana. "I finally understand where Archer gets his *out-there* sense of humour from." I can't believe I never put that one together before now. No wonder he and Nana get along famously.

The women somehow manage to laugh more, their cackles becoming wheezes as Nana turns her hand from side to side, finally taking a breath so she can speak. "He got his humour from *you*, dear girl. You just forgot how to have fun as you got older."

"I can still have fun." My face twists up as I go back to making my 'cock'.

"How many shots have you had, lovely?" Betsy asks, pushing the thick frame of her glasses up her nose.

"She's been *very* careful with her crotchet," Helen points out, her eyes widening.

"Well, *someone* has to stay sober," I argue. "I can't pick Archer up drunk, and I don't even know where Abigail got to. She just said she was meeting friends when we got back. I feel that I need to be ready for anything where she's concerned."

"Abigail's at the beach with Niall," Leo's says, hands in his pockets as he rocks on the balls of his feet. I can't help but notice the way his tan forearms bulge with muscle and sinew. He's so...manly. And I know I sound like I just stepped out of the fifties putting it like that, but it's just the best way to describe him.

Clearing my throat, I drag my eyes away from his forearms. Although I'm suddenly plagued with the memory of how those forearm muscles flexed when he was gripping my hips as I rode him.

*Focus, Darcy. Focus.*

I pick up the ball of wool I'm working with and start winding up the slack. "Abigail is with Niall? Alone?"

"No. A bunch of other kids are hanging out, swimming, windsurfing and making as much noise as possible. The usual thing." That makes me feel a hell of a lot better. If Leo had been given more input in how Niall was raised, I'm sure he'd be an awesome kid. But as things stand, I'm not sure I want him and Abigail becoming friendly. From what Nana has said, and things Leo's mentioned about his ex, the kid has been given the blunt end of the stick. I'd like to give him the benefit of the doubt, but I want to protect my daughter more. There's a bit of an age difference there, and I don't think Abby needs his kind of belligerent influence.

"You saw them just now?"

"Yep. I saw them on my way back from the workshop then I came straight in here. So, five minutes ago."

"You have a workshop?" I ask, frowning. When I meet Leo's eyes, my stomach flips. I have to say it feels near impossible living this close to a man you're attracted to while feeling unable to act upon it. It's been messing with my dreams. In a good, but frustrating way. I had a dream just last night, where I was taking a shower and he happened to join me, and well, I'm sure you can guess what happened next...

"It's where I work. Don't really have space for building furniture in my apartment. Don't think the neighbours would appreciate the power tools, either."

"You can show me your power tools any day, young man," Helen says with a wink.

Leo grins.

"Oh God, of course you have a workshop," I say. "You're a carpenter."

"That, I am." He's got this amused twinkle in his eye and all I want to do is slap my hand against my face. I'm so busy thinking about getting the man naked that I can't even hold a decent conversation. I must be ovulating or something. This is *bad*. I can barely look at him without heating up. And of course, Helen had to go and mention his *power tools*.

"I think most of us want to see your tools, Leo," Nana says, making things even worse.

"I want to know where this workshop is," Betsy adds.

"If we could visit to watch him work, we might make this cocktails and carpentry instead. You work shirtless, don't you, Leo?"

He tilts his head adorably to the side and chuckles. "Fully clothed, Betsy. Gotta watch for splinters, you know."

She pouts. "How disappointing."

Helen mutters something about sucking the splinters out for him and I close my eyes then cover them with my hand. *This isn't happening.*

"Oh God. Please stop," I say to them all. Of course, they just laugh.

"On that note, I better get to work," Leo says, taking the chance to get out before they start waving money at him.

I open my eyes to watch him walk away, because, well, he's got a *great* arse and he's wearing jeans. And I'm a bit of a perv.

"Oh, and Darce?" he says, stopping suddenly and turning around.

My eyes flick up to his face. "Hmm?" *Did he catch me?*

"If you need it, I don't mind checking in on the kids at the beach and grabbing Archer for you. He's at the community centre doing holiday club, right?"

"He is. But you don't have to do that."

"It's no trouble. I have the frame for the bed to bring in, but I should have it installed before he's ready."

"That is such a kind offer, but I couldn't..." I shake my head a little. I'm terrible at accepting help from people. I always feel like I owe them.

"For crying out loud, child," Helen says. "Let the man do something nice for you so you can have a few drinks and some fun. What's it hurt?"

I bite my lip and glance at Nana who's lifting her brow and nudging her head to the side in the most obvious *go on* look I've ever seen. "OK," I say on a resigned sigh. "As long as it really isn't a problem."

Leo laughs. "It *really* isn't a problem."

I pick up a shot glass and hold it to my lips. "In that case, thank you." Tipping my head back, I down the shot. Leo watches me with amused eyes while the other ladies chant, "One of us. One of us." I roll my eyes and laugh. Leo winks and my entire stomach does a backflip.

*Just friends, huh?* I don't think that's going to work out. Especially if he keeps looking at me like that.

"Have fun, ladies," he says, heading into the kids' room to get started.

"DO you think that if we turn up the heat, he'll take his shirt off?" Helen whispers a while later, which prompts a giggling Martha to get up from her chair and tiptoe dramatically to the thermostat, cranking it much higher than was reasonable on an already warm day. Still, not one of us gets up to fix the thing. We all sit there, drinking slippery nipples and watching Leo walk back and forth, lugging sheets of timber, his face getting redder and redder.

After spending nearly an hour in the bedroom,

drilling and hammering, he comes back out. And we all hold our breath.

"Esme? Is something wrong with your air conditioning? I swear it's blowing heat in there." He stands at the mouth of the hall, lifting the front of his shirt to wipe the sweat off his face. The action gives us a sneak peek of those washboard abs he owns.

We seem to sigh in unison.

Without a moment of hesitation, Helen cups her hands around her mouth and yells, "Take it off." Followed closely by a wolf whistle from Martha.

Nana and her friends are worse than teenagers.

"I see. The heat was turned up on purpose." Leo laughs while he shakes his head. "Is this what you're after?" He lifts the hem of his shirt, exposing his abs and flexing them a little.

I almost die a little as memories of sex with him hit me, while the ladies start hooting and hollering like they're at a strip club. I'm expecting those rolls of cash to make an appearance, but they do one better and put on that Pony song from *Magic Mike*.

"Oh my God," I moan, clapping my hand over my face. "This is *not* happening." Despite my words, I'm laughing. Never let it be said that an afternoon spent with a bunch of eighty-year-old women is dull. They're out of control.

Speaking of being out of control, as the vibration of the intro kicks in, Leo gets in on the crazy and starts dancing, putting on a show. He teases us all by lifting his shirt higher and higher then dropping it back to his waist again.

"No fair." Nana laughs, clapping along with the music.

Leo responds by turning a slow circle, before he slaps a hand against his own arse.

I'm smiling so hard my cheeks are hurting.

"Come on, Betsy." He grins, holding out his hand as he keeps moving to the beat. She takes it of course, and then he does this sexy little dance with her, rolling their hips together like they're doing the mamba or something. Now my stomach hurts from laughing, and I swear Helen is about to lose her voice if she yells any louder. But, like all songs, this one ends, and since Leo hasn't removed that shirt of his, fists thump against the table and we all chant, "Take it off. Take it off." Yes, even me. What can I say? I've been doing shots.

Locking his gaze with mine, Leo gives me a half-grin and a wink, then he grabs the collar behind his neck and whips the shirt over his head. He's standing there in his tanned and muscular glory while we all clap and cheer... and I squirm in my seat. *I know what the rest of that body looks like.* But then Martha grabs his shirt and sniffs it, which is a little too much if you ask me and kind of jolted me out of my heated memory, but the whole event is so over the top and funny that we laugh it off.

"Thank you, ladies, I'll be here for the next couple of hours," Leo says, taking a sweeping bow.

When he stands back up, I grab his shirt and toss it to him, "Back to work, mister," I say with a smile.

He salutes me then heads back down the hall while Carla and Helen shout "Encore."

"Let the boy work," Nana says, reaching for her

crochet hook, calm as can be, as if a strip show from the hot carpenter is a normal happening. "I'm not paying him to be pretty, you know."

We're back to giggling now, and Betsy picks up another shot and holds it out to me. "Looks like someone has an admirer." She lifts her eyebrows then lowers her voice. "Esme and I always knew you two wou—" She doesn't get to finish because Nana kicks her under the table and she drops the shot, liquid soaking my almost finished willy warmer. "Ow."

"Oh no." That was Carla, I'm not sure if she was upset over the spilled alcohol or the spoiled crochet. But we clean it up quickly, and I decide I'm all 'funned out' as Archer says.

"I think I might head out for a swim," I say, needing a cool down after Leo's show.

"You sober enough for that?" Nana asks, and I nod.

"Can touch my nose with closed eyes, and everything." I demonstrate by holding my arms out to the side and alternating the nose tapping.

"She's a grown woman, Esme," Betsy says, to which Nana shrugs, because she couldn't stop caring for people if she tried, despite her claims that people bore her.

"Have fun out there," Helen sing-songs as I leave. Then I hear, "You know, I'm a little warm after watching that dance too," and I walk away smiling. It doesn't escape me that this afternoon is the first time I've laughed that hard in months. Maybe even years.

## TWENTY-THREE

## LEO

This house is full of drunken giggling women.

I smile to myself as I listen to the rise and fall of their conversation and laughter. It amazes me how much alcohol a bunch of elderly ladies can put away. I think I'd be rolling on the floor if I ever spent an afternoon drinking one of their concoctions, and I've got a pretty good constitution. I reckon they could drink any one of my rugby buddies under the table. In fact, I'd put money on it.

Tightening the last couple of screws, I step back and place a hand on the side of the bed frame and give it a good shake. The anchor points in the overhead beam and floor aren't budging a bit. I've added shelves behind each bed to give the kids a place for their books, or iPads or whatever they like to have near while they sleep. There's also a couple of drawers beneath each bed for personal storage. I think if I was a kid, and my great grandmother had something like this made for me, I'd feel like the luckiest kid in the world.

Speaking of kids...

Checking my watch, I note that I still have about an hour before it's time to get Archer. Is it weird that I offered to get him when I'm no more than a friend to Darcy, the guy next door? At the time, I figured it'd be OK since helping each other out is what friends do. But would I help one of the guys out under the same circumstances? Hmm. Probably not. Having the desire to sleep with said friend seems to make my spirit a little more giving. Even without that possibility, for Darcy, I reckon I'd do it anyway. The woman needs a break. She's always switched on, and I got a real kick out of seeing her relax, laughing and pressing her knees together while I got in on the fun. Totally worth it.

*God, she has a beautiful laugh.* Music to my ears.

Shaking my head, I mentally groan. I suck at this friend thing. I want so much more.

I finish putting my tools away and flick the locking clips on the metal case. *Friends.* How do you even go back to being friends when you can't stop wanting the other person in your bed? I'm trying, and I'm struggling. She's so close yet she's so far away, and my fingertips burn every time I see her and don't touch her. It's not even just about sex. I want to be around her, wake up next to her, go to sleep with her being the last thing I see. I feel this great need to have her in my life, and I'm starting to get a little desperate.

Maybe I'm not as patient as I thought.

I heft my toolbox to my side then place a hand on the doorknob. I guess when you *really* want someone and want your connection to mean something, you have to push those physical urges aside and do everything you can to show her you're the guy she needs.

*The guy she needs...*

Yeah. I think that's who I am to her. It's not me being conceited. It's a feeling I have deep down in the centre of my being. We just...click. And I'm at the age where you don't pass that kind of thing up. You wait. Even if it means the only action you get is with *Mrs Palmer and her five daughters* for a while. Darcy is worth the wait. I'm sure of it.

Heading into the dining room, I brave the giggling gaggle. They're currently huddled around the oven, an empty box of frozen vol-au-vents filled with broccoli and vegan cheese on the bench. I figure they're watching the pastry turn golden, and why not? Vol-au-vents are pretty great.

"I'm all done in there, Esme," I say, doing a quick headcount and noticing that Darcy isn't among them. "Is Darcy getting Archer?" He griped about not being allowed to have 'slippy nipples with craft' when he and Esme walked past my place this morning. I told him he'd probably have more fun at his holiday club, but he was pretty adamant that hanging out with old ladies was the better choice. He's a funny kid that one.

Esme talks at the oven door. "She's at the beach."

"When did she leave?" Helen asks, looking perplexed and a little unsteady before she hiccups.

Carla speaks with a mouthful of celery. "Couple of hours ago."

"A couple of hours? Is she OK?" She was drinking, so I'm instantly worried.

Betsy shrugs. "Haven't heard any sirens, so I assume so."

"I'll go find her," I volunteer, figuring if all is well, a dip in the sea will be the perfect end to hours of hot work. I swear those women kept turning the heater back on.

"Be gentle with her, Leo," Esme calls after me and the rest of the women laugh like they're all in high school.

*Be gentle.*

Grabbing the set of binoculars I leant Archer so he could watch the yachts, (read, 'spy on his sister') I do a quick scan of the beach from Esme's deck. Niall and Abigail are in the group near the yacht club, lying around under the shade of their windsurfing sails. They're separated into boys and girls' groups, which makes their acquaintance sit better with me. I can see Abigail talking with one of the other girls as she applies sunscreen to the length of her arm. Niall is in the shade of another board, staring up at the sky. Moving on, I search the bodies littered along the stretch of beach until I find one that fits Darcy, lying on a towel on the stretch of beach closest to home. At least, I think it's her. She's got an arm across her face to block out the sun. But the black two-piece and those creamy thighs are definitely familiar. Something inside me shifts, and I need that cold dip more than anything now.

"Down, boy," I mutter to my crotch as I put the binoculars back where Archer left them.

Back at my place, I change out of my work gear and into a pair of board shorts, slinging a towel over my shoulder, Darcy dancing through my mind.

*Be gentle.*

She's going through a shitty break-up and I happen to have experience on that particular topic, so we've talked. We've talked about a lot of things—not only exes and kids. I like being around her, look forward to it every chance I get. I think back to the night we talked until we passed out on my couch. Nothing happened between us, but it felt so, *so* right. It was like the messiness in me mixed with the messiness in her and brought us closer. We started that night with a declaration of friendship, but we ended it as something else. I think it was hopefulness.

And the dancing.

Why did I do that? I haven't danced with a woman in years. Not like that, anyway. I think the last time I did it with any feeling involved was at my wedding. And I definitely haven't danced without music before, *or* created my own. She was vulnerable and sad, and she looked like she needed something from me, so I reacted. I loved that she trusted me with something so personal and hidden. That moment with Darcy, it was...intimate, special.

*Be gentle.*

I don't regret any of that night, although, when she made her mad dash for the door, I worried she'd go into full avoidance mode again—thankfully not the case—and I could have done without Niall's comments where he carried on like I have women on a revolving door. That couldn't be further from the truth. I've never once had a woman in the house around him. But I can't control the things Tash tells him. I swear her bitterness towards me has only gotten worse, which is fucked up given I forgave her for sucking my teammate's dick. You don't come back from fucking someone other than your spouse, so why she's punished me every day for that makes no sense. But God, I hate what she's done to Niall, poisoning his mind so he believes I'm someone I'm not. He used to be a good kid. Can still be one given the chance. I hate that it's never around me. I'm always the enemy.

Darcy has expressed similar sentiments over her strained relationship with Abigail. We both have our hands full with teen angst right now, and God help us both, because neither of us can figure a way out of it. It's hard doing what you feel is the right thing and getting nowhere.

So, yeah, Darcy and I have an interesting, possibly unusual bond. I didn't expect it, and I don't think she did either, but it's here and as much as I want to grab her tight and never let go, I have to *be gentle*. Because it's been *years* since my marriage broke down, and Darcy is going through it *right now*.

*Be gentle.*

I'm doing my best.

Walking across the road to the beach, I smile over the amount of sunbathing bodies. We're all told that lying in the sun is the worst thing we can do for our skin, and I'm inclined to agree, but it feels damn good to relax with the sun bathing you in its warmth. Animals do it all the time so it's only natural, I guess. In moderation.

Darcy looks pretty comfortable, her arm slung across her eyes and one of her knees bent up slightly. She's not wearing what I'd call a bikini, but she is wearing this two-piece suit that shows off a bit of smooth skin across her midriff. She's got a decent-sized rack—what? I'm a guy, we all call it that. Anyone who says different is a liar—her thighs are full and round, no thigh gap. I like a woman with thighs I can dig my fingers into, and Darcy's are perfect.

*Patience, Leo.*

Shaking off my lust-filled thoughts, I head straight for the water to cool off and calm down. It takes a lot for the water to warm up around here, and even in the second month of summer, it's still pretty bloody frigid. Enveloping my body in the cold cuts off any inappropriate blood flow quick smart. The last thing I need to do is approach Darcy with a bit of a chub.

I spend about ten minutes swimming between the rocky groynes before deciding to approach her. She's in exactly the same position, and it isn't until I get closer that I realise she's actually asleep. And she's burnt.

Really burnt.

Ah shit.

"Darce," I say, reaching down to touch her on the arm. She reacts with a start and flings her arm upward, slapping me in the face. "Crap." I stumble back, my eye feeling like it's about to pop out of my head. In my life, I've been tackled, punched and kneed in the face, but nothing hurts the back of your eyes quite as much as a slap from a woman. Why is that?

"Leo." She sits up and looks around like she's trying to figure out what she's doing here. "Oh God, did I just hit you?"

I blink a couple of times. "It's fine. But I really think we need to get you out of the sun." I'm trying not to show my reaction too much, but she has a brilliant white band across the centre of her face where her arm was covering. Everything below her nose and half of her forehead is bright red.

"Am I burnt?"

Grimacing a little, I nod. It's red now, but when the sun goes down, it's going to glow up a storm.

"How bad is it?" She looks at the back of her arm as she stands. "Oh crap."

"I've got a big bottle of aftersun cream at my place. You might need to bathe in it though."

"It's that bad?" She starts walking with her arms out from the sting. It reminds me of a penguin and I start laughing. "This is not funny."

"I know. I'm sorry." I wouldn't wish a bad sunburn on anyone. Well, maybe my ex... Nah. Not even her. Sunburn hurts like a bitch.

After waddling and whimpering across the street, she heads straight for my bathroom the moment we're inside. I call after her to tell her where the aloe vera cream is, but my words are cut off by the sound of her scream. My knee still isn't great, so I don't run for the bathroom but I do hop-race as fast as I can.

"What?" I'm out of breath. Hop-racing is harder than it looks.

"My face." Oh that. I was expecting a massive hairy spider after a scream like that, but I guess it stands to reason. Women worry a lot more about their looks than guys do.

I try to hide my smile as I take in her wide eyes and horrified expression. She's pressing hands against the red as if maybe that could push it back inside. I don't know.

Whatever she's doing isn't going to fix the problem. But slathering it in aloe vera is something that will help.

Pulling open the medicine cabinet, I take the large bottle of aftersun and squirt some in my palm. "Here," I say, gently smoothing the cream down her arm. "We can't fix it, but we can take out the sting."

She stops freaking out almost immediately and lowers her hands to the side. "I am such a mess of a person," she says, sighing as I run both hands down her arms then back up again.

"I happen to like messy people." Collecting more cream, I run my hand over the top of her chest, taking liberties. It's actually really nice to have her standing still and sober in front of me, allowing me to touch her. I feel this need to take care of her. From everything she told me about her ex and the way their separation went down, I think she's incredibly lost, floating about with no real direction or purpose. I want to be the one to ground her. And who wouldn't? She's adorable. A red and white-striped, pouting woman with big blue eyes that beg for you to adore her. Over the years I've lived next door to Esme, I've heard stories about Darcy. In many of them, she was featured as this woman who could do anything, had everything figured out. Seeing this catastrophe in front of me doesn't quite align with the preconceived image I had of her. This version of Darcy is far more human. Someone I can relate to.

"Well, you're in for a treat then. I don't know my right from my left anymore. Seems I'm not even responsible enough to put on sunscreen."

"Close your eyes and press your lips together," I say,

my voice way softer than I expect. She quiets and does as I tell her, shifting slightly from foot to foot as I apply the aloe vera to her face. That mind of hers is going a mile a minute. The moment I finish, she starts talking again.

"I've always had my shit together. This is so unlike me. Getting this burnt is something one of my kids would do. Well, not Abby. She's obsessed with skin care, so she'd never exit the house without using sunscreen first."

"We all have our moments." I sit on the edge of the bathtub and gesture for her to put her foot up on my thigh. Then I rub the cream over the burn on her legs. Her skin is really smooth, and it's possible that my mind is wandering to inappropriate places right now.

"I keep thinking about Archer telling you he's glad his dad isn't around." She shakes her head and changes legs when I tap her other knee. "I'm so saddened by that. I thought I was doing the right thing all these years, keeping the family together and placating everyone. But now I'm thinking that maybe I forced us all to live a lie... and I'm so confused. I mean, did I choose wrong in the beginning, or did things change as we grew older? He seems pretty much the same, actually, so maybe *I* changed. Or maybe my looks faded too much and..."

It isn't until I place my hand with the cool cream against her stomach that she reacts to my touch and meets my eyes. It's kind of strange, because I'm aware that she's messed up over some other guy, and I'm here rubbing cream on her like it's nothing and suddenly it is something. We lock eyes and I see the moment when she registers the intimacy of what's happening right now. Her pupils get darker, and her breathing changes a little, deepening as I take my time covering every millimetre of skin on her stomach.

"Your looks didn't fade, Darcy," I say, fully expecting that the words will be the defining moment, where we recognise there's more attraction than friendship and start doing something about it. But that's not what happens at all.

Instead, I'm met with laughter as Darcy looks at herself in the mirror, points at her face and says, "I look like a candy cane."

Standing up, I let the moment fall away as I wash the cream off my hands. "You're about a month too late for it," I say, grinning as our eyes meet in the mirror.

She laughs even more. "Maybe I'm just really early."

"Maybe." I grab a towel and dry my hands.

"It's going to peel and I'll look like a leper."

"You'll rock the leper look."

She gives me the side-eye and purses her lips. "I don't even think one of those models you date could rock that look."

I lift my brow. "You've googled me?" *Of course she has.*

The only way I know she's blushing is because she looks away and the white part of her face turns pink. "Gotta even the playing field. You already knew so much about me."

"It wasn't just to look at my pictures?" I tease.

She somehow manages to get redder. "I did it before I came back here. You have to know who you're letting around your kids. Archer has a thing for you." She shrugs and I don't know whether to grin or feel affronted. We only spoke recently about the shit Tash put me through after our divorce, and she acted as though she knew nothing. Those articles are still first-page results.

"Is that part of the reason you wouldn't talk to me when you came back? You were afraid the things Tash said about me were true?"

Her eyes go wide. "What? *No*. No, not at all. I read your wiki page and looked at your pictures. I don't ever read those gossip rags. I like facts and they thrive on bull-shit, so I figure if there's nothing in a legitimate news source, it's nothing of concern and to be honest"—she lets out her breath—"I was mainly just perving on your pictures." She drops her eyes like admitting that is a bad thing. "You're *really* good-looking."

The tension falls from my chest and I'm suddenly smiling again, wanting to hug her and let her take all the pictures she wants. Hell, I'll even get naked for them. "Give me your phone number."

Her eyes meet mine, surprised by my response. "What?"

"I want your mobile number."

"Um, it's..." She rattles off her digits and I nod as I commit them to memory.

"You don't want to write that down?" Her voice is breathless, and I want to kiss her so badly right now.

"I've got it," I say, tapping my head.

"Oh, that's a good skill to have. I have to use the same password for everything and I can barely keep that straight. Um, what do you want my phone number for? We live right next door."

Pulling some hair that has stuck to her cheek free, I tuck it behind her ear. "So, I can send you pictures."

Her mouth forms an O and her pupils grow larger, her breathing more rapid. "What, um... what kind of pictures?"

I lean close so my lips are brushing against her ear. "The kind you can touch yourself to."

"Holy fuck," she breathes out, her hand pressing against her chest. She's breathing so rapidly now, and I'm sure there's a delicious wet pool of arousal gathering between her legs. I have to close my hands into fists to resist the urge to reach out and discover the truth for myself.

"I like you way more than a friend should like a friend, Darcy Field." I'm getting hard for her and fuck if I can care enough to hide it.

Her eyes flick down and she swallows hard before closing her eyes. "God. This is way too soon," she whispers, as if saying those words is actually painful.

"I know it's too soon." I stand close and slide my fingers down the length of her spine and she shudders, her full lips parting as she places her hands against my bare chest. "I can't stop wanting you, Darce. Can't stop thinking about you." I'm not being gentle. I'm not being patient. I want her so much my gut aches. It's taking everything I have not to take her right here—and I'm primarily holding back because I'm mindful of her sunburn. I know nothing is going to happen, but fuck, I *want* it to. She needs to understand what being near her does to me. We don't have to act on it now, but I *need* her to comprehend the size of my hard-on for her.

Her breath catches and she looks away, although she doesn't stop touching me. In fact, she digs her fingers in, holding on harder. "It would be so easy to give in to this." She releases a sigh. "But my kids, Leo. I can't be selfish with the way things are. I'm sorry. This is just... it's bad timing."

"Then I'll keep waiting until the timing is right."

She looks at me and searches my eyes, her brow knitted. "Why?"

I shrug. "Because I want you and I'm willing to wait until I can have you. Do I need more of a reason?"

"Yes," she whispers.

"I'm happier when I'm around you. You make me feel hopeful again. I think you're beautiful."

"I'm a mess."

"A beautiful mess."

She presses her lips together. "You can't really think that, Leo. I am nothing like those other girls."

"What girls?"

"The ones in your photos online. The women you normally go for. Even your son was shocked you'd choose someone like me."

"Niall was an arsehole that morning. He's never even seen a woman in my apartment, so he was speaking out of his arse. Those photos? That time in my life...it was vacuous. No real emotions, no substance. I'm not that man anymore. I haven't been for years. I want... I want substance, Darcy. I want you."

She shakes her head and laughs. "You think *I'm* substance?"

"Yes. I do. And if you don't think you are then that's a

problem with your own self-worth, not with what I find valuable."

She stares at me for a moment with curious and intense eyes.

"You barely know me." She sighs. "This is so crazy." Then she rolls her eyes as she looks away, but I let that go because she's in a bad place right now. I know that. In her head she's been beating herself up for weeks, wondering why she wasn't good enough for that arsehole to stay. She's amazing, so he's the biggest idiot on the planet. It only took one afternoon with her to see the truth in what Esme had said for years. She's everything.

"You know," I start, taking a breath before I run my teeth over my lips. "Sometimes, you meet someone and you click. It may not make a lot of sense at the time, but it *feels* right. This—you and me—it feels right, Darcy. Am I wrong?"

"Leo." She moves her fingers against my chest, playing with a scar I got after a rough day on the field, and looks into my eyes. I can see her fight. Can she trust me? Even though I've been nothing but straight with her since the day we met, I understand why trusting me is hard.

"Tell me I'm wrong."

She hesitates then closes her eyes and says, "You're not wrong. The *timing* is."

I place my hands over hers and hold them to my chest. "There's this event I have to go to—"

"You know I can't go on a date with you, Leo." There's so much struggle in her voice.

"Just hear me out before you say yes or no. There's an

event. It's in August, an awards night I have to present at. I want you to go with me."

"You're asking me to an event that isn't happening for seven months?"

A grin pulls up one side of my mouth. "You think you can be ready by then?" I let my eyes wander over her sunburnt face and she rolls her eyes.

"What if this is simply hormones and we hate each other by then?"

"It's *not* hormones."

"*What if?*"

"Then we won't go. Simple."

"Simple? So why ask me now? Why not wait until then?"

"Because I need you to understand that I see us together in the future. I'm not going anywhere. I'm here and I'll wait for when you want me." *God, I need her to feel the same.*

She closes her eyes. "You know I want you, Leo. It just isn't as easy as what I want."

I lean in and press a chaste kiss to the tip of her nose. She smells like a health food store from all the aloe.

"It never is."

"OK," she says with another sigh, placing her hands on either side of my face then lowering them down to her side again. "We have a date in seven months. But if I don't think the kids can handle that, you'll have to take some pretty young thing you know from your regular life."

"This is my regular life, Darcy, and you are the pretty young thing. I'd rather go stag than take someone else."

Her expression softens slightly. "I'll accept the pretty —despite my current state—but I am *not* young."

I shrug. "Younger than me. Is that a yes?"

She takes a deep breath as she moves her head from side to side then laughs a little. "OK. It's a yes."

"Yes," I say, grabbing the back of her hair as I plant a kiss on her cheek. Except it doesn't land on her cheek, because she turns at the wrong moment and I catch the side of her mouth. We share a split second of surprise. Then our bodies take over, lips colliding, teeth clashing and fingers grabbing. I have her up on the vanity with her legs wrapped around me before I even comprehend what we're doing.

"This doesn't feel like friends," she gasps as I unhook the back of her swimsuit and it falls down her shoulders.

"We were never just friends."

*Beep, beep. Beep, beep.*

I freeze. Fuck.

*Archer.*

"Archer," she whispers against my mouth as I stop the beeping of my alarm. I slide the straps of her suit back up to her shoulders, careful not to aggravate her sunburn more than I already have.

"Yeah. Time to go get him." As much as I don't want this moment to stop, I'm not about to ignore a little kid when I promised to pick him up.

She reaches behind herself and clips her swimsuit up. "It's OK. I will. I should—"

"Have you seen your face?" I start to laugh.

She closes her eyes. "Oh shit. You're right, I can't go out in public like this."

"I'll meet you back at yours?"

She nods then worries at her lips with her teeth.

"You OK?"

"Yeah." She frowns. "It's just, we're not very good at this waiting thing, are we?"

A laugh bursts from my chest. "No. Our self-control could do with some work."

"I feel very out of control around you," she agrees.

"Perhaps we can be good at being careful instead?"

While she's still frowning, she also nods. "Yeah...I don't know how that will look, but I think maybe... perhaps we should only be around each other when no one else is. That might be best. Or maybe we should *only* be around each other when there are other people. I'm not sure which."

Pressing my lips against her forehead, I grin. "We'll work it out."

She wraps her arms around my waist and lets out a sigh. "I hope so," she whispers.

I leave to get Archer with my chest full of hope. Our defining moment is a sunburnt kiss.

## LEO

"Let me guess." Archer sees me waiting for him and places his hands on his hips. "They're both *drunk.*" He rolls his eyes and shakes his head, disgusted. I let out a small laugh and hold my hand out for his backpack.

"Nah, man. Your mum spent a little too much time in the sun and your Nana is still having fun with her friends."

"Drinking *nipples.*" His response is *just* loud enough to attract the attention of some mothers who are also picking up their kids from holiday club. One shoots me daggers, but another snickers and keeps her kids moving. It's time to get out of here.

"Come on, big guy. We're walkin'."

"Your kid's cute," some woman says to me as I'm opening the door. I don't know whether she's a mum or one of the workers, so I nod and say thanks.

"Why'd you say I'm your kid?" Archer asks as we walk along the footpath. He slips his hand into mine and scuffs his feet on the concrete. I miss this age. I remember when Niall couldn't go anywhere without holding hands. Now he barely wants to stay in the same room as me.

"I didn't say you were my kid. I just didn't correct her because I didn't know who she was."

"She's the girl who makes the sandwiches."

"She works for the holiday camp?"

He starts jumping from crack to line, his little body tugging on my arm as he leaps. "Yeah. She said that she knows how to make ham and cheese and that I didn't have to tell her how. But she put too much butter on, and the cheese was too small for the bread. I don't think she's very good at her job."

"I guess she makes them the way she likes them."

He stops jumping and starts hopping. "I guess so. Does your knee still hurt?"

"Only when I get up in the morning." It aches most of the time, actually. But it's been a problem for so long, I'm used to it.

"What about when you're walking?"

"A little. But that's why I wear this brace. It helps with the hurting."

"Nana said you need an operation for it. Is it because I knocked you over?"

"No, mate. I hurt it when I used to play football."

"Oh, so it's not because I hurt you." He looks at me, his eyes hopeful. I realise that he's actually been worried that he might be responsible for some long-term damage. Darcy might not feel it most of the time, but she's obviously a brilliant mum.

"Not at all."

"Because I'm sorry, you know. I didn't mean it."

"I know that. You were just having fun. But maybe keep the tackling to the footy field, huh?"

"I'm not allowed to play football. Mum says only meatheads play football and she doesn't want them to put meat in *my* head."

I grin. "That's what she says?" I would never have picked Darcy for a jock-hater.

"Yep. And Dad *hates* all sport. He only likes computer games, and he swears at them *a lot*."

Every piece of information I get on this guy is painting a picture of a man who deserves to be taken down a dark alley. And not with friends.

"Do you like playing computer games?" I ask, trying to keep things neutral. I'm not going to engage in any sort of negative conversation about the kid's father. Even if I do think the guy's a douche. I mean, who treats a woman like Darcy and two fantastic kids, who obviously love him to death, like he did?

"There's this game called Roblox that's really fun."

"What's that about?"

We stop for ice cream and talk about block-shaped people and 'OP' weapons for the rest of the way home. It makes me miss my own son even more. I could have had this. *Fuck, Tash.*

"ARCHIE." Abigail rushes across the side street just before we turn onto Beach Road. Normally we'd use the deck entrance, but Archer wanted to help his nana by checking the mailbox.

We stop and face her direction, waiting until she reaches us. "Where are you going with *him?*" Him being me, I assume, since she inclines her head my way but doesn't even acknowledge me. When Niall saunters up behind her, hands in pockets and gives me a nod, I understand why. *Great.* He's obviously been telling Abigail what an *awesome* dad he thinks I am.

"To check the mail. Where are *you* going with *him?*" Archer shoots back, and I have to fight a grin.

"Home," she says. "You should come too." She holds her hand out to Archer and glances at me, distrust in her eyes. *Jesus.*

"But I wanna check the mail." Archer squints up at her.

She leans in close, but speaks loud enough that I can hear. "You can't just pick some random guy to stand in for Dad, Archer. It's weird."

Clenching my teeth together, I tell myself not to react. Like Darcy, Abigail is going through her own shit too. I feel sorry for her. Her dad is a fuckwit.

"I'm not doing that," Archer argues, pulling away from her. "He's my friend."

"That's even weirder." Abigail stands back and crosses her arms across her chest. She's wearing a string bikini top and a pair of denim shorts, the local beach attire. She'll be a stunner like her mum when she grows up, but I have this strange inclination to tell her to put a shirt on. I don't think I'd handle having a daughter in this day and age. I'd lock her up until she was thirty so guys like my son couldn't even look at her.

"Why don't you go with your sister, Archie?" I tap lightly on his shoulder. "We can check the mail later."

"But that doesn't make sense when we're almost there."

"Just go with your sister, mate, OK?" I hold out his backpack.

Archer rolls his eyes and takes it, stomping off with Abigail. I follow along a few steps behind them, Niall walking beside me.

"I'm really not the guy your mother says I am," I say as they push through Esme's deck gate. I can hear them bickering.

"I'm yet to see any different," Niall responds, disdain in his tone. "Seems you'd rather hang out with the neighbour's kid than your own son."

I stop walking. "You wanna hang out? Let's hang out. Anything you wanna do."

He glances back, not stopping. "Nah. I'm good."

When he pushes through our gate and lets it slam instead of waiting for me, I grit my teeth and count to ten. I don't know how to fix this.

"Hey, thanks for grabbing Archer," Darcy says, leaning over the railing on Esme's deck. She's wearing a blue and white summer dress now and has put some makeup on that lessens the red on her face.

I walk a little farther and stand on the footpath in front of her. "I hear you think football players are meatheads."

She smiles and one eye twitches a little. "That doesn't sound like something I'd say."

"I can tell when you're lying you know. Your eye." I lift my hand, pointing at her tell.

She places her hand over it. "Can you tell now?"

Laughing a little through my nose, I take a step back. "I should go."

"Because I thought footy players were meatheads? Present company excluded."

I shake my head. "I've been called far worse."

"Was Abigail rude to you? Archer was ropable when she brought him in. I'm sorry if she overstepped."

"She's angry."

"At us all, it seems."

"Understandably. This all takes time. But we knew that already, didn't we?"

"Yeah," she says with a sigh. "See you later, and thanks for the bunks, the aloe vera, and..." She bites her lip and smiles, causing the silence to remind me of our moment in the bathroom. I want to suck that lip from her mouth and bite it with my own teeth. Pity there are people around.

"Always a pleasure," I say, trying not to smile too broadly and give us away. "See you soon."

"I hope so."

Giving her a nod, I make my way over to my gate and head inside. Niall is already locked in his room and I stand at the kitchen counter, my hands braced on the cool marble as I hang my head, overwhelmed. This afternoon, I was feeling hopeful and positive. The attraction I share with Darcy feels so right and I was longing to explore that. But there's so much in our family lives we need to sort out before we can even consider anything more than a few stolen moments together. How are we supposed to build something meaningful if we're always worried about other people? How do we do this without messing everything up? Jeez, this is complicated. So damn complicated.

# TWENTY-FIVE

## DARCY

*I happen to like messy people.*

I can feel the dopey smile spreading across my face, but I can't seem to stop it.

Leo *wants* me. *Me.*

Leo Murphy. Forty-five. Australian Rugby royalty. He played fly-half for over one hundred test matches on the national team—twenty of those as captain. Since retiring in his mid-thirties due to an ongoing knee injury, he's one of the few football personalities to be hand-picked by Network 10 as a commentator. He also did a stint as a morning radio personality in Melbourne, but has taken a step back from the limelight in recent years to focus on other pursuits.

If that sounds like an excerpt from his wiki page, it's because it is. I often read it to remind myself what a big deal he is. He seems so down to earth to me, and reading the history of his accomplishments only serves to strengthen my observations about him. He could be a cocky bastard with a past like this, but he isn't. He's wonderful, which leads me to ask the question: why is he interested in me? I saw photos of the models he used to date, the model turned actress he actually married. And I'm nothing like any of those women. I'm straight-up regular past-my-prime kinda pretty. It doesn't make a lot of sense, but I've gotta tell you, having a guy as gorgeous as Leo kissing me and tearing at my clothes like he can't control himself is a huge ego boost. If the sunburn wasn't already doing it for me, I'd be glowing.

Oh, how I want him. I want his hands on my hips, his mouth on my skin...

If only life wasn't so complicated, I'd get the chance to enjoy the way being near him feels, revel in the memory of his hungry eyes. But that's not how my world works. The moment I turn around to head back inside, I'm faced with a pursed-lipped, arms-crossed, toe-tapping teen.

"You spent the night with him?" It isn't a question as much as it's an accusation.

I glance over at where Nana and Betsy are sitting at the dining table, sewing up willy warmers. Helen, Carla and Martha have gone home, too drunk to continue. Nana lifts her brow and I'm not sure if she's trying to communicate that I need to come clean about everything, or if she thinks I need to tell Abigail to mind her own business. My instinct is to go with something in between.

"No, Abigail. Not in the way you're insinuating, anyway."

"But you were *with* him. At least now I know why we moved here. For *him*." She flings an arm in the direction of the shared apartment wall.

"You've got this all wrong. We were talking and I fell asleep on his couch. That's all."

"Talking," she scoffs. "So you'd be fine if I stayed up all night and fell asleep wth Niall?"

Now I'm pursing my lips and folding my arms. "You're a fourteen-year-old girl and he's a seventeen-year-old boy. Absolutely not."

"But if nothing happened, what's the harm?" she shoots back.

"It's not about harm. It's about risk. I'm a grown woman, and you're a teenage girl. They're *very* different things, young lady, and you're twisting this whole thing around."

She narrows an eye and shakes her head. "You're not even trying."

"Trying what?"

"To get Dad to come home. He's barely been gone a month and you're just moving on." Tears fill her eyes and I release my arms with a sigh.

"He chose to leave, Abby. I didn't make him go."

She balls her fists at her sides as she leans forward and hurls words at me. "But you didn't try to make him stay, either."

"Abby." I'm talking to her retreating back, so I press my lips together, slapping my hands against my thighs in frustration as she slams the door to her room. *Damn you, Kevin. This is all your fucking fault.*

"I don't know what to do with her," I direct towards Nana and Betsy.

"Not much you can do," Betsy says, glancing up from

her stitching. "She's angry at her father. But he's not here, so she's taking it out on you."

I pull out the chair across from them and pick up a completed willy warmer, shaped like a dragon. It's kinda cute, actually. "I've tried to call him, text him, Facebook message him...he's just gone." I look between both Nana and Betsy as I talk and they craft. "And I really did just fall asleep on Leo's couch that night. Nothing happened." I press my lips together as I finger the woollen flames coming out of the dragon's open mouth. "I'm trying to do the right thing here, make the right decisions. I know this isn't easy on the kids, but..." I let out a heavy sigh. There's too much going on to summarise with a single *but*.

Nana puts her willy warmer down, a snake with a forked tongue. "Let's be blunt here. This whole situation is a shitfight, and the only one handling it well is an eight-year-old boy. It's obvious to all of us that you and Leo are interested in each other, and there is never going to be a right time to explore that if you're always tiptoeing around other people. Do what *feels* right and the rest will work itself out."

"It's not that easy, Nana."

"Why? Because Abigail will throw a tantrum? She'll get over it. Tell her to talk to her father if she's angry. You didn't do anything wrong."

"But that's not what Abby thinks. She thinks this is on me. That I didn't do enough to make him stay. I didn't get that chance, Nana. *He* walked out on *us*, and he's not talking to *any* of us."

"Then tell her *why*. There's no sense in protecting their relationship with a man who didn't even have the decency to say goodbye to them. He's ruined that for himself, and you're too damn nice for your own good. Be selfish, Darcy. For once in your life, be on your own side. What will make *you* happy?"

"You should listen to her," Betsy says, nodding slowly. "She knows a thing or two about living for other people and missed opportunities."

"What do you mean?" I look at Nana whose eyes have misted over.

She waves a hand dismissively. "At my age, we all have a story of the one who got away."

"I'd like to hear it."

"Some other time," she says, looking to the hall where I find Archer standing against the door frame. "Just remember that when you're happy, your kids are happy too."

"I don't think Abigail will ever be happy," Archer says, walking over to me and sitting on my lap. "She's a dark cloud of teenage hormones." He shakes his head, so serious.

I release a small laugh and hug him tight. "She kick you out of the room?"

"Nah. That new bed is really cool and we can't see each other, but she kept huffing and puffing so I thought I'd come out here. Is there any food?"

"I'm making veggie burgers and sweet potato fries for dinner," Nana says. "Wanna help get it ready?"

"Sure." His eyes light up and he jumps off my lap before stopping and giving me a big hug. "I think Leo is really cool, and if you want to have a sleepover with him, then that's OK too. I like the way he makes you smile."

A lump forms in my throat, and I run my hand over his soft hair then cup his chin. "I love you lots, kiddo."

"Love you too, Mummy." He falls against me, giving me a tight squeeze. "I'm pretty sure you're one of my top five mothers."

"Top five?" I pull away a little so I can see his face, a grin tugging on my mouth. "How many mothers do you have?"

"Only you. I'm talking about all the mothers I've had in my other lives. I'm pretty sure you're one of the best."

## TWENTY-SIX

## DARCY

In the quiet of the evening, I stand outside the door to Archer and Abigail's room and place my hand on the doorknob. Both kids have been holed up in there since dinner, enjoying the privacy that the new bunk bed gives them.

At dinner, Abigail didn't speak to me. The advice Nana keeps giving me about telling her why Kevin left keeps rolling around in my mind. But would it even help? Or would she just blame me even more? Perhaps she'd tell me I didn't do enough to keep him with us...I don't know. I almost feel that no matter what I do right now, she's going to hate me. Like Betsy said, she's angry and Kevin isn't here, so it's all directed at me. It's hurtful. I understand it, but it hurts me. She's always been my girl. We had a good relationship before, and most days she'd talk my ear off. But now...

I rake a hand through my hair, getting my fingers caught in a tangled knot and wincing while I pull it free. I really am a mess these days. Kevin's betrayal has turned everything about my life upside down and inside out. Gone is the confident woman and mother I believed I was. I've been replaced with a sunburned, scraggly haired version of myself who spends her days not knowing her left from her right and struggling to function. I don't know who I'm supposed to be anymore. It's like my identity is gone. I was a wife and a mother, and while I'm still a mother, I feel like I'm being pushed away. Archer is so self-sufficient, and Abigail doesn't want anything from me.

Still, I need to keep trying with her. If I keep allowing her to storm off in anger, we'll never resolve anything.

"Here goes," I say to myself, turning the door handle as I tap lightly on the door. The way the bunk was installed, I'm faced with a large wooden panel. If I walk to the left, I'll find Archer on the top bunk; to the right, I'll find Abby on the bottom. The room is fairly dark save for a soft glow of lamp light coming out of each pod, and since it's almost nine thirty, I head to Archer first to say goodnight.

"Hi, Mummy," he says with a smile, his voice sleepy as he rubs at his eye with his index finger.

"What's this about?" I point to the black and orange-covered book he just put down.

"Bad Guys episode one. It introduces the characters and their personalities at first. Then they go searching for trouble and they find a cat stuck in a tree and they try and get it down. It ended *horribly* but they still got it down. And then they went to a restaurant and got some food, and they all admit they want to be a good guy instead of a bad guy because it makes them feel better. Wolf called it the Good Guys club."

"I thought the book is called Bad Guys."

"It is. They're bad guys in a Good Guys club."

"Oh, that sounds complicated. Who's your favourite good-bad guy?"

He taps his finger on his chin. "That's actually a very hard question. But probably Snake."

"Why Snake?"

"Because he's very straight to the point. I also like Wolf because he's dumb, and it's really funny."

"I like that you like to read."

"I like that *you* like that I like to read."

We giggle as I give him a hug and a kiss then blow a raspberry into his neck. He giggles again then lies back and sighs, his fingers twisting through his hair. "I really like these bunk beds."

"They're amazing, aren't they?" If I didn't think Leo was a catch before, the fact he can create something this beautiful with his bare hands is an even bigger turn-on than his looks. Oh, and that sexy voice of his. I *really* like the sound of his voice. Soft and deep, it sends chills over my skin. And his *kisses*. My God, I have *never* been kissed so toe-curlingly well. Ever. I've really been missing out.

"I made Leo a thank-you card." He twists and digs between the books on his shelf, coming out with a sheet of folded paper. "Do you think you can give it to him?"

He hands it to me and I smile as I take in the drawing of what I assume is of himself and Leo holding hands and eating ice cream. Inside it says, "Thank you for the bed.

You are really good at building. You can build stuff in Roblox too."

"This is beautiful, Arch. But, why don't you give it to him yourself tomorrow? I'm sure he'd like that."

He shrugs. "Abby said it's weird that I like hanging around him."

"I can hear you, you know," Abby says from the other side.

"You shouldn't say things you don't want people repeating," Archer shoots back.

"Enough, you two. It's not weird that you like talking to Leo. He's a very nice man."

Abby scoffs, but I choose to ignore that.

"How about we drop this off to him before we go to holiday club tomorrow? Would that work?"

He grins and nods rapidly.

"OK. Night, kiddo. Lights off at ten."

"OK, Mummy. Love you."

"Love you too."

Moving around to Abigail's side of the bed, I hold my hands out to the side and wait until I catch her eye. "Do I need to wave a white flag?"

She rolls her eyes. "No. You just need to give me my phone back." With all her attitude and sass at dinner, I confiscated it again.

Taking the rolling chair out from under the desk, I pull it closer and sit down beside her. "Do you think yelling at me and storming off is the way to earn it back?"

Her jaw tightens as she flips the page on her Cosmo magazine, an article about hooking up in airports. I'm not sure I want her reading that at fourteen, so I reach out and close the magazine, pulling it onto my own lap as I say, "We need to talk about this friction between us."

"No, Mum. You need to quit taking my stuff." She pulls on the corner of the magazine, but I clamp my palms down on it so it doesn't budge. She huffs and rolls onto her back, placing her palms against her forehead.

"What happened to girls your age reading Girlfriend and Dolly, anyway? This stuff is way out of your age group," I say, flipping through the pages and almost dying when I spot the sex tips.

"Those magazines are for kids."

"Disney princesses are for kids, Dolly is for teens, Cosmo is for women in their twenties."

"And That's Life is for over-the-hill women who get off on doing puzzles."

I gasp. I happen to love That's Life magazine—and not for the articles. When did she become so cruel?

"Abigail," I sigh.

"Mum," she mocks.

"What do you want me to do here? What's going to help?"

"Going home. Getting Dad to come back."

"It's not that easy. The house isn't even ours anymore."

"We could live with Granma or Aunty Jo."

"I don't think that would work, sweetheart." I love my mother and sister both, but living under the same roof is another story.

"Well, that's what I want. That's what will make me feel better. Getting my life back."

"I need you to understand that I'm not trying to keep your father away from you."

"Then why won't he call?"

"I don't have an answer to that. In fact, I've been calling and messaging him daily, asking—*begging*—for him to at least call and talk to you and Archer, to explain why he left. And I can't even express how sorry I am that he hasn't. It breaks my heart, because I *know* you need him, but I just don't know how to get him to you. I'm doing the best that I can here, Abs, and I really need you to cut me some slack. My husband left me, so I'm hurting too."

"Is that what you talk to Leo about? How hurt you are?"

"Yes, actually. He's been a good friend to me. And he's trying to be good to you, too. He built this for you, didn't he?" I tap the side of the bunk bed.

She rolls her eyes again. "So Dad's out and he's in? Just like that?"

I shake my head. "No, sweetheart. He's my friend."

"He doesn't look at you like a friend."

"Well, he can look all he wants, but it doesn't mean I'm ready to jump into a new relationship. Your father leaving has been huge for us all, and I think we need some time to ourselves before we let a new man into our lives. I'm here for you."

She narrows her eyes a little. "So you aren't dating him?"

I shake my head. "No. But I do like being his friend. Do you think you can handle that much?"

"I don't know. Why does he have to be around at all?"

"Because he lives next door, idiot," Archer snaps from the other side.

"Archer," I snap.

"Sorry," he mumbles.

"Doesn't mean he needs to hang around or pick Archer up from holiday club. What if Dad comes over, sees him here and gets the wrong idea?"

"Oh honey." I drop the magazine on the floor and lean forward a little, placing my hand over hers. "I know you want your dad to come back. But I don't think he wants to or he would have called."

"You said he just needs some time on his own. He could realise how much he misses us and decide to come back any moment now."

"I shouldn't have said that." I lift her ponytail and run my fingers down the length of it. I miss her. I miss the relationship we had before Kevin exploded our world. When she would come home from school and talk about maths class and yogurt disasters. This version of her is so far removed from the happy-go-lucky kid she was before, and I hate that I can't fix it. The hardest part of this is trying to work through my own grief and watch out for my kids' too. It's like a constant uphill battle I wasn't ready to trek, and I feel like I'm wearing the wrong shoes.

"Then why did you?"

"Because I didn't want to hurt you with the truth."

"What truth?"

I take a deep breath and steel myself. "I don't think he's on his own, sweetheart."

Her eyes flash, and I know I've gone too far. There's such a fine line dictating how much information is for adults and how much is for children. Despite Nana's assurances that Abby needed the truth, I think I just crossed it. "You're *lying*. He wouldn't do that. He wouldn't just leave without telling us. You've done something to stop him from calling, I know it. He wouldn't just leave. He wouldn't leave us for another woman. He *loves* us."

"Of course he loves you, Abby. I don't think anything will ever get in the way of that." *God, I hope I'm right, because Abby deserves a father's love.* "But you need to understand the truth here. He chose to leave, and until that moment when he told me he was leaving us, I had no idea he wanted to. I haven't heard from him even once. It's his choice to stay gone. No one is keeping him away."

"Can I have my phone back so I can see if he's called me back? He might not want to talk to you, but maybe he's just had no way to charge his phone and the moment he does, he'll call *me*."

"OK," I whisper, pulling her phone out of my pocket and handing it over.

She practically snatches it from my hand and powers it up. For a moment, there's hope in her eyes, and I see my little girl again. Sweet. Innocent. Not spoiled by hurt and betrayal. But when the only notifications that come through are from her friends, my little girl disappears. *I hate this.*

"I'm sorry, Abby."

"No, you aren't, Mum. It's easier for you this way. He dumped you and he's gone and you don't have to see him after he hurt you. But he's my dad, and it matters to me that he isn't here. It matters to me that our whole life has changed because you couldn't deal with him leaving. If you really cared about us, you'd let us go back to Bairnsdale, and you'd do something more to find him than make a few phone calls. You're not trying hard enough. I need two parents. And ever since he's been gone, I barely even have one."

I recoil like I've been slapped in the face. I didn't realise she was seeing the separation this way. I mean, I knew she was angry, but I didn't consider this. I was too focused on my own heartbreak, my own confusion. And she's right, it is easier for me to be away from Kevin, from our house, and from all that was familiar about our life with him. Life got hard. I ran. And I dragged them with me. It really hurts that she's throwing it all in my face.

"I've tried, Abigail," I say, not really knowing what else to say at this point. "I'm sorry it hasn't been enough for you."

"Just stop. You've done nothing but lie, and I don't believe you anymore. You said we were just here while the house was fixed up. You said Dad was away on business. You keep saying things—lies—that are all bullshit."

"Watch your language with me. I know you're upset, but you don't get to speak to me like that."

"What the fuck does it matter what you want?"

"Abigail." Since when did my daughter start speaking like this?

"You haven't once asked me what I want. You've just dragged us away from everything and everyone and you keep lying about why. Did he even really leave you, Mum, or did *you* run away? Or worse. Did you—"

"Don't you dare insinuate that I caused this. *He. Left.*

I'm your mother, not your emotional punching bag. I'm sorry you're hurting, Abby, I really am. But I didn't make your father leave. He did that all on his own. Think about that before you start slinging insults at me next time."

I stand up as calmly as I can, even though my entire body is shaking. I don't think I've ever been as angry with her as I am in this moment. What's worse is hearing Archer's sniffles as he tries to hide his tears.

I walk over and stand by his bed, sweeping his hair from his forehead before I plant a kiss above his brow. "We'll be okay, buddy," I whisper, even though I'm not really sure right now.

Wiping at his eyes, he sniffles as he nods. "I don't like it when you fight."

"Me either." A small part of me hopes that Abigail is listening to this and feels guilty for upsetting her little brother before bed. If she could only step outside herself for a moment, maybe she could see all the love she has right in front of her. My heart hurts for us all. "Sleep tight, OK."

He nods and I head to the door, saying to both of them, "Goodnight, I love you," before I close it and cover my face with my hands. *Fuck. Fuck. Fuck.*

"Everything OK in there?" Nana's voice nearly makes me jump out of my skin.

I shake my head then shrug, a stray tear sliding down my cheek.

"Why don't you come into the kitchen? Betsy is making espresso martinis as a test for our next craft club."

"Haven't you two had enough to drink today?"

"We're so old, we need the alcohol to preserve our organs."

That actually gets a smile from me. "I think maybe I'll take a shower first. I'll be out when I calm down."

With an understanding nod, she reaches out and rubs my arm in comfort. "I stand by what I said before. Your happiness matters too." I press my lips together and I nod, trying to be strong. But I feel so... broken. Nana pulls me into her arms and rubs my back. "You're a wonderful mother, Darcy. Don't forget that. It's hard now, but this will pass. I promise."

God, I hope she's right.

And that's when the tears fall.

Because, what if she's not?

## TWENTY-SEVEN

## DARCY

Once I'm showered and slathered in moisturiser to ease my sunburn, I pull on a pair of harem pants and a loose tank top before heading into the living area. Nana stands at the kitchen bench, putting lids back on liquor bottles while Betsy carries an impossibly full martini glass, her eyes wide and her mouth saying a silent, 'ohh' until she sets it proudly on the table, somehow managing not to spill a drop.

"This one can be yours," she says. "There's supposed to be a coffee bean on top, but you'll have to pretend this time."

"Thanks, Betsy," I say, taking a seat. She watches with keen eyes as I pick up the glass and sip. It's so strong it punches me in the back of my sinuses. "Whoa, that's got a kick." I gasp and sniff, blinking rapidly, because I think it's knocked out my vision a bit too.

Nana takes a sip of hers, gasps and wheezes. "Maybe a little less liqueur in the next ones, Bets."

Betsy takes a brave mouthful and smacks her lips together. "Really? I think it's perfect."

Nana and I shake our heads, still struggling to breathe properly. "If you like drinking battery acid," Nana says.

Betsy shrugs.

"You look like you're about to head out," I say to Nana when I can talk again, giving her a head-to-toe look. She's wearing a blue and red kaftan with jewels sparkling around the hemline. Her hair is neatly twisted into a French roll, and her lips are a bright red.

"Oh, I was just going to pay my friend Bob a visit. He got his hands on one of those little blue pills and wants to give it a spin."

"Best inventions ever," Betsy adds with a wink, her tongue snaking out to find the side of her martini glass before she downs over half of it.

"What happened to George?" I ask of the naked old guy I haven't seen since our first night here. "Did you break up?"

"Oh, no. It's just not his turn," she says like I should already know this. And come to think if it, I probably should. This is Nana, after all. "I try not to spend too much time on one man, dear. They get too comfortable and next thing you know, you're washing their underwear and vacuuming under their feet."

Betsy nods as she reaches for Nana's unfinished cocktail.

"Well, I guess you shouldn't keep Bob waiting too long. Wouldn't want the effects of that pill wearing off without you." I smile, hoping that one day I'll have

Nana's zest for life. She never lets anything get her down.

"He *can* wait. You're upset."

I let out a sigh. "I'm at a loss with Abigail. We keep going around in circles. I don't think she's going to be OK until I find Kevin."

"Do you think finding him will change anything?"

I shrug. "Not for me. But for the kids—especially Abigail—yeah. It'll give them closure."

"How do you think *you'll* feel finding him again?" Betsy asks.

"Honestly, in the beginning, I wanted to yell at him until I went hoarse, but now I just want him to talk to his kids, explain to them why he stepped out of their lives so effortlessly. It wasn't a snap decision. He planned it. They need to know it wasn't because of them, and nothing I ever say will convince them of that. Especially not Abby."

"Hmm," Betsy says, her chin resting in her hand. "I think that cleansing spell worked really well."

A laugh bubbles out of my chest as I remember their chanting and candle lighting. It seems so long ago now, but it was only a couple of weeks.

"You and your spells," Nana says, standing to take Betsy's empty glass into the kitchen. I have no idea how Betsy is going to stand after drinking hers *and* Nana's, so I hand Nana mine to spirit away to safety.

"*My spells*?" Betsy scoffs. "Oh, I see how it is now."

Nana gives me a smile and a wink, and I assume there's some inside joke going on between the two of them. Then she kisses me on the side of the head as she passes. "I'll be back in time for breakfast. I'm not taking my phone, but if you need me, Bob's number is in the little black book next to the phone on my nightstand."

I smile. "Your little black book?"

"Can't let the men be the only ones to have them." She leaves the room in a dramatic flair of silk and rhinestones.

"Always ahead of her time, your nana," Betsy says, slurping down the last of Nana's espresso martini.

"I like that she's a free spirit."

"You could be too."

"I have too much responsibility to be a free spirit."

"What a load of poppy-cock. Being a free spirit isn't about being selfish; it's about finding your bliss, being happy in any given situation. It's about embracing joy."

"Embracing joy?" She makes it sound so easy.

"That's all Esme does, you know. She lives a simple life, and she pours all of her love into the people around her. In doing that, she's surrounded by joy. You should try it."

"So, I just...love everyone? Just like that?"

"Yes. You let go of your judgement and your anger and you look for the good."

"Doesn't that only open the door for shitty people to come into your life?"

"The universe gives back what you put in, Darcy. If you express joy, joy is what will return."

"I can't imagine seeing me joyful is going to help Abigail much."

"No." She smiles like she knows everything. "But loving her will. Here"—she leans to the side and rummages through her handbag, pulling out a worn leather pencil case—"I think it's time to read your cards."

"Do you really think these work?" I ask, sceptical as I watch her gnarled fingers work at the zipper then pull out a set of tarot cards that appear to be as old as Betsy herself.

"All depends on what you want to know." She looks me in the eye as she shuffles the deck with an expert hand. I swear this woman is impervious to alcohol.

"Honestly, I just want to know how I'm supposed to get through this."

She holds the deck out to me. "Then shuffle the cards and ask them to give you direction."

With a heavy sigh, I take them from her hand and do as she says, closing my eyes and focusing on the movement of my hands and the searching in my heart. Who knows if a bunch of cards with pictures of them is going to hold any sort of answer?

"OK," Betsy says when I'm finished shuffling. "Cut the deck then select three cards." She points at the table, and I place each card in front of her finger. The first in the centre, the second to the left, the third to the right. "These represent your present"—she points to the card in the middle—"your past"—she points to the one on the left —"and your future"—the one on the right. "Flip your present first, and we'll talk about where you are right now."

I do as she asks and I find the image of a man wrapped in a cloak with golden cups on the ground around him. "What does that mean?"

"It's the Five of Cups. It's a dark omen that warns of

loss and disappointment. You're experiencing setbacks, but it's important to remember that this emotional pain and heartache will pass."

"No big shock there. My life is primarily disappointment right now." I've gotta say, it's uncanny how spot on this is already.

"In the present position, it suggests you should explore new paths. But if you're avoiding truths, any satisfaction you find will be short-lived. The only solution is optimism and honesty."

I narrow my eyes. "Are you just saying all this because you know about my situation?"

All I get is a knowing smile. "I don't deal the cards, my sweet. I simply tell you what's in them. Now, turn over your past."

Taking a deep breath, I flip the card on the left. It's a skeleton riding a red-eyed horse. "That doesn't look good."

"Well, it's not. It's the Death card. It doesn't necessarily mean that someone will die. It's mostly indicative of massive change. Something happened that will flip everything about your life on its head and there'll be no going back to it."

"You're shitting me?"

She grins. "I'm not. And since we already know about Kevin leaving and the ensuing bankruptcy, I think it's fair to say that when we look at your past and present cards together, you're in the midst of change. And where you go from here will be entirely up to you. Do you embrace those feelings you're having for the handsome rugby player next door, or do you live like a spinster, at the mercy of your daughter's temper for the rest of your life? Joy or anxiety." She lifts her brow. "Want to find out?" She taps the final card.

"This is making my life sound like a soap opera. And I have to admit, I'm feeling a little manipulated right now. You have prior knowledge while you read these."

She laughs. "Look up the meanings online when we're done. I assure you, I'm not twisting them."

"Cleansing spells and mystical tarot cards. You'll all have me addicted to my horoscope next. My mother would lecture me for days if she even caught me considering this kind of stuff."

"You're forty years old and you worry about what your mother thinks?"

"All the time," I say with a shake of my head. "I can't even talk to her right now for fear of judgement. We converse via text."

Betsy smiles in a way that tells me she's not even touching that subject. "Turn over the final card, Darcy. Let's see what this nervous, worried woman in front of me has ahead of her."

"Nervous and worried," I mutter. "Yeah, that pretty much sums me up. I'm constantly in a tizz about what everyone around me thinks or feels. But no one's really thinking about me, are they? Not even me, it seems." With a shrug, I flip over the card. It's a robed woman sitting on a throne with a crescent moon at her feet.

"The High Priestess." Betsy says this with a reverent breath and shining eyes.

"That's good?" Admittedly, I'm getting a little excited here. I've always thought this was such mumbo-jumbo, but the fact that the first two cards were exactly right gives me hope that this future card is right too. And there's nothing wrong with hope, surely.

"It is. And it's one of my favourites. It's all about feminine influence and wisdom and suggests that you have excellent intuition. If you'll let your head trust the wisdom of your heart for a change, you'll find yourself on a much better path than before."

"That's easy to say. But when my heart and my head are both hurting, I'm not sure I can trust where any of these instincts are coming from."

Reaching across the table, she pats her hand on top of mine. "You already know what your heart wants, Darcy. Your head is telling you to be cautious. In this future position, the High Priestess suggests that you're on a course to receive great rewards, which I believe you will. But, as with all paths that lead to success or happiness, there will be attempts to steer you off course, or push you back where you started. You need to reject those attempts, put yourself first for a change, and stay the course. Only then will you find your ultimate happiness."

"Even if my happiness results in my child's *un*happiness?" I pull my hand from hers and place both in my lap. "I don't know if that's something I can do."

Pressing her lips together, Betsy collects the cards, shuffles them again and places the deck in front of me. "Cut it," she says.

I do. Then she selects the card on top and places it in front of me. "The Lovers," she says, and I actually roll my eyes.

"Did you go through this and only put cards in there that tell me I should give this thing with Leo a shot?"

"Is that your interpretation of things?" she asks, lifting her brow. "The Lovers actually means that you have a decision to make: a fork in your road. One leads to happiness, and one...does not. Take from that what you will, but the cards don't lie."

"They don't know everything either."

She shrugs. "And yet they keep saying the same thing: your happiness lies with understanding how incredible you are, Darcy. How beautiful you are on the inside and out. You are incredibly loveable. While a man won't *make* you happy, having a man who sees the *real you* and loves what he sees will make all the difference. We all want and need love, Darcy, but *happiness* includes feeling buoyed by someone who *values* you, walks *beside* you and loves you unconditionally."

"And you believe that man is Leo?"

"Yes. Your nana and I have *always* believed it's Leo."

## TWENTY-EIGHT

## LEO

"So, you're telling the neighbour's kids that I'm a shitty person now?" I ask Niall as I sit beside him on the couch. He's watching some movie on Stan, staying out of his room for a change. I take it as an opportunity to talk, placing a tub of Ben & Jerrys in front of him to get his attention. No matter his mood, the kid can't say no to *The Tonight Dough*.

He picks it up and tears through the plastic, his spoon in there before he answers. "We were talking. The topic came up. Didn't say anything that wasn't true."

"I think your version of the truth and mine are two very different things."

He shrugs. "I just call it like I see it."

"And how do you see it?"

"You fucked up your own family, and now you're moving in on theirs."

I sigh and wipe a hand over my face in exasperation before grabbing the TV remote and hitting pause. "I don't want a substitute family, Niall. What I want is to fix my relationship with the one I have. But I don't think you want to give me the chance."

"Well, forcing me to be somewhere I don't wanna be isn't helping your case, Leo. I had plans these holidays."

I don't really know what to say to that. "I wanted to spend time with you before you go off to uni and can't find time to come out here anymore."

"You mean before you can't exercise your parental rights and force me here?"

"Force." I drop my eyes to the palm of my hand and run my thumbnail over a callous there. "Is it really that awful spending time with me?"

"I don't know, man. I'm not the one who abandoned his family when they got in the way of his big football career."

"You think I left because of my career? A simple Google search would tell you that wasn't the case."

"It told me how mentally abusive you were to Mum. How you made her live like a pauper and wouldn't let her have a career."

"None of that is true. I gave her everything she needed and more. I've continued to give her more. All I've ever wanted, Niall, is more time with you."

"Then maybe you shouldn't have left. Maybe you should've gotten a different job."

"Yeah. Maybe I should have." I bounce my shoulders and shake my head. I can't say that I've never thought about that option. It would have been a hell of a lot easier on my relationship with my son. But what kind of a lesson would I teach him, staying in a loveless marriage with a person I can't stand? I fucking hate these hopeless situations where you lose no matter what.

Sitting back, I run my hands through my hair and let out my breath. "Listen, we only have a couple more weeks before these holidays are over and school is back. How about we call a truce, spend some time doing fun shit together, and see if maybe we can get along?"

He shoves a spoon of ice cream in his mouth and talks around it. "Can we go skydiving?"

"If that's what you want, sure. I'll take you skydiving."

He thinks for a moment, eating, thinking, then nodding his head. "OK." He holds out his hand. "We'll call a truce."

I take his hand and we shake on it.

"Do you think you could try not to stir things up next door? Despite whatever reputation you think I may have, I like Darcy a lot."

"iPhone XR a lot?"

"Excuse me?"

"Do you like her enough to get me an iPhone XR?"

"To keep you quiet?" Just when I thought we were getting somewhere.

He shrugs. "You want something. I want something. It's a win-win."

"Jesus Christ." The apple doesn't fall far from the tree. It's like he's channelling Tash. "I'm not bribing you, Niall. I'm asking you to do the right thing and not spread rumours. The rest is up to you."

"And I'm asking for a new phone."

I ease out my breath to stay calm. No one said this was going to be easy, and exploding at him when we just called a truce isn't going to help. "What happened to your other phone?"

"I lost it."

"When?"

"I don't know. Sometime this week." He shrugs like it's nothing.

"And you're only telling me this now?"

"I was going to tell you earlier but you were too busy playing daddy to someone else's kid."

I choose not to let that barb get to me. "OK. I'll take you to get a new phone."

His brow quirks upward. "An iPhone XR?"

"A 7 Plus. That's the best I'm willing to do for you."

"Not even an 8?"

We spend a few minutes haggling over which phone he wants. He talks me into an 8 Plus, and I trade him for visiting at least once a month and spending one week of the Easter holidays with me. It still feels a hell of a lot like bribery, but I'm trying to look at it as compromise.

"Don't make me regret this truce thing," he says after a while, giving me a sidelong glance.

I laugh a little. We sit in silence, watching some martial arts film while I take what time with him I can get, happy for the absence of slammed doors and the loneliness that comes with sharing space with someone who won't talk to you.

"MORNING." I sit on the bench next to the privacy screen when I see Darcy's silhouette through the thatching, pulling my runners on my feet. "Not like you to be out here this early."

"I feel like I've been out here for hours. What time is it?"

"A little after six."

"The sun is coming up," she says, taking a seat on the bench on her side. We're sitting back to back. When I look over my shoulder I can see pieces of her through the diamond shapes in the thatching. Her eye, her mouth... glimpses of beauty.

"Something on your mind?"

"I'm sure you heard the yelling yesterday."

"I did. Change isn't easy on kids."

"Unless you're Archer."

"Yes, well, he's a fifty-year-old man in an eight-year-old body."

She chuckles. "A regular Benjamin Button."

"He's good fun though."

"He made you a thank-you card for the bunks. He thinks they're really cool."

"I'm glad. I'll put it with the John Cena figurine he gave me."

"He gave that to you? I thought he still had it."

"That's a different one," I say. "Long story."

"It's always a long story where Archer's concerned. What are you doing up this early?"

"Going for a run."

"Can your knee handle that?"

"It's a very slow jog, so yeah. I'm staying off the sand though."

"If you turn it into a walk, can I come with you?"

I take a moment to study her eyes, they seem wide and conflicted, like there's something she isn't telling me.

"Sure. That won't get you into trouble though?"

"My kids don't get up until eight. We've got some time."

"A walk it is then."

By the time she grabs her shoes, I'm on the footpath outside her gate. She's wearing a black pair of baggy pants that cuff at her ankles. Harem pants I think they're called—don't ask me how I know that. She has a pale yellow tank top on that hangs loose to her hips. Her blonde hair is pulled into a messy bun, and her sunburn isn't as angry-looking today.

"Don't mind the face," she says with a half-smile. "I haven't had the chance to cover it."

"I could never mind your face," I say in return, wondering for a second if that came out as a good thing to say or a bad thing. "I meant that I like your face no matter what."

She laughs. "Well, thank you. I like your face too."

We walk in quiet companionship until we reach the track that runs along the edge of the beach. There are a few people out running in the early morning light, but mostly, it's just us and the birds.

"We should do this more often," I say after a while, catching her hand in mine and feeling my chest stutter with relief when she responds by entwining her fingers with mine.

She takes a deep breath. "I think Nana and Betsy did some sort of spell on us," she blurts out, and that's the last thing I expected her to say, so I laugh in disbelief.

"What?"

"They did this chanting spell thing on New Year's Day. They said it was to help cut emotional ties with Kevin and open my heart to new beginnings."

"OK?" I'm all for a little crazy, but crediting this thing between us to a spell is a little beyond my level of acceptance. "Do you believe in, uh, witchcraft?" I choose my words carefully.

"What? *No.* That would be nuts." Thank God we're on the same page here. "But I think they do. And they keep letting it slip a few times that they've always thought you and I would be good together, like they're patting themselves on the back or something."

"You think they got their little coven of witches together, cast a spell to make sure we found each other, and it worked?" I study her eyes a little closer, wondering if she's been smoking her grandmother's wacky-tobacky.

"God, it sounds so ludicrous when you put it like that. I don't think that, but it is weirding me out how quickly I've come..." She stops talking and presses her lips together, keeping her thought to herself.

"You mean how quickly we've come to care for each other?"

We stop walking and she nods, turning to face me. "Is that jumping too far? I mean, we've had, um—"

"Sex," I offer because I've grown used to her stumbling over her words and withdrawing a little every time our conversation focuses on anything intimate.

"Yes. And, well, we've you know..."

"Kissed, hugged, danced, held hands, slept against each other, and every time we touch it feels amazing?" I hold up our entwined hands as evidence, pressing a light kiss to her knuckles. Her eyes flutter closed.

"Yes," she whispers, and I can't help myself. Lifting her chin with the index finger of my free hand, I press my lips to hers, sucking lightly, tasting the sweetness of her minty toothpaste and waking my body up in a way that only a kiss with a beautiful woman can.

"Do you really think a spell created this, Darcy?"

She keeps her face tilted up to mine and her eyes closed. "I'm struggling to care even if it did."

With a laugh, I brush my fingers along her cheek, being careful so I don't abrade her tender skin. "I don't think it was a spell. If those kinds of things existed, I don't think we'd have a choice in the matter. And we certainly wouldn't be capable of showing restraint for the sake of the children."

"I think you're right. But do you want to know something strange?"

"You know I do."

"Betsy read my tarot cards last night, and it was so eerily accurate I couldn't sleep."

"What did they say?" My interest is definitely piqued here. Spells are bullshit as far as I'm concerned, but tarot is a different beast.

"She got me to choose three cards. One each for past, present and future. Basically, they all said that I'm going through a huge change. That life as I knew it is over and I have a choice to make. One choice will lead to my happiness, and the other to, well, not my happiness."

"And you saw that as making a decision about you and me?"

"Yeah. Well, wouldn't you? I mean, if you believed in that stuff?"

I gesture towards the park bench and we both sit, our bodies facing the power of the ocean, our knees pointed to each other, my arm draped behind her. It feels natural. Good. *Real.*

"You know my mother passed a while back. A long battle with lung cancer. It was partially why I chose to quit playing. To take care of her."

"I'm so sorry."

I give her shoulder a squeeze. "She was almost eighty when she died, which is why I think I get along so well with Esme. She reminds me of her."

"She does?"

I nod. "We were very close. It was just her and me growing up, and she was...everything a mother should be. Patient, understanding, clever and funny. She always lived life outside the box. Never one for convention."

"I can definitely understand why you like Nana then." She smiles.

"Yes. Well, my mum also *loved* tarot and runes and horoscopes, stuff like that. She said it wasn't magic, just a way to read the energy of the universe to help us make decisions. She even threw runes the day I had to choose which rugby club to play professionally for."

"Did you do what the runes told you?" She looks up

into my eyes and I can't help but lift my free hand to brush a few unruly strands of hair behind her ear. It feels so natural, this desire to take care of her.

"I did. See, the thing about runes and tarot and whatnot, is that there aren't any definitive answers. Each stone, or card, is open to interpretation and there are positive and negative connotations for each. The symbols appear, and they make these vague suggestions, but it's you who gives them meaning."

"Are you saying the cards could have meant anything?"

"I'm saying they mean different things to different people. Everyone has some kind decision to make in any given moment, and what the cards do is bring your focus to that particular decision. Think of it like a therapy session."

"A therapy session?" Now she's looking at me like I'm the crazy one.

I laugh. "Just hear me out, OK? Say you find a counsellor and tell them you need help because you've just gone through a marriage breakdown, and now you're faced with choosing between what you think is right for your kids and what you think is right for yourself."

"That's exactly what I would say to a counsellor."

"And it's the question you were asking when Betsy read your cards too, wasn't it?"

She tilts her lips down a little and nods once.

"When the cards were flipped, what they did was guide you to the answers you already had inside you—same as a therapist."

"You think people should consult tarot instead of seeking therapy?" She narrows her eyes.

I laugh and cover my eyes with my hand. "That's not what I'm saying at all."

"I know that." She pulls my hand back down and presses a kiss right in the centre of my palm. I want to close my hands and hold on to the sensation of the soft touch of her lips as long as I can. "I just don't know what *my* answers are."

I stretch out my legs and cross my feet at the ankles. "Well, lucky no one's forcing you to make a decision right now then, huh? We've got bunches of time."

She rests her head on my shoulder with a sigh. "No one really knows how much time they have, Leo. This past year, thinking Kevin might die at any moment taught me that."

"What are you saying?" God, I hope she's saying what I think she's saying.

"I'm saying that I want this: you and me."

"What about the kids? I thought you wanted to wait."

"Well, the kids do make this tricky. But, I realised we're not the only single parents who have gone through this. I was reading some parenting forums while I couldn't sleep, and the general consensus online is that you don't tell your kids about your dating life until you know it's serious and long-term. You and I can't figure out if we're serious or long-term until we've dated like a normal couple, right? We just have to find a way to date without any of them knowing."

I nod slowly. "Are you suggesting we sneak around?"

She meets my eyes and swallows hard. "Well, yes.

But on top of that, I think, um, I *need* for us to get a hotel room."

*Do not get a hard-on. Do not get a hard-on.*

"You know. I think I've got something better, at least a little more convenient. Think you can get away at lunchtime?"

## TWENTY-NINE

## DARCY

As we walk back to the apartment building, a small figure can be seen waiting for us on Nana's deck. *Archer*. My chest stutters a little. I'm walking a good metre away from Leo, but my mind naturally wonders what I'd feel if that was Abigail standing there. We'd spend the day screaming at each other again.

Archer smiles and waves when we're close, and I can see he's got the card he made Leo in his hand. "Abby's still asleep," he says as I open the gate. He's a little out of breath because he's also jumping up and down, but I appreciate that this beautiful little guy wanted to calm my nerves.

"Thank you, lovely boy," I say, placing my hand on his head to stop the jumping so I can kiss his cheek. "Good morning."

"Morning, Mummy." He starts jumping again and waves the paper card at Leo. "This is for you."

Leo remains on the footpath as he reaches out to take

Archer's offering. "Wow. Is this us?" He points to the picture drawn on front.

Archer moves on to hopping. "Yeah. We have ice cream."

"I can see that." He opens the card and reads the over-sized writing. "Well, thanks. I'm glad you like the bunks, mate."

Archer switches legs. "They're so cool. I can't wait to tell my friend Louis about them. He thinks he's so great because he has a bed with a desk under it. Mine is so much better. Do you think he can come over and see it, Mummy?" He holds his hands together in prayer, finally standing still as he looks up at me, eyes big.

"I'll check with Nana, but I can't see why not." I laugh.

"Who-hoo," he yells, turning on his heel and running into the apartment.

"He has far too much energy for this time of the morning," I say, shaking my head as I turn to Leo. Then my stomach does an excited little dance. This is really happening. "See you around one?"

His eyes darken as he inhales slowly and nods. "I'll text you the address."

I bite my lip to keep myself from smiling too much. "Can't wait."

He gives me this look that says he feels the same then makes his way to his deck. I watch him until he's inside and we keep giving each other knowing smiles the whole time. It's a bit silly, but I can't bloody help it. I want him. Bad.

"Hello there." I yelp and just about fall backwards when an elderly man appears in front me.

"Where did you come from?" I ask, pressing my hand to my chest to calm my heart.

"That way." He smiles and points towards the beach. He's quite pleasant looking as he stands in front of me, his hands behind his back. He kind of reminds me of that actor Christopher Plummer with white hair, a prominent nose, and eyes that look like they're always smiling.

"Can I help you?"

"Yes, as a matter of fact you can. The name's Arthur. I'm here to see Esme if she's available."

"Oh," I say, wracking my brain to see if I remember a mention of an Arthur amongst Nana's men. I come up blank, but that doesn't mean a lot. Nana knows so many people. "How about you wait here and I'll go see?" I gesture for the bench seat against the privacy screen.

"Thank you." He gives a polite nod as he lowers himself onto the bench.

"Be right back." I flash another grin and head inside. "Nana. You up?" I call out. I know she came home early this morning after spending the night with her other friend Bob, but she may still be sleeping.

"I'm right here, pet," she sing-songs as she breezes into the living area looking fresh as a daisy. "I tell you, I feel like a girl again after last night. Nothing like a good org—" She stops dead in her tracks, her gaze landing on the figure sitting on the bench seat outside.

"Ah, you have a visitor," I supply.

"I can see that." She presses her lips together and runs a hand over her hair as if she's nervous about her appearance. It's funny, because I've never actually seen Nana do something like that. She's normally so devil may care about this kind of thing. If I didn't know her better, I might think that Arthur makes her nervous. "How long has he been here?"

"He just arrived. Should I send him away?"

She places a hand against her cheek. "No. It's fine. I'll, uh, talk to him."

"Is everything OK?" I study her expression carefully. She's definitely not afraid of this Arthur character, but I don't think she really wants to talk to him either.

"It's fine, dear. Really. Arthur, he...he wants more from me than I can give. And well, he's being quite persistent." She gives a little giggle.

"Do you need me to come with you?"

"Oh no. He's no danger. He's just..." She giggles a little. *Giggles.* "He's rather charming."

"That's a bad thing?"

"Traditionally, no. But when I'm the butterfly and he's the collector, I've a fear of being pinned down."

"I see," I say, the lightbulb turning on. "He wants to be exclusive."

"Mmm." She gives me a tight smile. "And as you know, three marriages were enough for me." She moves towards the door. "Wish me luck."

"Good luck, Nana."

She opens and closes the sliding door, and I try not to watch her interaction with Arthur, but as I'm getting Archer ready for holiday club, I'm struggling to tear my gaze away. This is the first time I've seen Nana behave like a regular woman who gets nervous around the men she's attracted to. It's fascinating.

"What are we staring at?" Abby asks as she slips onto a stool on the opposite side of the island bench. Archer and I are both on the kitchen side of it trying to look busy while we spy.

"Nana has a new boyfriend," Archer whispers, and I smile as I watch her eyebrows shoot up as she almost breaks her neck trying to get a good look at Arthur. It's nice having this moment where things feel somewhat normal with her.

"Oh God. I hope we don't have to see him naked too." She makes a face as she turns back to us and starts pulling strawberries out of the open punnet on the benchtop.

"Me too," I say, sealing Archer's lunchbox since he doesn't like the food they supply at the community centre. "Although, this one is better looking than the last one, don't you think?"

She looks again and grimaces. "I can't tell. Too many wrinkles."

Archer giggles and I catch a rare smile from Abigail as she bites into her strawberry. *This is so much nicer than the venom she was spitting last night.*

"What are you doing today?" I ask her, keeping the conversation going while it's pleasant.

She swallows. "Me, Gabby, and Steph were thinking of catching the train to Chadstone. The big Westfield is out there."

"Shopping, huh? You got enough money?"

She nods. "I have the money Granma and Aunty Jo

sent for Christmas, and I didn't spend all my birthday money either."

"You're probably richer than me then," I joke. "Just make sure your phone is charged in case something happens, OK?"

"Of course, Mum. I'm not twelve." She's bristles, so I'm backing off at this point and calling this morning's interaction a win. Small victories.

"OK. Well, you have fun with your friends," I say, collecting Archer's and my bag. "I'm going to walk Archer to the community centre then do a little shopping," I say. *Then I'm going to come home and have a long hot shower where I scrub and shave myself smooth in preparation of what's to come.*

Just before I leave, my phone buzzes in my pocket, letting me know I have a text alert. While Archer slips his backpack on, I sneak a look and find a picture of Leo waiting for me. No shirt, his running shorts riding low on his hips so I can see that secret little trail of hair that points to what I want so badly my insides ache from longing. The caption reads: **This one is for looking. See you at 1.** Followed by an address. I exit from the pic almost as fast as I see it, but it's already committed to memory. I can't stop smiling.

## THIRTY

## DARCY

"Your workshop is better than a hotel room?" I walk through the open roller door of 'Murphy's Carpentry' and my butt cheeks prickle, imaging the splinters I could get from sitting on any surface in this place.

Don't get me wrong, it's a beautiful workshop. Big rustic-looking workbenches and tools lined up perfectly along the wall. There are a few pieces of completed furniture set up for display, a sitting area where I imagine he takes lunch or chats with clients, (and possibly plans to fuck me) and he's even made a beautiful cabinet to hold various samples of wood.

As far as workshops go, this is well organised and tidier than one would expect. However, when he said he had somewhere for us to go, I thought maybe he had a second house or could borrow a mate's place or something. I wasn't expecting to be on my hands and knees with the wood shavings. I'm going to smell like I've been rolling around in the scrub.

Leo sets the chisel he was working with to the side as

he smiles my way. "There's an apartment upstairs. Lunch too if you're hungry."

"Oh?" Now I'm all excited again. "Does anyone live there?"

"I did for a while after my split. I was still playing at the time, but I've always had this place for something to do in the off season. Sometimes it's handy having a bed upstairs for somewhere to crash when I work late."

"OK," I say, taking a deep breath, because I'm nervous and think that maybe I've jumped too far too fast. I want to have sex with Leo. Badly. But now my hands are all clammy and I'm not even a little bit drunk, so I'm more nervous than I thought I'd be.

"Come here," he says, eyes happy, mouth curved upward, strong hand held out to me. My heart flutters in my chest and my stomach twirls like a little girl in a dress. When I reach him, he gives my arm a gentle tug then wraps an arm around my waist, swaying gently from side to side. The motion puts me instantly at ease as I melt against him. How does a man I've known on and off for a month understand me better than the man I spent twenty years of my life with? The two men are very different people, and I'm glad. It's the first time I really feel like I'm being romanced. Leo makes me feel like I'm worth the effort.

"Remember the first time we did this?" he asks, inhaling my scent as he nuzzles my neck.

"How could I forget? It was seriously the most romantic thing that's ever happened to me."

I feel his smile against my skin. "I wanted to kiss you so badly."

"You should have. I wouldn't have objected."

Lifting his head, he meets my eyes and I feel like I'm falling into the murky green warmth they contain. "It wasn't the right time."

"Was the bathroom the right time?" I ask, smiling as I recall our crazy clash of teeth the day before.

"Probably not. But I think we can both agree that we're terrible at waiting. We rushed into this at the very start." *Yet it felt so good. So...right.* How could I ever be strong enough to say no to *this*. It's perfection.

Sliding my hands up to his shoulders, I lace my fingers behind his neck, gently teasing the back of his hair with my fingertips. "Do you think we're rushing into this now?"

"No," he whispers. "I think we've finally found the right time."

I smile up at him. "You know, I still haven't taught you how to cook the perfect steak."

"After this, I'll take you out and buy you the perfect steak," he whispers, just before his lips connect with mine, and suddenly I'm a puddle, melted at his feet.

"You know just what to say to win the ladies over." I smile as he brushes his nose against mine and chuckles.

"It's all about waiting until they're craving—"

"Do not say a hot beef injection." I push away slightly, covering my mouth as I burst out laughing.

Leo laughs and shakes his head. "There is no way I was going to say that. I was actually going to say that I had to wait until you were craving meat and tempt you with a steak dinner. But if we're going to the gutter, a hot beef injection's exactly what I'm going to give you." He hits a button so the roller doors start sliding closed.

"Oh God, is it bad that I'm salivating over the thought of a steak dinner now?" I snort from laughter as I back away playfully. "Better watch out, mister, I might bite."

"I hope so," he says, opening a door to my right.

I go through without hesitation, finding a narrow set of stairs that leads to the second-floor studio apartment with a small kitchenette, a turquoise fridge, a handmade table with two chairs, and of course, a bed.

*Gulp.*

"It's nothing spectacular. But it's clean, and no one's going to bother us up here. In fact, I don't think anyone knows about it except me."

Sucking a lungful of air through my nose, I lace my hands behind my back as I look around. "I'm nervous," I admit.

He grins. "Really? I couldn't tell from that whole beef injection conversation downstairs."

I wince. "That was a little weird, wasn't it?"

"I like your brand of weird. But if this is still too soon for you, we can slow things down, have lunch and talk. No pressure."

I take in another breath and bite my bottom lip. Physically, I am more than ready. This man not only turns me on, but he's revealing the deep-seated loneliness I've obviously overlooked until now. I heard Abby's cries of anger and sadness—fear of me choosing Leo over her dad—but this moment is about *me*. Like Nana said, it's time to be on my own side for a change. I'm not OK with only being

Leo's friend. I want more, the same way he wants more from me. This is about us. *Our* pleasure. *Our* happiness. And since we're adults, I think we get to choose that. We can have our cake and eat it too.

"I really don't want to wait, Leo," I say, my voice breathy, breasts heaving. I want this. I've wanted him to touch me from the moment I laid eyes on him. And ever since our first time together, I've dreamt of little else but his hands on my skin. I crave him. "I want this."

"OK then."

He moves towards me and catches me in his arms again, hands on either side of my face as he brings his mouth to mine and we kiss, slow and long. His tongue is minty fresh as it glides along mine, telling me he brushed his teeth before I got here. Strangely, it's that small consideration that has me swooning, wrapping my arms around him, deepening the kiss.

He hums his pleasure, fingers finding the zipper in the back of my dress and sliding it down my back until the bodice feels loose around my body and he's pushing it from my shoulders, fabric floating down and pooling at my feet.

"You smell so good," he says, tongue on my pulse point a moment before he sucks on my skin, hands flattening against my back and pulling me against him. I inhale.

"So do you." And he does. He smells as you'd expect, like the wood he works with, a subtle spice of cologne, and those pheromones that make women do silly things like sneak away to a workshop in the middle of the day under the guise of running errands. "Take off your shirt."

I help him with his buttons, both sets of hands rushing to find bare skin. I gasp at the contact, my hands running over his muscles as his warmth presses against mine, and our mouths are once again connected. And we're walking, kissing, touching, making our way to the bed. His fingers work open the clasp of my bra just as the backs of my legs touch the foot of the bed, and he grins, eyes darkening as he peels the silk and lace away, dropping it to the floor.

"You are an exquisite woman, Darcy."

I want to laugh, because I don't *feel* exquisite. But I believe he truly thinks I am, and that's a very sobering thought. This man. This *stunning* man, thinks that I, Darcy Field, am an exquisite human being. I release a giggle as he pushes me so I'm falling back on the bed, landing with a bounce in the soft clean-smelling bedding. Then he slides over the top of me, bracing his weight on either side as his mouth and tongue leave magical kisses across my stomach.

"I have plans for you," he says, taking my right nipple into his mouth and teasing it with his tongue.

"Are you talking to me or my breast?" I ask with a gasp and a smile, my fingers sliding into his thick hair.

"Both." He blows cool air on my wet nipple, causing a tight, hard peak to form.

I giggle again as he moves to the other side and does the same, his free hand moving down my side, taking a handful of flesh as he presses his fingers possessively into my thigh.

"Oh God. I like that."

"This?" He does it again, his strong grip pulling my

thigh so I'm physically wrapped around him and our pelvises are pressed together.

"Yes. I love the possessiveness of it." I also love that I feel comfortable enough to tell him that. I never would have done that with he-who-shall-not-be-named-while-my-legs-are-wrapped-around-my-new-lover. I'd have feared being mocked or teased. With Leo, I don't have that fear. I don't think he'd ever make me feel less than.

"I want to possess you, Darcy." He speaks in a low whisper and runs his mouth, nipping and sucking, from the centre of my breasts to the base of my ear. "All of you."

My whole body comes to life as I moan in response. The funny thing about Leo is that he's always so restrained. In general life, he's patient and calm, quiet even. But get him alone and wanting and he's a bit of a beast. I like it.

*No.*

I love it.

"All of me?"

"Mmm." He returns to my nipples. "We might be here awhile."

"I have all afternoon."

Lifting his head, he gives me a wicked grin. "Excellent."

When he's finished doing delicious things to my nipples, he makes his way down my stomach, nipping, licking and sucking my skin until he reaches my parted thighs and nudges his mouth right against my apex.

"You might wanna remove those first," I say of my

underwear, while I press up on my elbows to get a better view.

He meets my eyes and smirks. "Soon." Then he places his mouth over the thin silk and blows his hot breath against my centre, heating it to point where I'm gasping and sliding my fingers into his hair.

"What the hell?" I let my head loll back.

"Good? Bad?"

"Wonderful."

He runs the tip of his tongue right at the point where my thigh becomes my pelvis, and I shudder.

"Oh, that's good too." I release my hold on his hair as he pulls my underwear from my body, dragging it down my legs in slow-motion torture, the aching between my legs insistent and intense.

"Leo," I whisper, reaching for him as he sits back and takes a moment to look at my body. I feel thoroughly loved by his eyes, the way they take in every part of me with such hunger. I forget to worry about the way my breasts sag or my stomach crepes. I forget about the cellulite and stretch marks and the broken veins that normally bother me when I see them in the bathroom mirror. In his eyes, I feel every bit as gorgeous as he tells me I am. "I need you inside me."

"Soon." He quirks one side of his mouth. "I'm in no hurry here, Darce. I want to touch and tease you until you're so far gone you can't think straight. I want you to lose control again."

"Oh God, Leo." I place a hand across my forehead, trying not to let that initial embarrassment I felt after our first time get the better of me. "I haven't had enough wine for that."

"Who says you need wine to let go? All you need is trust and enough time riding the edge that you forget to stop yourself."

"You sound like you've done this kind of thing before," I say, half-cheeky, half-knowing. It's silly to think of a man his age and background and not understand he's slept with far more women than I have men, and while it doesn't bother me, it does make me feel inexperienced. He's so sure of himself and I still feel like giggling every time he pays me a compliment.

"With you"—he slides his hands up my legs, gripping my thighs as he pulls me closer to him—"everything is new again." He settles himself on the bed, face settled between my thighs so he's looking directly at my most private parts. When he inhales, my stomach does this crazy flip. Not because I'm shocked, but because I'm turned on by the way he seems to really get off on my scent. It's carnal. It's animal-like. And I fucking love it. "That moment when you grabbed your breasts and licked your own nipples..." He hisses his breath in through his teeth as he places a hand on my mound and runs his fingers over my neatly trimmed curls. "I can't tell you how many times I've jacked off thinking about that." He slips a finger between my folds, moaning when he connects with my juices then pushes inside.

"Oh God." My cheeks burn while my insides clench around his fingers. It's a strange sensation, my mind telling me to be embarrassed while my body sighs with arousal. "You've been...um"—I struggle to maintain focus and flick my gaze to his tented pants—"over me?"

"Unashamedly." He inserts another finger, pressing a kiss between my legs, right on my clit. "Didn't you?"

Pressing my lips together, I nod, shocking myself that I'm admitting it. There was a particular video of him on YouTube, dominating the rugby field, that really got me going. "Yes."

He flicks his tongue over my clit. "Now we're getting somewhere. I'd like to see you touching yourself."

"You would?"

He nods as he places his mouth over my core and sucks back on my clit.

"Oh God." I grab a fistful of the sheet. "Don't stop."

He chuckles, and I feel the vibration shoot right up to my nipples. "This'll be over too soon if I don't." Pressing a kiss on the inside of my thigh, he keeps his fingers moving as my clit pulses with need.

"Show me what you do when you're thinking about me," he says, taking a hold of my hand and disconnecting it from the sheet. We lock eyes and I'm instantly nervous. But there's such heat in his gaze that I allow myself to be spurred on as he guides my hand between my thighs and urges it to join his as it pulses inside me. "Yes, Darcy." His slick fingers slide with mine, his breathing thickening as he watches the show. "Show me what you do when you're alone."

With my eyes on his rapt expression, I slide my fingers up to my clit, circling it before I slide them back inside to join his. Up and back. Up and back. My breasts grow heavy and everything tightens. "Leo," I gasp, losing focus.

"Let go, Darcy," he instructs. And I do. My hips lift as my body shudders and a moan tears from my throat. The moment the orgasm rips through me, Leo moves my hand and replaces it with his mouth and tongue, sucking and swirling on my clit until I'm pulling at his hair and gasping out his name. Wave after wave hits me, and he doesn't stop, doesn't let go until I throw my head back, my body wrapped in heavenly fire as I scream, "*Leo.*"

With soft gentle laps, he brings me back down, kissing his way back up my body, tasting my neck until he captures my mouth, tongue demanding as he shares my flavour with his passion. "Is that what you imagined?" he whispers against my lips as I wrap my arms around his neck.

"It was better," I whisper back. "Way better."

"I love it when you scream," he murmurs, just before he slips his tongue into my mouth and takes over my mind with the hunger in his movement. My head spins and my body comes back to life, calling as though it hadn't just been given the orgasm of its life by the hottest man I've ever met.

"Leo." I can still taste that hint of toothpaste from before, but mostly there's a carnal sweetness on his tongue that I don't hate. It tastes like sex. I reach for his pants, eager to get them off and feel his hardened length in my hands.

Keeping our mouths joined, he shucks his pants and I feel the weight of his penis hit against my thigh. "I need you inside me." I reach down and take him in my hand, pressing my fingertips into the throbbing vein on the underside, my palm gliding up and down his length, thumb finding his slick, precum-drenched tip. He moans and I quicken my movement. "Leo, please. I want you."

"Condom," he says, finally breaking free from my mouth.

I whimper, because I don't want to stop holding him in my hand, but at the same time, my insides are throbbing. I want him to fill me.

"Roll onto your side," he says, and I roll, not having the slightest bit of hesitation in his instruction. *God, I love how sure of himself he is.*

He slips into bed behind me, lining himself up with my entrance then pushing inside, his hand flattening against my stomach as he does. I moan as every nerve ending I possess comes to life, and my brain decides that it doesn't need thought anymore. Just feeling.

Reaching back, I pull his hair and turn my head, kissing him over my shoulder as he thrusts in and out of me, his big cock angled perfectly. "Leo," I gasp, the connection almost transcendent as I spiral towards yet another orgasm. "I'm so close."

He pivots his hips, pressing his lips against my shoulder. "Hold on, baby. I'm almost there. Wait for me."

"I'm trying. Oh God. You're so big. You feel so...*ohhh God.*"

"Holy fuck," he grunts, pushing hard against my core as he pulses in my depths. "Fuck, Darcy. That was—"

"Transcendent?" I offer, grinning as he places soft kisses against my shoulder.

He chuckles before taking my chin between his

fingers and bringing his lips to mine. "Fuck yeah, it was," he says, kissing me in a way that makes my heart sing. Then and there, I decide that Leo's workshop is my absolute favourite place in the world. Like Betsy said when she read my cards, "while a man won't *make* you happy, having a man who sees the *real you* and loves what he sees will make all the difference." And it does. My God, it really does.

## THIRTY-ONE

## LEO

"How are the kids feeling about starting a new school?" I ask Darcy as we walk along the beach path before the sun comes up. In the two weeks since we decided to give this relationship a red-hot go, we've taken to spending this quiet time of day together before our kids wake up. It gives us time to walk and talk without the worry of teenagers kicking up a storm over seeing us together. And it's been incredible. Building a friendship from scratch. She's even more amazing than I already knew.

"Archer is excited. He's made some good friends through holiday club, so he's keen to make more. Abigail is being very tight-lipped about it. She's more relaxed now that her uniform has turned up, but she's been moaning a lot to her friends back home."

"Eavesdropping, huh?" I nudge her arm with mine, giving her a teasing grin.

"Me? Never." She laughs a little and then she sighs. "It's the only way I learn anything about her these days.

She's stopped yelling at me every chance she gets, but she's still very withdrawn. I'm thinking she might need some grief counselling? I don't know. I'm hoping school will help her settle in more. Seems we won't be leaving Nana's any time soon, so she'll have to get used to being here."

"No news on the job front?" She's been applying everywhere she can, hoping to find something entry level that still gives her time with her kids. Not an easy feat.

She shakes her head. "And my single parent benefits are taking forever to process. It's been a nightmare trying to get that off the ground. Although, the lady at the café on the main road said she might have a couple of days for me when school goes back. But how that's supposed to pay rent and support two kids, I'll never know."

"Ez is cool with you staying though?" I couldn't imagine Esme ever pressuring Darcy and her kids to leave. She loves having them there.

"Of course. She'd keep us forever if she could. I just feel like I'm taking advantage. She pays for most of the food and I'm not contributing to bills."

"It's not taking advantage when it's freely given, Darce."

"I know. But it still doesn't feel great. I love Nana, I do. But I want my own place again. I want my independence, and the kids need their own space. That bunk set-up you created is amazing, but it's only temporary. I can't expect them to share a divided room forever."

A sly grin pulls at my lips as I stop walking and catch her about the waist, pulling her against me. "You could always give up your room and bunk in with me." Never going to happen. But I'd fucking love it if it did.

With her hands moving up and down my arms, she lets out a heavy sigh. "I've considered it, believe me. Do you realise how hard it is not to sneak out at night and knock on your door?"

I nuzzle close to her ear, inhaling her intoxicating scent. "About as hard as it is to fall asleep knowing you're only a few metres away."

She turns into me and touches her lips to mine. "Torture," she whispers before we let our need win for a few moments, kissing like teenagers while the cool wind sprays salt against our skin.

"Pure torture," I agree, dropping my forehead to hers before we release each other and continue walking, feeling together and apart at exactly the same time.

Keeping our relationship on the down-low is a necessary evil, but I'd be lying if I said it wasn't difficult. Living next door, seeing and hearing each other when you can't act on that need to be close is bloody hard.

When you first sign up for parenthood, you don't realise you're signing up to willingly put yourself second at every turn. But the moment that kid is placed in your arms, you realise that your child's happiness is more important than your own. We can try to make the two coexist, but when emotions are high, sacrifices must be made. Darcy's and my circumstances—our love for our children and concern for their well-being—insist we maintain our distance. For a while, anyway. We have to repair the relationships in our own homes before we introduce anything new.

"How about Niall?" Darcy asks after a few silent steps. "He's at one of those fancy private schools in the city, isn't he?"

I nod and then shake my head. I always wanted him in public, but Tash insisted on private. With the amount of trouble he's been in over the years, I wonder if that was the right choice.

"I don't know what that answer is." She laughs as she leans forward slightly to see my expression.

"The answer is yes. He's at a fancy private school."

"This is his final year. Has he given any indication how he's feeling about that or what he wants to do next?"

I shake my head. "Nothing. I took him out, paid for all his school stuff and that's about as far as that went. I know he's planning on going to uni, but I'm not sure even he knows what for. He's quit busting my chops though, so the truce is still working. We're actually going skydiving this weekend before I take him back to Tash." I'm *really* not looking forward to seeing her. She always finds some way to try and make me stay longer, and by the time I leave I feel thoroughly harassed and have a splitting headache. I can't handle being in the same space as her any more. We're chalk and cheese. And I often wonder what the hell I ever saw in her.

"Skydiving? Wow. His idea or yours?"

"His. It was one of the conditions of the truce."

She giggles. "Teenagers. Always trying to bargain over everything. You know, Abby tried to get me to agree to buying her this really expensive backpack for school last weekend. Said she'd clean both hers and Archer's side of the room for a month if I let her. Of course, I said no. I'm too low on funds these days to think about a three-hundred-dollar backpack, but I had to give her points for trying."

This is the point where I don't know whether to keep my mouth shut or open it. Darcy is a proud woman, and if I offer to give her money she could take that badly. But she's struggling for cash and I have plenty after always being careful and investing my earnings over the years. I know I can help, but the question is, will she let me?

"If you're struggling, Darce, I can help." I chastise myself internally the moment the words are out there. And the way her eyes bug slightly tells me I probably should have kept my damn mouth shut, but it happened, so we're gonna deal with it.

"No, Leo," she says immediately. "I can't take money from you. And it's not because it's coming from you. I can't take money from Nana either. She tried to give me a credit card the other day." She rolls her eyes and laughs, trying to brush her discomfort off.

"Why?" I ask. Not because I want to force her to take my money, but because she's refusing help altogether.

"To help pay for things."

"No," I say. "Why won't you let us help? We know what Kevin did to you, we know your situation, and both your nan and I have the means to help you. There are no strings attached. You don't need to worry about money and count pennies when you have two people who care about you and *want* to step up, Darcy."

"Leo," she says, a slight edge to her voice. And I know I'm pushing a little hard, but I don't see the sense in this for the sake of something as fickle as pride. Maybe it's that superman complex, but I want to do this.

I stop walking again and face her, sliding my hand against her cheek as I look into her clear blue eyes. "I *want* to take care of you, Darcy."

"Leo," she says again, but this time it's a soft whisper as her tongue snakes out to lick her lips. It makes me want to kiss her, and only serves as a reminder as to how hard I've fallen. There's no turning back for me.

"I mean it, Darce."

She shifts her gaze between my eyes as she chooses her words carefully. "I love that you want to take care of me, Leo. It shows how wonderfully kind this big heart of yours is. But I need to do this for myself. And before you object, I need you to look at this from my point of view. Relying on someone else to take care of me and the kids is *exactly* how I got in this situation. I need to stand on my own two feet. Even if I'm just waiting tables." She flattens her hand over my heart. "Can you understand that?"

Pressing my lips together, I release the air through my nose as I nod. "Yeah. I do—I don't want to—but yeah, I get why you need that."

She smiles before pressing a quick kiss to my lips. "Good. Then let's move on to talking about fun things like when I'm going to get the chance to visit you at the workshop again." Pulling her lip between her teeth, she takes a step backwards then we start walking again. I'm amazed by her ability to face a problem without turning it into a confrontation or letting it spoil our time together. *Where has she been all my life?*

"Let me see if I can fit you into my schedule," I tease,

flashing her a smile as the tension in my chest melts away. Years upon years of senseless arguing with Tash has taught me to brace myself whenever I bring up a touchy subject. It's refreshing to be with someone who can communicate her objections without getting pissed off. Darcy keeps me grounded and I'm in awe of her at every turn.

"You'd better make time for me." She bumps her shoulder against my arm. "Although, with the way things are this next week, I'm thinking we're not going to get a moment to ourselves until the kids are back at school on Monday."

I stop walking as a sudden idea hits me. "What if I offer you a job?"

It takes her a second to realise I'm not moving before she halts and turns around. "What do you mean?" Her brow is furrowed but her eyes show intrigue.

"I could give you a job. At the workshop."

She grins then starts laughing. "Oh, I get it. Is this a *sexy* kind of job? Are you going to fit the upstairs apartment with a pole so I can dance for you? 'Cause, I've gotta tell you, buddy, I don't possess that kind of coordination."

A chuckle bounces out of my chest as I shake my head. "Of course not. I mean a legitimate paying job."

"What kind of job?"

"You've been organising your family for years, right?"

"Ah, yeah?"

"OK. So, why don't you transfer those skills to organising me?"

"Organise you, how?"

"This may surprise you, Darcy, but I'm shit at paperwork."

"I'm listening."

"I haven't put anything in a filing cabinet for years. It all gets tossed in the back office and forgotten about. Whenever I need something, it's a fucking nightmare. If you think you're up to the task, I could do with the help. We'll call you the office administrator and you can work school hours, so you're home when the kids are. We'll set it all up legitimately through my business manager and I won't overpay you at all."

She's smiling now. "I like that you added that last part, because I'm going to hold you to it." She holds a finger up, pointing at me with a stern look on her face.

"I will pay you whatever the going rate is. I won't even control that part, my accountant will," I promise, holding up my hands to show I'll have no part in that decision.

Her hands move to her hips and she nods slowly. "That could work," she says. "But no hanky-panky unless it's our lunchbreak, all right? You don't get to pay me to have sex with you."

I grin. "I'll be a total gentleman. I promise." *Most of the time.*

She nods. "I'll have to think about that some more. Can I think about it?"

"Of course. You say the word and the job is yours."

"What happens if I say no?"

I shrug and rub my hand over the back of my head. "I find someone else to do it?"

"So you *really do* need someone?"

I laugh. "Yeah, it's a disaster in there. I actually put an ad on SEEK last year, but quickly learnt that giving out my name brought out the crazies, not people actually looking for a job. I truly need help, and I believe your skills are what I'm missing."

When we take to walking again, she asks questions about what I'll need her to do and when I'd need her to start. We agree to three days a week at first to see how we go, and by the end of the conversation I'm feeling as though she's seriously considering the offer. To me, it's the perfect solution. She gets a job with the hours she wanted, and I get the assistance in the office I need while helping *her*. And it certainly doesn't hurt that I'll get to see her for a few hours each day. All she has to do is say yes. But, like with all our decisions, we have to take our kids into account. Niall won't really give a fuck. He'd be weird if I suddenly had Darcy in the apartment all the time, but he's not going to object to me working with her. Archer is the most accepting kid in the world and will probably want to come and see us working because he'll consider it fun. Then there's Abigail. And Abigail won't like the idea at all...

## THIRTY-TWO

## DARCY

"Leo offered me a job today," I tell Nana while we're straightening up after the kids have gone to bed. She's making us a pot of tea while I clear up the board games Archer and Abby have been playing all afternoon. A storm rolled in at about two o'clock and the rain hasn't let up since. It was actually nice seeing them spend time playing together. I've missed seeing their interactions since we moved here. Hearing them giggle together—and even squabble—was like music to my ears.

"Oh?" Nana says as she fills the pot with hot water. "Is that what you kids are calling it these days? I've always preferred to go with the technical term, cunnilingus."

"Very funny." I slip the games into the storage drawers of her wall unit then return to the kitchen to fetch mugs. "It's an admin job at his workshop. Doing all of the paperwork and filing for him."

"Oh, well, that sounds like it could be a wonderful

solution for you. And I suppose if it's a disaster, it'll still give you something to put on your résumé." She can put a positive spin on everything.

"I'm hoping it does work out. He said I can work school hours too. It'll be win-win."

"And you get more one-on-one time with your hunky beau." There was never any hiding the fact Leo and I were together from Nana. I swear she smelled him on me the moment I walked in the door from spending the afternoon with him. She feels like the greatest matchmaker on earth. "That makes it all the more enticing." She gives me a wink as she places the lid on the teapot and we both move to the table outside to enjoy the cool of the storm from our undercover vantage point.

"Do you think that makes it a bad idea, though? Being together and working together?"

She shrugs and pours our tea. "Lots of couples work together, sweetheart. And you and Leo don't really get to spend a lot of time together anyway. I say go for it, but I'm never one for caution, you know that. I'd prefer to burn hot for a short time over simmering slowly forever. What do *you* want? I think that's the only real question. What does your gut tell you?"

Lifting my mug, I blow on the steaming liquid. "It's telling me to be careful because things are good with Abigail right now. I don't want to mess that up by taking a job that could set her off."

"Pish, child. I understand your concern, but Abigail is a fourteen-year-old girl who needs to grow up. Her father turned out to be an arsehole and that's upsetting, but life goes on. She has a good life *here*. And you're already doing the right thing by the children keeping your romantic relationship with Leo out of their sight, but if you're going to let Abby's behaviour stop you from taking a job to support her and her brother, then that's taking it a bit too far for me. You are your own woman, Darcy. If she kicks up a stink, well, I'll have something to say about it. You take that job, pet. I'll have nothing else." She gives this nod of finality, resolution in her eyes as she stares into the dark rainy evening.

A smile curves my lips. This is the thing you should know about my nana: she's an incredibly determined woman whose wealth did not come from family or male companionship. Every penny she's made came by her own hands. Those kimonos she always wears? The patterned silk they're made from is designed by her and sourced by some of the top fashion labels on the planet. In her life and in her business, she's been scoffed at, joked about, put down and chided at every turn. And never has she allowed another human on this earth dictate their terms and sway her from her goals. Not her father, not her mother, not her husbands and certainly not her own son. She'd rather be alone than allow herself to be compromised. Which makes her pretty badarse in my opinion.

I think that's a huge part of why I came straight to her when my life fell apart. While my sister—and even my mother—would have taken us in, Nana is the one person I know who would pick me up and force me to get my shit together in the best and most loving way possible. I think that's what she's trying to do here, and I hear her.

Abigail is *my daughter*, so she doesn't have the right to tell me how to run my life. She can be hurt that her father has left, but ultimately, she needs to trust in the person who stayed—me. And I need to trust myself to make the tough decisions whether they upset Abby's balance or not. When the choice to support my children is between a casual waitressing job or a stable admin job, the logical and *best* decision is to choose stability. Nana is absolutely right.

"I'll take the job," I say, nodding along with my certainty. "It's the right choice."

"Of course it is, dear." Nana touches my arm then sits back, crossing her legs as she takes a sharp inhale. "I think I'm going to get a tricycle." That is probably the last thing I expected to come out of her mouth.

"A what?"

"A tricycle," she repeats. "Like a bicycle but with three wheels."

"I know what they are. Why do you want one?" Aren't they only made for small children?

"They have ones with motors on them nowadays so you don't have to pedal as hard. I can use one to get around town, pick up the shopping, visit people. I bet I could get Betsy interested in one too. We could go riding together. Start a gang." She grins, her eyes dancing as she meets mine.

The visual has me smiling. "And what would your gang be called?"

She thinks for a moment, her lips working together as her eyes narrow. "The Bayside Biddies. We could get T-shirts."

I have to put my tea down so I don't spill any as I laugh. "Oh Nana, I'd really like to see that."

"Good," she says. "Because I'm doing it."

THE RAIN CONTINUES into the next morning, and I lie in bed, listening to the pitter-patter when my alarm goes off at five. "No romantic walk for me today." I sigh, feeling put out because it's my favourite part of every morning. It's the only time of the day when Leo and I can be alone, touch each other openly, kiss... *oh God, how am I supposed to get through today without it?*

It sounds dramatic, I know. But if you'd been on the receiving end of one of Leo's all-consuming kisses you'd feel the same. I suppose it's going to be a great benefit of working with him, even if the weather is horrible I'll still get to see him. *And kiss him.*

My phone buzzes on my bedside, an image of Leo lying in bed, his hair all scruffy, his jaw coated in stubble. The caption reads, **raining** 😑

Using selfie mode on my own phone, I run my fingers through my hair, neatening myself before taking a picture to send back. **I've decided to accept your job offer** 😊

**If you'd told me this on our walk, I'd be picking you up and spinning you around. There'd also be kissing** 😉

**We could still go walking in the rain. Get**

**wet together** 😄 As my reply goes through, I study his handsome face and realise he's been shaving for me early each day. With a smile, I touch my finger to the screen, running my fingertip along the line of his jaw. When I sigh this time, it's filled with longing. I want him constantly.

**If you could hear through the walls, I groaned. I want to see you wet** 💦 **Also, I'm hard now so thanks for that** 🍆

I laugh as quietly as I can, mindful of the sleeping children in the next room. **I'm not exactly dry here** 💦💦, I type back, grinning like an idiot. I've never texted anything remotely dirty and this is fun.

**There's a pool in the building.**

I send back a question mark.

**We can go swimming**, he clarifies. **There's also a spa and a sauna, and there's rarely anyone down there** 💦🍆💦🍆💦

I reply with a gif of a woman almost falling over as she races out the door.

**I take that as a yes?**

I laugh and reply, **Yes. I'll meet you down there.**

Hunting through my drawers, I find my swimsuit and wriggle into it. I haven't put it on since my hideous sunburn occurred, although, my skin surprised me by not peeling as much as I thought it would. I did end up with a funny-looking tan line across my face, so there's that. I've been using that gradual tan moisturiser to make it blend in. It's working OK. And since that sunburn was ultimately responsible for what's going on with Leo and me right now, I have no regrets.

After I finish in the bathroom, brushing my teeth and whatnot, I tiptoe down the hall, grabbing a towel on the way. Once I'm out of the house without disturbing anyone, I smile and hug my towel to my chest. Today is looking to be a great day after all.

## THIRTY-THREE

DARCY

The pool and gym are located in the building's basement next to the car park. It's in a unique position, tucked away so that no one can see inside unless they physically enter. It's quite beautiful, really. This long echoey room that glows blue and seems to ripple along with the light reflecting on the water.

When I enter, the door makes one hell of a noise when it opens and closes, echoing like I slammed it. Leo is mid-lap in the shimmering blue of the twenty-five-metre pool and stops swimming at the sound, planting his feet and turning my way. He pushes the water and his dark hair from his face and smiles. My mouth goes dry, watching the water run in rivulets down his chest.

"You are a gorgeous man," I blurt out. Even my voice echoes in here, seeming to travel with the tiny waves as they move along the water's surface and reflect against the ceiling.

Leo smirks as I drink him in like a woman starved. "Get in here." We've had sex only once more since that first time above his workshop in the last two weeks. It was a frantic stolen moment when I stopped by while out picking up groceries. This early in our relationship, it simply isn't enough. I'd jump his bones daily—hourly—if I was able.

"Is it cold?" I ask, dipping my toe in the water to test it out.

He moves closer and flicks some at me. "Just dive in. I'll keep you warm."

I grin. "Here I come."

Bending slightly, I do a shallow dive skimming close to the surface until I reach the point where Leo stands. In my mind, I'm lithe and graceful. Then I stand and I'm coughing and spluttering, anything but classy.

"Oh angel," Leo coos, patting me on the back. "Did water get up your nose?"

I nod as I wipe a hand over my face, laughing and coughing—because I feel like an idiot—but I know how to laugh at myself.

"OK now?" he asks as I calm down and sink back in the water, bringing my knees up so I'm floating away from him.

I nod and smile.

"Where do you think you're going?"

I lift an arm and drag myself through the water. "I thought we were doing laps."

He catches my ankle. "We're *not* doing laps."

With a yelp, I'm dragged back to him, caught in his arms until I wrap myself around him, legs about his waist, arms around his neck. His hands grip my arse and squeeze. "It's like that, is it?" I look deep into his mirthful eyes, my heart thudding hard in anticipation. He excites me beyond measure.

"Kiss me good morning, Darcy."

So I do. Standing in the centre of the pool, he holds me while I kiss him with everything I've got, tongue exploring hungrily, tasting mint and feeling heat. I love the way his tongue moves with mine, as if it's encouraging me to take more, give more, be more.

Bringing my hands to the front of his chest, I pull back slightly and smile up at him as I run the backs of my fingers along his smooth jaw. "You shaved."

"Of course." He brushes his cheek against mine. "I reckon I'd cut your face up if I didn't."

"Ever the chivalrous one," I say, laughing as he twirls me through the water.

"Hmm, not really," he says, pushing the strap from my shoulder before sucking lightly on my bare skin.

Oh God, I could happily let this man do whatever he wants to me, whenever he wanted to do it, but having sex in a pool that is open to the entire building is probably a terrible idea—even if there is a noisy door to warn us. "I don't think we should do this right here," I gasp, hating myself for being a Debbie Downer and saying the words.

"No one's coming in here, Darce."

"Still," I say, placing my hand against his chest. "It's a little too open for me. How about"—I glance around and spot the door leading into the sauna—"we go in there?"

His eyes move with mine. "You want to have sex in the sauna?"

"Yes, Leo," I whisper, my arms going around his neck

again. "I *really* want to have sex in the sauna." I pull at his bottom lip with my teeth and he growls.

"Do you think you can do something for me first?" he asks, lips brushing against mine.

"Anything."

Sliding his hand along my left arm, he finds my fingers and wraps his around them, bringing my hand into the space between us. "Do you think you can take this off?" He twists the gold band adorning my ring finger and my stomach does a strange flip. *Shit.* I'm not even sure why I still have it on. My marriage to Kevin is now nothing more than a piece of paper tying us together legally. We've been separated for two months and both of us have moved on. The ring is unnecessary. Something I've kept on out of habit because it's been living on my finger for two decades.

"Does it bother you seeing it there?" I ask, studying his serious eyes.

He nods once. "I want you to be mine. It marks you as his."

I have a fleeting moment where I wonder if Kevin is still wearing his, but then I remember he took it off during his radiation treatment and never put it back on. *Why am I still wearing this?*

"OK," I say. "You can take it off." It's time to fully let go.

Pinching either side of the band with his thumb and forefinger, he wriggles it up my finger, millimetre by millimetre until it reaches my knuckle...and goes no farther. "I don't want to hurt you," he says, releasing the band so I can take over.

"It normally comes off just fine," I say, wedging my nails beneath the metal and wriggling it to lever it over the lump of skin it's caught against. "Shit. My finger has gotten fat."

"Maybe just leave it for now then," he says. "If it's stuck, we'll try again later. Ice it or something."

I keep trying. "I don't understand it. I've never had this problem." Hunching forward, I try pulling with all my might, the water making my grip slip, my hand hitting against the surface of the pool and spraying water all over Leo's face. "Oh shit. I'm so sorry."

He wipes his face and chuckles before he reaches out and takes my hand. "Don't worry about it," he says, his gaze earnest.

"But now I want it off." I pout. This is one of those moments where something that was normal a few moments ago suddenly bothers me. Like when you're going about your day feeling just fine then you look in the mirror and find out you have this massive zit on your chin and after that moment the zit is all you can think about until you can get home and pop it. My wedding ring is that zit.

Pressing his lips together momentarily, Leo lifts my finger to his mouth then sucks on it, moving his tongue around and around in a way that makes my body tingle all the way down to my toes. Then he places his teeth at the base of the ring and shifts his jaw back and forth until the ring pops free. When he removes my finger from his mouth, he's holding the ring between his teeth. I regret the zit analogy now, because it messed with the sexiness of the act. It was still bloody hot from where I'm standing, though.

Holding my hand in his, he flattens out my palm and drops the ring inside it. "Thank you," he says, meaning it. Never have two simple words meant so much. *Thank you for believing in us. Thank you for caring that the symbol be removed.* Thank you for wanting me.

I close my hand around the band and take a deep breath. It's a big thing, removing one's wedding ring. A symbolic moment where you recognise that your marriage is over and you don't need the symbol of it any more. "It's OK. I don't need it any more." Mind you, my finger feels weird now. It's been a long time since it had no ring on it, but at the same time, it feels as though one of those shackles Nana spoke about has been removed. I *really* don't need it any more.

I open my hand and let the ring fall, watching it slide through the water, side to side until it hits the bottom of the pool.

When I look up, I'm met with warm appreciative eyes followed by soft lips and a heated a tongue.

"You have a skilled mouth," I whisper when we come up for air, impressed by his kissing abilities *and* his ring removal technique.

"Get your arse into that sauna and I'll show you just how skilled it is."

Turned on, I'm anxious for him to do exactly that. "You had me at hello." I grin, I've always wanted to use that line.

He chuckles and pulls me closer, kissing me deeper, clutching me tighter. Then he releases me and I push away, gliding through the water until I reach the pool ladder.

Remaining in the centre of the pool, he watches as I climb out and collect my towel, wrapping it around my body before I unclip the top of my swimsuit and pull it free, swinging it over my head before I pull open the sauna door.

"*Holy shit.*" I yelp.

As the steam billows out the door of the small room, I'm confronted by the familiar sight of a half-naked elderly man.

"George?" Thankfully he's got a towel over his crown jewels, but the rest of his body is on full display—which is probably why I recognised him so fast. That image is burned on my retinas forever.

"Oh, Darcy. Hello there. Long time no see. Why don't you take a seat and I'll add some more steam?" He picks up the ladle in the water bucket and pours it over the heated rocks. They hiss and sizzle.

Leo appears behind me, placing his hands protectively on my upper arms as he lets out a relieved sigh upon seeing George soaking up the steam. "G'day, George," he says over my shoulder.

"Nice day for a sauna, Leo," George says.

"Sure is," Leo agrees as George shifts to the side.

"Come on in. Take a seat. There's plenty of room. And steam." He adds another ladle of water.

Not wanting to appear conspicuous, Leo and I step into the small area, only really big enough for four people. But with Leo's size, three feels like a squeeze.

With my towel tight across my chest and my hands

placed on my knees, I'm trying not to start giggling over the misery plaguing Leo's expression. George happily explains how his joints play up whenever it rains and he can't sleep. He finds the heat of the sauna to be a great help. Leo looks like he wants to beat his head against the wall. *I think he wanted to experience a different type of heat...*

Catching my eyes, Leo sees my struggle, letting his mouth quirk a little as his eyes drop to where my towel is covering my naked chest. Then he shrugs and stretches out as the steam surrounds us and George continues to talk. He tells us all about his ailments—the click in his hip and the fact he has to get up and pee about thirty times a night—for another ten minutes before the heat gets a bit too much for me and I excuse myself to use the showers. This morning tryst of Leo's and mine is an obvious bust. But it was fun nonetheless. At the very least, we learned the pool isn't as unused as we thought it was.

Smiling to myself over the whole George disaster, I turn on the rainfall shower in the ladies' room and hold my hand beneath the falling spray, getting the temperature just right before I hang my towel on the hook and strip off my swimsuit. Just as I step under the gentle warmth, a light knock raps against the door.

## THIRTY-FOUR

## LEO

"She yours, son?" George asks once Darcy has left the sauna.

I take a breath and nod slowly. "Partially."

"What the hell does partially mean?" he responds. "You're either together or you aren't."

"It's complicated. She's newly separated."

"Her ex still sniffing around?"

"Nah. He's fallen off the face of the earth. It's her kids. Well, one in particular. She's not taking the break-up well."

"So, you're sneaking around like a couple of teenagers?" He chuckles and I nod. "I don't envy you that."

I shrug. "It is what it is."

George smiles to himself then chuckles again. "I suppose my being here threw a spanner in your works."

"It's OK, mate. I've got a hand and a good imagination."

He has another chuckle before he goes quiet for a

moment. "Those showers have locks on the doors. You could always pay your lady a visit." His bushy eyebrows waggle suggestively. "Worst she can do is say no."

I get out of that sauna so fast the steam probably still has the outline of my body in it.

The sound of a running shower tells me exactly which of the two stalls Darcy is in. I go hard just thinking about her in there, wet and naked.

Trying not to groan, I tap lightly on the door. "Darce. Let me in."

The lock flicks almost immediately then the door cracks open and Darcy peeks through, grinning. "But this is the ladies' room, Leo Murphy. I think you'll find the men's is next door." Her eyes trail down the length of my body, stopping at my tented shorts before flicking back up to my face, that grin of hers turning wicked.

My cock jumps, desperate to sink itself inside that gorgeous body of hers.

I place my hand against the door and push my way in. "I don't give a fuck," I say, locking the door behind me. "I need you. I'm not waiting." Hooking my thumbs in the waistband of my swim shorts, I drop them to the floor and kick them aside so I'm as naked as she is.

With a heated grin, she reaches for me at the same time I reach for her, our mouths colliding as we move under the shower spray, kissing and touching in this tiny private space. My entire body aches for her.

"You make me feel desperate," I practically growl as I dig my fingers into the sexy curve of her hips and pull her flush against me, grinding my rock-solid cock against her stomach, showing her just how desperate I am.

She moans and moves her body against me, the water gliding between us and smoothing out the friction. I need to be inside her. Now.

"Do we need a condom?" she asks, reaching between us, her hand sliding along my length as she licks the water that runs off my chin. "I can't get pregnant. My tubes are tied."

*God, that feels good.*

"I'm clean," I assure her, hissing as I slide my fingers into her wet hair before I take her mouth aggressively, my tongue exploring, taking over. I want to devour her.

She releases this tiny sigh that sings to my cock, throbbing in her grip. "I want you, Leo. Please."

"Hold on." As I lean down, she releases me and grabs hold of my lats, digging her fingers in as I grip her thighs and lift, pinning her against the tiled wall with my torso and my thigh. It's not the easiest position, but I want to watch her face as I pump into her, see the way her mouth falls open when she comes.

Lining myself up with her opening, I push inside, almost losing focus as her warm soft walls tighten around me. "God, you feel good, Darce. So fucking good." I have to force myself not to blow my load then and there. I need this to last me until I can get her alone again. *Draw it out, Leo. Draw it out.*

I keep my hips still, dick buried deep as I take her mouth, kissing her with soft, slow strokes of my tongue. Every time she whimpers and rolls her hips, I almost blow, but then it passes and I'm ready to move again, drawing my shaft out then sliding it back in again. Slow at first then faster and harder as that hunger takes over, and Darcy's cries spur me on. She's so fucking hot, so fucking tight and wet. I'm dying here. I never want this to end. I want to stay just like this, frozen in time with Darcy in my arms.

"Leo. Leo, please," she begs, her nails biting into my skin as I tighten my grip on her thigh and pump harder.

"Darcy. Fuck, I needed this. I need you. Hold on, angel. Come with me. *Fuck.*"

"I'm close," she gasps. "So close."

I pick up my pace, hips pivoting, our pelvises colliding, almost violent in our frenzied need for release. "Darcy." I force her name through gritted teeth, her pussy tightening around me, pushing me over the edge. "Let go."

She drops her back against the tiled wall as she calls out my name, her body pulsing as I spill myself inside her, coming so hard my knees feel weak. Overcome, I whisper her name between kisses, telling her how beautiful and amazing she is.

"Leo," she gasps, pressing her lips to my shoulder as we stay joined, our bodies slowly returning to their normal state as our moment melts away and time starts moving again, the world calling, reminding us of our responsibilities. "We should get back."

"I hate that I have to hide my need to touch you," I murmur, not wanting to let go. And that's the crux of it really, the big fault in this beautiful attraction between us. We have to keep hiding it. And I don't know how long for.

"It'll be easier when the kids are back at school," she says, brushing her fingers through my hair as I withdraw from her body and lower her to the floor. "We'll be working together so we can see each other during the day. Maybe I can sneak over to you some nights? Niall will be back at his mum's so we won't have to worry about waking him. It'll get easier."

God, I hope so. Letting go of her feels so unbearable that I wrap her in my arms and bury my face in the curve of her neck. *It'll get easier.* She holds me just as tight, and I know she's struggling with this as much as I am. Because we're falling, and we're falling hard. *It'll get easier.*

Loosening my grip, I kiss her one last time, slow and tender before I step away and force myself to put some mental distance between us. When we dry off and get dressed, we leave the pool area ten minutes apart.

*It'll get easier.*

## THIRTY-FIVE

## DARCY

**I think we should download Snapchat**, I text to Leo a couple of days later. Our pictures to each other are getting hotter and I'm starting to worry about the kids spotting one when the text alert lights up my phone.

**Snap what?**

I send him the link to the app in the App Store. **A private way to send photos. Once you look at them they disappear.**

**Why would I want your photos to disappear? I need them to keep me company on lonely nights** 😴😈

Laughing at his blatant wanking reference, I type out my reply. **You can take a screenshot.**

I love that he's so open about the fact that he beats off over my photos. Knowing he gets off that way is a huge turn-on for me. In the past, masturbation was something hidden, especially when my ex was fond of porn while I preferred the arousal I experienced from a well-written romance novel. When we took care of ourselves, it wasn't something we shared. Ever. With Leo, being open about our sexual appetites feels normal. I didn't realise how much I'd love that.

**Then what's the point in the app?** he sends.

**So the photos don't show on the lock screen. Prying eyes...**

**Ah. Gotcha. Downloading now.**

Doing the same, I set up an account and send him my invite link. When he adds me, I strip to my waist and send a topless selfie.

*Murphy74 took a screenshot*

**I think I'm gonna like this app,** he sends via text.

**You can take videos too.** I send a short one of me fondling my breasts.

*Murphy74 took a screen recording*

**I love this app**, he sends.

*I love you*, I type, my fingers working before my mind catches up and thankfully deletes the words before I hit send. **I thought you would**, I send instead, my heart in my throat, because that was close. I am *not* in love. It's too early for something as huge as that. Way too early. And it can't possibly be the truth. Leo and I have been together such a short time. I'm in deep like, sure. But love? *No.* That would be crazy. It's too soon for that. Way too soon.

Before I can make an actual fool of myself, I make my excuses via the text feature on the app and put my phone on silent, rolling over to go to sleep. *Love.* The word makes me nervous. I've used that word for such a long time. To my kids, my sister, my mum... *my husband.* With Mum, Jo and the kids, every time I think the word my heart beats in joy without question. Yet, as I think of how I've said it to Kevin, I'm starting to see that my unquestioned, irrevocable *love* had evolved into... *obligation.* I wonder now if I need to rediscover what love actually means. Passion. Adoration. Romance. Tenderness. Intimacy. *Equality. Respect. Devotion...* Did I ever know that type of love with Kevin? I think the answer is no, and that makes me feel quite desolate. Yet... Yet now there's Leo, and our connection is so *different,* so new and exciting. But is it *love?* That's something I can't possibly feel already. Did I simply slip into an old habit without thinking? Yes, that must be it. What I typed doesn't mean a thing. I'm not in love.

"DID your mother tell you she got a job?" Nana asks the next morning. I'm pouring myself an obscenely strong coffee because I barely got a lick of sleep last night. My mind just wouldn't quiet.

"What kind of job?" Archer asks, his tone excited and interested, while Abby asks the same question with suspicion, like my working could possibly embarrass her.

"It's an admin job. Filing, organising, answering phones. Stuff like that." I shrug then take a sip of my coffee, glancing at Nana, who's obviously waiting for me to give the rest of the information. "It's, um, at Leo's workshop, running his office."

"You're working with Leo?" It's another case of same response, different tone. Archer obviously thinks it's awesome, and Abby is struggling to understand why I'd do such a thing.

"Yes," I say, taking my seat at the table. "It's good money, great hours, and since I have zero job experience, I think it's very kind of Leo to give me the opportunity. I haven't been so lucky elsewhere, and frankly, I'm running out of cash. If I don't take this job, there'll be no pocket money and no mobile phones any more." I look directly at Abby as I say this, and I watch the tension between her eyebrows fade.

"It's just a job though, right?" she asks. "He's not doing this just to get you alone?"

"It's just a job," I assure her, immediately drinking so I don't have to maintain eye contact.

"When do you start?"

"Monday, when you're back at school."

She presses her lips together as she nods. "So that's really it. We're here for good? There's no going back home?" Her bottom lip wobbles for a split second before she catches herself and straightens her back. My mummy guilt twists in my gut and pulls at my heart. *I'm doing what I think is best for all of us,* I remind myself, as I reach over and take her hand in mine.

"I know this is hard for you, sweetheart. Saying goodbye to your friends is never easy. But I also think a new school will be good for you. We're closer to the city, so the standard of education is higher. The opportunities are better here too. We lost everything in Bairnsdale, Abby. Here, we have a chance at a new start."

"But that's the thing, Mum. I didn't get the chance to say goodbye. We just left."

"Yes. And that was my mistake. I should have been clear with you over what was going on. But you need to understand that I was terrified at that point. I had no idea how we would survive."

"But why did you bring us here? Why didn't we go to Aunty Jo or Granma? They would have taken us in and I wouldn't have to change schools."

"You're right, they would have," I say, glancing up at Nana who is listening intently to our conversation. "I chose to bring you here because I needed Nana. She is the strongest, toughest, *bravest* woman I've ever known. If *anyone* is going to teach me how to be the resilient mother you need, it's Esme Sullivan."

"Oh lord, you're going to make me cry and ruin my makeup," Nana says, waving a hand at her face as she lifts her eyes to the ceiling. "I'm just doing what any decent grandmother would do."

"No, Nana, you're going above and beyond. You've saved us all, whether you realise it or not."

"Well..." She waves her hand in the air like it's no big deal.

To my surprise, Abigail is the first one out of her chair. "She's right, Nana. You're pretty awesome," she says, throwing her arms around Nana's neck. Archer jumps up and pretty much slams himself against her.

"You're the best, Nana."

"Oh." Nana's eyes mist over and the tears she's been trying to hold in, fall.

"Told you," I say, joining in on the group hug. "I'll be grateful to you forever."

"It was nothing," she says, sniffling. "Now let go, all of you. I'll have to go take off my face and start all over. I've got a hot lunch date today, I'll have you know."

We release her with a laugh and return to our usual morning routine while Nana floats off to her bathroom to fix her face with Archer trailing behind, talking snake bites and the best first aid methods for treating them.

"Hanging out with your new friends today?" I ask Abby in between the chat messages she's shooting off to friends.

She replies with a shrug, followed by a sigh. "Most of them have gone back home. They were only here for the holidays."

"Oh? You didn't meet any kids you'll be going to school with?" I was under the impression most of the groups she was with all summer went to the local high school. It's why I was a little more relaxed on my curfew, so she'd have friends once school started.

She puts her phone down for a second. "The locals don't hang out with the tourists, Mum."

"But you aren't a tourist if you're going to school here."

"Yeah, well, I didn't know that at the time. Some of the kids saw me coming out of these apartments and thought I was rich like them." She puts her head down and concentrates on her thumbnail.

"So, you just let them think that?" Suddenly a lot of

her behaviour makes sense. Not only was she grieving, she was also pretending to be something she wasn't. It must have been exhausting.

She meets my eyes for a second and shrugs. "I didn't think it would hurt. I didn't think we'd stay, either." Her mouth pulls up at the corner, and I feel so out of touch with her while at the same time feeling relieved that we're sitting here having an actual conversation. I'm caught between wanting to jump for joy and being concerned. But I think the point here is that Abby is talking to me. She's sharing her problems. Cheering is definitely something I'll be doing the moment I'm on my own.

"I can't say I'm happy you were pretending to be a rich kid, but I can understand how it happened."

"I didn't lie. I just didn't correct anyone."

I press my lips together. "It's kind of the same thing, really."

She shrugs. "Maybe."

"Well, what about Niall next door? Does he know you're staying here long-term and that you're not rich?" If he does, I hope he wasn't an arsehole to her about it because that would have been really stressful. I hadn't had many interactions with him—I'd actually gone out of my way to avoid him since he insinuated I was geriatric—but he did give off that entitled vibe of a kid who's never known any real struggle. It's hard for me to reconcile his personality with Leo's when Leo is so easy-going and down to earth. If it wasn't for their similar looks, I'd struggle to believe they were related.

She shrugs. Again. "Niall's fine." That didn't even come close to answering my question.

"Fine, meaning?"

Suddenly she frowns and I know this conversation is running out of steam. She's back to finding me annoying. "He wouldn't say anything, OK? Leave it alone."

I lift my hands. "OK. I'm just checking on you. Being an outsider is hard. Especially when people think you're something you're not. Hopefully when school starts, you'll meet some of the local kids so that next holidays, you won't have to pretend. You'll be able to relax and have fun, and we can forget this ever happened." I'm really not happy about this pretending to be rich thing, but I think I can let it go as long as it doesn't become a recurring problem.

She shrugs yet again, flipping her phone about in her hands. "Do you think we can go back to Bairnsdale? Just for a visit. Gemma is having a sleepover with everyone this weekend, and since it's the last one in the holidays, she's asking if I can come. If you don't want to drive me, I could always catch the train and Aunty Jo can collect me from the station."

"You're not catching a train all that way on your own."

"So, what, I can't go?" *Here comes the attitude...*

"I'm not saying that. If you want to go, I'll take you. We'll visit Aunty Jo and Granma while we're at it, and if there's anything you need from the old house, we can stop by the storage unit on the way home."

"Home," she repeats. "Meaning here?"

I nod. "Do you think you can handle that? Stop giving me so much crap?"

With a heavy sigh, she rubs one hand up and down her forearm before she nods. "Yeah, Mum. I get why we're here. I'm not super happy about it, but I like the beach, and if I can visit Bairnsdale sometimes, I think I'll be OK. I'm going to miss my friends though."

"Come here," I say, holding my arms out. She shifts on her seat and stands to give me a hug. "I love you, OK? Don't ever forget that." I hold her tight, rubbing her back and feeling about a thousand times lighter after this morning's conversation.

"I love you too, Mum."

I close my eyes. *Music to my ears.* The day Kevin walked out of our lives seems like a lifetime ago now, and I feel like we've finally turned a corner. I think we're going to be OK.

## LEO

On the Friday before school goes back, Darcy stops by the workshop so I can show her the shitshow that is my office. I like a tidy workspace, but since I spend as little time in the office as possible, it isn't kept to the same standard. I'm quite embarrassed frankly.

"Wow," she says when she steps in and looks around.

"It's horrible, isn't it?"

She turns to me and laughs. "Not at all. I was expecting cobwebs and big spiders hanging over yellowing piles of paper. This is a neat stack of archive boxes and an unorganised desk."

"Try and find an invoice from three years ago," I say. "Then you'll understand what I mean."

Placing her hands on my shoulders, she smiles up at me. She's so damn pretty. Her blonde hair is pulled into a ponytail, and she's wearing a pair of dark blue jeans and a flowery tank top. I want to sit her on this desk, yank that hair tie out, and peel those jeans from those delectable legs of hers. But I'm trying to be professional. I'm a man of my word, so I'll only fuck her on our lunch breaks.

"I'll have this all filed away in no time." She pushes up on her toes and plants a kiss against my lips. "See you on Monday, boss."

"Whoa." I catch her by the wrist before she can get away from me. "Where are you going in such a hurry? And why aren't I seeing you until Monday?"

She tilts her head slightly to the side. "I'm supposed to be picking up a parcel at the post office, so I can't be away long. And I'm taking the kids to Bairnsdale this weekend, remember? I told you about it on our walk this morning. I'm going to see my mum and Jo, pick up a few things from the storage unit. Plus, it's time I faced my mother's judgement over the whole Kevin thing." Oh shit. Now I remember. I was busy calculating the time and distance while wondering how I was supposed to get through that without knowing she was only a few walls away. I'm beyond attached to this woman.

"Hmm. I think I blocked that from my memory because I'm not looking forward to a full weekend without you."

Reaching out, she runs her fingers down the centre of my shirt, stopping to play with one of the buttons. "I'll send you Snapchats."

"Promise?"

She nods. "Naked ones."

"Videos?"

She laughs. "If I get enough time alone."

I groan then hook my finger in the front of her top, pulling it open so I can salivate over her gorgeous hard-on-inducing cleavage. "Just a peek to tide me over," I say as she giggles and play slaps my hands away. I slip my hands around her waist and pull her against me, kissing her hard until she whimpers in my mouth. I love that sound. The little noise she makes when her body succumbs to my touch. It's heaven. "If we had more time, I'd bend you over that desk and take you right here."

Darcy moans and my dick comes to life.

A throat clears not far from us.

I snap my head up, the hairs on the back of my neck bristling as I find the last person I expected to see standing in the doorway, leaning casually on the door.

"Tash?" *What the fuck?*

My dick instantly deflates. Nothing like the sight of your ex to be the cold spoon to your erection. I clear my throat as I straighten Darcy's shirt.

Tash smiles, her overly plumped lips struggling to fully curve, but I'm pretty sure I see a forked tongue poke past them. "Nice to see you too, Leo. I went by your apartment and no one was there," she explains with a shrug.

"Well, you found me. What do you want?"

Ignoring me, she turns her attention to Darcy. "This must be the Darla I've heard about. Niall told me Leo's got a new plaything."

"She's not my plaything," I correct. "And it's Darcy."

"Of course." Tash holds out her hand to a slightly rattled Darcy, who reaches out and takes it, giving it a timid shake. "Voracious in the sack, isn't he?" Tash's eyes flash as a malevolent grin takes over. Darcy snatches her hand back and frowns.

"Tash." There's warning in my tone. "What are you doing here?"

"Oh," she says, her eyes staying on Darcy, sizing her up. She stands a little taller when she's done, her dark hair falling in long fake waves cascading over her bone-thin shoulders as she pushes her fake breasts forward. It's like she's the peacock and all this so-called 'enhancement' she's had is the plume that makes her the most beautiful of all. I've got news for her... "I was in the area so I thought I'd pick Niall up and bring him home before school." No. That's not it. I know this woman, and my guess is she came here to do exactly what she's doing right now: try to intimidate Darcy.

I narrow my eyes. "His school doesn't go back until Wednesday. I have him until Sunday. We agreed I'd bring him to you."

She waves a manicured hand in the air as she looks around the office as if all of this is beneath her. "Well, I'm here now."

"I should probably go," Darcy says, pressing her hands against her thighs before picking her handbag up from the desk where she dropped it.

"Don't leave on my account, Dana." Tash places a hand on her chest to show 'true' concern.

"It's Darcy," I grind out. I really need her to shut the hell up and go away.

Darcy's mouth becomes a thin line. "I'm not leaving because of you. I'm leaving because I have somewhere else to be."

"Oh, of course, *Daisy*." Tash nods.

"Darcy," Darcy and I correct at the same time, although mine is more of a growl.

"I don't know why that name can't stay in here." She taps her head lightly and laughs.

Darcy's eyes narrow. "I think it's because you're purposely trying to belittle me, Tilly, I mean, Tanya. I mean, Taylor... See? I can do it too." I'm so happy right now, I want to clap. Then—and I couldn't admire her more—, Darcy does the best possible thing by smacking a goodbye kiss against my lips. My entire chest is bursting with pride. Darcy is more amazing to me every day. "I'll text," she says, giving me a secret smile.

I want to grab her and kiss her face off, but I settle for smiling back and waving as she saunters out of the workshop, her head held high as she gets in her car.

"Jesus, Leo. What the hell do you see in *her?*" Tash spits, reverting back to her venomous self the moment her audience is gone.

*I see strength. Honesty. Passion. Trust. Beauty.* Everything I *don't* see in Tash.

Leaning back on the desk, I fold my arms across my chest and grin. "My heart."

## THIRTY-SEVEN

## LEO

"I'd rather stay," Niall says as he stretches his long legs out in front of him, taking up way more couch space than necessary.

Tash's mouth falls open. "Are you kidding me?"

Niall shakes his head. "Dad's taking me skydiving on Sunday. I'm not missing that." I get that he's only staying because he wants to skydive, but he just called me Dad. It's been a really long time since he's called me anything but Leo so internally, I'm doing backflips. Today is the best fucking day.

"So I wasted my time? I thought you hated it here?"

"I just told you. Skydiving."

Tash huffs. "Jesus bloody Christ."

She looks to me like maybe I'll help her but I simply shrug. She's trying to cut into *my* time. Time I paid her handsomely for, mind you. "What can I say? I promised him."

Pinching the bridge of her nose, she lets out a slow breath before lifting her hands in defeat. "Fine. Come back Sunday." She looks at me, head to toe then back up again. I don't enjoy having her eyes on me. They're cold and make me feel as though she's searching for cracks in my armour. "Since I'm here, do you think we could go somewhere and talk?" She softens her expression, tilts her head to the side, making me even more wary than I was about two seconds ago.

"What about?"

"Important grown-up things that our child doesn't need to hear."

"I'm seventeen, Mum. I'm not a kid any more," Niall says.

"Still," Tash says. "Can we go for a walk or something? I could do with stretching my legs after all that driving."

"You live twenty minutes away, Tash," I reply.

"I came from set in Nunawading," she says, as if that makes it so much worse. Nunawading is only forty minutes away.

"After you then." I gesture for the sliding door and follow her out, knowing that the fastest way to get this conversation over is to go on this walk. I don't trust her. She's being far to amenable right now.

I start walking along the footpath and Tash insists we need to walk along the beach path because the air is fresher there. I don't particularly want to walk that path with her because it's something I do with Darcy, but I want Tash gone. Her presence is eating away at my good mood.

"Can we talk now?" I press after she's commented on the weather and state of the waves in the bay.

"Niall tells me you want him for the Easter holidays too."

"We called a truce and it was part of our settlement agreement," I state, my hands in my pockets as I kick at a small stone on the path.

"I was planning on taking him with me to London. I've got business in the UK and I thought he'd enjoy the change of scenery."

"I see. And how much is it going to cost me for you to let him stay with me instead?"

She stops walking and smiles that wolfish grin of hers. She's always working some angle. "Come now, Leo, I'm not always after your money."

"You sure about that?"

"I was actually going to ask you to come with us. We can set aside our differences for a couple of weeks, have one final family holiday before Niall is all grown-up."

I actually laugh. "Because we regularly have family holidays?"

"You know what I mean."

"No, actually, I don't. What's your angle? Is this because of Darcy?"

"What?" She laughs. "I couldn't care less about you slumming it with your neighbour. This is purely about us and our little family."

"There is no us, Tash. And you've gone above and beyond to destroy any sense of family we could possibly have. Cut the bullshit."

Hugging herself, she steps off the path and walks towards the water, stopping before she hits the tideline.

With a heavy sigh, I follow her. I feel like I'm in a

scene on her soap and she's preparing herself for some dramatic moment. "What's this about?"

"I might have to relocate," she blurts out.

"To London?"

"Yes," she says, an edge to her voice. "They're writing me out of the show. There'll be a fire at the Lassiter's Complex and I'll die. Do you understand what that means? There's no coming back from that kind of exit, Leo. I'll have no choice but to do the pantomime circuit in the UK or I'll go broke."

"Well, you're not Susan, Tash, you had to know your time on the show would come to an end at some point. Didn't you save in preparation for this?"

"No. And what's so special about bloody Susan? My character was rich and diverse and well loved." *Diverse?* "This is all because they were too cheap to pay me what I'm worth when my contract came up for renewal. I make that show, Leo. The ratings will plummet when I'm gone. They've made a huge mistake. I can't believe this." She puts her face in her hands and sobs in front of me. At first, I stand there, but then she basically falls against me so I catch her and give her back a slight tap in sympathy before I push her away.

"You'll be fine, Tash," I say. "You always land on your feet." *She engineers the fuck out of that landing though.*

She looks up at me, fisting my shirt, her cheeks streaked with tears, her makeup remarkably in place. "You really think so?"

"Yep. You'll work it out."

"Then you understand why I have to take Niall and why you need to come too, to keep the family together."

"No," I say, dropping my hands to my side as she straightens up.

"What?"

"He's under eighteen and you can't take him out of the country without my permission. I'm not leaving my life here, and I'm not OK with you relocating him to the other side of the world in his final year of school. It's too disruptive." I feel like my mother's voice is coming out of my mouth. She'd say exactly the same thing.

Tash's eyes go wide. "But—"

"No, Tash. You can't manipulate your way out of this one. I won't change my life for you, and I won't allow you to change our son's."

She pats at her crocodile tears with the pads of her fingers. "What if he wants to go?"

"Then he can join you after his exams. If you can't wait until the school year is over, then he can stay with me until he graduates. You aren't doing this to him this year. His school is too important."

She narrows her eyes at me. "This is because of *her,* isn't it? That's why you don't want to come too." *She is so fucking delusional.*

"No Tash. I won't move to England because I can't stand being around you. Darcy has nothing to do with that. You made that happen all by yourself." I step away, shaking my head at her gall. She was always crazy but this shit is next level. "I'll see you Sunday with Niall."

"This isn't over," she calls after me as I walk away.

I wave over my shoulder. "It never is with you." *Fuck.*

When Tash drives off in a total huff, Niall and I stand on the deck, leaning against the railing as her tyres skid against the road and leave behind a pissed-off cloud of smoke.

"What'd you do? Throw sand in her vagina?" Niall asks, squinting in the afternoon sun.

I look at him and frown. "You're talking about your mother."

"Still, doesn't take a genius to see you didn't let her get her way. What'd she want?"

"She wants to take you to London."

"For a holiday?"

"To live."

He frowns. "Oh."

"I said no. You need to finish year twelve first."

"What if I wanted to go?"

"Do you?"

He steps back from the railing and takes a seat at the outdoor table. "I don't know. It could be cool."

"Yeah. And it'll still be cool when your exams finish. You'll be eighteen then, and I won't be able to stop you from going, but despite your age, I do think you need to finish school before you change your whole life by shifting countries."

"When is she going?"

"April, I guess. She was talking about going during the Easter holidays."

"So, what will happen? I'll move in with you?"

I nod. "You can get a bus to school from here. It's not much farther."

"What about when I turn eighteen and get my license. I'll need a car to make my exams on time."

"Then I guess that's something we can discuss closer to your birthday."

He nods then wipes a hand over his face. "Why is she leaving?"

"They're writing her out of the show."

He stands abruptly, flicking his arms by his side in agitation. "I need to go for a walk."

Giving him a nod, I watch the way his face pulls tight and darkens as he stalks down the street. I'd be lying if I said I wasn't slightly happy about the fact he might come and live with me. It's what I've wanted all along. But in doing so, I'm keeping him from an overseas adventure. And depending on how much he wants that, depends on how much of a fight I'll have on my hands. Either way, I'm not backing down on this one. An education is far too important to piss away on following his mother around the UK while she cashes in on her fame before it runs out. If my mother taught me one thing in my life, it's that you need an education. You have that, it doesn't matter where life takes you, or what challenges you face, because you'll always have a good foundation to fall back on. I know I can't back down on this one.

"Hello there, Leo," Esme's voice sing-songs from the opposite direction, followed by the ringing of a bicycle bell. When I turn in her direction, a smile takes over my face. She's pedalling away, not on a bicycle, but on a tricycle, and she's wearing a shirt that has a granny on a Harley and the words 'Bayside Biddies' across it.

"Hey, Ez. What in the world is this?"

She pulls up on the footpath in front of me. "Oh, Leo,

this is my new trikey gang." She rings the bell on her handlebars twice.

"Gang? I hate to break it to you, but it looks like you're the only one."

"Well, of course. You've got to start somewhere. I'll have you know, I've been about town since lunchtime and I think I have at least two ladies ready to join up. I asked Betsy and she laughed. But she'll be begging to join in when she sees how much fun we're having."

I can't help but laugh. "I've no doubt."

"Well," she says, ringing her bell again. "I'm off. Lots of recruiting to do. Toodleloo, Leo, dear. Say hi to Niall for me." And with that, she pedals off again, the whirring of a little motor sending her down the path with little effort.

With a chuckle, I watch after her. She has me smiling through my frustration, and I love her dearly for lightening my mood.

A tricycle gang. Only Esme could come up with something as zany as that.

## THIRTY-EIGHT

## DARCY

"I really miss you, sis," Jo says, linking arms with me while we walk through the local park. Archer runs and jumps ahead of us, playing with Jo's brown Cavoodle, Dudley. "Christmas sucked with just Mum and me, and New Year's was...actually, I went out with friends, so that was OK."

I smile. "You know I miss you too."

"And Mum?"

"Eh, you know that's complicated. But I definitely miss you."

"Yeah, yeah," she says. "Just not enough to come back."

"I really need this fresh start. I think it's helped the kids too. Made the split more definitive for them."

"So, Abigail is back to herself again?"

"She certainly seemed herself when I dropped her at her sleepover earlier, but I imagine the Abigail I pick up tomorrow will be a different story. But she's not throwing tantrums any more, so that's a positive step. She's also stopped accusing me of hiding Kevin from her."

"Thank heavens for small mercies. Nana isn't driving you nuts yet?"

"Never. You know I love her randomness. She keeps things interesting."

"Yeah, well, you know me and order, I'd be rocking in the corner after a few days with her."

"She's not that bad."

Jo shrugs. I find it funny how two women who grew up under exactly the same conditions can be so different yet still get along. It's always been us against the world, and nothing has really changed that.

"Fetch," Archer yells, throwing a stick as far as he can. Dudley responds by sitting in grass and panting. "I said *fetch*." He mimes throwing the stick again. Dudley lies down. "Jo-jo, your dog is broken."

"Maybe he just needs you to show him how it's done, mate," Jo calls out.

"Shouldn't dogs just know this stuff?"

"Some need more help."

With a shrug, Archer runs after the stick, calling for Dudley to follow along. I expect him to pick it up, get Dudley to sniff it and maybe throw it again. But he gets down on all fours and picks the stick up himself—in his mouth.

"Yuck, Archer. Spit that out." I laugh. I can't help it.

"How else am I s'posed to show Dudley?"

"You hold the stick near his mouth before you throw it," I say.

"Oh," Archer says, pulling a piece of bark off his tongue. "Why didn't you just say that in the first place?"

"Boys are so gross." Jo chuckles.

My phone chimes in my pocket. When I pull it out, I see that I have a Snapchat from *Murphy74*. A small smile plays on my lips before I slide the phone back in my pocket, deciding to save opening it until I'm alone.

"Who's Murphy74?" Jo asks, spying on me.

Now my smile takes over my face. "A friend."

"Oh, I see. This is the real reason you aren't coming back. You're getting some."

"It's not like that," I argue before rolling my eyes. "Well, it *is* like that. But he's not the reason I'm staying. He's a bonus."

"*Rawr.* Who is he?"

I keep my voice low so Archer can't hear. "Remember the guy next door?"

"The one you licked your tits for?" She chuckles. "Yeah, I remember. Nana's neighbour, right?"

I nod. "And he's..." I let out a sigh, feeling like I did as a teen and I was crushing hard on Keanu Reeves after seeing him in Point Break. *Rawr.* Keanu also got better with age. "He's amazing."

"Amazing huh? I'll be the judge of that. Does he treat you right?"

"He treats me *exactly* how I want to be treated." I lift my brow and try not to giggle.

"OK, so he's great in the sack. What else?"

"He's a great conversationalist, works with his hands, he's a dedicated father, is amazing with Archer, respectful with Abigail and her moods, and he's been there for me. I feel wanted by him. He cares about me and after feeling second best for so long, that's bloody amazing."

"He sounds like the full package," she says. "What's wrong with him? Is he ugly?"

I shake my head and pull up a picture of him. One of the PG ones he sent. He's shirtless and lying in bed, but he's sexy and you can't see anything past his collarbone.

"Oh my lord." Jo stops walking and snatches my phone. "I think I just became hetero. He is *gorgeous*."

I snatch my phone back before she can swipe through the photos. "I keep pinching myself, believe me."

"Why does he look familiar?"

"He used to play rugby for Australia. Leo Murphy. He did morning radio for a stretch too."

"Oh God, *that's* what's wrong with him. He's a meathead."

"He is *not* a meathead, I assure you. He's mature, he's driven, and he's *kind*. My God, Jo, he's so many wonderful things."

"And the kids just instantly love him?"

"Archer thinks he's the sun, but they don't know we're dating. We're keeping that quiet until we know how serious it is. We've been together maybe three weeks?"

"Ah, you're in the honeymoon phase. Nothing is annoying yet, I know it well. It's when lesbians end up moving in together then struggle to split when everything falls apart. It's why I never invite anyone back to my place any more. Too risky."

"You don't want someone to share your life with?" I ask.

"I have Dudley," she says, looking at me like I should totally get this. "Why would I want a human?"

I shrug. "I don't know. For the hugs? The conversation?" *To carry one another's burdens?*

"Dudley provides both those things and rarely interrupts."

"Well, what about sex?"

Her eyes light up. "Did you just ask me about sex?" She whispers the last part like it's a naughty word, grinning because I've never been very open about my sex life.

"Maybe. And I didn't even blush."

"Wow," she says, pride in her eyes. "I like this guy. He's good for you."

"He's *amazing*," I gush.

"OK. I believe you. But what about his ex? You said he's a good dad, so there's a kid in there, and that means an ex. Unless she's—"

"Oh no, she's well and truly alive."

"And?"

"Well, the kid—he's a seventeen-year-old boy—is as you'd expect a spoiled teenager to be. His mother gives him everything so he's a bit of a brat, but then so is Abigail, so I can't really talk."

"And the mother?"

"I've only met her once. But, she's...difficult. She bad-mouths Leo to Niall and when she met me, she called me several different names but never Darcy."

"The ole 'You aren't important enough for me to remember your name schtick'?"

"Yeah. But I didn't let it get to me. I called her on it, gave Leo a possessive kiss, and left with my head held high."

"Good for you, sis. I'm proud of you. It's like you're finally becoming the woman you were always meant to be. Out from under Kevin's douchebag thumb, you're actually standing up for yourself. I never thought I'd see the day."

"I wasn't that bad, was I?"

She scrunches up her nose. "Yeah. You were pretty defeated, but you put on a good show, I'll give you that. But as much as I wish you were here, you're so much happier now. Maybe it's the sea air, maybe it's this new guy you're with, or maybe it's just the absence of Kevin. Whatever the reason, I think that day at the hospital was one of the best days. Even though it didn't feel like it at the time."

"I could've done without going broke, though."

"Yeah, well what are you doing about that? Do you need money?"

"No. I have a job now. And Nana's happy with us staying in her apartment. I'll be able to contribute and save towards hiring a lawyer to sort this all out, clear my credit rating so I don't have to file for bankruptcy."

"Good. I don't think it's right he gets off scot-free. Now that you're feeling stronger, you need to make him pay for his kids. He should be giving the money for them to you." I've been putting off dealing with the legalities of what Kevin did to our finances, but I know I have to do something. His actions have impaired my future. I can't afford to spend the rest of my life paying for his financial mess.

"I'd rather forget he ever existed, but you're right. What he did was unforgivable as well as illegal. Father of my children or not, I can't let him off."

"That's precisely *why* you can't let him get away with it. He's responsible for those kids too."

I let out a sigh. Yet another thing to worry about Abigail losing her shit over. If she finds out I'm planning on reporting her father for fraud, she may *never* forgive me. Nana's voice sounds inside my head, telling me I need to be brave enough to make the tough decisions that are right for the kids and my future. I have to stop worrying so much about Abigail. I have to do what's right. Become the strong and brave, *resilient* woman my kids need.

## THIRTY-NINE

DARCY

"Gram-Gram," Archer shouts, running up the front steps of my mother's house before he throws his arms around her waist and tells her how much he's missed her. And he would. Archer always sees the best in people and my mother hasn't given him any reason not to like her. She's a much nicer granma than she ever was a mother, which I think is often the way. The pressure of life and our ability to provide for our children while they're young often gets in the way of our enjoyment. I wonder if my children will feel this way about me when they have children too. Although, I hope I've never been as critical of them as my mother was of me. I'd hate for that to be a continuing legacy.

"Take a deep breath, sis," Jo says while Archer and Mum have a short exchange. "I'll buffer as much as I can."

"Thank you," I whisper, squeezing her arm, so grateful for her support. Jo and Mum have a very different relationship than Mum and I do. I think because

Jo is tougher and doesn't really give any fucks, Mum's criticism and judgement didn't affect her quite as much as it did me. Jo plants her foot and won't let it budge. She's similar to Nana in that respect.

"Well, well," Mum says, placing her hands on her hips after Archer has run inside. "Look what the cat dragged in." She has such severe features: sharp blue eyes, grey and white hair cut short to avoid spending much time styling it. With her lack of skincare, she looks much older than her sixty-three years, and while her lips have never been full, they seem almost pencil like as she eyes me with displeasure. I've been a terrible daughter in her eyes, skipping the usual Christmas festivities and dodging her calls since late November. But what more can I say? I couldn't handle her on top of everything else I was dealing with. I was on my own side for once in my life, as Nana would say.

I plaster a smile on my face as I step up on the porch and embrace her stiff body. "It's good to see you, Mum." *I will not bite. I will not bite.*

"Is it? I almost forgot what you looked like. No phone calls for the holidays, sending your sister to do your dirty work for you. You've been ignoring me for months. I practically convinced myself you were dead." *And she wonders why I avoid her...*

"It's barely been two months, Mum. December and January. And I've been texting. I just wasn't ready to talk about things yet."

"And I suppose now you are? Maybe I don't want to know any more."

I take a calming breath. "Then we can talk about something else. Or we can sit in silence. Your choice."

"Oh, there's plenty to talk about. Imagine my surprise when I drove past your house and saw the auction sign up. Since you weren't talking, I practically had to water-board your sister to get any information out of her."

"Waterboard her?" I laugh. "How do you even know what that is?"

"I have Netflix, Darcy."

"OK. You tortured poor Jo and she told you every-thing?" I glance at Jo and she's smirking, which means she's barely told Mum anything at all, and Mum is just being overly dramatic. *I wonder who that reminds me of?*

"I know that Kevin left you. Left you and the kids with nothing, so you packed up and went to live with your crazy nana."

I nod slowly. "That's about the extent of it."

"Why on earth didn't you tell me? I could have helped you. You didn't have to drag the kids all the way out here, upend their lives, and expose them to Esme's madness."

"Mum, don't."

"I simply don't understand it. I have plenty of room here. You could have come to me. I would have taken care of everything. Instead, you've cut me out."

"I needed to get out of here, Mum. Staying with you would have kept everything the same and I needed change."

"At the expense of your children? In times like these, they need stability and routine. Instead you've taken away everything they know. Did you see the way poor

Archer just threw himself at me? The poor child is beside himself."

I struggle not to smile in the face of her horribly inaccurate observation, which is interesting. Two months ago, her cruel words and criticism would have stung very deeply. *How wrong I was to cut Nana out of my life for so long.* Two months with her, and it's like my heart and mind have found strength I didn't know I had. Two. Months. *That's* love. "Archer loves living in Bayside, Mum. He was happy to see you. Just like I am. And since I'm here, I'll answer any questions you have about Kevin's and my split so you don't have to waterboard Jo again. However, I'm not going to argue with you and have you tell me I'm a horrible daughter or question my parenting. I did what I needed to do, and I'm sorry if that hurt you, but it wasn't about you. My world fell apart, so did my kids'. Going to Bayside allowed us a change of pace and the chance to heal. I don't regret going."

She lifts her chin while lowering her eyes to look me over. "You're looking well," she says, but it's more like an accusation. "Very tanned. I can't say I was looking so refreshed this soon after your father left me. But then, I didn't run away and laze about the beach for two months while my sister organised my life and my mother fretted. I never thought of you as selfish, Darcy, but now I'm wondering where I went wrong in raising you."

My mouth drops open and I suck in my breath. I was expecting her to be nasty, but the reality of it is something else. Spending the time since Kevin left within the loving environment Nana provides has certainly made me realise I don't deserve such hatefulness. I'm not a little girl any more. "You're wrong, Mother. You didn't go wrong in raising me. I grew into who I am despite your efforts to make me feel less than, and in spite of Kevin's efforts to do the same. *He* left me because no matter what I did, I wasn't good enough for him. And now you're poking me in the shoulder with your words because my actions weren't good enough for you. I said this only a moment ago, and when I say it now, I need you to hear my words: my actions had *nothing to do with you*. As my mother, you can choose to support me, or you can stand against me. Quite frankly, there's nothing anyone can do to rattle me at this point. I am doing what I think is best for me and my children, and I won't be swayed."

Mum's mouth opens and closes, flapping about like a fish out of water. I've never seen her speechless before. But, I guess I've never stood up to her like this before either.

Jo hides her own smile by wiping a hand across her face. "Something tells me that now would be a good time for tea," she says, stepping between Mum and me and guiding us inside. "Then we can talk about Darcy's new man."

Mum splutters. "New *man?*"

"What the hell?" I pinch Jo on the underside of her arm, the same way I did when we were kids and she did something like this. She flashes me an evil grin, telling me this is my payment for her running interference for me since I left town. I roll my eyes. Some things between sisters never change no matter how grown-up you get.

"Yeah, Mum. A rugby player too," she goes on. "You should be proud. At least one of your daughters can find herself a good man." Now she winks at me, always loving to tease Mum after she made the mistake of asking her if she was 'sure she was a lesbian and not just having trouble finding a good man'. Jo had replied at the time with, "The right man for me is a woman, Mum," and that was the end of that.

"Are you insane, Darcy?" Unfortunately, this is just the start of a tirade from Mum. I'm going to kill Jo when we get back to hers. "You've been single for one *second* and you're already *dating* again? Your poor kids."

"You'd better have wine back at your place," I whisper next to Jo's ear. I know she does this to stir Mum, but I think she also gets a kick out of torturing me too.

"You know I do." Of course she has wine. Jo's solution to everything is wine. Wine after five, tea any time before, and a joke to diffuse all situations.

"You're discussing *wine*," Mum splutters. "This is serious, Darcy. You're out of control."

Jo laughs again.

"Why is this so funny to you?" Mum glares at Jo.

"Because you think you can still control things. To me, that's hilarious. Darcy is a forty-year-old woman, Mum. It's time you realise you don't have the right to control her."

"But her life is a mess."

"Is it? She's living by the ocean, bumping uglies with the hottest guy I've ever seen, and she's no longer with that bastard who ran out on her."

"There was nothing wrong with Kevin." *What fucking planet has my mother been living on?*

"Now *that's* funny. The guy stole all their money and

left her for another woman, Mum. She deserves to go and have some fun. The kids are fine, she's enjoying herself with this new guy. Who cares if it's too soon, or if it's serious or just a rebound fling. The point is, your daughter has had a horrible couple of months and she's actually found some happiness within it. So how about we skip this tea and pop the bubbles, because we should fucking celebrate that. Don't cha reckon?"

For the second time in a short while, my mother's mouth falls open and flaps. And I no longer want to kill my sister, I want to hug her. But that was my relationship with my big sister in a nutshell. Up and down, but always together. And I loved her.

## FORTY

## LEO

"I'm glad you called," I say, phone pressed to my ear as I lie back in bed with Darcy on the other end of the line. Besides a couple of texts and Snapchats, I haven't had the chance to see her or speak to her since Tash rudely interrupted us yesterday. I've been dying to tell her how amazing she was while also wanting the reassurance that Tash's bitchiness hasn't affected her any.

"I needed to hear your voice," she says with a sigh.

"I was worried you'd be a bit put off after meeting my ex."

"What? No way. She was just playing bitchy-girl games to scare me off."

"As long as it didn't work."

"No. She was intimidating for a second, but then I realised that she doesn't want you, she just doesn't want anyone else to have you either."

"I think I'm a tree she's never been able to cut down."

"Ha. Good analogy. I want to come home."

I smile at her sudden subject change. "Home. I like that you're calling Bayside home these days."

She makes a small agreeable sound and I hear the fabric moving over the receiver. "This isn't home for me any more. I feel like I've been arguing and justifying my actions all day. I think I drank my body weight in wine to get over the stress."

I chuckle. I thought she sounded a little chatty. But I like Darcy when she's chatty. She forgets to filter what comes out of her mouth. "Visit to your mum didn't go well?"

"That's an understatement. She was at me the moment I arrived, then Jo dropped the *you* bomb and Mum almost fainted."

"The U bomb?"

"No. The *you* bomb. Jo told her about *you*."

"Your mum knows about me?" I smile, because that also means she was talking about me to her sister. Knowing that makes me feel...great. The more people that know, the less of a secret we are. The more *real* we are. I want to have something real with Darcy. And this conversation, the fact she's told other people, the fact she calls the place where she's with me home, is a huge leap forward.

"She does. And she thinks I'm a terrible role model because of it. I could have killed Jo for saying something. But she was getting me back for taking off and leaving her to deal with Mum all alone over the holidays. So, fair's fair, I suppose. I love her to death, but my sister is a shit sometimes." She lets out a chuckle. "You should have heard my mother, Leo. She can't believe I...how did she put it? That I could throw myself at 'the next good-looking man who came along'. Tried to make me out to be an absolute harlot and said some horrible things about Nana. But I was proud of myself at the end of it, and you'd be proud too, Leo, because I didn't let her make me feel bad about leaving Bairnsdale, or for my decision to date you." I'm smiling as she babbles in my ear. "I'm forty years old and I'm finally grown-up enough to stand up to my mother." She laughs at herself and it's the most beautiful sound. "But I can't wait to come home. Do you think I can sneak over to your place on Sunday night? I'm dying to see you and these Snapchat messages won't be enough."

"I would love for you to sneak over to my place on Sunday night. I'll even leave the door unlocked."

"Good," she says, the word a sigh that seems to trail off as her breathing changes and I'm pretty sure she just fell asleep on the phone. I laugh to myself, listening as her soft breath becomes a gentle snore.

"Good night, Darce," I murmur. When she doesn't respond and her breathing doesn't change, I stay on the line, thinking about how much this woman means to me and that my life wouldn't be the same without her. My chest fills up with emotion and I can't help the words that come next. They must be said. "I think I'm in love with you, Darcy."

"Hmm," she responds, her voice sleepy as the receiver muffles. I think her phone falls away from her ear, but I do hear what comes next, a soft murmur. "I love you, too."

I'M on a high the entire next day. And it's not because Niall and I jump out of an aeroplane—although, what a rush. If you've never been skydiving, I highly recommend it—it's because I feel it. The deepest kind of connection a man and a woman can have. It's taken me forty-five years to find a woman who makes me feel this sure, but better late than never. Maybe we weren't ready for each other before now.

I know I'm getting ahead of myself here. Darcy was mostly asleep and she was also drunk last night when she murmured those words. But, experience has taught me that Darcy is most honest when she's drinking. It's how I learned she was interested in me in the first place, so I'm not going to discount it. I'm just going to keep it close to my chest until she's ready to say it sober, and it's going to be the reason I'm smiling from now until forever. Because she's it. I've found my one. And better still, she's coming over tonight so I can show that beautiful body of hers the love it deserves.

"You're acting so weird today," Niall says when we pull into the driveway at Tash's and I whistle to myself while I grab his bags from the boot.

"It's a good day to be alive."

"My God. Did jumping out of that plane give you a come-to-Jesus moment, because I'm out if it did. Truce over."

I clap him on the back and laugh. "We've had a great day. Can't I be in a good mood?"

"I guess."

"I'm serious, Niall. This is one of the best days I've had in a long time. And that's because it was with you."

He looks really uncomfortable, but fuck it. I want him to know that I love him and saying those words would probably tip him over the edge right now.

"OK. Well...I gotta go. But thanks for today. It was pretty lit."

"See you soon, mate."

He laughs a little. "Sure, Dad."

Even Tash's attitude can't bring me down from this high I'm on. She opens the door and says hello to Niall, then she looks at me and asks if I've changed my mind, and when I say no, she slams the door in my face. Normally that would piss me the fuck off, but today, I laugh.

She tried to intimidate Darcy and she failed. Darcy is falling for me, I'm falling for Darcy, and nothing's gonna stand in our way. We're going to make this work. Because when it's right, it's right.

When nine p.m. hits and the sounds of next door quiets, I flick the lock open on my door then go outside to watch the stars come out, a beer for company as I wait for my favourite person on the planet to join me. I don't expect her till at least ten, so I have some time to kill. And I don't want to sit inside thinking about what I'm going to do to her or I'll meet her at the door with a hard-on. No, some time spent stargazing and contemplating will do me good. Especially when things are looking up in all aspects of my life.

I received word late Friday afternoon that my quote for this killer treehouse design has been accepted. The job came in via an old rugby buddy of mine and I start work within the week. It's exciting because it's a literal copy of the main house being installed in the backyard. I'm building every bit of furniture, every fixture from scratch. This kid is obviously spoiled, but it's a cool job for me. I'm really looking forward to it.

Speaking of spoiled kids, Niall seems pretty chilled out over the idea that he might be staying with me for his final months of high school. It's the first time I've ever spoken with him about a decision his mother and I were at odds over, and he actually agreed with me. I'm pretty sure he'll be on a plane to Heathrow the moment he closes his final exam booklet. But the fact that he chose to remain at school gives me hope that he really does have his head screwed on properly. Insisting he spend these holidays with me has turned out positively.

I'm about a third through my beer when Esme pokes her head around the screen and offers me a sympathetic smile. "I was wondering if I could get your help over here?"

"Anything," I say, a little wary as she gestures for me to come over to her side. Taking the long way, I step onto her deck and the first thing I find is Darcy, passed out on the couch.

She's so peaceful there that I can't even be disappointed. She's had a big weekend, and we'll get other chances.

"I think she's knackered after driving all afternoon. She really wanted to come and see you, but the poor love couldn't make it. Thought you might be able to carry her to her bed. At least then you get the chance to say goodnight."

Taking a deep breath, I smile at Darcy's sleeping form then give Esme a kiss on the forehead. "Thanks, Ez."

I crouch down beside Darcy, sweeping my fingertips through her hair to push if off her forehead. "Hey Darce. I'm just going to carry you to bed, OK?"

"Hmm." She leans into me, all softness and warmth as I slide my arms beneath her.

"You love her, don't you?" Esme asks as I lift Darcy off the couch, taking care not to put too much pressure on that knee of mine.

"What makes you say that?" I ask as I bring Darcy to my chest. She barely even stirs.

"Just a feeling I have. I'm good at noticing these things."

I'm filled with warmth as I look into Darcy's face. In the grand scheme of things, she's so new to my life, but I feel as though I've known her forever. "She's very special to me."

"I'm glad you two found each other," Esme says as I start for Darcy's bedroom. "Oh, and if she wakes up and you two start getting frisky, don't hold back on my account. I won't listen in. Much."

With a chuckle, I shake my head and carry Darcy down the hall, setting her gently on top of the single bed in her room. She seems so small and peaceful as I remove her shoes before she rolls into her pillow and sighs as I pull her covers up to her shoulders. "Thank you," she murmurs, her eyes still closed.

"Sweet dreams, angel," I whisper, pressing my lips to her forehead. Before I leave, I hover at her door, watching her sleep for a split second while wishing I could fall asleep next to her. *Soon, Leo. Be patient.* Then I thank Esme, and head back through my open front door, flicking the lock and getting into bed myself. And despite missing out on spending time with Darcy tonight, I'm still smiling. Because tomorrow she starts work, and I'm going to be near her all day. I'm not gonna lie here either. I'm *really* looking forward to our lunch hour. Not that an hour will be long enough for what I want to do to her...

## FORTY-ONE

DARCY

"Do you hate me?" I ask Leo as I walk into the workshop after dropping the kids off at school. "I hope you don't, but just in case, I brought a peace offering. Coffee and croissants. Can't hate a girl who comes bearing pastries." Twice I've fallen asleep on him now. Once over the phone, and again last night. When I said goodnight to Abby and Archer, I thought I'd wait until ten to make sure the kids were definitely asleep before I left. I'd been so keyed up about seeing him that I closed my eyes for ten seconds to calm myself down. The next thing I remember is waking up this morning. Nana filled me in on the rest, this impish little grin on her face as she explained how strong and careful Leo was when he carried me to my room.

Leo stops what he's doing and smiles at me, this brilliant grin that brightens his whole face and touches his eyes. My stomach flips and dances because he looks at me like I'm his world. It's both terrifying and exhilarating. "Get your arse over here," he says, setting aside the blueprints he was working on as he gestures for me to move forward.

"Are you asking as my boss, or my beau?"

He chuckles. "Who even says beau these days?"

"Nana and Betsy. I think it should be used more. I like the sound of it."

When I'm level with his feet, he grips my hips and hoists me on his drafting table, spearing his fingers in my hair as his mouth reunites with mine. With a whimper, my body sighs and relaxes, and I almost forget I'm carrying coffees, catching myself just before his plans are ruined and I've got a whole lot more than a missed sexcapade to make up for.

"Mm, is that how you welcome all your new employees?" I ask when he releases me then takes the coffee tray from my grip.

Setting the cardboard tray aside, he hands one cup to me and keeps one for himself. "Since you're my first employee, I'm going with yes." Opening the paper bag, he pulls out a croissant and takes a bite, eyes sparkling as he chews.

I touch the side of his face, longing for this ability to reach for him freely. He turns his head and kisses my palm.

"You have such happy eyes," I say as he hands me my croissant and we start eating.

"That's because I'm happy around you." He grins as he chews. "In case you haven't figured that part out yet." He moves a few papers that are a little close to where I'm sitting and places them a safe distance from our meal.

"What are those for?" I ask of the plans drawn on

them. It's looks like cut-outs for a house.

"Big job creating a miniature version of a one-hundred-year-old farmhouse. It's going to be stunning."

"Oh wow. Do you have a picture of the house you're recreating?"

"I sure do." He steps away for a moment then returns with the photo of an old colonial-style farmhouse, yellow and terracotta, with a pitched roof, moulded handrails and brick chimney running up the side. "It's beautiful. Are you including the chimney and the second storey?"

"I am. The fireplace will not work, of course. But I'm even making copies of some of the antique furniture." He shows me a few other pictures. "It's a really exciting project." I'm so engrossed imagining a downscaled version of this house that I don't see someone standing in the entryway until Leo says her name.

"Abigail?"

"What?" I immediately put the pictures down and jump off the drafting table, frowning as Abby stands in her new school uniform, long hair plaited down her back, bag over her shoulder. "I dropped you off at school almost an hour ago. What's going on?" *Did I get the wrong address? Did school not start today? How is she here without my permission?* Handing my coffee to Leo, I move closer to check that she's OK.

"Why where you sitting on his desk?" she asks, a knit in her brow as she looks from Leo to me.

"I was looking at the plans and pictures for his miniature house project. It's rather cool if you wanna see."

"She's still married. You know that, right?" She directs that at Leo.

"Abby," I chide. Not that it makes much of a difference. She's been much quieter, less talkative since I picked her up from her sleepover. She said she had fun, so I've put it down to her feeling out of her comfort zone starting a new school.

"Her ring is gone, but legally—"

"I'm aware," Leo says gently.

"Good," she replies, before her eyes return to me. My expression is waiting, trying not to become annoyed that she's already skipping on the first day. "I need my sports uniform."

"Oh," I say. "Why didn't you just text me?"

She shrugs. "It's just assembly then recess. I thought I'd come see you at work."

Spy on me more likely. "OK. Well, this is the place. The workshop is here and the office is over there. I'll mainly be in there."

She looks at Leo, her eyes moving over his button-up shirt, jean-clad legs, and booted feet. "And you're out here, building a little house?"

Leo rubs his hand along his jaw. "Actually, I was about to go to the hardware store, so if you need that sports uniform, I can drop you on my way. Your mum has work to do."

"Uh..." Her gaze flicks between us, like she's really trying to wrap her head around the fact that work gets done here—or, at least it will. "Sure."

"Let's go then." Leo grabs his keys and lets me know he'll be about an hour. He takes control and diffuses the situation so easily that I'm grateful for his experience with difficult teens.

Once they drive off, I stand still for a moment while I contemplate what Abby's visit meant. I don't buy for a second that she came here to do anything other than check up on Leo and me to make sure we weren't doing anything non-work related. Thank God she came when she did, because ten minutes earlier and we would have been busted. When she became such a suspicious person, I'm not quite sure. But it's something I'll need to watch. I'm not ready to introduce Leo as anything more than a friend just yet. I don't want to rock that delicately balanced boat because she's obviously not ready, and I've worked too hard to go backwards with her.

Moving into the office, I open each drawer in the four filing cabinets along the wall to see what space I have to work with and find them mostly empty. "Well, that makes things easy."

Starting on the first box, I go through each bit of paper and sort it into categories while I think about this past weekend and the difference in my life from Bairnsdale to now. Besides the fact that I have two children, everything about my life has changed, and as Jo pointed out, I'm definitely happier for it. Kevin's leaving was a blessing in disguise and maybe the kick in the pants I sorely needed to get my life on a different, more fulfilling path.

Archer has been amazing. He's the most versatile kid and has thrived moving to Bayside. I hadn't noticed quite how subdued he'd been around Kevin until I saw the contrast in his behaviour at Nana's. He's much more outgoing and gregarious now, and I love that he's gotten that opportunity while he's still young enough to enjoy it.

Then, of course, there's Abby. She misses her friends. And she misses the stability of before. I've mentioned that she isn't very adaptive to change, and I have to say that I'm proud of her for accepting our new circumstances when I know she'd rather resist. It shows a level of maturity I didn't think she possessed yet, and if we can keep the status quo moving forward, there's no reason I can't take her back to Bairnsdale fairly regularly to see old friends. We can make this work for everyone.

This new development of leaving school to check up on me is interesting though. And I'm not sure if it's because she doesn't trust me alone with Leo, or if she was so nervous about going to school today that she made up an excuse to delay arriving. Either way, I'm happy she left with Leo with minimal fuss. I also love that he stepped up and volunteered to drive her, like it's no issue to be helpful or go out of his way for another person. I think if we can have more 'normal' interactions like this between her and Leo, we'll be that much closer to being able to introduce him as being more than a friend. I do feel we're months away from involving the kids in our relationship. That parenting forum I read suggested I wait until I've been seeing Leo on my own for at least three months. Because if I allow the kids to accept him as family and things don't work out, it can be more damaging than keeping my relationship a secret from them. And I'm trying so hard to get this right.

I let out a sigh as I collect another stack of papers from the box. Maybe this thing with Leo is all a pipe dream and I'm putting too much pressure on us to become something more than we are. We're together, but anything more than that seems to be a logistical night-mare. We're a series of stolen moments and hidden conversations. I wish we were more, but the one thing my mother was right about is that this is too soon. I can't run from one committed relationship to another. As Abby pointed out, I'm not even divorced yet. And I won't be for at least another year. Should I even be contemplating a real known-to-the-world relationship with Leo when I'm still married to Kevin?

This is all so complicated. Logic versus emotion. In my heart, I want something amazing to happen with Leo. But in my head, all I can see are problems moving forward. Meaning we're stuck as we are now. The question is, will the occasional heated moment and quiet morning walk be enough?

I have to admit I had a dream over the weekend that Leo said he was falling in love with me. I'd fallen asleep while talking on the phone so his voice was fresh in my mind, and I was wishing I was with him instead of in Bairnsdale. In the dream, we were cuddled up in bed—something I'm craving—and he was pressing kisses against my shoulder then he paused and said he thinks he's falling in love with me. Then I said I love you back. No pause, no thought, I just said what I felt. And now I'm trying to imagine a world where that level of emotion can be a reality without creating problems with Abigail, possibly Niall, and definitely Tash. The way she treated me on Friday was simply off-putting. She and Leo have been apart for thirteen years. She has no claim over him any more.

God, the idea of our relationship becoming public

knowledge scares the crap out of me. And not only because of the reactions I expect, but because I'm afraid to trust this feeling. I mean, I loved Kevin all those years and was completely blindsided when it was over. I wasn't enough for him. What's to say that when the initial attraction wears off that I'll be enough for Leo? What if I give my heart again, fight to have a life with him, and then he wakes up one day and realises that *I'm not enough*? It would destroy me. What I feel towards Leo burns hot and bright in my chest, and I desperately want to believe that the last twenty years were designed by fate to lead me to this perfect man who complements every part of me. But what if I'm doing exactly as my mother suggested and throwing myself at the first eligible guy I found because I'm scared to be alone? *Lawd. This hurts my head.* Nana isn't wrong in her encouragement to live a life with joy and happiness and all things Leo. But she is in a very different stage of life than I am, and I do need to juggle her open way of thinking with the wisdom it takes to raise stable and emotionally healthy kids. Jo isn't encumbered with that responsibility either, so as much as I love her, she doesn't know what this is like.

I'd like to think fate lead me here, but as I look around at all the paperwork across the desk, spreading to piles on the floor, I'm so overwhelmed. The chaos in front of me eerily matches what I'm feeling inside my head. *In my heart.* I'll be able to make sense of all the paperwork in front of me, but my heart? I don't think I trust myself to make any sense of that.

## FORTY-TWO

## LEO

"I get the feeling you don't like me much," I say to Abby as we drive towards the high school. We've stopped off at the apartments to get her sports uniform, said a quick hello to Esme while she sat and had tea with Arthur—I thought she broke up with him, but I struggle to keep up with her harem members—and made it halfway back to the school with barely a spoken word.

"I don't know you, Leo. You're just some guy who lives next door and keeps showing up like you have a reason to."

"I get it," I say. Her words are simple, but they're telling.

"I doubt it."

"You're worried I'm making moves on your mum and trying to take the place of your father."

"Hanging out with Archer, giving an unqualified woman a job, building an elaborate bunk set for us. All signs are pointing to yes."

"Do you want the truth, or do you want me to lie?"

"Truth."

"I like your mum. A lot. But she won't let me have the kind of relationship I want with her until she's one hundred percent sure you kids are going to be OK with it. Which is a beautiful thing, because it shows how much she loves and cares for you."

"So that's why you gave her a job, because you're into her?"

"I gave her a job because she needs money to support you and Archer and she needed a break. I offered money, but she wouldn't take a handout because she's proud and she's trying to teach you how to be strong and resilient when the chips are down."

"Doesn't explain why you're all buddy-buddy with Archer."

I sigh as I shift gears to turn the corner. "Archer comes to me because he likes to. I don't make him, but I do listen when he talks. Which is ultimately what I think he's after. He's a good kid, maybe if you spent some time with him, you'd see that for yourself. And as far as the bunk build goes, I'm a carpenter. Building things is my job. A job your Nana paid me for. So, maybe you can stop looking at me like I'm some kind of threat to you. Maybe sit back in the knowledge that your mum loves you guys above everything else in the world. And every decision she makes is based around what's best for the both of you."

She leans back in her seat and scoffs.

"You don't believe me?"

"I do. It's just that you say you don't want to take the place of our dad, but that was the biggest dad speech I've ever heard. You said you'd tell the truth." *That's* the longest dad talk? *Holy shit*. The man is such an arse.

Pulling up outside of the high school, I sigh. "I don't want to take the place of your dad, Abigail, and I'll tell you why. That guy up and left, and I don't live my life that way. I stand up, I show up, and I don't give up. I'm not going anywhere, I don't lie, and I certainly don't cheat. I *really* like your mother, Abby. So we can either get along and let your mother be happy, or we can fight each other and force her to choose."

She lets out another scoff. "You think she'd choose you?"

I shake my head. "Not for a second. She'll always choose you. What you have to decide is, are you going to make her do that? Or are you going to let her be happy?"

"HOW WAS Abby going back into school?" Darcy asks when I return a little over an hour later. The tray of my ute is laden with supplies, and she grabs a can of paint and a box of random fixtures to help me unload.

"She was OK. Wanted to know my intentions." I feel a smile kicking up the corner of my mouth. I don't hold any resentment towards Abby. In fact, I think that her reactions are very typical of a girl her age going through the collapse of her typical family unit. I've been through a stack of tense moments over the years with Niall, so I'm an old hand at navigating the hard questions. No kid wants their parents to split and anyone outside the immediate family is viewed as a threat.

"Towards me? What did you tell her?"

I stack sheets of plasterboard against the far wall and gesture for her to put the box and paint can on the workbench. "A version of the truth. I didn't out us as together, but I did tell her I care about you. I won't lie to anyone about that."

As she inhales, her back gets straighter and her hands go to her hips. "And how did she respond?"

"She asked if that's why I gave you a job." I keep moving so she has to follow me back to the ute if she wants to continue this conversation. I have no objection over relaying my conversation, but we're working here.

"And what did you say?" She jogs a little to catch up to me, concern knitting her brow. I've obviously overstepped in her book. But the way I see it, I didn't tell the girl anything she doesn't already now. I just took away a little doubt and I'm not going to apologise for that.

I pull a stack of two-by-fours off the tray, and she catches the end of it—adorably, because I can totally carry this myself—and carries with me while I relay what was said about the circumstances of her job, that she wanted to know why I spent time with Archer, and what my motivation for making the bunks was. The only part I left off was when I spoke about not taking the place of her dad. I think that part of the conversation was between me and Abigail, and if she wants her mum to know that's a concern of hers, then I'll let them have that conversation on their own.

When we place the wood on the rack, she pushes her hair back from her face. "And she was fine with those reasons?"

Moving to stand in front of her, I slip my finger into the belt loop on her jeans and pull her closer. "Yes. I also told her what an amazing mother you are and how your first thought in all you do is for your children's happiness."

"You think I'm an amazing mum?"

I nod. "Uh-huh."

"Well, thank you. That means a lot to know you think that."

"It's true. And do you know what else I think?"

She grins, catching the soft change in my tone. "What else do you think?"

"This may not be the best segue, but I *really* missed you this weekend. I think we should close up the workshop and take a nice long lunch break to celebrate your first day."

Her hands glide over my shoulders, fingers lacing behind my neck. "I've barely done any work, but, I've missed you too and I'd *really* like to connect in that way with you again."

"Oh, angel. I'll give you a connection you'll never forget."

It takes about five seconds for my thumb to find the remote and hit the button so the roller doors slide down and we're blissfully alone. *Finally.*

## FORTY-THREE

DARCY

The alarm sounds on my phone, letting me know it's almost time to pick up Abigail and Archer. I press my face into Leo's chest and groan. "I don't want to get out of this bed."

Tightening his arm around me, he places a kiss on the top of my head. "Me either. I want to ravish you, fuck you, sleep wrapped up with you then wake up and do it all again. Repeat. Repeat."

"Sounds heavenly." I brush my fingers through his chest hair, listening to the sound of his heart and his breath. "What would we eat?"

"That's easy. Each other."

I chuckle. "And what would we drink?"

"Hmm, there are options. But this could get really gross really fast."

My chuckle becomes a grossed-out giggle. "We should probably get out of bed then."

"Hmm."

We're in agreement, but we don't move a muscle. It

feels too damn good being alone with him. But the tick-tick of time is forcing my heart rate to quicken, moment by moment slipping away. The outside world demanding attention.

"OK. I'm getting up," I say, forcing myself to sit.

"Come back." Leo pulls me to him and I happily fall against him, laughing and kissing before I push away again.

"I really have to get up. I need a quick shower before I grab the kids, or the mothers at the primary school will smell you on me and think I'm a hooker. That won't be a great first impression."

"I think you smell wonderful. Not hooker-like at all," Leo says, running his fingers up and down my bare back. I close my eyes and enjoy his touch for a split second longer. "Want some company in that shower?"

"Yes. But we'll never get out of there, so no. Stay right here." I hold a finger up as I stand and head for the small but functional bathroom. It has white tiled walls, blue tiled floor, a decent-sized shower, and a small vanity and toilet. Everything you need.

As I wait for the shower to warm, I take a quick look at myself in the mirror. Kiss-sore lips, bright eyes, messy hair, and pink cheeks. I look thoroughly fucked, and the grin curving my lips confirms it. The man is amazing in the sack.

When I have the water temperature right, I step under the stream and call out to Leo. "Hey, I know I'm not supposed to work tomorrow, but I'm thinking I might come in and do the work I should have done today?"

"Sounds good to me," he says from the doorway, giving me a sudden fright that causes me to laugh.

"What do you think you're doing?"

He grins with only one side of his mouth. "Saving water. There's a drought."

"In New South Wales. Not here."

He slides the glass door of the shower recess open. "Doesn't hurt to conserve, Darcy."

When he takes me in his arms and kisses me, I feel his hard length awaken against my stomach, causing fluttering inside me in response. "Oh God, Leo," I gasp, wrapping my arms around him as his kisses move down my neck and shoulders. "I don't have time. We don't have time."

"How long until you need to leave?"

"Maybe ten minutes."

He hoists me against the wall and grins. "Challenge accepted."

IT'S TAKES the full five days of the week to complete the fifteen hours' worth of work I would have done in just three had Leo and I been capable of sticking to our sex at lunch rule. The fact that we could close up the workshop at the click of a button proved too tempting for us when we've previously struggled to find a shared window of time. We were like kids in a candy store with very dirty minds and large appetites.

Truth be known, it's been a wonderful week and I regret none of it. Even the part where Abby turned up and demanded to know what Leo's intentions towards me were. Turns out, that conversation with Leo did put her mind at ease. She hasn't made one snarky comment about him to Archer all week. She's even said hi to him a couple of times when he's been on his deck when we've left the apartment. That's progress in my eyes.

Both of the kids have had a fairly decent first week at their new schools. Archer loves the new-to-him play equipment at his school and thinks his teachers are 'the best', and Abigail seems to be slotting in with a new group of friends. Some girl called Rachel has taken her under her wing and is introducing her around. I overheard them chatting to each other online the other day while they were doing homework, and there were a couple of other kids in on the conversation too, so it felt like some semblance of normal to me and helped me breathe a little easier. I knew school would either make or break our move to Bayside for Abby. I'm keeping my fingers crossed and holding them over my heart, hoping this improvement continues and my smiling, relaxed daughter returns to me.

"I thought we'd go into the main street and get something really yummy for afternoon tea," I say to both my kids after school on Friday afternoon. "I got paid today, so we can celebrate making it through our first week of school and work."

"Can we get cheeseburgers?" Archer asks. "Or chicken nuggets? Something that involves meat."

"Sounds good to me. What do you think, Abigail?"

She gives me a shrug, but I can see she's interested. "I

actually don't mind the vegan food Nana cooks, but I think I could definitely go a burger."

I smile. "Let's make it an early dinner then. We'll even get dessert. I feel like going all out. I've never had a payslip before. I feel so grown-up."

"Never?" Abigail says, shocked. "You've never had a job? What about your Etsy business? Doesn't that count?"

"That was a hobby. It took me five years to save the money we've been living off this past couple of months and it's almost gone. So, I don't count that as a job."

"Can we live off this money?" Archer asks.

"Well, we can't move out of Nana's. But it'll pay for everything else."

"Good. Because I like living at Nana's."

"I'd like it better if I had my own room," Abigail says.

"I know, darling," I say, glancing her way as I find a spot to park. "I'm working on it, OK?" I finally have a meeting with a lawyer who specialises in debt relief next week. I'm hoping they can point me in the right direction so I can clear up my credit rating and find out what Kevin did with all that money he syphoned away.

"Can I sleep over at Leo's, Mummy?" Archer asks from the back seat. "He's got a room that's completely empty. We can have a boy's side and a girl's side."

"That's super inappropriate, Archer," Abigail shoots over her shoulder as we get out of the car.

"I have to agree with your sister on this one, mate. It would be very inappropriate to ask Leo if you can have a room in his house," I say, although I certainly wouldn't mind sleeping over at Leo's place myself.

"But he wouldn't mind," Archer argues. "And you could still come and say goodnight. You just walk through the door and pretend like his apartment is the other half of Nana's apartment. I do it all the time."

Walking towards the café, I slip my arm around Archer's shoulders and pull him against my side. "I'm sorry, honey. It's not something I'd feel comfortable asking of him. You and Abby will have to share for the time being. We're doing OK with the bunk dividing the room, aren't we?"

"It's fine," Abby says. "*No one* needs to sleep over at Leo's. I don't mind sharing."

Later at the café, we've finished our meals while Archer regales us with tales about the cool trick his friend Nicholas can do with an elastic band and a handful of gumnuts. I don't think homemade slingshots are allowed at school, but Archer assures me the gumnuts are quite harmless. I may need to test this 'trick' out to check for myself.

Abby messages with a friend on her phone, looking up occasionally to listen in or add something to the conversation.

"What does he shoot the gumnuts at?" she asks before frowning towards the magazine rack on the wall of the café, holding newspapers and, of course, magazines for café customers to enjoy. "Is that *Leo* on the cover of New Idea?"

"Huh?" I turn around and squint at the neatly stacked magazines, my eyesight not as good as it once was. "Which one?"

"That one," she says, pointing. "Second from the left

on the third row. It has yellow writing about a Neighbours star reuniting with her— Oh." She sits back in her chair, blinking. "Maybe it isn't him."

"Yes, it is," Archer says, jumping up and grabbing the magazine. "Look. It says his name right here under the photo. Who is he hugging, Mummy?"

"Don't look at it, Mum. It's probably nothing," Abigail says as I take the magazine from Archer's hands as my chest squeezes tight. Sure enough, Leo's on the cover, standing on the beach with his arms wrapped around his ex-wife. *So much for hating each other*. The headline reads 'Star-crossed lovers: Neighbours Star and Retired Ruby Legend reunite after thirteen years.

A lump forms in my throat. Based on the outfits they're wearing, this was taken a week ago, after I left them alone at Leo's workshop. This means they went for a walk along the beach together, hugged after whatever they were discussing, and Leo didn't even think to tell me. *I didn't realise they were on hugging terms*. God, I hate this. I hate this jealous feeling that's taking hold and making me crazy. It's a hug. That's all. There's nothing wrong with hugging the mother of your child. Maybe she had some really bad news? There could be a very obvious reason and the magazine is just blowing this all out of proportion. He's not Kevin. He's *not* Kevin.

"Mum, just put it down. You're always saying how those magazines are trash anyway," Abigail says while I flip through to the article.

"I, um...I just want to see what it's about. I, ah, I didn't realise Leo was so close to Niall's mother." I plaster on a smile as I look up and meet her eyes. They look sad.

Like she feels sad for me. And of course, she does. She has a heart, and she knows there's at least an attraction between me and Leo. In teenage speak, she's sitting across from me while I discover the boy I like might like another girl more than me. But he can't.

*This isn't true. They're making it up. He wouldn't...*

God. I feel sick.

Desperate to see if they have any actual evidence, I flip the pages until I find the main article containing more pictures. They're mostly innocent and taken on the same day, showing them walking along the path together, Tash resting her head against Leo's chest while his hands stay by his side and then there's the one where he's holding her, but blown up on the page, it's more like he's comforting her, not embracing her. And I'd feel a thousand times better if that's where the article ends, except there's more. In a smaller, circular frame, there's a grainier picture taken with a night-vision lens showing him kissing...someone. The magazine caption claims it's Leo and Tash, but I know my own picture when I see it. The woman he's kissing is me.

"Holy shit," I say, slapping the magazine closed.

"Wait," Abigail says, trying to take it from under my hand. "Was that picture *you?*"

"No," I say, stretching the word out. "It wasn't. We're just friends."

"It's definitely you, Mummy," Archer says, somehow managing to get his hands on another copy of the same magazine. "Look, that's your bum." He points to the picture then scrunches up his face. "Why is Leo grabbing it so hard? Grown-ups are weird."

"I..." I look from Archer who seems delighted and Abigail who looks set to explode, and I shake my head. "Itsnotwhatyouthink," I say in a rush.

Abigail glares at me, her eyes fighting tears as her jaw pulls tight. "You're a liar," she whispers. "So is Leo." She stands up. "No wonder you like each other." And walks out.

"Wait." I go to chase after her, but the owners of the café call out because I haven't paid my bill. With frantic hands, I throw some money on the table as fast as I can, grab Archer, then rush out into the street. Looking both directions, she's nowhere to be found. "Abigail," I yell, my head swivelling left and right, searching faces and figures. *Fuck.*

"I think she's gone, Mummy," Archer says. And I think he's right.

Shit. Shit. Shit.

FORTY-FOUR

DARCY

"She's home. She's safe," Nana says, hand held out to me as I arrive home in a mess. I've been driving around town searching for her ever since she took off this afternoon. I'm an absolute wreck.

"Oh, thank God," I cry, landing in her arms and allowing myself a moment of weakness as I bury my face against her shoulder.

"Everything will be OK, pet," she soothes, patting me on the back.

Lifting my head, I blow out my breath, tears burning my eyes. "We keep saying that, don't we? But it isn't getting better, Nana. It feels like it is and then it gets worse."

"Oh, Darcy." She looks at me with utter sympathy, but I know she sees it too. I keep taking one step forward and two steps back, trying to give everything to everyone around me, including myself. But I'm failing. I keep trying to do the right thing yet I'm failing every step of the way.

"Is she in her room?" I ask, touching my fingers to my forehead as I collect my thoughts.

Nana nods. "For about fifteen minutes.

"OK. I need to talk to her. Can you distract Archer for me? He's upset too."

"Of course, dear." She holds her hands out to Archer, suggesting he shows her how his Roblox game works.

"Is Abby OK?" he asks, his voice small.

"Oh, she's fine. We need to give her and your mum some time to talk it out." I don't hear much more past that. My blood rushes in my ears as I try to calm down. I don't want to go in there yelling at her, but I'm furious for the way she's reacting, running off like a spoilt child, not answering her phone, and scaring the living daylights out of me. It's immature and unkind, and *I* want to rant and rave at her, maybe shake some sense into her. But those are all things fuelled by anger and a sense of powerlessness. I won't let my own frustrations fuel my conversation with her, as it'll only make this shitty situation worse.

"Here goes." After a few calm breaths, I wipe my damp palms on my thighs and approach Abby's room, knocking on the door before entering.

"Go away," she says, sniffling.

"You ran off, Abby. I was worried sick. We need to talk about that."

"Why don't you go and talk to Leo? I'm sure he'd love to hold you while you cry. Just ask his ex-wife."

Ignoring her jibe, I pull out her desk chair and take a seat on the fluffy cushion, my hands between my knees as I press my lips together. How are we supposed to get past this point where she quits being angry and I get to be a human with feelings? I feel like I'm forever walking on eggshells, never knowing which one will break and set her off.

"You can't run away when you're upset, Abby. It doesn't fix anything. You need to learn to stay calm and communicate with me."

"You run away when you're upset, Mum. How do you think we got here?"

"That's a very different situation and you know it. I've faced any number of problems in my life by standing up and talking it through."

"So talk then," she snaps, hugging a pillow to her chest.

"Do you want me to explain my relationship with Leo?"

"What's the point? All you do is lie. You already said nothing was going on, that you were just friends with him, but that was a lie. Leo at least admitted he likes you but he said you weren't going to be together until Archer and I were cool with it. That was a lie too. Because you *are* together, aren't you? You're just lying about it and hiding it. You're as bad as *Dad*."

Ouch. Low blow.

"This is nothing like what your father did to us."

"Isn't it? Because it feels the same. You're sneaking around, leaving the room when you get a text message or a call, lying about what you're doing. It's the same, Mum. You just don't wanna see it."

"How dare you," I hiss, my voice low and hurt. "How dare you compare what he did to this. How dare you throw that in my face." I'm too raw and angry to give her accusation the proper analysis it deserves. *This is fucked.* "Yes, I was sneaking around with Leo. But I wasn't cheating on anyone. I was just doing what any responsible parent would do by making sure Leo and I were serious before I broached the subject with you. I have the right to find love again, Abigail. Your father left us and I was so blindsided it practically destroyed me. But I've done everything I can to get strong enough to survive this. Having Leo as a friend has been really good for me. He is a good man, and he actually makes me happy. I think I deserve to be happy, don't you?"

"You love him?" She narrows her eyes in disbelief, and I sit back with a sigh.

"I don't know, Abigail. Maybe."

"More than us?"

"What do you mean?" *Is this some kind of test?*

"Do you love Leo more than you love me and Archer?"

"What kind of a question is that?"

She locks eyes with me for a solid moment. "A serious one."

I actually smile, because I can't believe she's questioning my love for her. "You and Archer are my children, Abby. I love you both more than anyone, *anything*. Surely you know that."

"Do you love me enough to stop seeing Leo?"

The bottom of my stomach drops out and a tightness forms in my throat. "Is that..." *Why is she doing this?* "Is that what you need from me?" Bile rises up my throat. I don't want to give him up.

She looks me dead in the eye and I can see the

moment her resolve strengthens. It comes a second before she nods emphatically. "Yeah. I do. Dad left. He won't talk to us. And I guess I just... I need you to choose me." Her lip wobbles and a tear slides from her eye. "I feel like I'm in the way of you living your life. Like it'd be easier for you if I just went away."

"That's not how it is at all, Abby." A tear slides out from my eyes.

"It's how it feels. That you're just waiting until I'm out of your hair so you can run next door to him."

"Oh honey, that's never been the case. I love you. You're my child, I'll always choose you."

"Dad didn't choose us." Her tears come fast and hard now, her words getting lost in her heaves. I gather her in my arms, my heart breaking as she cries against me and begs me to pick her.

"Mummy, please. *I need you.*"

What am I supposed to say to that? She's my daughter, and I know how much she craves stability. And right now, she needs me to provide that for her, to focus on her needs. *Fuck you, Kevin.* He really did a number on our baby girl, and my hatred for him is renewed as I close my eyes and nod over Abby's shoulder. "I'm not going anywhere, honey. I'm here. I'm choosing to be here. We're going to get through this together, I promise. I'm here."

ABIGAIL CRIES so hard that she falls asleep, her eyes puffy and red. I don't imagine I look much better since

I've been in here crying along with her, lamenting Kevin and his selfish behaviour. It gives me renewed strength to seek justice over what he did to me and the kids financially. He doesn't get to live happily in his new life while I pay literally and emotionally for the damage he caused. Even though I thought he took everything when he left, and he's still taking—destroying—especially in the abandonment issues he's created in our daughter. I will never forgive him for this. Never.

When I emerge from the bedroom, I find Nana sitting on the couch with Archer curled up asleep on her lap, the poor kid also having gone through the wringer of late. He's just so strong and capable that he doesn't let anything faze him for too long. He has the ability to see the bigger picture even though he's so incredibly young.

"How is she?" Nana asks. "And how are *you*?"

"Wrecked," I reply, letting out a huge sigh because I'm really struggling not to start crying again. I don't think I'll ever stop.

"Maybe a shower and a stiff drink will help you sleep. Everything will look better in the morning."

I shake my head. "Not this time, Nana."

"Why ever not?"

"Because despite my efforts, I really can't have it all. I need to go and speak to Leo. Tell him I can't see him any more."

She sucks in a breath and places her hand against her chest. "No, Darcy. Talk to her some more. Don't give him up because your daughter is throwing a tantrum."

"It's not a tantrum, Nana. She's deeply, emotionally affected by Kevin's abandonment, and she *needs me* to place my focus on her. And while I'm with Leo, she feels threatened. She's afraid I'll abandon her too." I sniff and wipe my nose with the back of my hand. "And you know, I don't blame her. I have been distracted lately, daydreaming, counting down the time until I can see him again. I'm not doing my job with her. I need to be better."

"So, you're ending things with Leo, sacrificing your own happiness so she feels validated?"

I nod.

"Darcy, I think you're making a terrible mistake here, pet. Your children need you happy so you can focus on them. Being miserable isn't going to fix this."

"I know, but I have to do something, Nana. I'm losing her. She's my daughter. I'd do anything for her."

"Don't give up the man you love."

I give her a small smile. "I'll see you soon, Nana."

"Darcy."

With a copy of the New Idea in my hand, I stand in front of Leo's front door. "Tear off the Band-Aid," I say to myself, placing my hand against my forehead. *I can't do this. My heart has never felt so ripped in pieces.*

Closing my eyes, I lift my shaking hand and knock on the door three times, my heart in my throat as I wait for him to respond. As if in slow motion, the handle turns and the door pulls open, revealing a freshly showered Leo wearing a clean white Bonds shirt and a checked pair of pyjama shorts.

"Angel," he croons, voice smooth as silk, his face lighting up when he sees it's me. My heart sings at the sight of him, and I want to throw myself in his arms and hold on tight until all of my problems sort themselves out.

"Oh, Leo." I clap my hand over my face and burst into tears, the pain in my heart too much to bear. *I don't want to do this.*

"Hey," he soothes, pulling me into his arms and steering me into his apartment. Once gathered against his chest, I cry and hiccup and clutch at the fabric of his shirt. I can't even speak. "What's happened?"

Managing to push myself away from him, I hold the magazine up and his expression falls as he sees his ex-wife on the cover smiling with the headline that tells the world they getting back together.

"This is why you're upset? Not a word of that is true, Darcy. You have to know that. This is just one of her bullshit power plays. And I should have known it was coming when she insisted we talk at the beach. She's pissed at me because I won't let Niall go to the UK with her."

"I...I..." I can barely get a word out through my hiccupping. "I know there's nothing between you. It's... it's the picture in...inside."

"Let me get you a drink," he says, lowering me to the couch where he pushes my hair back from my face then touches my check lovingly. "Then we can talk this out."

A fresh wave of tears comes. "Whatever you have that's strongest."

His brow draws tight as he grabs a tumbler from the kitchen cupboard along with a bottle of tequila. He pours some in a glass and hands it to me. "Want that mixed with anything?"

I shake my head. "Straight is fine." Lifting the glass to my lips, I knock it back in one gag-inducing gulp. "It burns so bad." I gasp and splutter as Leo takes the glass from my hand and sets it on the side table.

"Show me this picture," he says, sitting down on his coffee table so he's directly across from me.

With a short nod, I thumb through the magazine and open it to the article, handing it to him as I point at our photo. "Abby saw it."

"She did? Shit."

"Yeah. Shit. She flipped out in the middle of the café, ran off, and I've spent all evening trying to find her."

He covers his mouth. "My God. Why didn't you call me? I could've helped."

"It's okay. She's home now. We've been arguing and talking and, well, she just completely hates me right now. I've lied to her. Again. And I guess when everything is considered, I can't blame her. She needs me and I haven't been there." I press my lips together and meet his eyes, filled with a growing concern.

"Don't say it, Darce," he says, shaking his head slightly. "I know where this is going, and I really don't want you to say it."

I reach out and take his talented strong hands in mine. "I'm so sorry. We got carried away, Leo. I forgot who you are in this world. I forgot that people—gossip magazines—care about what you do." I let out my breath, close my eyes and shake my head. "I got so caught up in *you*, in *us*, and I *really* don't want to do this," I whisper.

He lifts my hands to his lips, pressing his mouth against them as he speaks. "Then don't."

I meet his beautiful eyes, my heart cracking open, raw and bleeding. "You know I have to. I have to choose my kids. Kevin did so much damage when he left and Abby needs someone—me especially—to choose her above everyone else."

He nods, bringing my hands to the space between us before letting go. "So, you're breaking up with me?"

*Shit.*

"I don't want to break up. I just want to press pause. I care about you, Leo. I care about you so, so, *so* much. But we knew this might happen. We were pushing our luck as it was, being too eager. We should've waited. We always knew we should've waited. From the very beginning. We got carried away."

His eyes flash, and he stands, head shaking in disbelief. "How do we press pause on this, Darcy? How do we go backwards when we were so close to moving forwards? Do you have any idea how much you mean to me?"

My eyes burn and I press my palms together and try not to get hysterical. "Probably as much as you mean to me."

"Jesus." He wipes a hand over his face, jaw tight as he looks away. "How long, Darce? How long do you want me to wait? A month? Two? You want me to ask you on that date in August and see if you're still free? Or do I wait forever? What do you want? *Tell me?*"

I jump a little at the intensity of his words, coated in hurt and frustration. My tears fall and I can't do anything to stop them. I hate that I'm doing this. But when a child is in pain, a mother will literally do *anything* to take that pain away. *It's the way we're built.*

"This is not about what I want, Leo," I cry, pushing to my feet. "It never has been, don't you get that? I was always a mother first, your lover second. And I'm sorry, OK? If I could have it both ways, I would. But we tried that, and I can't lose my daughter because I fell in love with you too soon. We would never survive that." This was never how I wanted to tell him how I felt. But there it is, the truth, raw and too late.

"You love me?" He stops moving, frozen in place as he searches my eyes with his.

I nod as I wipe at my tears with the backs of my hands. "I'm sorry."

He blows out a loaded breath as he places his hands on his hips. "I'll wait," he says finally.

"Really?" The tiniest seed of hope burrows itself in my chest and takes root there.

He nods as he moves closer to me, wrapping his hand around the back of my neck as he presses his forehead to mine. "As long as it takes. I'll wait. I'll always wait."

Placing my hands on his stubbled cheeks, I let out my breath in a gasp, wanting to cry again, but this time from relief. "It won't be forever, Leo. I promise."

"I know, angel." He presses his lips against my temple, gathering me in his arms as he inhales my scent, holding tight. "But even if it does take that long, I'll still wait. You're the only future I want."

As he presses a sweet, tender kiss to my lips, my tears fall harder as I wonder if we can survive this when this already feels like dying. It's one thing to say you'll wait for someone. It's another to actually do it. My father didn't stick around. My husband didn't stick around or even fight for us. And Leo? He could have any woman he wants, why wait an indefinite amount of time for me? I'm not that special.

"I should probably go," I whisper, this moment feeling far too much like goodbye.

Swallowing hard, he nods then kisses my forehead once more. "God, I'm gonna miss you."

"Yeah," I say. "Me too. I'll be seeing you."

When I walk back inside Nana's apartment, I lean against the closed door and put my face in my hands, sobbing just once before I take a deep breath and wipe my exhausted eyes. "I'm OK," I say, straightening my shoulders. "I'm going to be OK."

By the time I reach the living area, I have my face-anything smile on. I find Nana still sitting with Archer asleep on her lap.

"Tell me you didn't," she says, concern in her eyes.

I lift my chin and try to harden my resolve, but when I speak, my voice wobbles. "I really don't want to talk about it, Nana. I want to get this guy into bed then go to sleep myself if that's OK with you."

"Of course, dear. We can talk whenever you're ready."

"Thank you," I say, pressing a kiss to her cheek before I lift Archer from beside her and carry him to his room. I'm not quite strong enough to get him into his bunk, so I need to wake him a little so he can climb up himself.

"Goodnight, buddy," I whisper, kissing his sweet head.

He rubs a balled-up fist against his eyes as he yawns. "I would've said yes, Mummy."

"To what, sweetheart?"

"If you'd asked me about Leo, I would've said yes."

Pressing my lips into a sad smile, I brush my fingers along the round curve of his cheek. "Well, that's where I went wrong, I think. I didn't ask."

"You're the mum. That means you don't have to."

A ball lodges in my throat. "Sweet dreams, OK?" I force out, before I get out of the room and place my hand over my eyes. I can't stop crying. Needing the confines of the shower, I push on the bathroom door and flick the water on straight away, biting on my knuckles as I sob and sob. My chest burns like an open wound. I feel like the best part of me has been torn away. This hurts so much more than before. So much more.

FORTY-FIVE

DARCY

You know when you're young and you're dating some guy and your relationship gets to this point where something needs to change, but you don't *really* want to break up, so you ask for a 'break' in the relationship aka Ross and Rachel? After about a week or two, you realise it's the best decision you made, so you fully break up. Yeah? That isn't the case here. Weeks have passed since I put Leo's and my relationship on hold and each day has felt like agony without him. Like I've been torn in two and struggle to exist without my other half. This is nothing like what I felt when Kevin left. It's been weeks, and I'm still feeling so raw. I've become a zombie. Drifting through life like I no longer have a soul in my body, craving something but unable to get it. I skip the brains eating part—because that's gross—in fact, I mostly skip the eating part all together. Instead, I fill the void in my heart with work and kids. Not work at the workshop. We couldn't work that close after...you know... so I gave that up too. I work at the café now. At first, I was only working a couple of days a week, but when I showed them my technique for making melt-in-your-mouth steak, they took me on in the kitchen full-time. It means I have more money in my pocket, but less time with the kids because I tend to work into the evening. But I do my best to be present and spend time with them when I'm home, helping with homework and whatnot. And I take them on outings on my weekends off. I like to keep busy.

And the kids seem fine. Archer misses Leo, of course, but he's got his school friends now, so that helps. And Abby, well, she's Abby. I can't really say if she's better or worse, but she does pick a hell of a lot less fights with me. She's still got that fiery attitude, but she's quieter if that makes sense. Although, I wish I could say the same about her relationship with her brother. Those two seem to snipe at each other a lot more of late. They squabble over the smallest inconvenience and I'm forever breaking up their bickering, but until I can save enough to get a place of our own, I don't see that improving. They need their own rooms to provide some distance, I think.

God, this single parent thing is hard. I'm being the best mother I can and it still doesn't feel like I'm enough. But, I devote every free moment to them. My focus is on them. I'm doing the best I can. The best I'm capable of.

*It's been eight weeks.*

Leo is...well, it seems he's missing. I don't see him out on the deck any more, and on the rare occasions I see a light on in his apartment, the shades are down and the TV is on all night. I know this because I don't sleep a lot. Whenever I try, I end up crying until I pass out and then I wake up with swollen eyes and a headache, and I'm no good to anyone that way. I've taken to making my notebooks again—the ones I used to sell on Etsy when I was with Kevin—and I'm getting really good at making the binding perfect, and my watercolour technique is really coming along. They keep me busy when the kids have gone to bed so I don't have to pause and think. I can focus and work until I physically can't keep my eyes open. I've woken up with a watercolour painting stuck to my face more than once.

The days are semi-easy because of the endless activity of work and home. It's the nights that get me. Nana and Betsy sit with me a lot while I create my notebooks. They crochet willy warmers to sell at the fete, and they chatter along and try to include me, try and get me to laugh with them. But I can't muster the energy to do much more than smile and nod a few times. I'm so exhausted from wearing my mask of coping all day that I simply can't keep it up at night.

"You chose the wrong path, love," Betsy says to me one night.

"No, I didn't," I reply. "I just chose the one that hurts me more than it hurts my kids."

"Want me to read your cards again? Maybe those paths will join up again in the future."

"I hope they do, Bets, but I think I'm going to pass on the reading if it's all the same to you." The last thing I need is hope right now. Hoping for my circumstances to change will just make being apart from Leo harder. What I need more of, is focus. That way, I can keep going.

*God, I miss him.*

"Well," Betsy says. "They're in my bag if you change your mind."

I smile and nod. But I don't need my cards read. I know what my problems are and only time and patience can fix them.

Some nights are worse than others. I get restless and stalk the house, back and forth. Nana tells me to go out, take a walk or a drive to clear my head. One of those late-night drives is how I learn Leo is back on the radio. I weave my way through the streets, mindlessly listening to Nova when an ad comes on promoting the morning show. I hear his voice. My chest jolts as though a hand reaches inside and takes hold of my heart. I'm forced to pull over so I can breathe.

In a cruel twist of fate—or perhaps at the hands of my pining heart—the place I've stopped across the street from is his workshop. I didn't realise this was where I was headed, but I'm not shocked either. At the end of the long driveway, the roller shutters are up, and the lights are on inside. I can see his distant form, bent over his work while he carves a piece of spinning wood. A second revelation hits: he's working into the night and sleeping in the studio upstairs. *Does he feel as empty as I do?*

I can't tell you how much I wanted to go to him that night, sate this aching hunger by diving into him and staying there. But that will only put us back to square one, and I made promises I can't break this time. So, I stayed put and just watched him from afar. I downloaded the podcast version of his show and listened to his smooth voice and glorious laugh while I stared at the workshop until he closed up. Then I waited until the all the lights went out before I left. So, yeah, I'm a stalker now.

*EIGHT LONG WEEKS.*

"Darcy, dear." Nana's voice snaps me to the present as I clear off one of the outdoor tables. It's not really part of my job now that I'm in the kitchen, but sometimes we pitch in on the floor when we're a little short-staffed. Today is one of those days.

"Hey, Nana," I say, smiling as I take in the state of her. She's sitting perched on the seat of her electric tricycle, her Bayside Biddies shirt proudly displayed as she leads her growing 'Trikie Gang' as she likes to call it. She's co-opted Betsy and Helen so far and is working on the remaining two ladies in the craft circle. "Were you after something to eat?"

"Well, yes, but that's not why I said your name."

"It isn't?"

"No. Now, I understand you're very busy right now. But I was wondering if maybe you could take a short break so we can have a talk."

"Uh..." I look inside. There's only a few customers having a late breakfast and the lunch service doesn't start for another hour, so I can probably spare some time. "OK. Do I need to be worried?"

She laughs and shakes her head. "Not at all." Still, there's something about the way she smiles at the end of that makes me think I'm about to get harangued—while they circle me on their trikes so I can't get away. "Meet us around the corner?"

"Ah, sure."

Betsy salutes me as they all motor off, and I tell my boss I'm going on break and will be back in thirty minutes.

"What's going on?" I ask when I find them in a small parking lot standing next to their trikes, their colourful helmets hanging on the handle bars. They form a straight line with Nana in the middle, Betsy on her left and Helen on her right.

"We're staging an intervention, dear," Nana says as she takes my hands.

I snatch my hands back. "I'm working."

"You're *always* working," Nana returns.

"I don't need an intervention."

"Yeah, you do," Betsy says. "I hate to say this, kid, because I love you like my own family. But you're a fucking drag these days. I literally feel my lifeforce slipping away whenever I'm around you."

My mouth falls open as Nana and Helen agree with sympathetic nods.

"You pulled me out of work to tell me I'm boring? What the hell, Nana?"

"Oh, sweetheart, it's not that you're boring. It's so much worse than that. You're being a martyr. And if you don't do something to get off that high horse, soon you'll be stuck up there all alone, and Leo won't be around to help you down."

"I don't need a man to help me down. I'm a strong independent woman who can do everything on her own.

Leo is...he's a luxury I can't afford right now. The kids—"

"How long are you going to keep that excuse going?" Helen asks, finally speaking up. "Seems to me you're using them as a shield to keep from getting your heart broken. Your husband left and he was no Leo, so what's to say Leo won't get bored and take off too? Is that your thinking?" She lifts her brows and I choke back a gasp. Is this an intervention or some kind of voodoo ritual where they stab pins into my heart?

"Slow down, Helen," Nana stage-whispers out of the side of her mouth. "We weren't supposed to bring that up yet."

"Yes, I was," Helen whispers back. "It was tell her she's being a martyr, warn her that Leo won't wait forever, then ask her is she's scared of rejection." Helen counts them off on her fingers.

"No," Betsy says, also in an overly loud whisper. "It was the martyr, the warning, her mood, the kids, and *then* the fear of rejection."

Nana frowns. "I thought we had a thing about working too much and contacting her lawyer too."

They exchange glances before Betsy holds a finger up and tells me they need a moment. I let out a sigh as I fold my arms across my chest and listen as they squabble over a piece of paper and the order in which they need to tell me my life is crap. In a nutshell, I need to fix things with Leo to quit being such a downer.

"I'm not making excuses," I say finally, deciding to take control of this thing myself. "I haven't handled any part of this past few months well. I've lied, I've hidden the truth—which is sort of the same thing—I've been self-ish, self-involved, and I've stuck my head in the sand and hoped instead of doing what I knew I should have done and faced my problems head-on. I ran away from every-thing and everyone when I should have been knuckling down and focusing on my kids. I hurt them when I took them from what they knew. And I really hurt my daughter when I decided to focus on what made me feel good instead of being the mother she needed. I'm *trying* to fix that. And I miss Leo so fucking much, but this is something I need to do. And he understands that. He said he'll wait." I whisper the last part, a fact I've been clinging to in all my darkest moments. As the weeks have gone by and our communication has ceased, my fingers have been slipping, yet I still hold on. I need to feel like there's something for me on the end of this difficult road. And yet, I feel guilty just thinking that focusing on my kids is a difficult road because they deserve better than that. They deserve a mother who is one-hundred-percent committed and fulfilled by them, and I know I'm not cutting it, but I'm trying. I'm trying so fucking hard.

"Men don't wait like women do," Helen says, her head tilting a little as her kind eyes give me a hard truth.

"He promised," I argue. Clinging. *Clinging*.

Betsy steps closer and places a hand on my elbow. "There's a For Sale sign on his apartment, Darcy. It went up this morning."

I stumble back and hold my hand up when they try to catch me. I don't want to be touched right now.

*Eight weeks.*

"He's leaving?"

All three women nod.

I shake my head. "Eight weeks," I whisper. "That's it? That's all he could give me?" What happened to forever? What happened to me being worth it? *Eight weeks.*

Holy fuck.

"Darcy," Nana says, her voice stern as she cuts into my internal freak-out. "I know you think you're doing all this to help your daughter. But while you're hurting yourself, all you're doing is teaching her that tantrums win. You've been an absolute shell of a person since you let Leo go. You're so broken that you don't see what's happening. Your kids are constantly bickering. Archer puts on a brave face but hates Abigail for forcing you to push Leo away. And Abigail knows what she did was spiteful and wrong, but she's too damn proud to admit it and try to put things right again."

"Sound like somebody you know?" Betsy asks, eyes aimed at me.

I can't quite catch my breath. "I—"

"Do you know how I know that?"

I swallow back the tears, because I do know. It used to be me. Every day. After school.

"Please don't say it, Nana."

"Honey, they're missing you. You thought you were absent before, focused too much on Leo. You weren't. You were there. Now, you're just...you're gone, Darcy. There's no light in you anymore."

"But—"

"This nonsense stops today, Darcy," Nana insists. "And I don't want to hear any bullshit about Leo not waiting long enough or Abigail not being ready for you to have a man in your life. You and Leo make each other happy and you're miserable apart. I can't stand it. Abby and Archer need a happy mother. It's the single best thing you can do for them. So, quit pushing your man away and go fix it. Go and be happy, or-or I swear to you, Darcy, I'll dig that cauldron out of my storage cage and we'll all put a hex on you. I won't stand by and watch this self-destructive behaviour one moment longer. Go to him, child," Nana insists. "Go and talk to him before it's too late and you lose him for good."

I place my hand on my chest. It's the first time Nana has ever been this harsh with me. I don't know what to say.

"You heard the woman," Betsy says. "Go."

Helen just smiles and shoos me away with a flick of her hands.

I step away, my brow knitted as I try to wrap my head around the fact that I just got owned by a gang of old ladies. *Leo has put his apartment up for sale. What the actual fuck?*

"Oh, and Darcy," Nana calls out as I stumble away. "There's one more thing. You might want to give your lawyer a call. He keeps leaving messages saying he's found what you've been looking for. Said something about a settlement. While you're sorting your life out, you might want to get on that too."

## FORTY-SIX

## LEO

"I can't believe this is our last show with you, Leo," Chrissy, one of my co-hosts says on-air. My fill-in position on breakfast radio is coming to an end and I have mixed feelings about it. It's been good for me to be forced out of the workshop, to get out of my own head and interact with people. "I'm really going to miss seeing your pretty face across from me each morning. It's been great having you on the show this past month."

"Thank you, Chrissy," I say with a laugh. "I actually spoke to Dave yesterday, and he's feeling a lot better now. He told me to make sure I put his chair back the way he had it."

"That's right, people. Dave Hollis is back on Monday morning," the other co-host, Hamish adds. "Leo Murphy has been kind enough to keep this show a trio in Dave's stead. And I'm sorry to see him go, but I have to admit I've missed Dave-o. Poor guy looked like he went a few rounds with a sledgehammer when I saw him last. Dental surgery is not kind to the face. Not that it was a particularly pretty face to begin with..."

Chrissy laughs. "Oh, Dave's not that bad. But, I do have to wonder, because you played rugby with Dave, didn't you, Leo?"

"I did," I reply. "He was hooker, and I was fly-half when we toured with the Wallabies. We exchanged the captaincy between us for a bit, but yeah, I've known him my entire career. Back when we were kids playing club footy."

"OK," she continues. "Then how come he came out of the sport looking beat-up and you came out looking like a dream?"

"I think she has a crush on you, Murph," Hamish says with a laugh.

I laugh too, rubbing a hand over my stubble before I answer. "Well, that's got a lot to do with the positions we played. Dave spent most of his career in the centre of the scrum and it gets really rough in there. The guys tape their ears and wear headgear, but there's only so much friction your head can take before you get things like cauliflower ears."

"You weren't in the scrums?" Chrissy asks.

"I don't think she followed your career, mate."

"No. My position made me a half-back. Basically, we're the guys outside the scrum who get the ball and run it up the field. We take our fair share of hits, but we don't get the retired boxer look about us when we make a career of the game."

"That's interesting. See, I always thought you all got in on the scrum, goes to show what I know." Chrissy chuckles at herself before she continues. "Now, you had a pretty big career with the Wallabies, Leo. But you always worked two jobs, didn't you? You managed to get yourself an apprenticeship that you completed in the off season, even when you played professionally. What was the thought process behind that?"

"Nothing complex, I was simply raised to have a backup plan. I felt so incredibly lucky to be playing professionally, but I was aware that even the best players retire in their thirties, so I needed a steady business to fall back on."

Hamish shakes his head, his expression filled with wonder. "That's admirable, man. You had this massive career in rugby, and you could have retired and lived off your name for the rest of your life. Yet you work as a carpenter."

"He still commentates games," Chrissy adds.

"Yeah, but that's a few months a year," Hamish counters. "The rest of the time he's banging together a bunch of wood." Chrissy covers her mouth and giggles. Hamish rolls his eyes. "You know what I mean. And my point is, if I'd been in Murphy's shoes, I would be taking things a hell of a lot easier. The guy has a killer work ethic. Our listeners won't know this, but we get to the station around five each morning, leave around ten, then we go home and relax or whatever. But Leo goes back to his workshop—"

"Murphy's Carpentry and Cabinetry." Shameless plug.

Hamish laughs as he keeps talking. "And he works with his hands all day. I just admire your dedication. You could be riding the fame train, but you're the most down to earth guy I know."

I'm also desperate to fill every waking moment of my day so I don't go all caveman on Darcy and throw her over my shoulder, but I won't be talking about that on-air. No. Today we're clearing something else up.

I give Hamish an appreciative nod. "Thanks, Hamish. I think my mother deserves all the credit for that. She always kept me grounded. And I do enjoy my work. It's not a very imaginative business name, but I'm good at what I do and I like keeping busy. I like working with my hands." I shrug. "Once I'm finished up here—"

"I don't want him to go," Chrissy mock-cries.

"—I've got this job I want to finish up then I can get started on a passion project."

"Oh," Chrissy says, perking up. "Do tell."

"I'm doing up an old house. My son is coming to live with me, and my life is heading in a new direction, so it's time to make a few changes."

"This is the son you had with Tash Murphy from Neighbours, right?" she asks. It's the question this whole segment has been leading up to.

"She wasn't on Neighbours at the time, but, yes."

"Now, you've been divorced for a long time—thirteen years—and she kept your surname because she wanted to have the same name as her son?"

"That's right."

"Several weeks ago, the No Idea magazine ran a story that you two were getting back together again. Was there any truth to that?"

"Absolutely not." I laugh again, although this time it's

uncomfortably. I'm nervous doing this on-air, but I'm bloody tired of letting someone else narrate my story. "Tash and I, we've always had a strained relationship. I've tried to keep fairly tight-lipped where the press is concerned, but even after all these years, she keeps coming at me and I'm tired of staying quiet, Chrissy."

"Do want to break that silence today?"

"Yeah," I say, holding her gaze while nodding. "I do."

AFTER DETAILING over a decade of manipulation and deceit, I walk out of the radio station feeling like a huge weight has lifted off my shoulders. My mother always said that it took two to quarrel and only one to end it. So, I've never been a man to speak badly of others in public, always preferring to take the high road and refuse to play petty mud-slinging games. I thought that if I could endure Tash until Niall turned eighteen, I'd be free of her. But I'm done from her latest bout of Machiavellian behaviour—she's petitioning the Department of Foreign Affairs to approve 'special circumstances' so she can take Niall to London without my permission.

"You have two choices, Leo," she said over the phone when I confronted her. "Come to London with us or watch me take him away for good."

"You're out of line, Tash. He doesn't even want to go. This is pure spite and I won't let you do it."

"Then I suppose I'll see you in court."

I've been forced to re-open our custody case to fight for what's right for Niall's education and block her from taking him out of the country. Meanwhile, she's been talking to the press, concocting this story that I convinced her I wanted to get back together, just to gain Niall's trust and force her out of the picture. I think she's been getting pointers off the writers of her soap, because this is her most convoluted tale yet. It's a nightmare. And it couldn't have come at a crappier time. I'm under the pump at work, I'm heartsick without Darcy, so I can't take any more. Tash's bullshit needs to stop, and after finally speaking out, unloading years upon years of her bullshit, I feel bloody brilliant. I know this won't be the end of it, but I'm not backing down this time. This is for me. And it's for Niall. And hopefully, eventually, it will be for Darcy too.

"Great show in there today," Hamish says as he follows me out into the carpark.

"Thanks for helping to make it happen."

He holds his hand out to shake mine. "It's the least I can do. You're a good man, Murph. Don't let the media shit-fight get you down."

I give him a nod before he claps me on the shoulder then breaks off to walk to his own car. When I get inside mine, I pull my phone from my pocket and look at the dark screen, taking a breath to prepare myself before I turn it back on. The Apple symbol appears before the onslaught starts. Journalists. Reporters. Tash.

And Niall.

*Shit.*

His is the only call I return. *I hope he doesn't hate me for outing his mother.*

"Son," I say as I hold the phone to my ear, holding my breath until I hear his voice.

"I only have one question," he says by way of greeting. There's anger in his tone, which is to be expected.

"Ask away." For the first time in his life, I'm an open book.

"Was all that true?"

I let out my breath. "Every word. I can prove it all."

"Then I need you to come and get me. The lawyer said I can choose who I live with, and I don't wanna live here any more. She told me you didn't want me, Dad." The stress in his voice makes him sound young again, and I close my eyes, glad this didn't backfire, but pissed it's what it came to. Even more so that it took me this long to fight dirty in return. But when her selfish actions are threatening every relationship I care about, there is no choice. It's my turn to be in control of the story.

## FORTY-SEVEN

## DARCY

"You'd better have him home by Sunday night, Leo, or I will sue for breach of orders. That will fuck up your plans." Tash's shrill voice can be heard through the closed doors of Leo's apartment. *At least I know where he is now.*

After I left the café, I went to the workshop looking for him, and when he wasn't there, I came here instead.

"If you could for once, stop thinking about yourself and worry about your son for ten seconds, you'd realise that he *chose* to come here," Leo yells back.

"Because you're spreading lies," Tash screeches. And I'm surprised the windows aren't rattling.

"It was the truth," Leo booms. "You want the proof? I'll show you the fucking proof."

I really shouldn't be standing out here listening to this. It's obviously none of my business and I should go inside and pretend I can't hear a thing, but my feet don't want to move. When Tash screams something indecipherable and storms out of the apartment via the sliding door, I'm caught on the footpath, kicking myself. I could have at least made it to the privacy of Nana's deck before I started eavesdropping.

She stops in her tracks when she sees me, levelling me with a cold stare that causes my hair to stand on end. "He's not worth it," she says to me before she stomps off and gets into her Mercedes convertible, speeding off.

Mouth open, heart thudding, I turn back to the apartment building and find Leo standing in the open door, tension radiating off his body. We lock eyes and I'm shocked to find his hard.

My distress over the sale of his apartment falls away, replaced with concern for his well-being. "Is every—"

"Not now, Darcy," he snaps, raking his hands through his hair, nostrils flared.

"I—"

"Please. I can't talk to you right now." I blink rapidly as he turns away and locks his door. Distress shudders its way through my chest. I'm rattled by the anger in his tone and his reaction to my presence. There was a time not so long ago when we'd sit on our decks, talking through the privacy screen, using it as a confessional as we worked through our problems like life-long friends. Now he says, 'not now' and locks me out. *Eight weeks.*

*What the fuck just happened?*

Niall appears on the other side of the glass door, avoiding my gaze as he reaches up and lowers the blind so I can't see in. I'm being shut out. Shut out and pushed away.

*Men don't wait like women do.*

Stepping back, I snap my mouth shut and turn away, not stopping until I'm back in my car, returning to work. I spend the rest of the day putting one foot in front of the other, going through the motions while my mind reels. If Leo is selling his apartment and he doesn't want to talk to me, does that mean I'm too late?

*Fuck.*

CAN WE TALK? I send the message later that night after the kids are asleep, and I can't stop fretting over the way Leo snapped at me. Nana offered me a puff of her joint, but I don't need to get high. I need to find out where I stand with Leo.

It takes almost thirty minutes for a response to come through. **Has anything changed?** he sends, followed quickly by: **Are we pressing play again?**

**Not yet. But I'm worried about you. There's a For Sale sign outside your place.**

I bite my lip as I watch the dots dance then stop. Dance then stop. They stay motionless for a good five minutes, and just as I'm about to give up watching, they start again.

**I'm sorry. I'm dealing with my own shit right now. I can't do this.**

*He can't do this?* My thumbs fly over the screen before I hit send: **Do what? Talk to me?** After the message goes through and changes to 'delivered', I stare at the screen, waiting for the dots. Time ticks once and my heart beats twice, a pressure building in my chest and buzzing in my head as I wait, and I wait. But the dots don't come. The message doesn't even change to 'read'.

*He's ignoring me.*

Covering my face with my hands, I drop my phone off the side of my bed, pull the blankets over my head, and cry myself to sleep.

*"I'm dealing with my own shit right now. I can't do this."*

He can't do this.

*Fuck.* When the hell will this get any better? I'm not sure how much more I can take.

OVER THE NEXT WEEK, I see Leo twice. And each time he's wearing a suit. The first time he doesn't see me. He's getting into his car in the parking garage, that tension I saw outside his apartment still there as he speaks to Niall as the two of them leave together.

The second time I see him, it's late evening and I'm standing on the deck drinking tea while Nana is visiting Arthur. It's a bit of a shock when I spot him, dragging his feet as though his whole body weighs a ton. There's stubble covering his jaw, dark shadows under his eyes, his jacket is slung over his arm, and his tie is hanging loose around his neck. He looks such a wreck that I open my mouth on instinct to ask if he's all right. But then we lock eyes, and all I can hear are the words, *not now*, so I lower my gaze and step back inside, locking the sliding door behind me.

I know what's going on with him. The problem with having any sort of celebrity in this country is that your personal drama is quickly splashed all over the papers: *Neighbours Star and Rugby Legend Locked in Bitter Custody Battle*. The media loves calling them that—as if their real names are of no real consequence—and each day of the emergency proceedings gets its own column in the paper, complete with photos of a distressed-looking Tash and a furious-looking Leo. Things in the courtroom are getting really ugly with mud-slinging back and forth. I can't understand why the court is not convinced that Niall should stay in Australia. He only has seven months of school left. Not to mention that Leo has provided evidence showing that he's been manipulated, disparaged, and blackmailed—essentially—for many years. It's as though because Tash seems to be able to conjure up fabricated bullshit and accusations of abuse and neglect, *there must be truth to it.* I'm upset for Leo as much as I'm upset for Niall. This can't be easy on either of them. Especially with the media frenzy it's created. Everyone is waiting for the day when Niall gets to tell his version of events, and since I don't know Niall very well, I'm incredibly nervous for Leo. Despite the radio silence, I wish him luck the night before:

**I'm rooting for you.**

The message sends through, but the status doesn't change. And I'm left lying in bed only metres away from him, feeling further away than I ever have before. I love this man with my flawed and desolate heart. If only that could be enough to hold him up. However, right now, Leo's fighting a battle he's fought on his own for a decade. What I want to write is *I'm rooting for you. I love you.* But there's little point. Leo Murphy is in fight mode, and he's relying on what he knows best—himself.

## FORTY-EIGHT

DARCY

"Sit down, please." I gesture to the seats on the opposite side of the dining table from where I'm standing. Nana sits at the head of the table with a steaming cup of tea in front of her, and there's a plate of her oatmeal raisin cookies ready for the kids. At the sight of this, both Abigail and Archer hesitate before slowly taking their seats.

"What's going on?" Abigail asks, looking between Nana and me. "Is someone dying?"

"Oh no." Archer slaps his palm against his face. "Is it Nana? She's so old."

Nana quirks a smile. "No one's dying, sweet boy. Your mum needs to talk to you about something, and I thought it would be easier if I eavesdrop right here. Have a cookie." She pushes the plate towards him and he grabs two. Abigail refuses when offered, preferring to fold her arms on the table.

"I want to talk about your father," I say, still standing because I feel better this way. As much as I don't want to have this conversation with them, I know it's well over-due. I've been putting it off and putting it off, but now that things are escalating legally, I don't want to put it off anymore. I promised them I'd be honest moving forward, so here it is.

"Has he called?" Abby asks straight away, and it jolts in my chest that she's still hanging on to that hope.

"No," I respond, keeping my voice gentle. "This is about some legal proceedings I've been looking into."

"Like what?"

"Well, as you know, we lost the house and when we came to Nana, we didn't have much money."

"But then you got a job," Archer supplies.

"Yes, well, it's why I had to get a job quickly. I couldn't support you both on my own. But what I want to talk to you about is the way your father lost the house and what it means for us if we do nothing. And what it will mean if we do something."

Abby frowns. "OK."

I pull out a chair and sit, clasping my hands in front of me. I still think the kids are too young to understand our position, but I can't keep fighting with Abigail every time she discovers something about my life I haven't told her about. So, I'm going to live my life like Nana does: as an open book.

"I'm on the verge of personal bankruptcy. That means I owe more money to the bank than I can possibly pay back. If I do this, it blocks me from doing anything that involves credit. Like if our car dies and we need a new one, I can't get a loan, and it'll make it harder for us to get our own place. It's not the end of the world, but it's difficult, and really, it's not fair. You see, I never took out a loan, and I never owned credit cards. As far as I was aware, the mortgage was almost paid off and our finances were looking up. And I thought that because it's what your father told me. He looked after our finances, and while, yes, he was the main provider in the house, he was also the one who insisted that I didn't go to work after having you kids. So, it was his job *and his choice* to provide for us. He's not allowed to take all of that away. But, when he decided to leave, he took all the money out of the mortgage on the house, and he also took every dollar from our family accounts and hid it somewhere. I'm guessing in an account in his name." Abby's eyes go wide and Archer actually gasps.

"He did *what?*" he yells.

"He took all of our money. Slowly, over many months, so he could use it to start his new life." That's as matter-of-fact as I think I should get with them. The truth without the nitty-gritty details. Because it goes so much deeper than just taking all of our money. He did work outside his company on the sly and declared that income as though it was mine. Then he used those false tax returns to secure credit cards and personal loans that he cleaned out and didn't pay back. This was a calculated attack, designed to leave me completely destitute. And I don't understand why. More so, I cannot believe this reprehensible monster was my husband...and I had no clue who he really was.

"He *stole* from us?" Abigail asks, her eyes misty as her brow pinches.

I nod. I feel bloody awful telling them this. I never

wanted to reveal Kevin for the cheating thief he is, but he's left me little choice. I refuse to work to pay off money he's benefiting from when he can't even be bothered to support his kids.

"What an arsehole," Archer yells.

Nana giggles. "You're right about that one."

"Language, young man," I say before continuing with my speech. "The reason I'm telling you all this is that I'd like your input on what to do about it."

"If he stole, will he go to jail?" Abby asks, and I shake my head.

"The lawyer says the most he'll get is house arrest, but that's only if we get the police involved."

"You've been talking to a *lawyer*?" Abigail's expression shifts to indignant teen, like she's about to yell at me for not telling her sooner, and I'm so tired of it that I just snap.

"Of course I've been talking to a lawyer, Abigail. What the hell do you think people do in this situation? We are adults with responsibilities and commitments, and when those responsibilities and commitments aren't met, lawyers get involved. Now, if you'll shut up and stop behaving like the fourteen-year-old child you very obviously are, I'll give you what you want, which is a vote in what we do next. Do you want that? Or do you want to get your knickers in a twist over a detail I really didn't have to share with you? Because I don't have to tell you a damn thing, Abigail. About my finances *or* my impending divorce besides the custody arrangement, which I'm pretty sure is fairly obvious to you. I'm doing this as a *courtesy* to treat *you* with respect, and if you can't give me the same in return, then I will make every single decision about my life, *and* your life without consulting you at all? Do I make myself clear?"

Her mouth opens then closes and she gulps before she nods. "I'll listen," she whispers. "I want to know."

As I let out my breath and push my hair away from my face. I risk a glance at Nana, who's lifting her teacup to her mouth as her eyes spark with pride. Besides her comment during her recent intervention, she's been unusually quiet over how I've been handling my conflict with Abigail. Now I see she's been waiting for me to stand up and assert myself as the parent, and I have to admit that it feels pretty damn good. I gave up a beautiful burgeoning relationship for Abigail, and I don't regret putting my child's needs over my own. But I do think I've given her the misguided impression that her voice has power over my actions; that she has the right to berate me when she doesn't like my choices. That was my mistake. One thing my mother said growing up that has stuck with me: 'I'm not here to be your friend, I'm here to be your mother.' And while that pissed me off at the time, I understand and appreciate it now as a mother myself. My role as my children navigate the difficult space between child and adult is to teach them how to be a decent human being, to guide them in their choices, to show them that actions have consequences and that we all have our place in this world. You can't behave like a toddler then expect to be treated like an adult. You can't snap at your mother and expect her to smile and take it on the chin. But what you can do is show respect to earn respect, and I think that's a really important lesson to learn.

"OK," I start. "There are a few things I can do to fix our situation. First, I let it go. I declare bankruptcy and we all let Dad live his new life and have all the money. Or, I go to the police, which is justified because what he did was illegal. It'll fix everything, but it'll get drawn out and Dad will have a police record, which could affect his ability to work. *Or,* I get my lawyer to try and recover the money and clear my credit so we settle this without getting the police involved at all."

"I don't want Daddy to get in trouble with the police," Archer says, as I expected he would.

"What would the settlement do to him?"

"Nothing really. Your dad would have to agree to pay child support for you guys and pay back the money he took. Then I'd sign papers to say I won't press charges, and that would be it. We'd go our separate ways."

"Will that make you divorced?" Archer asks.

"No. We can't divorce for about a year. But it will mean he's agreed to help take care of you, because that's what dads are supposed to do."

"Will it mean he visits us? Can we put that in there?" Abby asks.

"I..." I start then press my lips together. I'm so far removed from Kevin that I would be happiest if I never saw him again. But it's different for the kids. They need two parents and if I can do this for them, I have to try. "I can ask."

"What if he says no?" Archer asks.

"Why would he say no?" Abigail directs at him.

"He stole our money and he didn't call at Christmas *or* on the first day of school."

"Maybe he's scared we hate him now," Abby says.

"I *do* hate him. Dads aren't meant to steal, Abby. It's come-on sense."

"Don't you mean 'common sense', dear?" Nana asks.

"No. It's like when someone does something really dumb and everyone shouts, *'come on'* at them because they should have known better. *Come-on* sense."

Nana lifts her eyebrows and tilts her head, understanding his logic. Weirdly, it made total sense to me too.

"Hate is a very strong word, Archer," I add. "And if your dad decides he wants to spend time with you, he has every right to ask for it."

"That's dumb. What about what I want?"

"Well, that will be considered too. We'll have to get something called Parenting Orders to decide how that would work, but first, I think we need to see what your father is willing to agree to. I can't force him to visit, but I can force him to pay."

"Then that's what you should do," Abby says, nodding her head. "It's not right that he stole from us, and it's not fair that he keeps all the money. ."

"OK." I nod, feeling a sense of relief that this has turned out OK, after all.

"Why'd he decide to steal the money anyway?" Archer asks.

"Mum already said, dummy. So he could start a new life."

"Yeah, but Mummy said it took months for him to steal it all. He didn't just wake up and decide 'oh, I want a new life today.' He *planned* it." I suck my breath in awe. This kid is so damn smart.

Abby frowns and swings her gaze my way. "That is really messed up."

Closing my eyes for a second, I breathe deep through my nose, preparing myself to unload. The truth. The whole truth, *so help me, God.*

"Then I suppose I should go back to when everything changed," I say. "You see, your father found a lump..."

"THAT WAS BRAVE IN THERE EARLIER," Nana says later when the kids have finished asking a thousand questions before finally going to bed. "It could have gone very differently, but you handled it superbly. I'm proud of you."

"Thanks, Nana," I say, taking a sip of my wine, sorely needed after that marathon explanation session. I'm absolutely exhausted, but I'm glad to be free of the secrets I was keeping on Kevin's behalf, while also deciding on a road we can move forward on. I think we became a tighter family unit tonight.

"I was surprised you didn't talk to them about your relationship with Leo."

"What relationship? We've barely spoken in nine weeks now. I've tried reaching out during his custody hearing but..." I shrug.

"So that's it? You hit a roadblock and you're through? I thought you loved him."

"I do. But you should have seen him, Nana. That day I came to talk to him, he was so angry that I could feel it coming off him in waves. I wanted to be there for him, but he shut me out."

"Maybe he couldn't handle missing you while he fought for his son?"

"I don't know, Nana. I could have at least provided comfort or an understanding ear, like he did for me when my life was falling apart. But he told me to go away. That doesn't sound like he wants a relationship to me. It sounds like he wants to be alone."

"That Tash is a devil of a woman," she says, obviously wanting to change tack. "Did I ever tell you about the time I overheard her telling Leo that she would fabricate a story about him beating on Niall if he didn't give her money? She turned on the tears as an example of how believable she'd be to the press, and poor Leo felt so backed into a corner that he gave her what she wanted." She shakes her head, her mouth in a tight line. "Terrible, vindictive woman."

"She hasn't been too pleasant lately either. The papers are having a field day."

"Luckily, I had my phone on me at the time, and I recorded the entire conversation. Can't be submitted as evidence to support Leo, of course, but I think the anonymous email I sent multiple media outlets might go a long way to discredit her in the court of public opinion."

A grin spreads from ear to ear. "You didn't."

"I certainly did. Horrid woman. I always said I'd find a way to help Leo and Niall, and I'm glad the opportunity finally arose for me to do just that." She pulls a joint out of her pocket and lights up. "Celebratory puff?" She offers it to me.

"Don't mind if I do." Inhaling deep, I hold the smoke in my lungs as I hand the joint back. "You know," I say as the smoke billows past my lips. "No matter what ends up happening between Leo and me, I'm really glad he has you."

She takes a long contemplative drag before she speaks. "Don't give up on him, sweetheart. He needs you to wait for him just as much as you need him to wait for you."

*Then why won't he even look at my messages?*

## FORTY-NINE

## DARCY

A media circus erupts the next morning when the video hits mainstream news outlets. Paparazzi and news vans are parked outside Leo's apartment, which means they're outside ours too. We can't go out on the deck without being asked a torrent of questions about Leo and Tash. I just say, "No, thank you" and go back inside while Archer stands at the glass windows, his phone on its side as he records them.

"This is gonna be awesome for my YouTube channel," he says, tickled pink.

Nana, Carla and Betsy sit at the table crocheting and Betsy uses a willy warmer covered-hand to wave at the cameras. Abigail is mortified and pulls our blinds to the floor, claiming it's so she can watch TV in peace.

"I'm off to work," I say at ten thirty. It's one of those Saturdays when I have to work the lunch shift. When I went full-time, I bargained with management to give me alternating Saturday and Sunday shifts with one full weekend off a month. It was the best compromise I could come up with to make money and spend time with the kids. And I'm lucky that Nana is here to supervise when I can't. The woman is surely a gift from God.

"Make sure you take the front door, dear. The vultures will get you if you leave via the deck." Nana nods her head towards the closed blinds while Betsy complains about them ruining the view.

There's chatter around town when I get to work too. Locals have noticed the news vans parked along Beach Road and they're lamenting the disturbance to their "quiet enjoyment of a suburb we pay a high price to live in," I hear one of them say.

The woman with her leans across the table, head nodding with enthusiastic agreement. "Although that footballer is moving soon. Saw the For Sale sign myself this morning. Can't come a moment too soon if this is the kind of malarkey he brings around. Shameful these young people can't manage their relationships properly. In my day, you got married and you stayed married. For better or worse we said. Far more worse than better if you ask me, but we still kept at it."

Hating the reminder that Leo is leaving, I shoot my breath between my lips and thank my culinary skills for landing me in the kitchen. At least I won't l have to listen to the gossips my entire shift.

"You're late," my boss, Karen says as she rolls a falafel salad wrap in cling film.

Dumping my bag, I grab my apron and tie it behind my back. "Damn press is taking up all the available parking. It's a nightmare out there."

"That's right. That football guy lives in your building,

doesn't he?"

"He sure does," I say, moving to the fridge and pulling out a stack of steaks and a tub of sour cream.

"You see him much? He's a bit of a looker." The dormant butterflies that live in my stomach burst to life as my mind forces a very specific montage of Leo smiling at me, looking with hungry eyes.

I have to close my eyes to calm my heart. *I miss him so much.* "Not as much as we used to," I say. "His, um, place is for sale." Just saying that out loud causes my butterflies to fall to the pit of my stomach and still. I can't wrap my head around the fact he's leaving.

"Just as well, I guess. He can take the media attention with him. Although, it will probably die down soon. I'm sure another soap star will embarrass themselves on film before you know it." She smiles as she clears her work area then joins me in preparing the steaks. "I still can't believe a sour cream marinade is the secret to these," she says. "You can't even taste it."

"It's the acid," I say, brushing the sour cream over each steak. "Breaks down the protein."

"I'm kicking myself for not booking a stall at that big fete the hospital is having tomorrow. We would have made a killing with your sandwiches."

"It sounds like a really big deal. Nana and her friends have been working non-stop preparing for their stall." Finishing with the last steak, I pop it in the container with the rest then cover it up.

"What are they selling?" she asks, taking the container to the fridge where it'll stay for the next hour.

Turning on the tap, I pump two squirts of soap into

my palm as I smile about Nana's stall. "Some sort of crocheted pouch," I say, being intentionally vague. They're still planning to pretend they're coin purses so they can act like innocent grannies when they're called out on it. Archer's filming the whole thing, of course. He's calling it a 'social experiment'.

"Oh, that's sweet. I hope they do really well. Are you taking your kids there? It should be a fun day."

"Well, Archer is going with Nana, but I think Abigail already has plans to go there with her friends." I shrug.

"Wow. A day off work *and* no kids for the day, what will you do with yourself?"

"Oh, I don't know, I'll probably go to the fete too."

"Or you take a long hot bath and relax. Take some time for yourself. You work too hard, Darcy. I should know, I'm your boss," she says with a wink before collecting the tray of wraps and taking them to the display cabinet out front.

*Relax.* I go back to prepping ingredients for the lunch service. *Who has time to relax anymore?* I always think it's such an easy thing to say to another person; *relax.* But it's not as simple as sitting back in a hot bath and enjoying the quiet. With the quiet comes time to think. And with thinking comes remembering and longing, and I don't want to feel that. So, I keep going instead.

WHEN THE CAFÉ quiets down in the afternoon, Karen takes the opportunity to go on break, leaving me to run things with one other staff member. We're mostly making coffees and selling cakes and slices to the afternoon tea patrons. The noise level has dropped to a low murmur, and I can actually hear the radio as it plays hit songs from the nineties. I hum along to Lisa Loeb's *Stay* as I bring some more milk from the cool room to put in the barista fridge.

"Hey." A gentle rumble cuts out all other sound as it enters my ears and tugs gently on my heart. I stop what I'm doing and turn to the voice.

"Leo," I say, standing so I'm a little closer to his eye level. He looks good enough to eat in jeans and a grey T-shirt that hugs his muscular chest, peeking through the open zip of his worn-looking leather jacket. He's scruffy along his jawline, like he hasn't shaved in a couple of days, the salt and pepper bristles revealing his age while making him look deathly sexy at the same time. There's a pair of aviator sunglasses pushed back into his dark hair, their mirrored lenses probably chosen to help shield him from the cameras. Although, I'm surprised he risked leaving the apartment with the mob waiting on him.

"I hear you make a killer steak sandwich here," he says, and when he lifts the corner of his mouth in an attempt at a smile, I notice how tired his eyes seem. He has the look of a man starved and hungry but unable to eat. I recognise it easily since I see it in the mirror every day.

*Has anything changed? Are we pressing play again?*

I remember his text messages before he told me he *can't do this* then went silent on me. Discomfort twists in my belly and I lower my eyes before clearing my throat.

"It's too late in the day for steak sandwiches." I try to

keep my voice even as I reach for an order pad. "But I did promise you the recipe once." I scribble it down and tear the page off for him. "You can make it at home. Or in your new place. Whatever works for you."

He takes the paper from between my fingers and looks at it, nodding slowly. "Tash is backing off," he says, meeting my eyes. "She's going to let me keep Niall here. Maybe you can thank Esme for the video for me? I assume it was her."

"It was. But I think maybe you should thank her yourself. You were friends first, and you do live right next door. For now, anyway." I keep flicking my gaze from him to the pen I still hold in my hand, struggling to have this conversation. There's so much we should be saying, but we're not saying any of it. We're talking like nothing is happening but the worst thing possible *is* happening: we're letting go and I hate it. *He said he can't do this and he pushed me away.* I close my eyes for a moment to bolster my emotions.

"I'm not staying in the apartment anymore. I have a new place closer to the city. Since Niall is moving in with me, it'll be easier for him to get to school..."

My chest hurts. It's tight and sore like the unspoken words are lodging themselves between my heart and my rib cage, squashing my lungs. "It must feel good to get what you've always wanted."

He doesn't respond at first, just locks eyes with me before giving me a tight-lipped smile. "How are your kids?"

"They're fine. I got a lawyer and he found Kevin, so Abigail is hoping we'll be able to create a communication agreement." His eyebrows shoot up. "I don't know that it'll work, but she's happy something's happening. Archer is the same. He asks about you a lot."

He nods. "Tell him I said hi."

"OK," I whisper. *I'm not going to cry. I'm not going to cry.*

He takes a breath and steps back. Then he pauses, frowns and steps forward again.

"No. I'm not leaving like that," he says in a rush. "I feel like we've made a real mess of this, Darce. I miss you like crazy, and I hate that you're standing right in front of me but there's this gulf of distance between us." He gestures between us then reaches across the counter, plucking the pen from between my fingers. "We need to talk or...something." He pulls the notepad closer then scrawls an address on a fresh page. "I don't know what we're supposed to do, but doing nothing feels like..." Knitting his brow, he shakes his head. "Will you meet me here?" He pushes the pad and pen across the counter. "Tonight. Please? We can talk, and"—he shrugs—"I don't know. I just need to talk to you. Because I'm waiting, Darce. I'm still waiting. OK?"

Picking up the pad of paper, I hold it to my chest as I nod. "I'm still waiting too, Leo."

"Yeah?" His eyes brighten as he lets out a relieved breath.

Smiling for what feels like the first time in months, I let out a charged breath. "Yes."

"Tonight then?"

I nod as he grins and steps away. He looks so relieved that I almost laugh. I also nearly cry because I'd let myself believe he didn't want me anymore. But he's still waiting. *He's still waiting.*

## FIFTY

## DARCY

"I need to talk to you," I say to the kids when I'm home from work. We've had dinner and I brought home brownies for their dessert, so I feel they're sufficiently sweetened up before I broach the subject of Leo.

"Again?" Abigail asks, her dessert spoon still in her hand. "There's more?"

"What did Dad do this time?" Archer asks.

"This isn't about your father. This is about me."

Archer's eyes go wide. "Are you dying?" he whispers.

"What? No. No one is dying. I want to talk to you both about Leo."

Abigail places her spoon in her bowl. "What about him?"

"I think you should marry him," Archer blurts, bouncing in his seat. Abigail turns and shushes him before turning her full attention to me.

"You want to date him?" she asks, her eyes wary.

"I do." It's time to be honest. "It won't stop me from being here when you need me. You guys are both my number ones. But it will mean that I'm a lot happier because while I love being your mum, I'd also like to have someone who loves me."

"We love you, Mummy," Archer says with a smile, and I grin back.

"I know you do, buddy. But with Leo, it's a different kind of love."

"The kind that makes you glow," he replies, wriggling his fingers next to his face as he says it.

"I suppose that's one way to describe it."

"That's how I know you and Leo love each other. You glow when you're together. And he makes you smile. And your eyes get all sparkly. You're like the angel on the tree at Christmas."

My cheeks heat as I lose my battle with a smile, because that is probably the most beautifully innocent way I've ever heard someone describe an obvious attraction.

"You love each other?" Abigail asks, her expression still guarded as she listens to Archer gush.

With an inhale, I nod. "I think we do. Yes."

"Well, I vote yes," Nana says as she walks down the hall with a bag of willy warmers. "Life is short, and you and Leo are perfect for each other. As someone who loves you, Darcy, I only want you to be happy. Leo makes you happy." She places the bag on the floor against the wall and claps her hands together. "Oh, this makes me so happy."

"I'm happy too," Archer says, jumping out of his seat and doing a random little jig.

Nana dances around with him, singing 'Love is in the

air', and I try not to smile too much, because Abigail hasn't responded yet.

"Are you going to be OK with this?" I ask, focusing on her. I've done everything I can to do right by her, but I'm at the point where I need to make this decision for myself, to stand up and fight for what makes me happy. Because ultimately, it's going to teach my kids that love— real love—is worth the fight. I know in my heart that once Abigail gets to know Leo properly, she'll think he's as great as Archer does. She just needs to give him a chance.

"Do I have a choice?" she asks, narrowing her eyes slightly as she watches Nana and Archer dance about. "It looks like I'm out voted."

"Of course. This is a decision we need to make as a family, so I'd like a unanimous vote. But, first, I want to tell you what it's like to find that one person who completes you in here," I say, tapping my hand over my heart. "And once I've told you that, I want to tell you what it feels like when you're apart from that person. When I'm done, then you can cast your vote."

Nana and Archer stop dancing and turn their attention to the table as I begin, hedging my bets while hoping to God that I've raised a compassionate and caring daughter. Our little family's happiness depends on it.

## FIFTY-ONE

## LEO

A light from the street hits the curtain and I'm immediately craning my neck to see if she's here. We didn't set a time. But it's almost ten and I'm expecting her any moment. *If* she's coming.

"Shit." I get up and rake my hands through my hair, pacing back and forth when I realise it's just some random car using my driveway to turn around.

"Relax, pops," Niall says, clicking away at his Xbox controller in the study that connects to the living room. "She'll be here."

He seems so sure. But honestly, I'm not. That distance I was talking to her about in the café, I caused it by pushing Darcy away when everything blew up between Tash and me. I've been missing her so damn much that the idea of being in the same room as her, not being able to touch her, to bury myself inside her when my emotions were on edge...it was more than I could bear. I needed her beside me and it felt like a knife in my gut that I couldn't have her.

It sounds like all I wanted to do was fuck her until I felt better, but that wasn't the case at all. I wanted *her*. All of her. I wanted the comfort, the closeness, the connection. And I knew I couldn't have that, so I pushed her away. And now I'm freaking out that my invitation to work this out wasn't enough of an olive branch. *I should have told her I love her.* That might have made the difference, shown her what she means to me. *Shit.*

"Oh my God, Dad," Niall says, putting his controller down and getting up. "Have a drink and calm down, you're giving me anxiety." He gets up and grabs a beer from the fridge, popping the cap, and handing it to me. "She's maybe five minutes away."

Wrapping my hand around the cool glass bottle, I frown before bringing it to my lips. "How do you know that?"

"Abby told me." He sits on the couch opposite and pops the ring pull on a can of Pepsi Max.

"You two talk?"

"Yeah." He shrugs. "We DM on insta. We have a decent streak going on Snapchat."

My eyes pop at the mention of Snapchat. "You do *what* on Snapchat?"

"Streaks. You now, take a random picture and send it through. You get a score for keeping it going. We're up to ninety-something days now. I have streaks with heaps of people."

I frown, feeling really old all of a sudden because I don't know what the hell he's talking about. "And the DMs?"

He looks at me like I've sprouted an extra head.

"Direct message. Like texting, but no one uses regular texts anymore."

The tension eases in the back of my head slightly. "So, there's nothing...uh...racy about the stuff you send each other?"

Now his eyes bug out and he chokes a little on his Pepsi. "No," he practically shouts. "She's fourteen, Dad. A kid. Do you think I'm that stupid?"

"I...ah...I don't...um, pretend to know what teenagers are doing with these apps these days."

"It's not that. Well, it *is* that. But only with girls our own age."

"That's a relief. I'm glad you're being responsible."

He chuckles a little. "Let's call it that."

I take a long pull of my beer and study his face. It's uncanny how much he looks like me at the same age. Sometimes he holds his expression a certain way, and I see an old picture of myself mirrored right back at me. He's smaller than me though, has a slimmer build that comes from Tash's side. He's more suited to AFL than rugby, not that Tash would ever let him do either. She'd claimed it was because she didn't want me forcing my passions down the boy's throat, but I always felt it was just her way of making sure I had as little in common with my own son as possible. I've often wondered if she hated the fact that he looks so much like me, or whether it gave her pleasure, seeing me in his face and knowing he gave her control over me. Jesus, who knows what goes on in that woman's head? She was so intent on destroying me a couple of days ago but the moment that video surfaced, she did a complete one-eighty in an attempt to save face. To anyone else in Tash's position, that video could ruin their career. But Tash has this magical ability to turn any and all attention to her advantage. I have no doubt she'll go to the UK and become an even bigger name than she is now. She's just going to have to do it without Niall. And definitely without me. I won't be fodder for her attention-seeking schemes anymore.

"Have you been talking to Abby this whole time?" I ask suddenly, remembering that while Niall is my son, he's Tash's son too. I remember the look on his face the day he and Abby came back from the beach, causing a scene when they saw me walking with Archer. And I have this sudden and awful feeling he's been playing games to spite me.

"Yeah, Dad," he says, voice soft as he shifts the ring pull on his can back and forth with his index finger. "We've been in touch this entire time."

My mind clouds over. "What do you talk about?"

"Lots of stuff. School. Friends. Mostly parent stuff."

Sitting back, I balance the bottle on my thigh. "I'm guessing you weren't very kind in your assessment of me?"

"She hated you just fine on her own. But I didn't help you out, either."

I tighten my jaw. "I see." I don't want to believe this, because we had a truce in place and I'd asked him not to stoke the flames of Abby's dissent. But it makes sense, the timing, the sudden insistence. It has Tash's influence all over it.

"You've gotta remember, pops, that this was before I knew the truth about Mum. I've spent my whole life thinking you were a lying prick, and she was angry about her dad, so we'd vent to each other."

A thud resounds in my chest as pieces fall into place. "And I made the mistake of telling her that her mum would choose her over me."

"I'm sorry, Dad. I told her to test it and see if it's the truth."

I close my eyes and will the blood pumping between my ears to calm down. I want to grab his shoulders right now and yell, 'why would you do that?' but I already know the answer to that. He did it because he's been angry all his life and he wanted to hurt me. Living with Tash, you're bound to pick up some manipulation skills. It's how she deals with any and all conflict. *I should have gotten him out of there sooner.*

"I really am sorry, Dad," he says, and I know his words are sincere because the previous venom in his tone is gone. It's just me and him and the truth now. I have to own the fact that I allowed Tash's reign to continue for far too long. Had I outed her publicly sooner, perhaps things wouldn't have gone this far. My silence and my pride did a huge amount of damage to my relationship with my son. But that needs to stay behind us. With Tash leaving the country, we need to establish a new kind of relationship, one that doesn't contain any shadows of the past machinations. It's going to be difficult, and it's going to take work. But this is the road I always wanted to travel, one where I have my son walking alongside me. I don't need to be angry here. I'm *trying* not to be angry, but my reticent silence has him rushing to explain himself. "I did it because I was

pissed off that you wouldn't come to London with us."
*What?*

"I didn't think you wanted to go. I thought you wanted to stay here and finish school. Like we discussed."

"Yeah, well that was before Mum convinced me you two had reconciled. I know this sounds dumb, but she said you'd been talking a lot in secret to see if you could have a better relationship for my sake, said you fell in love again. Then the magazine article came out. And I guess I wanted it to be true, so I believed her."

"You didn't think to call me and ask if it was real?"

He offers a self-deprecating smile and shakes his head, laughing at himself in a disappointed way that twists my insides. *I should have fought harder for him.* That was my mistake. I should have protected him from her instead of protecting his relationship with a toxic-minded person. Sometimes two parents aren't better than one.

"That probably would have helped," he says. "But to be honest with you, ever since I was a kid I wanted Mum to say those words to me. You were always so angry at each other and I used to think, if only they could love each other again, we could all be happy. For years, I wished on birthday cakes and stars and dandelions and any shit you could use to make a wish. And it never happened, and I quit caring, until…" The ring pull snaps and he hooks it on the tip of his finger. "I can sit here now and know it was really dumb to believe, but I think that's part of why I was so angry, and why I told Abby to make her mum choose. I was angry at myself for hoping my parents could love each other again, like I was still that little kid believing my wishes would come true." Dropping the ring pull inside his empty can with a *ting*, he meets my eyes with a sullen smile playing on his lips. "For what it's worth, I also told her I was wrong. That I've been playing the role of the unwitting accomplice for years, which is so messed up, because we were studying that trope in English last year and I didn't see it. I sat in class and thought, what a dope." He laughs. "But here I am, a sorry dope who hopes you can forgive him for messing with your life."

*Wow*. It's the first thing I think when he explains his thought process. And then, when the words settle, I feel pride. Because it takes a big man to own up to something that huge. Pressing my lips together, I release my breath and hold out my hand. He lines his up with mine and we shake before I pull him up and hug him. "Thank you," I say over his shoulder. "It took guts to tell me that."

We release each other and he looks into my eyes, surprise in his. "You're not angry?"

"Oh, I'm angry. Some of that anger is toward you, a lot of it is toward your mum. The lies she told you... I've always wanted more with you, Niall, and it fucking sucks that she filled your head with poison about me. Having said that, I'm also angry at myself for not acting earlier. But I'm letting it go. This is a new start for the both of us, and I don't want to bring any of the bullshit of the past along with us. Sound fair?"

He nods. "That works for me. And, I understand why you did what you did all these years—you wanted me to have both a mum and a dad—but I think if you had have done this a few years sooner, I probably wouldn't need all the therapy I'm gonna need. My head is seriously messed up over all of this."

"Do you want to see a therapist?" I ask seriously. I hear the joke in his tone, but I want to make sure it's just that before I laugh and brush it off.

"I don't know." He shrugs. "I think the truth has made a huge difference in the way I think about every-thing, but it is a bit weird up here. I'll think about it and let you know."

"OK, son," I say, clapping him on the shoulder.

Then he laughs. "This is weird too. We used to never talk and now we're having constant DMs."

I frown. "Direct Messages?"

"Nah, man. Deep and meaningfuls. Different context."

"Why can't you kids just say the words instead of abbreviating everything?"

"Showing your age, pops." He chuckles as he pats my back and walks away. "I'm gonna make myself scarce before your girlfriend knocks on the door. I think I just heard her pull up."

"She's here?" My heart picks up and thunders against my ribcage as I look towards the front door, moments before I hear a knock.

Niall chuckles. "I'll leave you to it. Don't do anything I wouldn't do."

Nodding as I hear him head up the stairs, I stare at the door and take a calming breath. This is it. The moment that will make or break Darcy and me. Do we give this relationship our all, or do we let it go and spend the rest of our life wondering? *God, I hope it's the former.*

## FIFTY-TWO

## DARCY

Leo's new place is situated halfway between the Bayside apartment building and the Melbourne CBD. It's a large sixties-style brick home, painted white externally with extra angles in the façade where the windows are set back and the bricks create a pillar-type vibe. As a kid, I would have looked at this house and thought it was a mansion, especially since it's directly across the road from Port Phillip Bay and would have cost Leo a pretty penny. But it seems to be in a state of disrepair. There are piles of building materials covered with tarps on the overgrown front yard, and there's a lot of peeling paint around the windows and gutters. He's obviously bought himself a project home.

Picking my way over the broken pathway, I make my way to the front door and stand still for a few seconds, checking that my hair feels smooth and my breath smells fresh. I've gone a little overboard in my appearance, putting on a dress and heels like we're going somewhere fancy. But I was nervous and getting dressed up helped me feel a little more in control of my emotions. I'm less likely to burst into tears if I have eye make-up on, and I'm less likely to chicken out and run away if I'm in heels. Plus, this outfit makes me feel pretty, and I want to be pretty for Leo. No. I want to look pretty for me. I've hated every minute away from Leo, but in some ways it's been the break I needed so I could understand myself better. And love what I see, something I'm still working on. So, this dress is for me...and hopefully, Leo will like it too.

Taking hold of the brass door knocker, I tap it against the heavy oak door, my heart thud-thudding as I wait. There are voices inside, then the creak of floorboards and footsteps coming my way. *This is it, Darcy. Make or break time. Don't fuck it up.*

A deadbolt turns then Leo is right in front of me like a dream and in the jeans and T-shirt he was wearing earlier. His eyes light up as they drink me in, making me so glad I took the extra care in my appearance.

"You look—"

"I want to press play on our relationship again." The words burst from my mouth before he can invite me in or even say hello. A premature declaration.

His eyes fly up to mine, and a second later he catches me about the waist and pulls me against him, kissing me so hard my head spins and my body sings, missing this man with every fibre of my being.

"Does that mean you want to press play too?" I ask, breathless when we come up for air.

A chuckle rumbles out of Leo's chest. "Get in here,

Darce," he says, stepping aside to let me inside his new house.

The furnishings are a little sparse, but I see the potential here. High pressed-metal ceilings, glossy oak floors, and large living areas with a fireplace in the living room.

"You're fixing this up?" I ask as I look around and spot a fabric tarp on the floor where he's been fixing a cornice in the dining room.

"It's my passion project," he says, his chest inflating as he looks around like he's seeing it with me for the first time. "I started in the kitchen. Redid all the cabinets—even installed a radio."

"A radio?" I smile, and he does too.

"How else does one dance while washing up?"

Tears fill my eyes. "I suppose you could dance to no music at all," I say, my heart filling up. *He remembered.*

Taking my hand, he gives it a gentle tug. "Let me show you around some more. I have something special I want to show you."

He shows me the first floor, detailing the beautiful work he's doing in each room before he takes me to see the main bedroom.

"It's in here," he says, pushing the door open.

My heart almost bursts as he directs me so I'm standing in front of a stunning handmade dressing table. "You made this?" I ask, running my hand over the stained wood.

"For you. I wanted to create a space here for you. For all of you. There are three bedrooms upstairs. One for each kid. So, when you're ready, I am too."

My eyes fill and I blink rapidly. "That's what this is?"

I ask, my voice almost a whisper. "You bought this place for all of us?"

He nodded, concern in his hazel eyes. "Is it too much?"

I shake my head. "No. It's perfect. It's..." It's thoughtful, it's unexpected, it's a testament to this man's heart, because he's made space for me and my children in his home. Even though we were apart and our future seemed uncertain, he built his life around us as a family. He didn't just wait for me. He *planned* for me. Planned emotionally, physically *and* financially. For us. All of us. *How did I come to deserve such a man?* Overwhelmed, I turn in his arms and kiss him with every emotion I possess. "I love you, Leo" I whisper. "I love you."

"Oh, angel," he whispers in return. "I love you too. So much it hurts."

Then we fall onto the bed and make out like a couple of teenagers, keeping it clean because we know we aren't alone. Niall is upstairs, and while there isn't anything terribly wrong with having sex while he's here, I think both Leo and I want our first time back together to be as private and unrestrained as possible.

Instead, we spend the rest of the night and a lot of the early morning talking. We talk about ourselves, our kids, our relationship, the mistakes we've made and how we simply can't exist without the other in our life. No matter what comes from this point on, we walk our paths together.

"So, what do we do now?" I ask, curled up beside him, loving that I'm in his arms again. After months without this closeness, I finally feel like me again.

He slides his hand over my hip and presses his fingers into my flesh, dragging me a little closer. "We hold on and never let go. I don't think I need to remind you of the agony these past couple of months have caused."

"No. When Betsy read my cards and told me you were my key to happiness, she never mentioned how painful the path without you would feel. It was like living with only half a heart."

"Or soul," he says, brushing his fingers along my jaw.

"Do you believe in soulmates?"

"I didn't. My mother did. She said once you've found your one, you'll never want another. I didn't believe that for a long time. But now I know what she meant."

"Do you think that's why she never married?" I ask, knowing very little about Leo's mother besides the fact she was a lot like Nana and fiercely independent during a time when it wasn't easy for a woman to be so.

"She only ever said that she loved a man once, and that was enough for her."

"How sad."

"If she spent her life feeling half as bad as we've been feeling, it's tragic."

"I agree. I never believed in soulmates before now either, as I thought we learned to love the person we're with. But now, I truly believe that when you find your other half, you become one. I don't want to ever be without you again."

He wraps me in his arms and kisses the top of my head. "You don't have to," he says. "I'm not going anywhere."

I smile and nuzzle my face against the intoxicating

heat of his chest, listening to his heart, his breath, the soft vibration of his voice, and I feel like I'm finally home. Home in the arms of the man I love.

I WAKE up early the next morning in almost exactly the same position, rejuvenated from the first decent sleep I've had in weeks upon weeks. It's funny how you can go your entire life not knowing a person exists, then a few weeks after meeting them, your hearts and souls are intrinsically tied together in a knot so tight even death can't break it. As I look up to Leo's sleeping face, I run my fingers along his stubbled jaw, thinking how lucky I am to find such a man. One who had enough faith in our relationship to weather the storm of my angry teenager and his bitter ex. He never gave up on us once—even though his confidence wavered for a moment there—the evidence of his certainty in the dwelling around us, big enough to fit both of our families under one roof.

That's right, he bought a house for us, one that's halfway between Niall's school and Abby and Archer's school. It's why he put his place up for sale, so he could move in here and work on repairs while he waited for our paths to align.

"What if they didn't align until the kids were grown?" I asked.

"Then we'd have a nice big house for when the grandkids visit."

"I love how sure you are."

"The moment I drove past and saw the sign out front,

I knew this would be the place we grow old in. It may not be today or tomorrow, but you will live here with me. I've no doubt of that. This is our home."

I like the sound of that. A home with Leo. When both of my kids are comfortable with Leo in our lives and Niall is comfortable with me, I'd love nothing more than to merge our families into one big happy one.

"I love you even more than I did yesterday," I whisper, pressing a kiss beneath his chin. He makes a small noise, but he's so fast asleep that I don't want to disturb him, so I slip from beneath the covers and visit the ensuite bathroom before heading into the kitchen in search of coffee.

I'm messaging Nana to check on the kids as I round the corner and almost drop my phone when Niall says, "We have to stop meeting like this."

Just like that time when Leo and I fell asleep on the couch, Niall is sitting at the table eating cereal while I walk around barefoot. "Good morning, Niall," I say, giving him a smile before asking where things are.

"Let me show you," he says, getting up from his chair and walking into the kitchen to start up the coffee machine and show me where all the pods are. "There's a bunch of flavours in here. Dad prefers the Italian roast. I like the French, personally."

"Thank you, Niall," I say, collecting a mug for myself. "Would you like me to make you a cup?"

He has the exact same half-grin as his father. "Never thought you'd ask," he says before he grabs the milk and helps me work through the steps of the machine since it's much fancier than my freeze-dried coffee and a kettle version.

When we're done, we sit down together and take a sip of the liquid gold in our hands. "I feel like my brain is finally waking up," I say.

"That must be something. Mine never seems to go to sleep."

"I read that the teenage brain doesn't rest properly until about three a.m.. It's why you have trouble getting to sleep then feel tired in the morning."

"Hmm. Then how come adults are always tired?"

"Because we're practically geriatric," I say, fighting a smile.

He at least reddens as he rubs at the back of his head. "I was a bit of a douche that day."

I shrug. "We've all struggled, I think. Don't feel too bad about it."

"Did he...did Dad tell you about my, um, misplaced advice?" he asks, eyes glancing between me and his mug as I make a noise in the affirmative.

"Yes. And like your dad, I hope we can all move on from this. Your dad and I just want to be happy, and I think if you kids can give our relationship a chance, then we can all be happy together."

"You don't just date the woman, you date her family too," he says with a nod. "I read that in a magazine at the doctor's office once. I forgot my phone."

I'm starting to feel like I'm listening to a seventeen-year-old version of Archer. No wonder Leo likes him so much. "Well, it's very insightful."

He shrugs. "It applies to men too, I guess, since you

have a family and Dad has a family and we're all gonna live here one day."

"You know about that?"

He squints a little as he scratches behind his neck. "Yeah. And I don't mind. I've never had siblings, but it'll be cool."

"I'm not sure when it'll happen, but it's good to know you're OK with it."

"I'm going to uni next year, so I won't be home as much, but there's plenty of room here. We can make something here that none of us had before: a functioning family."

"I like the sound of that, Niall," I say, just as hands slide over my shoulders and Leo kisses me on the neck.

"I like the sound of that too," Leo says, taking the seat next to me. He picks up my coffee and takes a sip. "Nice to see you two chatting."

"I had to apologise for calling her your geriatric lover the last time she slept over. Which, judging by the fact you two are *both* wearing the clothes you wore last night was completely innocent again. Lame guys, lame." Niall shakes his head as he stands with his now empty coffee cup and places it in the dishwasher, while I wonder how he knew what clothes I was wearing last night but decide not to ask. It's probably evident by the fact my dress is crushed from sleeping in it.

"Hey, we were thinking of heading to the hospital fete a bit later if you want to tag along," Leo says as Niall excuses himself.

"Yeah," he says. "What time?"

"Twelve? We've got to go back to Darcy's first then

we'll head over. I can grab you on the way through if you want."

"Nah, I'll come with you to Darcy's." He grabs the back of his neck again and frowns. "I...um...I'm *really* sorry, Darcy. I've been a total dick to you. Watching you with Dad, it's really obvious that you two are cool together. I've never seen him like this. So, yeah, if I can come with you, that would be cool."

## FIFTY-THREE

## DARCY

"There was a bag sitting right here," Nana says, pointing at the empty spot on the floor. "It was *full* of willy warmers. Does anyone know what happened to them?"

"What bag? I know of no bag," a croaky voice comes from the direction of the couch where a little hand is poking up, using the dragon willy-warmer as a puppet.

"Perhaps it's a cave to you, Mr Dragon," I say, grinning at the silliness of this moment. "Do you have many friends in there?"

"He has me. *Ba-gock!*" Archer's other hand comes over the back of the couch and it's got a rooster on it—the penis part is over his fingers and the ball part over the rest of his fist. "I'm here for dinner. But he doesn't seem to have any food." He's using a high-pitched voice for the chicken.

"Well then, what are you going to eat?" I ask, playing along.

The dragon talks again. "I don't know about you, but

I'm having chicken. NOM NOM NOM!" He throws the chicken to the side while Nana and I laugh at his antics.

Abigail looks at her nails and rolls her eyes. "There are so many things wrong with this." Then she gets up and takes the crocheted animals off Archer's hands and throws them back in the bag.

"Hey, Mummy," Archer says, running over to hug me good morning.

"Hi, Mum," Abby says as she hands the bag of willy warmers to Nana. "I thought you'd have Leo with you." I smile because I love that she's being considerate and understanding when getting to this point was difficult for her. Sure, Niall egged her on, but the dissent was already there. He couldn't have made her do anything she didn't want to. Abigail and I needed these past weeks to see each other as human beings as well as parent and child. As much as I missed Leo, our time apart led us all to this moment.

"I did," I say, stepping to the side as Leo appears in the doorway with Niall right beside him.

"Leo," Archer shrieks, jumping off the ground in hyperactive joy before he launches himself at Leo and almost bowls him over. I have flashes of Leo going down and twisting his knee again, but thankfully that doesn't happen.

"Hey, buddy." Leo laughs, hugging him back. "It's so awesome to see you."

At the same time, Abigail's eyes light up. "Niall," she says, rushing to him and landing against him in a hug that isn't nearly as ferocious as Archer's. "It's good to see you."

"Same to you, little sis. Thought I'd come over and make sure you stay out of trouble."

They release each other and Abby laughs, her hand over her mouth. "Oh God, don't call me that. It's so weird."

Niall shrugs. "Better get used to it. These two lovebirds are the real deal. So that makes us family."

"So, I'm getting a big brother?" Archer asks.

"Do you want a big brother?" Niall responds.

Archer tilts his head in thought. "That depends, will you give me money?"

"No." Niall laughs.

"Archer," I admonish, trying not to laugh, because I never know what's coming out of his cheeky little mouth.

"That's exactly something a big brother would say," Archer says unfazed. "You can stay."

"My lord, we're all jumping so far ahead of ourselves," I say. "Leo and I only just started dating properly."

"Oh, sweetheart," Nana says. "They're not jumping the gun, they're facing facts. You and Leo are together and this"—she gestures with her hand to everyone in the room—"is your happily ever after. Enjoy it, and don't waste any more time fighting it. Lord knows, you've already done enough of that."

"I guess this means you can put your hex book away," I joke. "No need to pull out the cauldron."

"Pish." She waves a hand about. "A good cauldron should always be handy for when the need arises."

"I'm not even going to address that, are you?" Leo asks out of the side of his mouth.

"Not on your life," I say back while we watch Nana gather her things and ask Archer if he's almost ready to go. He runs off to get his portable charger so his phone battery doesn't go flat during filming.

"What time does the fete start?" I ask Nana, who is going through the bag of willy warmers one last time to check they're all there.

"Nine. Although Helen and Norma are already there, getting things set up."

"Norma?"

"Yeah. She's new. Martha is out. She has osteoporosis, had a fall, so now her son has put her into a nursing home in case she shatters a hip or something."

"That's terrible. She didn't fall because she was drunk, did she?" The amount those ladies drink during their crafting sessions could pickle the whole ocean.

"Not that I'm aware of. I think she slipped coming out of the shower. Poor woman was lying there for two hours before anyone found her. Lucky. It could have been days if she didn't have all of us."

"Who found her?"

"Leo, actually." She smiles at the gorgeous man beside me with absolute fondness. I'd called her to see if she wanted to go for a walk and she wasn't answering. We check in on each other every day, you see. At our age, you have to so the cats don't eat your eyes."

"You don't have a cat, Nana."

"Neither did Martha."

"A cat *ate her eyes*?" I can't think of anything more disturbing.

"No," Nana says. "But one would of if Leo hadn't come to help when I called."

I turn to Leo and nudge him lightly in the side with my elbow. "Saving old ladies while working two jobs and fighting for custody of your son. Is there anything you can't do?"

"I think we established that I suck at barbecuing steak. But I have your secret recipe in my wallet, so pretty soon I'll be awesome at that as well."

"First he'll take over Bayside," Niall teases. "Next stop, the world."

We all laugh as Leo says, "You better believe it."

Archer comes running back in with his charger and phone. "I'm ready," he gasps, puffed from his haste.

"What are you doing with that?" Niall asks. "Is that an iPhone?"

"Yeah." Archer holds it up. "It's just a six, and I can only take videos and call Mum, but that's OK."

"OK?" Niall says. "That's awesome, I didn't get a phone until I was in high school."

Archer shrugs. "That's because you're older than me. Everyone has phones now. You should probably get with the times."

Niall laughs. "This kid is great."

"I'm smart too," Archer continues. "I'm filming Nana's stall to put on my YouTube channel. I reckon it'll be like those social experiments with the homeless people that go viral. You make ten thousand dollars for a viral video, you know? *American* dollars. That's more in Australian money, isn't it, Mummy?"

"Yeah, mate. Around fourteen thousand, I suppose."

"How's it gonna go viral, Archer?" Abigail asks. "You only have like, thirty followers."

"Thirty-five," he shoots back.

"OK, thirty-five. *Sorry*. I'm sure it'll be a sensation." She lifts her phone and looks at the screen. "My friends are meeting at the beach before we walk to the fete. You coming with?" she asks Niall.

"Yep," he says. "See you all there." Then they wave and they're off.

"Are we going to have to worry about them?" I ask Leo as we watch Niall and Abby walk along the footpath talking animatedly.

"I don't think so," he says, slipping his arm around my waist. "Niall understands the age difference and if he's calling her his sister already, I think he's drawing a line in the sand."

"That's good, and I'm glad they're getting along. This morning has been so wonderful. I woke up in your arms, the kids are happy and getting along, and I can't stop smiling." I press my hands to my cheeks. They're warm and round under my palms.

"I want to wake up next to you every morning," he replies, leaning down to kiss the tip of my nose. "The moment you're ready, I want you to move in. Esme is right. I think we've waited long enough."

"Of course, I'm right," Nana says as she bustles towards the door. "I don't understand why anyone would think otherwise." She stops in front of us, a big grin on her face as she looks from Leo to me before taking in the way we're embracing. "Now this, *this* is what I wanted for you all along, my dears. Both of you. Why don't I take

Archer on my own and give you the opportunity to have a few moments of peace? You can come by the fete a little later." She gives us a wink and nods as she hustles Archer out the door. The decision is made in her mind, so she doesn't wait for us to respond. It's not like we were *going* to object. A moment *alone*? What kind of heaven is this?

"See ya, Mummy," Archer says, rushing out with Nana with his phone in his hand and his grin in place.

"Be good, OK?" I say to the dust in his wake.

"We'll be fine," Nana says with a waggle of her eyebrows as she closes the sliding door, leaving Leo and me to the quiet.

"We're alone," he whispers.

We stand still for about two seconds before we're kissing and pulling at each other's clothes. We get his shirt off and the zip of my dress is undone before I place my hands on his chest and pull back. "Wait, wait. Let's not rush this," I say, panting, fingers caressing his deliciously warm skin.

His chest rumbles and I smile up at him in a coy way. "I am desperate for you, angel."

"Hmm, I like it when you call me that."

"Good, it's what you are to me." He bows his head and teases the lobe of my ear with his tongue.

"You still have furniture in your apartment, right?"

"I do. I left it behind so the real estate could stage the room or whatever it is they do."

"Then let's go over there. I feel a little funny doing this in my Nana's apartment—not that she'd care. In fact, she'd probably give me a trophy." I laugh, excited and nervous to be on the precipice of reuniting our bodies as one, and I want to get myself ready, make this special, and go somewhere we aren't going to be disturbed. "How about you give me a minute to shower and freshen up for you and I'll meet you there?"

"Hmm." He narrows his eyes in thought. "Can I wait for you naked?"

"You can wait for me any way you want."

"All right," he says, reluctantly stepping back. "Just don't take too long." Have I mentioned how much I love the way this man's eyes shine when he looks at me. I mean, they twinkle. *Twinkle.* I feel like I'm the literal light of his life.

"I wouldn't dream of it."

## FIFTY-FOUR

## DARCY

"You still have your pants on," I say when I walk into his apartment and find him drinking from a bottle of water while he watches the yachts in the bay. He's quite a sight to behold—tan muscular torso, jeans that hug his arse perfectly. I have this urge to lick him all over, slide my fingers between the ridges his muscles create. I want to grab him, bite him, devour him. *My lord, it's been too long.* He turns his head towards me and gives me the benefit of his soft green gaze, warm and fuzzy as it settles inside my chest. Now mine is bursting, I could write an entire book describing my feelings for him and it still wouldn't be enough. He's my one.

"The unwrapping is part of the fun." He grins and offers me some of his water. I shake my head as I pull the sash open on my silk dressing gown, letting it fall open just enough to show him there's nothing on underneath. "Holy fucking hotness," he says, capping the water and throwing it on the couch before he comes straight for me. "I don't think I've ever felt this happy before, Darcy." His hands slip underneath the silken material, rough, warm and strong against my skin. I'm total mush.

"Me either," I admit, biting my lips as I try to control my smile. This is so crazy, feeling so strongly towards a man who, in the grand scheme of things, I've known for such a short time. But after all we've been through, it feels like we fought a lifetime to find each other. This is the real thing, that connection they write love stories about, the one you'd do absolutely anything for. "I love you, Leo."

"I love you too, angel."

With his fingers settling about the flesh on my waist, he pulls me close and wraps me tight as his mouth meets mine and we lose ourselves in a soul-searing kiss. The world around us slips away as my body remembers what it's like to be alive, to have his hands on me, his tongue exploring, his need pressing. In one of his delicious displays of strength, he scoops me into his arms and continues kissing me as he carries me to the bedroom, bumping into the wall before he sets me on my feet at the foot of the bed.

"That floor is deceptively flat," he says as he pushes the robe off my shoulders and kisses my smooth skin before he lets the material float to the floor. He steps back for a moment to admire the view. "This is my favourite outfit of yours."

"I have to agree. I prefer you with a lot less clothes as well." With a laugh, I pop the top button on his jeans, sliding down the zip before reaching my hand inside to find... "Um. What am I feeling right now?"

He grins, eyes shining with mischief. "You'll have to undress me to find out."

Taking a seat on the edge of the bed, I push his jeans down his hips then just about choke when I find one of the willy warmers covering his dick—a crocodile to be exact. I fall back on the bed, clutching my stomach laughing.

"You like that?" he asks, kicking his jeans off the rest of the way so he's standing there in nothing but the willy warmer.

I lift my head and take another look at him, dropping back on the bed as I laugh some more, my stomach hurting as I force out the words, "You look so ridiculous. Oh my God." I'm crying. "I love you so much."

He leans over me on the bed, his eyes intense as he looks down at me. "I will love you, every part of you, until the day I die," he declares, turning this crazy moment into one filled with absolute, heart-swelling joy. "You are the woman of my dreams and I never want us to be apart again."

I place my hands on either side of his head, fingers sliding into his hair as he leans in and kisses me, soft at first, then deep and possessive until he's completely stolen my breath.

""I never want to be apart either," I say, sliding my fingers down the muscles on his back before they catch on the cord that ties the willy warmer to his waist. "But this"—I pull on the string and loosen it—"I can part with."

With a laugh, he brushes his nose next to mine. "It's surprisingly comfortable."

"Really?" I say as I pull it from between us. "I'd have thought it'd be all scratchy from the wool."

"Whatever they used is incredibly soft. It's like a good quality sock."

"A cock sock," I say, laughing all over again.

"Hmm, I love the sound of your laughter." He wraps his arms around me and we roll until he's on his back and I'm on top, his hands go to my breasts, squeezing before he crunches up and takes my nipple into his mouth, sucking back and doing these fantastic flicky things with his tongue. "I love everything about you."

*Everything.*

I moan and scrape my nails up his back, through his hair, my hips grinding as my craving for friction gets the better of me. "I love everything about you too. I've missed you so much."

With a low groan, he pushes me back on the bed, placing his hand at the base of my throat before dragging it all the way down to my mound where he pauses then detours until he's gripping my hip. "Promise me you'll never leave, Darcy."

"I promise," I say, my chest feeling full as I drink him in. My perfect man. He has a few scars on his body from years of sports scrapes, and if I squint, his nose is a little crooked, so I suppose, if I really look for it, I can find tiny flaws to convince myself that this man isn't too good to be true. Because that's how he seems. He makes me feel as though it's OK to just be me, to be a little crazy, to want the things I want, to not be perfect and to sometimes be selfish. He's been nothing but supportive and present, and I'm honestly thinking I've found my soulmate. Like

Leo, I hadn't believed they were real, but when I'm in the presence of a man who simply *gets* me without any added bullshit, I feel sure they do exist. It's like he's been made for me. I know I keep saying it, but I love him. I love him.

"Come here," he says, pulling me by the hand until I'm sitting up with him, my arms wrapping around his neck as our mouths connect, kissing while he holds my hips and guides himself inside me. Everything fits together wonderfully, and I moan into his mouth as I push through my thighs rising and lowering to meet the mutual movement of our hips.

"I will love you forever," I whisper, my body tingling, our breath mingled, fingers pressing into skin.

"Forever and then some," he returns, holding me tight as he lowers me back on the bed, hooking one thigh over his shoulder as he drives in deeper, just the way he knows I like it. "You feel so good, Darcy. Touch yourself for me, I want to come together."

"I want that too," I gasp, sliding my hand between us and using my middle fingertip to swirl my arousal around my clit.

"God, that's hot," he grunts, curving his body so he can see the movement of my hand and the in and out of his thrusts. "Tell me when you're close."

"I'm close," I gasp, my breasts growing heavy, my insides coiling. "So close."

"Holy shit," he hisses, straining through gritted teeth.

"I'm there. I'm there."

With a rumbling hum, he thrusts in deep, grinding our hips together so our connection is as deep as possible.

"I love you," he whispers as he kisses me, both of us floating down from our combined orgasm.

"I love you too. So much."

We spend a little more time kissing and touching, revelling in the afterglow of great sexual chemistry and honest emotion. I feel so complete in this man's arms, knowing he's in my life for good now. I'm never letting anyone mess with our happiness again.

## FIFTY-FIVE

LEO

"What were you like when you were playing rugby?" Darcy asks, lying next to me on the bed in my apartment. We're doing that thing where you lie in each other's arm and play with each other's hands. She's currently running the pad of her thumb over the nail on mine, slowly learning how to recognise every part of me by touch. I inhale her hair, scenting her shampoo and the sunshine held there. I love the way she smells. Vanilla and sea breeze.

"I don't think I was too different from how I am now. I was very driven back then, focused on training. I guess I was a little more intense, definitely shallower. My priorities were messed up in those early years but by the end of my career, I was pretty much the same man I am now."

"I can imagine it would be easy to get caught up in the fame and attention in the beginning."

"The attention leading up to and during the season was intense. We were treated like we were something more than just a guy who was lucky because he was born good at sport. So yeah, we all got cocky and thought we were kings. Did a lot of stupid, immature stuff that guys who are constantly competing with each other get up to. People recognise you, ask for your autograph, your photo...it's a different world with different standards. It was very surreal."

"Even now people think you're important. You should have heard the way everyone in town was talking when the cameras were here yesterday."

"Hmm. Lucky they realised I wasn't here anymore and cleared out, or we would have been fighting them again today."

"They would have loved taking shirtless photos of you while you were watching the yachts before."

I chuckle. "Wouldn't be the first time."

"It must suck knowing that someone could snap your photo and put it in a newspaper or magazine at any given moment."

"For a while, I hated it. But it doesn't happen much anymore. There's a bit of attention here and there, especially during the season when I commentate and a little more during the awards season, so unless Tash is stirring up trouble, I'm yesterday's news. And I prefer it that way."

"You must be glad she's stopped fighting you."

"I am. This is what I've wanted for so long: the chance to be the best father I can be to Niall. But I don't like that I had to out Tash's behaviour publicly to achieve it."

"Do you think you would have won the court battle if Nana hadn't released that video?"

"I think so. I had evidence of her manipulative behaviour coming out of my ears. She had absolutely nothing on me. However, I *really* appreciate what Esme did. It ended something that could have dragged on for weeks, if not months."

She rolls to her side so she's facing me, and I rest my hand in the curve of her waist, moving my fingers lightly against her skin. I love the shape of her. The curves. The softness.

"I'm sorry I wasn't with you when everything was falling apart."

"I'm sorry I pushed you away when you tried," I tell her honestly. "But in the end, I think we both needed to clear out the demons from our past so we could come together without any bullshit holding us back. We have a stronger foundation this way." I hug her to me, feeling ridiculously happy and complete with her lying naked in my bed.

She takes a deep breath, then slides her hand up my arm before transferring it to my chest, just over my heart. "You are so incredibly amazing, Leo Murphy. I hope you realise that."

"I'm really not," I say with a chuckle.

"It's true. I mean, look at you. You're Mary Poppins."

"Mary Poppins?" I laugh, not sure if that's a compliment or a jibe.

"'Practically perfect in every way,'" she quotes.

"I am definitely not perfect."

"I beg to differ here. Let's start with your looks."

"That's not at all shallow."

"I'll go deeper." She smiles and presses up on her

elbow as she moves her fingers up and down my chest. "You're older than me but you look even better now than you did in your twenties."

I laugh because this is absurd.

"It's true. You have a body to die for, the face of an Italian suit model, and the smile of the quintessential Aussie guy. Even your toes are good-looking."

"My toes?"

"Yes." She laughs. "And then there's everything else about you. Your personality is calm and rational. You're scary as hell when you're angry, but you're *controlled*, which I really admire. You're *amazing* in bed. So good in fact, that if I heard one of my girlfriends bragging about her husband or boyfriend doing the same, I'd think she was making it up. And on top of all of that, you're great with my kids. Archer loves you. He cried with happiness when he saw you again, Leo. *Cried*. And even Abigail never disliked *you*. She just didn't like sharing me."

"Wow. I think I want to date me now."

"I'm serious, Leo. You're wonderful. And I think Nana was right before."

"About?" Esme is right about so many things I need clarification here.

"About us waiting for each other long enough."

"Does this mean you want to move in?"

"I'll talk to the kids about it, and if they agree, then yes. I want to be crazy, in love, living as a family with you."

Without a second's hesitation, I grab her by the back of her head and kiss her hard, rolling us both so she's lying beneath me and I'm showing her how goddamn happy she makes me feel. She might think that I'm all kinds of wonderful, but I feel almost unworthy of someone like her. She loves with everything she has and doesn't even think of herself before making a sacrifice to benefit someone else. "I am far from perfect, but I will spend the rest of my life trying to be the man you deserve, angel."

"You're already so much more than that. You're a gift."

I laugh before kissing her again. "There's plenty wrong with me, I assure you."

"I can't see it."

"Give it time. I'm sure that six months down the track, we'll piss each other off over something stupid like leaving a pair of shoes in the middle of the floor and we'll have a huge fight where everything little seems to get on our nerves and we're not sure if we're even compatible anymore."

"Oh God. I *do not* want to have that fight," she says, wrinkling her nose. While we're still so in bliss mode, it's hard to contemplate being that annoyed with her. But I'm a realist. Both of us have been married before—well, technically, Darcy still is—so we know we're going to piss each other off at some point. However, I have no doubt that each roadblock that life throws our way will be something we get through together. I've never felt this strongly about someone who wasn't my own flesh and blood before.

"It'll be OK. Because that'll mean we get to make up. And since we already know I can be a bit of a closed-off arsehole when I'm pissed, I'll probably have a lot to make up for."

"OK, I'm liking the sound of this a lot better now."

"Will it make you feel any better if I tell you I'm super anal about tidiness? I'm terrible at sharing. I'll get jealous if you so much as smile at another man, and you already know I can't cook."

"That does make me feel a little better. And I'd list my bad traits for you, but I think you've already seen most of them. I'm not the best at hiding my bad side."

"Your so-called bad side is nothing. Believe me. You've met Tash, and you, my angel, are a walk in the park by comparison."

"Oh." She grins. "Is this the part where you tell me how amazing you think I am?"

I smile as my hand slides around her waist and I grip her arse, pulling her flush against me. "This is the part where I fuck you while I tell you how amazing you are." I grind my hips against hers, my growing need pressing into her thigh.

"See what I mean? You're always going that extra mile," she says, before I silence that beautiful mouth of hers with a kiss, thanking my lucky stars because this gorgeous, perfect, funny and precious woman is mine. I can't wait to spend every day of the rest of my life with her.

## FIFTY-SIX

## DARCY

"There are so many more people here than I expected," I say as Leo finds a parking spot near the fete. We've been circling around for almost twenty minutes trying to find something.

"It's a huge deal around here. Lots of wealthy retirees and families with kids live around here. It's a good way to give back to the community, appease the guilt of capitalism, and have fun at the same time."

When he pulls into the car space, we jump out of his ute and he holds out his hand for me to take. I smile because this is the first time I've been able to hold his hand in public. We've always been such a secret before now, skulking around in the dark and in quiet corners. As I slide my fingers between his, a sense of freedom and belonging envelops me. I have 'I love him, I love him' running on a loop inside my head.

"I wonder how Nana and her Bayside Biddies are doing." As we cross the street, I can hear the thump of bass in the air along with the hum of a chattering crowd.

The air smells sweet and feels light while fete goers mill about, children carry fluffy pink fairy floss on a stick that's almost bigger than their heads, and parents are weighed down with bags, exhaustion in their eyes.

"Holy shit." Leo laughs and covers his mouth as a group of raucous teen boys burst through the seam of the crowd. That in itself isn't so unusual, but the energy of the crowd around them, the intakes of breath, the giggles and the pointing are what draw our attention.

"Oh my God." I'm covering my mouth too, because each and every one of them is wearing a little crocheted animal on the *outside* of their clothes, zippers open so they fit correctly of course.

Leo's chest rumbles with laughter as he swipes his free hand across his face. "Looks like the willy warmers are selling well."

"Maybe you should have worn yours?" I meet his eyes and we both burst out laughing as we spot a few more young guys walking around wearing them.

"They've started a new trend," I say as we weave our way through the crowd, finding roosters, dragons, snakes, and elephants. *Definitely of various shapes and sizes.* I can barely keep a straight face.

"Hey, mate." Leo taps one on the arm. "Where'd you get your decoration from?"

The kid laughs and tells him some old ladies are selling them near the food trucks. "I'd hurry if you want one. They didn't have many left when we were there."

"Thanks for the info."

Weaving a little farther through the throng, we spot Nana and her ladies laughing up a storm while they rearrange the table. At a glance, it looks like they only have about six warmers left.

"Successful day?" I ask as we reach the table.

Nana beams. "Can you believe it? We made about a hundred of these things and there's hardly any left."

"You're a roaring success."

"The hospital fund will love us."

"I bet they will. Where's Archer?"

"Oh, Helen took him to the Mr Whippy van for an ice cream cone."

"Is this your granddaughter?" A lady I've never seen before leans in and smiles at me.

Nana places her hand on the woman's back in a friendly gesture. "Oh yes, Norma, this is Darcy. Darcy. Norma."

Norma holds her hand out to me. "Your son is the most adorable boy," she says. "He's been really helpful all day."

"I suppose he hasn't managed to get the sensational video he was after?"

"Oh, he's been filming on and off. We've been having such a lovely time. Is this your husband?" she asks, gesturing towards Leo who's chatting with Betsy at the end of the table. He gives me a wink.

"Not my husband," I say with a smile. "But he is mine."

Nana leans in. "Darcy split with her shit stain of a husband late last year. Leo is her reward for almost twenty years of servitude."

"Nana," I chide, still not liking the idea of putting Kevin down to raise myself up. If it wasn't for my marriage to him, I wouldn't have my children, and I certainly wouldn't have been in the right place at the right time to find Leo. In the end, everything has worked out as it should.

"Ah yes," Norma says, a knowing look in her eyes. "I used to say that about my fourth husband. Not that he was a shit stain, that he was my reward for being with the wrong men for decades before."

"You're not married anymore?" I ask, feeling a slight pang in my chest at the idea her fourth marriage didn't work out either.

"Widowed," she explains. "He passed last year. So, I'm here trying new things, trying to live for the both of us until my time comes and we're together again."

"That's really beautiful, Norma."

"She's going to join the Bayside Biddies," Nana says. "I'm taking her trike shopping tomorrow morning, and we've already ordered her shirt."

"I've actually got an embroidery machine, so I'm going to make us patches to go on our leather jackets for winter," Norma adds, and I immediately know that she and Nana will become fantastic friends. I can just see them both sitting on Nana's deck smoking weed while Betsy sucks down cocktails and reads everyone's cards.

"Who's in charge here?" an angry voice demands, cutting into our conversation.

"I am," Nana proudly proclaims. "Is there something I can help you with?"

"Yes. You can pack up your table of filth and get out of here. Shame on you, selling these, these *things* to innocent people, claiming they're money pouches. You're old enough to know better."

"But they are money pouches," Nana says, her eyes wide and reassuring. "You see, the notes go in here." She pokes a finger into the penis pocket. "And your change goes here." She wiggles her fingers in the testicle pocket. I cover my mouth as I try not to giggle, Nana's innocent act is just too good.

"I may be younger than you, madam, but I wasn't born yesterday. There's no way you don't see that for the penis pouch it is. For crying out loud, there are young men all over the fete wearing them through their zippers." *Penis pouch. Hahahahahahahhahaha.* Oh God. I'm wheezing.

"What young men choose to put in their money pouches is their business. I can't force them to use it for money when they'd rather use it to contain their willies."

I wipe a tear away and bite my lip to keep from cackling, and the woman splutters. "It's indecent."

By now a crowd has gathered around the table, and Leo has moved into a protective position, standing beside the table with his arms folded as though he's security keeping an eye on things. Niall appears on the other side —the Murphy security detail.

"What's going on?" Abigail asks as she slides in next to me.

"This woman is trying to take on Nana," I whisper.

"Oh," Abby says. "That's not going to end well for her." If a fourteen-year-old girl thinks an old lady is a badarse, you'd better believe it's the truth.

"Can you see any skin?" Nana asks the woman. Her face remains the picture of seriousness.

"That is not the point. Just look at what you've done." She sweeps her arm behind her, and sure enough, everywhere you look there's a guy wearing a cute animal puppet over his dick. "Just *look*." She points to Niall's crotch as her last piece of offered evidence. Abigail giggles because Niall is standing there wearing a rooster.

"Oh, you look wonderful, Niall," Nana says in response, and I can see the pride in her free-spirited eyes.

"This is an outrage."

Nana returns her attention to the red-faced woman. "Ma'am, if you've purchased one of our pouches and aren't satisfied with the product, you're welcome to return it for a full refund."

"There's no way I'd hand good money over for something as...*disgusting* as this."

"Then I'll kindly ask you to move along." I am so impressed with how calm Nana remains.

"I'll move when you pack up and go."

"There's nothing indecent about animal underwear, and as far as I'm aware, there's also no law against wearing your underwear on the outside of your clothes, otherwise no one would ever be able to go out in public dressed as their favourite superhero. So, I think we'll stay." Nana folds her arms and sits back in her seat, a challenge in her eyes.

"Then I'll call the police."

"Go right ahead."

"Aw come on," some guy says from the surrounding

crowd. "Leave the old ladies alone. They aren't hurtin' anyone."

The woman doesn't even acknowledge the guy and pulls out her phone, dialling the local police station. "Yes, I'd like to report several counts of indecent exposure," she says when she's connected.

"Hey, hey. Now, that's unnecessary," another onlooker says. "You're the one causing a disturbance."

"I won't be bullied by you, young man." She holds up her finger like she's talking to a naughty child.

"Put the phone down," the guy says, reaching forward to stop her, which is when Leo steps in. Despite the fact that this woman is the cause of the scene, he's not about to let some other guy put his hands on her. It's swoon-worthy stuff and I'm falling in love with him all over again, *and* filled with very lusty thoughts.

"Why protect her, bro?" the young guy says. "You with her?"

"Not on your life. But we don't need to give her a reason to play the victim here. The moment you touch her, she'll cry assault. It's easier to stand by and let her make a fool of herself off her own back. Don't you agree?"

The young guy pulls out his phone and nods. "Yeah, man. You're right. She'll make a great 'Get me the Manager' meme." He snaps a couple of pictures of her.

Leo shakes the guy's hand. "I don't know what that is, but it sounds like a good alternative."

There must be police on site, because it's only minutes before they arrive, and the woman is animatedly telling them how disgusted she is with the willy-warmer stall. She's gesturing at the young men wearing them, shaking her head so that her blonde bob is flicking left and right along with her wobbly cheeks. She's gotten herself into quite a tizz, so much that her face is bright red and I'm a little concerned she's going to stroke out.

"We're going to have to ask you to move along," one of the officers says. "We're a coastal community, ma'am. There's nothing being shown that you wouldn't see on the beach. In fact, they're wearing *more* clothes than they would on the beach."

The other officer picks up a crocheted lion and holds it out to Nana. "How much?"

"Ten dollars," she says, trying not to grin but failing miserably like the rest of us.

As the officer reaches into his pocket to pay the money, the crowd cheers and a few of the guys tell the woman to push off.

"This is ridiculous," she splutters. "You people, you're what's wrong with this world." Then she turns and grabs the table, tipping it so the rest of the willy warmers go flying along with the cashbox. Money spills everywhere. Chaos ensues as some greedy bastards grab for what they can. Thankfully, the crowd has more good people than shitdicks in the mix, and those trying to abscond are stopped and hauled in front of the cops to be reprimanded. In the end, the police leave the area with three people in tow—the original woman, who caused the scene, and a teenage boy and girl who tried to take the money. As far as I know, they let them all off with a warning and asked them to go home.

"That was so awesome," Archer says, appearing at my

side with his phone held between his hands. "When can we go home so I can edit this? It's gonna be so cool."

Leo and Niall put the table back to rights, while Abigail collects the fallen willy warmers. "I think we'll head off fairly soon, mate. Nana is almost finished here. Have you had fun?"

"This has been the best day," he says, a massive smile bursting past his cheeks.

"Oh, I'm definitely finished," Nana says, standing with the cashbox tucked under her arm. "I just have to take this to the money tent to donate to the hospital and we're good to go."

"Can I come with you, Nana?" Archer asks, bouncing on his toes.

"Of course, my boy," she says with a smile.

"I think I'll go too," Leo adds. "Just in case the vultures come back around."

"Me too," Niall says, joining them.

"See you guys back here," I say as they wander off, my heart doing a happy little skip when Archer slips his hand into Leo's and starts skipping alongside him.

"Leo's really good with him," Abby says, watching them with me.

"He is," I say, slipping my arm around her waist and hugging her to me. "I think Archer reminds him a lot of Niall as a boy."

"He's good with you too, Mum. I can already see how much happier you are being back with him. I'm sorry I came between you."

"Oh, darling," I say, hugging her a little tighter. "I understand how much you were hurting. It was unfair of me to think I could start up a new relationship when you were struggling so much with your father leaving."

"Have you heard anything back from your lawyer?"

Releasing her, I reach up and tuck a strand of her shiny brown hair behind her ear. "Not yet. But I don't want you to get your hopes up, OK? I don't want you hurt again."

"I'm OK, Mum. I guess I just miss him. I mean, I know he did some crappy things, but he's still my dad."

"Yes," I say. "And he'll always be your dad. I just don't know if he can be the kind of dad you need him to be."

She takes a big breath and sighs. "I'll be all right if he can't. I just wanted to try one last time, you know?"

"I definitely know," I say, understanding more than she knows after going through my parents' divorce when I was close to Abigail's age. My dad didn't disappear the way Kevin has, but due to his alcoholism, he wasn't the most reliable to be around. There were many weekends when he didn't even bother showing up.

After we finish helping the other ladies pack up, we carry most of the gear to Leo's ute and stack it in the tray.

"Looks like your paths joined again after all," Betsy says with a smile once I've hooked the cover back in place. She gives me a bit of a fright because she's so small and I almost elbowed her as I turned around.

"Or maybe this was the path I was always supposed to travel along," I suggest. "When you read my cards, you said I'd have to make some tough decisions to ensure my future happiness, and I think that's what I did. It sucked, but while Leo and I were apart, we both managed to sort out our family problems so we could be together without hurting anybody. I think both our families are stronger as a result, and we can start again with a blank canvas."

She winks. "That's a good way to look at it. Of course, I saw that in your cards all along. I just kept it to myself."

"Of course you did." With a laugh, I link my arm with hers as we walk back towards the fete with the others. "Can I ask you something, Betsy?"

"Anything."

"Did you...this sounds really silly." I wave a hand to wave it away.

"Spit it out, child. I'm getting older by the second."

"It's just...you did that chant spell on me in January. I've always wondered if maybe you and Nana cast a spell to bring me and Leo together."

Reaching the cleared trestle table, Norma hands Betsy her handbag before announcing that she and Helen are taking off. We say a quick goodbye before continuing our conversation.

"You think a spell could cause that amount of chemistry?" Betsy asks, looking far too amused to be taking me seriously.

"No. But, you've both made comments about how you knew we'd fit together. Then the tarot cards were so on point. I just need to know if it's all us or if you and Nana called for some universal guidance."

She reaches up a hand and pats me on the cheek. "No spells, sweetheart. Just plain old interfering match-making by some old ladies who think they know better."

"What do you mean?"

"You don't think it was a coincidence that you met Leo at the beach the exact moment he was out running with his shirt off?"

"That makes a lot of sense," I admit, remembering how Nana had specifically called him over before Archer decided to wipe him out. "I hope she didn't ask Archer to tackle him too."

"Oh, I doubt that. But I also wouldn't put it past her. When Esme gets an idea in her mind, there's little any of us can do to stop it. The moment you called and said your marriage was over, operation Leo and Darcy was in full effect. She's always said she thought you'd be wonderful together. And she was right."

I don't know whether to be annoyed or laugh. I choose to laugh. "Well, I suppose her heart was in the right place. And it's not as if she made Kevin leave me, so I can't really fault her anywhere."

"Oh, no, darling. She'd never do that. That scumbag husband of yours did that all on his own. Your life is going to be so much better now without him. I saw that in the cards too."

I lean in and give her a tight hug. "Thanks for being you, Betsy."

"Don't get too soppy with me, child, or I'll cry out the few remaining tears I have left and shrivel away to nothing."

It's at that point that Nana arrives with Leo, Niall, and Archer. "I've just had the most magnificent idea," she says, clapping her hands together.

"Spit it out, woman," Betsy says.

"Picture this." Nana holds her hands up in front of

her face. "A Bayside Biddies recruitment drive. We travel around the state, maybe even the country, recruiting other biddies to join our trikey gang. We can have yearly retreats where we tour wine country and drink ourselves silly."

"Will they have to patch in?" Betsy asks. "Because I want to be VP if we're doing the patch system."

Nana's eyes light up. "Yes," she says, almost in a hiss. "And I'm president. This will be perfect. Come with me, Bets. There's a biker stall set up near the cash tent. But don't worry, they're not the bad kind of bikers, they're called grey warriors or something like that—retired people travelling and having fun as a group. They can point us in the right direction to get our trikey gang out of Bayside and around the country."

"Let's take it to the world," Betsy says as they toddle off together, arm in arm.

"Oh no, Bets, we'll be dead before it gets that far. Be logical, we've got maybe ten years left in us."

"If you can't take over the world in ten years, Esme Sullivan, then I don't even want to know you," Betsy retorts.

"Fine, we'll take it to the world then," Nana says and that's the last we hear before they disappear into the crowd.

"Those two are nuts," Abby says, laughing.

"I think they're lit," Niall says, chuckling.

"You know, if I ever wrote a book about these women, no one would believe the things they get up to," I say.

"They'd have to," Archer says from beside me. "I have it all on video."

I place my hand on the top of his head and ruffle his hair. "I suppose you're right. Ready to go?"

"Hells yeah," he says, changing it to, "heck yeah," when I give him a stern eye.

"OK, let's go," Leo says, gesturing for Abby and Niall to leave too. This simple moment of walking towards Leo's ute as a single unit makes my heart happy.

"How'd everything go handing the cash in?" I ask Leo as we all climb into our seats, three kids in the back, Leo and I in front.

"Great. They donated over eight hundred dollars to the hospital fund."

"Who knew a bunch of cock socks would prove so popular?"

"They're bloody hot on your nuts though," Niall says from the back. "I had to take mine off or I reckon kids would be off the cards for my future."

"Maybe they're more of winter a thing," I say, also hoping Archer doesn't ask how warm nuts impedes making babies.

It doesn't take long before we're back at Nana's place, carrying the displays and supplies from the stall up to the deck. Archer is talking animatedly about how he's going to edit the video of the day and pretend he's a 'man on the news' reporting a story. He asks Leo if he can borrow a tie and Leo says sure thing, and everything is feeling as perfect as can be until a figure stands from Nana's outdoor table.

"I was wondering how much longer I was going to have to wait in this heat."

"Kevin?" I say, the bottom of my stomach falling out.

## FIFTY-SEVEN

## DARCY

"Dad." Abby grins and breaks into a run, slamming against her father's chest with the same ferocity Archer ran at Leo earlier this morning. By contrast, Archer remains by my side, holding my hand as he looks on.

"Why is he here?" he asks.

"I'm not sure," I say, my voice shaking because after all this time, I honestly didn't think I was going to see him again. And I don't know how I feel right now. *It's definitely not happy...*

"Hello, Archer," Kevin says as he releases Abigail and puts her about an arm's-length away from him. It hurts to watch because she's smiling, grateful that he's here, and he's already distancing himself. He's not here for his children.

"Hi, Dad," Archer says, holding tighter to my hand.

"Darcy." Kevin's eyes move to me then to Leo and Niall. "Who's this?"

"I'm none of your business," Niall snaps immediately,

his eyes narrow, nostrils flared as he takes in the scene as it plays out in front of him. It makes me realise how protective he is of Abigail already.

Leo steps forward. "Leo Murphy," he says, holding his hand out for Kevin to shake. "I'm Darcy's fella."

Kevin pulls his head back like he's surprised or perhaps disbelieving that anyone could actually want me when he didn't. Over these past few months, I've learned to let go of a lot of the anger I held towards him, but now it's all there, a pressure in my chest that has me wanting to yell at him until my voice is hoarse.

"Don't I know you from somewhere?" He studies Leo's face as he shakes his hand. "You're that guy in the papers. The footballer who married that Neighbours chick. Why the hell did you give *that* up?" *Is he insinuating what I think he is?* I feel like the unspoken 'for her' is hanging in the air.

Still holding on to Kevin's hand, Leo smiles in the way a fox would smile before eating a rabbit, then he leans in and says something I can't hear, something that makes Kevin's face pale.

"I'll leave you and Darcy to talk," he says when he pulls back, patting Kevin's shoulder before he releases his hand. "I'll be right next door." He directs the last part at me.

"So will I," Niall says, looking from me to Abigail.

"And so will I," Archer says, following along.

"Archer," Abigail says, the look on her face telling him to get right back here.

"No, it's good," Kevin says, nudging her on the shoulder. "You should go over there too. Give your mum and me the chance to talk."

"Will I get to talk to you too?" she asks hopefully.

"Maybe," he says, a flippant tone to his words. "We'll see."

Then Abby's expression falls along with her shoulders and she nods. "Goodbye, Dad," she says, bringing tears to my eyes, because this isn't any old goodbye. It's the goodbye of a girl who just lost hope.

"Yeah, bye, Abs," he says. Her face crumbles and she turns away from him, keeping it together as she dashes from Nana's deck to Leo's. I touch her arm in comfort as she flies past me then clutch at my chest when I see her land in Leo's arms and burst into tears as Niall closes the sliding door, shaking his head.

"You're an arsehole," I say, walking up onto the deck and dropping my handbag on the bench seat. "What is wrong with you?"

"You're blackmailing me and I'm the arsehole?" he says, sitting back down on Nana's outdoor setting. He has an earring now, a little diamond stud. His teeth are also whiter, and I'm pretty sure he's coloured his hair to cover up the grey. And he's been working out. He's even wearing a fitted T-shirt to show off his newly acquired muscles, tiny compared to Leo's, but they're there, along with his spray-on tan. *Who is this man?*

"It's not blackmail, Kevin. That money belonged to the family, not you. And you committed fraud. All I'm asking is for my fair share so I can pay out the debt you created in my name, support our children, and move on with my life."

"You didn't work for any of it. I supported you and your *hobbies* for twenty years."

"*What*? You never let me have a job. You stopped me from going back to uni after I had Abby. You didn't give me a choice. Jesus, Kevin, what is wrong with you? What is so wrong that you can't appreciate that you literally had it all. Kids who loved you, a devoted wife. I took care of you, I did everything you ever wanted of me. I nursed you through *cancer*. And the minute we left the oncologist's office, not only did you dump me callously, but you were *ready* to run. You had already taken *everything* and left me with *your* debt. What kind of monster does that? I was destitute, Kevin. *Your children* were destitute."

He crosses his legs at the ankle. "You were never going to go without. Your family was always going to step up and take you in, and it looks like that rich nana of yours jumped at the chance. You don't need or *deserve* my money."

"Your money? *Our* money. We're married, Kevin, so legally, it's half mine. Not to mention the fact that you're also responsible for two children we created together."

"You've got a substitute dad for them now too. You're doing just fine."

"No, Kevin," I say, my voice rising. "I'm not 'doing fine' off the back of someone else. I'm here working my arse off to provide for our kids. Don't you dare make out that I'm some money-grubbing bitch who's jumping from person to person with her hand out. Don't you fucking dare."

"Whatever, Darcy. You're not doing it hard."

I press my fingers against my temples and take a deep

calming breath. "Why are you even here? Is it to see the kids? To tell me how much you resent our life together? What?"

"I want the shoebox."

"The what?"

"The shoebox you took from the house. It was in the garage, full of receipts and stuff." Oh, the box Jo found with all the paperwork in it.

"The proof you committed fraud?"

He grins, and I stand here wondering what I ever saw in this man. He's by no means ugly to look at, but he is ugly on the inside. Ugly and selfish. I've had enough time away from him to realise how much he used me and kept me down. Now I feel free *and* loved, and my whole world is so much brighter now. I just want him to go away.

"If you want me to agree to a settlement, you're going to have to hand it over so I know you won't use it against me in the future."

"It's with my lawyer, Kevin. When you sign the paperwork, we'll hand it over."

"How can I be so sure of that?"

"How can I be so sure you'd sign if I handed it over now?" I shoot back.

"Because I'd give you my word."

"Well, your word is bullshit. You promised yourself to me in front of God and you walked away without much trouble. Forgive me if I don't trust you."

He actually laughs. The bastard *laughs*. "Does your meathead boyfriend know you still have a thing for me?"

My mouth falls open. The gall of this man.

"Sorry, Dar, I'm just not interested any more." He

stands up and brushes his hands over his too-tight jeans. "Just give me the box and I'll go."

"I told you, I don't have it. But let me give you this instead: if you don't leave, I'll skip the settlement altogether and hand it over to the police. I bet you'll look real pretty in orange."

"I wouldn't go to prison for that."

"You sure about that? Willing to test it out?"

Taking a deep breath, he narrows his eyes and looks me up and down. "You've changed. I don't like it."

"I don't give a fuck about what you like any more. You're someone else's problem now."

He holds his hands up like he used to when he claimed I was being hormonal. "Then I guess our lawyers will sort this out. Tell the kids I got called away, or something."

"How about you say goodbye yourself this time?"

He scrunches his nose a little. "Nah. I don't do messy."

Then he gives me a nod and heads for the gate, pulling it open before I call after him. "I need to know one thing," I say.

"What?"

"All those conferences, the late nights, the paintball tournaments; were they actually real?"

He runs his tongue along his top lip before he answers. ""I reckon you already know the answer to that one." I do now. Without a doubt. And I once trusted this scum...

"Why? Why did you?"

He chuckles. *The bastard.*

"Why not?" Another brazen shrug. "You had no clue the first time. No. Fucking. Clue. It was too easy. And too fucking good to stop." This time, I don't cry, even though my heart is hurting, I have no more tears left for this man. I feel heat rising up my chest and all over my body, that anxious energy that causes your skin to burn. I'm so angry. So, so angry. He made his choices, and quite frankly, we're all better off without him. As he walks away, I hope we *never* see him again.

## FIFTY-EIGHT

## LEO

"This is Archer, reporting from sunny Melbourne. Make sure you give me a thumbs up at the end of this video, and if you really liked this, click subscribe, and I'll bring you more local news as the shenanigans unfold."

*Shenanigans.* What eight-year-old boy says shenanigans?

Niall gives him the real-life version of a thumbs up as he finishes the recording.

"Did you get it all?"

"Sure did," Naill says, shifting to the side as Archer moves to sit beside him on the couch. If you'd told me a week ago that my closed-off, arrogant, and angry son would be sitting in my house being kind and thoughtful to my girlfriend's little boy, I would have scoffed. It's as though being away from Tash has given him a broader perspective on life. And although he has every right to still be angry and ill-tempered as he deals with the lies he was fed for years, seeing him offering a little boy kindness is making me feel so damn proud. There is good in him.

He and Archer have been recording his voice-over and on-screen news reporting since we got back. It's been a good distraction for whatever is going on with Darcy and Kevin next door. Well, it is for Archer and Niall, anyway. Abby and I are sitting at my dining table with a storm cloud above our heads.

"Are you OK?" I say to her after we've both taken time to calm down.

With a bounce of a shoulder, she leans her head on one hand. "I thought that when we saw him again, it would be like this big happy reunion. But he acted like he didn't even care we were there."

"I'm sorry he behaved that way," I tell her, reaching across the table to pat her arm gently.

A tear falls from her eye but she swipes at it pretty darn fast. "It is what it is. I mean, it's no real shock since he hasn't returned even *one* of my messages in a hundred and twenty days...or whatever," she mumbles, as if embarrassed she knows that detail. *That stupid fuck doesn't deserve this girl.* "But I hoped he'd realise he missed us and he'd visit. I don't know..."

"There's nothing wrong with hoping for the best," I say.

"Well, if he was a real man," Niall puts in, "he'd step up and be a father to his kids. No matter how much you and Mum hated each other, you were *always* there for me, Dad."

"I don't even want him to be my dad," Archer says with a scowl. "He left without saying goodbye and he stole all our money. I'd prefer no dad at all."

Abby's face clouds over as she listens to the boys'

comments. "You're right. I know you're right. I just need to let him go." She pushes her hands away from her like she's shoving something away from her chest. I can see Darcy's strength in her.

"I hear your nana's friends do a pretty good cleansing spell. They did it on your mum on New Year's Day. I don't believe it's magical as much as it's symbolic. But maybe it'll help."

She shrugs. "Maybe."

"Hey Dad," Niall says, loading Archer's video onto his computer so they can cut it all together. "What did you say to that guy when you leaned in?"

"Oh," I say, sitting back in my seat. "I just told him I didn't give up anything with Tash. I found something great with Darcy. Then I thanked him for messing up because his loss is my gain. And I warned him that if he ever does anything to hurt any of you, I'll, ah...make sure he feels very sorry for that." I flash a quick smile as I recall the actual words I used, 'If you so much as upset the hair on their heads, I'll break every bone in your body.' Not my finest moment, but it felt bloody good after watching him push Abigail to the side like that. It took everything I had not to take that pointy weasel face of his and smash it into the ground. He's lucky I'm a calmer man these days.

"You really did that?" Abby asks. "You thanked him for messing up?"

"I did," I say with a nod. "And I meant it. Because if he didn't walk away, I wouldn't have met your mum, and I wouldn't have met you. And I wouldn't be getting a second chance to have a happy family. I have everything I ever wanted in life right here in this room." I let my gaze land on each of the three kids.

"And next door," Archer says. "You can't forget Mummy."

"Oh, I'm not forgetting her. She's standing right there." I point to the hallway where Darcy stands, leaning against the wall as she watches me interact with our kids. And I'm saying *our* kids now, because the moment I fell for her, I welcomed these kids into my life. While I don't want to say I'm going to be a better dad to them than Kevin was, I'm still going to, because these kids deserve something better. We all do.

"Mummy." Archer jumps up and runs over to his mother, wrapping his arms around her as Abigail does the same, crying against Darcy's shoulder. She holds her tight, apologises for Kevin's douchiness, and promises everything is going to be OK. *She's such an amazing mum.*

My heart goes out to them. I never knew my dad, so I never felt the sting of rejection when he walked away. But I did feel the absence of a father figure growing up. My mother was amazing, don't get me wrong, but there's something inside boys that longs for an older man to show them how to navigate this world as a man. It's why I never stopped trying with Niall no matter how hard Tash pushed. And I'm pretty sure girls need men around to teach them how *they* should be treated by the opposite sex. Fathers are important to kids in so many ways. I missed out, and I refuse to let these kids miss out just because Kevin is a fucktard. There was never any doubt in my mind, but I make a vow here and now that I will always treat Abby and Archer as though they're my own.

"Let's give them a moment." I turn to Niall and incline my head towards the sliding door. We move out onto the deck, giving Darcy a chance to talk things through with her kids. Sometimes, being there for someone means knowing when to step away.

"You've got it *so* bad," Niall says, rubbing a hand against his chest as he stretches his legs out in front of him.

"I told you, son, she's the *one* all the stories tell you about. We think they don't exist, but they do. And I swear, your whole body knows about it. Like these little tentacles come out of you trying to grab hold and..." I stop talking because Niall is looking horrified.

"Don't ever describe it like that again. Not to your son, anyway. I don't want to know anything about your tentacles trying to grab hold of her...whatever." He shudders. "*Yick.*"

"Hello," Esme sing-songs from her deck. I hear the sliding door move along the tracks. "Where is everyone?"

"Over here, Ez," I call out before she pops her head around the privacy screen.

"Thought you wouldn't be far. Darcy's bag is inside."

"She's inside mine talking to the kids."

"About moving in to the new place?"

"Their arsehole dad was here," says Niall.

"Oh dear. What did he say to them?"

"Absolutely nothing," I say. "Barely said hello before he wanted to talk to Darcy."

"I hope he doesn't expect she'll take him back."

I shake my head. "I'd say it had something to do with the settlement. He left pretty quick. Kids are upset."

She sighs, her mouth curving down. "What a cretin of a man. I hope he gets gonorrhoea. Or something worse than that. What's worse than gonorrhoea?"

Niall shrugs. "Flesh-eating bacteria?"

"Yes," she says. "I knew there was a reason I adored you, Niall. That's exactly what that man needs. But in his dick so it falls off and he can't use it. I wonder if I have a hex for that."

"Ouch," Niall and I say in unison.

"Remind me never to get on your bad side," Niall says, adjusting in his seat.

Esme holds two fingers at her eyes then turns them to indicate she's watching him.

"Want to join us over here?" I ask. "I don't have much to offer besides water, but the company's OK."

"The company is supreme," she says. "But I'm afraid I have to love you and leave you. I'm meeting Arthur for dinner."

"Arthur? Isn't he the one you thought was getting too serious? Or was that George?"

"No, it was Arthur. He's my only one now."

I can't keep the grin off my face. "Well, well, well. This is a complete one-eighty from the Esme I know. Who are you?"

She lifts her brow in a show of her cavalier attitude. "A woman who's entitled to change her mind. He was very thorough in his wooing techniques and well, he won me over."

"May you have a long and vivacious journey together," I say.

With a grin, she bows her head in thanks. "I appreciate you not putting a label on it, dear. You know how I hate those things."

"I do. Have fun tonight."

"You too. I'm sure you'll have to think up something wonderful to take everyone's mind off he-who-shall-not-be-named."

"Did she just make a Harry Potter reference?" Niall asks, chuffed.

"Of course, I did," Esme says. "I'm old dear, not dead."

"I love her," Niall says as Esme goes inside. "She's the best old bird I've ever met." *She is.* I've watched her take a special shine to Niall, as if knowing that he needed a nana just as much as Abigail and Archer. How she knows exactly what everyone needs is beyond me. Maybe she really is some kind of magical?

"I'm going to miss not living next door to her. But I think we'll see her plenty. She's Darcy's grandmother, after all."

"Hey, I just thought of what we can do tonight."

"What's that?"

"It requires a backyard and a weird-shaped ball," he says as he rubs his hands together. "It's something you're really good at."

"Backyard footy?" I laugh. "I haven't played that with you for years."

"It'll be fun. We can initiate the new kids to the Murphy way of life. Plus, it'll give them a chance to see the new house so they get used to the idea. What do you think?"

"I think we can run it by them and see what *they* think."

"That's the way, pops," he says, slapping me on the arm.

"Hey, Niall," I say a second later.

"Yeah, Dad?"

"Thanks for embracing all this. It means a lot."

He gives me a nonchalant shrug. "It's no biggie. I like seeing you happy. I've given you a lot of misguided crap over the years and this is my way of making up for it. And I've always wanted siblings, so it's about time you sorted that shit out." He finishes with a cheeky grin and I laugh. I love this more relaxed version of my son.

## FIFTY-NINE

DARCY

"Look at me, I'm a meathead," Archer yells, running over the grass with a football under his arm. Abigail races after him, lunging forward to pull the piece of torn material from the back of his shorts.

"Got you. You're tagged," she says, a huge smile on her face as she waves the green cloth in the air.

"Aw man," Archer complains, moving back to where Abby stands so we can get the game moving again. He tucks the material back into his shorts then Niall and myself line up behind him with Leo and Abigail on the other side.

Archer taps the ball on his foot then passes it to Niall, who runs at Leo then fakes left but passes the ball to me instead. I shriek and fumble, all thumbs, before I get hold of the damn thing and run for the plastic chair that marks our goal line.

"Eeek," I shriek, laughing as I'm caught around the waist and lifted off the ground by Leo.

"No contact," Archer yells. I kick my legs, laughing hysterically as I clutch the ball to my chest and Leo tackles me to the ground.

"I'm never letting go," I yell as he tries to tickle it from me.

"Stacks on," Niall yells, and the next thing I know, I've got an extra three bodies landing on top of me.

"This isn't what I signed up for." I cackle, as someone manages to get the ball from under me and we all fall apart in a laughing heap on the soft lawn.

"Having fun?" Leo asks, offering me a hand to help me up.

There are grass stains on my pants and my hair is in my face, but I nod. "I am."

After Kevin left, I had a heart-to-heart with the kids, telling them I didn't think we should make spending time with him a part of the settlement agreement. Instead, I wanted a parenting order drawn up that would give me full custody and release Kevin from any further monetary obligations. "I think that if he doesn't want to be a part of this family then we shouldn't make him," I said.

Archer cried and asked why he didn't just stay away, and surprisingly, Abby said the same. It really hurt her to have him dismiss her the way he did when she was so obviously excited to see him. I don't want to give him the chance to do that to her again.

"What if he changes his mind and tries to see us when we're older?" Abby asked after I explained his reason for coming to Bayside, hating that I was left to do his dirty work yet again.

"That's something that will have to be up to you. I'm not going to stop you from seeing him altogether. But I do think he'll need to put in some effort before he wins you back. No chasing people who don't want to be caught, OK?"

"OK," she said.

When Leo and Niall suggested a welcome-to-the-family BBQ and a game of backyard footy to get the day back on track and lighten the mood, not a single one of us said no. Archer begged to sleep over at the 'new house' since Niall had told him and Abigail about it earlier, and Archer wanted to see his new room.

"Are you OK with this?" I said to Abigail as we grabbed overnight bags.

"It's my own room, Mum. I'm more than OK with it."

As we line up across the backyard, ready for me to take a free kick since Leo broke the body-contact rules and tackled me for the ball, I take a moment to appreciate the people around me and how much my life has changed in such a small amount of time. That day in the hospital car park feels so long ago now. Long gone are the days when I was little more than an inhouse servant to a man who didn't appreciate me. Now I feel loved, I feel happy, and my children's laughter fills my heart. The way I look at it now, I didn't lose anything when Kevin left. I simply dropped the deadweight in my life and gained a wonderful man who complements me as much as he completes me. With him comes an exuberant young man who I'm liking more with every moment I spend with him. Together, our tiny single-parent families make one big family of five. To an outsider, this development would seem really sudden. But if they understood how hurt we'd been—how much we had to fight to get to this point —they wouldn't blink twice, because this, this joy, this laughter, this *light*, is the way it's meant to be.

"Come on, Mummy," Archer groans. "Just kick the ball already."

"All right, all right," I say, pulling my foot back and releasing an almighty kick that sends the ball spinning through the air.

Right into Leo's nuts.

"Oh my God," I cry, covering my mouth as he groans, clutches his privates, then drops to the ground in a moaning heap. "I'm so sorry." I rush to his side, skidding to a stop beside him as I drop to my knees.

"Wrong goalposts, Darce," Niall says as we gather around a red-faced Leo. He leans to the side and coughs, and I reach out and place my hand on his arm.

"I'm so sorry, Leo. Do you need me to get some ice or something?"

"Oh God. No. No ice," he gasps, slowly pushing up on a shaky arm. "Not after last time."

The memory of the first time I tried to help him flashes in my mind. I copped him in the gonads that time too. Suddenly I'm laughing. "I promise I won't throw it at your crotch again," I say.

He shakes his head, glancing my way with the shadow of a smile. "I'm OK," he says, making it to a sitting position. The kids band together to help him up, then I wrap an arm around his waist and walk with him inside the house.

"Did you hurt your knee too, or is it just your balls

this time?" I ask, wondering how full circle we actually came.

"Just my nuts," he says with a chuckle as we lower him to the couch and Niall hands him a bottle of beer that he uses to press against his crotch. Then the kids excuse themselves to go upstairs where their rooms are located. Besides Niall's room, the other two only have a bed and a chest of drawers in them at the moment. But there's already talk about how they plan to decorate.

"I'm so sorry, honey," I say, giggling a little once I hear the kids upstairs. I love hearing their excited chatter.

"You're lucky I love you so damn much," he says, lifting the beer bottle from his crotch to take a drink. "No other human on this earth could get away with clocking me in the balls twice."

I move closer to him and pout. "Do you want me to kiss it better?"

"I do, actually. But I'm going to need a bit before it's in working order again." He holds his arm out and I snuggle in a little closer, draping my arm across his waist as he offers me a sip of his beer.

"It's all yours," I say as I rest my head on his shoulder. "I think you need it more than me." I smile up at him, watching the way his Adam's apple bobs as he takes a drink. "Have I told you how much I love you today?"

"You've listed some very positive traits you believe I possess, and loving me was definitely one of them. But don't let that stop you, I'm happy to hear it all again."

He turns his head so his nose brushes against mine as we both grin like lovesick goofballs. "I love you," I whisper.

"I love you too, angel," he says, touching his lips to mine. "Welcome home." Then he kisses me, slowly, softly, completely. And finally, after months of struggle and piles of hardships, our paths have fully aligned, and the only way forward is together.

## EPILOGUE

### DARCY

*One year later*

"All right, everyone." Leo taps his glass as he stands and raises his voice above the din. "Before we bring the dessert out, I have something I'd like to say."

As the voices quiet and all eyes turn our way, I'm thankful I have a master craftsman to call my own, because without him, there's no way I'd fit this many people around a regular dining table. Leo built me this beautiful extendable table that is perfect for whenever we have company, which is often, because what would our family dinner be without Nana and Betsy joining us? Oh, and Arthur. Seems the dashing older gent has worn Nana down, and she's decided to try a committed relationship one last time. To the chagrin of those in her little black book, for the last twelve months, she and Arthur have been exclusive. And, might I add, utterly adorable. When

I asked her what it was that made her decide to give love another chance, she said that Arthur had a hard-on like a rock and that he took his teeth out for cunnilingus, which made him top of her *to-do* list. After a moment of making it all about sex, she added that he always made her pancakes the next morning and would massage her temples whenever she had a headache. I took that to mean she'd fallen for him and quietly cheered for her. I don't know what happened during her marriages to turn her against the idea of commitment, but I'm very pleased she's found someone to share her life with during her twilight years. We all need someone to love.

"Quick, Leo. Say something or Mum is going to fall asleep waiting on you," Jo says with a laugh, giving Mum a bit of a nudge with her elbow because my usually stoic mother has had a little too much to drink. Somehow over the last twelve months, the woman who ran our lives with military precision growing up, has learned to relax and enjoy some of the finer things in life. Maybe it's because she's visiting Bayside more often and succumbing to the fun-loving influence of Nana, or maybe she's finally mellowing. Either way, our relationship is a hell of a lot better, and I don't dodge her calls as much any more.

"Yeah, get on with it, pops," Niall says with a laugh as Leo waits for everyone to calm down. "Dessert is the best part."

"I'm trying here, son. But if you'll all just shut up for a second, I could get a word out." Each syllable is uttered with a smile on Leo's lips and spark of joy in his eyes. Seeing everyone who means something to each of us in one place is a dream come true to him. Over the past year, he and Niall have become as close as a father and son can be. Having their clouded history cleared up and living under the same roof without Tash's truth-bending influence has been the salve to heal all wounds. Niall knuckled down and completed his final year of high school, achieving such incredible results that he was accepted into the university of his choice to study sports medicine, which is something he's always been interested in. His interest was cemented when Leo had his knee operation, though. They spent countless hours working together on his physio, and Leo is walking and running like a twenty-year-old again.

"I can't be quiet," Niall responds. "Abby is trying to eat mushrooms like they're a burger and it's all wrong. I feel like she's eating mould."

"Well, they are a fungus," Nana says, giving Abby a nod in comradery, because she fully supports Abby's move to veganism. She's had a wonderful time teaching her some of her favourite recipes, the jackfruit pulled pork substitute being the favourite for all of us.

"You could probably do with some more vegetables in your life with all that junk food you shove down your gob," Abby returns with a smile. I've watched my daughter go through a great deal of change this past year. After settling in to her new life in Bayside, she's come out of her quiet, high-grade-chasing shell and become the outgoing, outdoor loving girl I see before me now. She's still doing great at school, but she's found a balance that has room for fun and of course, her first love. She's been dating a boy called Jayden for about six months now, and while I worry incessantly about her, I'm assured by both

Leo and Niall that they both read the boy the riot act. If he so much as touches a hair on Abby's head without her permission, he'll take a long walk off a short pier. But despite being frightened by two giant men, Jayden is sticking around and Abby smiles more than she ever has. She even sits with me at least once every day and talks incessantly about the happenings in her day. We had our rocky road in the months after Kevin left, but once I stopped trying to hide the facts and became open and honest about our situation, our closeness returned. *I have my little girl back*—even though she's growing up now. She'll always be my girl.

"Oh," Archer yells above everyone. "Niall and I are going to Maccas this week to see how many cheeseburgers he can eat before he pukes. I'm going to film it all for YouTube and when he does puke, it'll be in a KFC bucket. Funny, right?"

Remember that video Archer made about the willy warmers? Well, just as he was sure it would, it went viral. All of a sudden, his YouTube subscriber count blew up, and he's become this tiny entertainment entrepreneur who plans out his programming to keep his viewers entertained. Niall helps him out while keeping a watchful big brother eye on the social media aspect of it. It's been a wonderful bonding project for the two of them, and I really appreciate the time and effort Niall puts into it. He's a very different young man than the crass, judgemental arse I met that first morning. It's no surprise that adding a good helping of love into a kid's life brings about positive change. He doesn't have much to do with his mother, but when he does see her or even talk to her via

FaceTime, he's often quite angry and aloof for a few hours afterwards. Sometimes days. Grief takes time to heal from.

As much as I enjoyed working at the café, I returned to work with Leo at the workshop. Despite having a really sexy co-worker, the actual work is more engaging, and it has really good lunch-time perks. Like, *amazing, mind-blowing* perks if you catch my drift. Leo is a master craftsman, but he always struggled with the paperwork side of his business, which is where I come in. I may have gotten my dreamer side from my father, but my organisation skills, inherited from my mother, are top-notch. Leo's filing cabinet didn't know what hit it.

"Before we go off on another tangent," Leo says over everyone. "I want to propose a toast." He lifts his glass and smiles. "To Esme. Without whom, not a single one of us would be in this room today. You brought us all together, coached us to see the beauty in the universe, and to grab on to love with both hands when we found it." He looks at me and beams, taking hold of my hand and pressing a kiss against my knuckles. "We definitely found it," he says, looking into my eyes. I almost cry, because my heart is so full it may actually burst. "And I'm never letting go."

Leo is the man of my dreams, the filler of my heart. He's taken my children under his wing, and he treats me like I'm the absolute light of his life. That date he wanted to take me on was actually in Monte Carlo where he was presenting the World Rugby Award for Try of the Year— something he himself won in his heyday. It was absolutely magical to fly first class and be given the star treatment. But it's the everyday Leo I'm in love with most. The one who likes to take care of me, support me, and be the person I need from one moment to the next—even if he still hasn't figured out how to cook a decent steak.

"*I love you,*" I mouth, and he kisses my knuckles again.

"Tonight marks the eve of the one-year anniversary of when we decided to become a family. Fittingly, it's also the day Darcy's divorce has come through."

"I'm officially single and looking, guys," I tease, laughing when Leo scowls. "Oh look, I found him." He laughs and gives my hand a gentle squeeze.

"I asked you all here today to celebrate family," Leo continues. "To celebrate the best twelve months a man could have, and to thank you all for being a part of that. Here's to many more years together." He lifts his glass of beer in the air and we all lift our various glasses in return and say cheers before we drink. It's a loving sentiment from a loving man. I have to agree with him that the last twelve months have been the best I've had. Once we got over Kevin's abandonment and let Leo and Niall into our lives—our hearts—nothing seemed like it was too much of a burden. We just worked so well together and nothing about us was difficult or a chore.

That's not to say that everything is perfect all the time, we certainly have our tiffs the same as any other couple. But at the crux of things, we know there's nothing we can't overcome. And I think that's what makes the biggest difference. Our love is certain.

"I would also like to say something," Betsy says, rising from her chair as Leo sits down. We all turn our attention to the small woman with her slight hunch and sharp eyes as she looks at us with pride. "I never had a family of my own. But through Esme, I've experienced the love of one. I consider all of you my kin, and getting the chance to watch you come together and blossom has been a great pleasure for this old woman. Especially since I saw all of this in the cards. I was very confident that this day would come, just like I'm very confident about what's in store for the future." She lifts her glass and gives me a wink. "I'd wish you all happiness, but what's a wish when my predictions keep coming true and I already know?"

"What's going to happen?" Abby asks, leaning her chin on her upturned palm, elbow on the table. She loves it when Betsy reads her cards.

Betsy gives her a knowing grin. "That's something I'll let you experience for yourself. But the one thing I'll tell you is that in the next year there'll be a ring. And I'm pretty sure there'll be a puppy too." This time she winks at Archer.

"Oh Betsy," Nana says, shaking her head while she laughs at her friend. "Any one of us could have told you these two will be married in a heartbeat. Your cards are just telling you what we already know."

"You didn't know about the puppy," Betsy says, taking a mouthful of wine.

"Archer's wanted a puppy for years and Leo's been fixing the fence in the backyard," Nana returns, and she and Betsy bicker back and forth while Archer sits there getting more and more excited by the second.

"I think we're visiting the pound next weekend," Leo says, leaning close to my ear.

"And a quick trip to the altar it seems," I add, laughing at Betsy's and Nana's insinuations. Leo and I haven't even discussed whether or not we'll marry. We're happy just being together.

"Yeah, I don't know how they found out about that," he says, pulling a small black box out of his pocket. "I literally bought this on a whim this morning."

"What. Is. That?" My eyes go wide and I simply stare at the box as Leo gets off his chair and kneels in front of me. Suddenly, the bickering stops and the entire table goes silent.

With a beautiful half-smile kicking up the side of his full mouth, Leo holds up the box and looks deeply into my eyes. "Every day since I've met you has been better than the last. You're the light in my heart, and the other half of my soul. When I think about the future, I can't imagine a moment without you in it. So, if you'll have me, I'd be honoured if you'll be my wife. Will you marry me, Darcy, my angel?"

He doesn't even get the chance to open the ring box before I fling my arms around his neck and yell, "Yes! Of course, it's yes. A thousand times."

"Does this mean I can call you Dad now?" Archer yells, wide-eyed and excited, and the next few minutes are filled with kisses and hugs and tears and everything that should come when the man you love asks to marry you in front of all the people who love you both in return.

Archer cries the most, tears of happiness, because despite his bravery over Kevin's decision to leave us, he's still just a little boy wanting to be loved.

Abigail moves in front of Leo and gives him a tight

hug, tears in her eyes. "I hope this means I can call you Dad too?"

"Really?" He pulls away a little and takes her cheeks in his hands, obviously staggered by her request. When she nods, a tear slides from his eye. "I'd be honoured," he says. Both of my children hug him at once, and I think I fall in love a little more. Their father left, and while we know where he is, none of us have tried for a relationship with him because he dealt a lot of hurt and doesn't want a relationship in return. Somehow, in that huge void of pain, Leo stepped in and loved on us so hard that we forgot to be angry anymore. It reminds me of the story Nana tells of the dog I rescued as a child, who'd been feral until I showed it love and gained its trust. That's what Leo did for us. He loved us when we were broken, put up with us when we were a mess, and gave us proof time and time again that we could trust him. He'll be right there whenever we need him, which really, is everything you want in life.

When Leo and I first started out, I spent a lot of time worrying that he'd wake up one day, look at me and see that I wasn't the model or the actress type he'd previously dated. He's reassured me over and over that I'm beautiful in his eyes, but I've struggled to believe him, until he told me that one day we'd be so old that no one will remember what we looked like young. Looks fade, but hearts stay the same. He was attracted to my looks, sure, but what he's in love with is my heart. And that, ladies and gentlemen, is the most beautiful thing anyone has ever said to me.

As I stand with my hands clasped together and happy

tears in my eyes, Leo reaches an arm out towards me and another towards Niall and pulls us in so we're all squished together in a happy-family sandwich.

"I helped him choose the ring," Niall informs me when we finally part. "And I'm glad you said yes. I'm going to call you Mum the Second, because it sounds fancy and will match your new bling." He nods towards the box that still hasn't been opened. And I give him a hug and a kiss on the cheek.

"I'd really like that, Niall."

"Oh, can I put the ring on for you?" Archer asks, looking up at Leo.

"How about we both put it on your mum's finger together, huh?"

Abigail moves to my side and slips her left hand in my right while Leo and Archer kneel on the ground together and pluck a beautiful diamond and emerald ring from the box. "Did you know about this too?" I ask her as she grins happily, nodding.

"It was so hard to keep secret. I had to help them with your ring size since we have the same size fingers."

"Oh, what the hell, I'm joining in," Niall says with a laugh, getting down with them. "You marry the man, you marry the family, right?"

"Right." I laugh, remembering our conversation the first morning I woke up in this house. Leo and our kids were package deals, it was all of us or none of us. It was the only way this could work.

As we gather as a unit, Leo and the boys hold my left hand and the ring slots into the small divot on my ring finger that never seemed to fill in after I removed the gold band Kevin had given me.

Leo stands and takes my face in his hands. "I love you so much," he says.

"I love you too," I return, feeling on top of the world as he kisses me and everyone around the table claps.

Betsy's quick to add, "I told you. The cards are never wrong."

And I have to agree, because my life has never felt more right.

Sign up to the Lilliverse Newsletter to discover more titles, limited offers, and upcoming releases by Lilliana Anderson
https://www.lillianaanderson.com/newsletter

Lilliana's next release is A Beautiful Destination the final instalment of her Beautiful Series.

## ALSO BY LILLIANA ANDERSON

**Preorders (2019)**

Darcy Comes First (Love is a Beach)

A Beautiful Destination

Lying Game

**Cartwright Brothers**

Fool Me Twice

Fools Rush In

Foolish Games

Fool's Errand

Fool's Paradise

**47 Things**

47 Things

One More Thing

**Standalones**

In the Wind

Till There Was You

Never Again

**Drawn Series**

Drawn

Drawn 2 – Obsession

Drawn 2 – Redemption

## Drawn to Fight

Zac & Evie

Hugo & Meg

## Beautiful Series

Too Close

A Beautiful Struggle

Phoenix

A Beautiful Forever

Commitment

A Beautiful Melody

A Beautiful Rock

Devotion

A Beautiful Star

A Beautiful Taste

A Beautiful Danger

## Entwined Series

Our Hearts Entwined

Our Lives Entwined

## The Confidante Trilogy

Confidante: The Brothel

Confidante: The Escort

Confidante: The Madame

For more information on upcoming releases visit

www.lillianaanderson.com/preorders

# ABOUT THE AUTHOR

Bestselling Author of the Beautiful Series, Drawn and 47 Things, Lilliana has always loved to read and write, considering it the best form of escapism that the world has to offer.

Australian born and bred, she writes New Adult Romance revolving around her authentically Aussie characters with all the quirks you'd expect from those born Down Under.

Lilliana feels that the world should see Australia for more than just it's outback and tries to show characters in a city and suburban setting.

When she isn't writing, she wears the hat of 'wife and mother' to her husband and five children.

Before Lilliana turned to writing, she worked in a variety of industries and studied humanities and communications before transferring to commerce/law at university.

Originally from Sydney's Western suburbs, she currently lives a fairly quiet life in suburban Melbourne.

*For more information on Lilliana and her work:*
www.lillianaanderson.com
info@lillianaanderson.com

*To join her Facebook reader group and talk books*
https://www.facebook.com/groups/438800699591852

facebook.com/LillianaAndersonAuthor

twitter.com/confidante_lili

instagram.com/lilliana_anderson

## ACKNOWLEDGMENTS

Time for thanks! This book was truly a labour of love, and I am eternally grateful for the patience, understanding and effort that came from my team. I rarely miss deadlines, and as this book grew and grew, the motivation and understanding that was sent my way was heartwarming.

To, **Marion Archer**, I thank you all for your keen eyes, your amazing patience and funny comments. **Margaret Neal** and **Helena Cullen**, thank you for dropping everything and helping to proof the final copy. As my knuckles get worse, I make more errors and your eyes are my saviours!

To my author friends, blogger friends and readers who share my posts, you're all so wonderful. I don't ask you to do what you do, but you see something I post and share it far and wide. I'm eternally grateful. Thank you all so much. I love you!

To every blogger and reviewer who has an ARC – I

thank you too (please like it!) You are the first step to announcing my work to the world. No author can do this without you, certainly not me xoxox

Also, a big thank you to Wade, my husband. He's very understanding of the long hours and the effort I put in to each book and never moans when I say I'll be finished on the weekend but I'm not finished for another week. I really appreciate his unending support and encouragement.

Thank you to my kids for being my cheer squad and for being so patient while I type and type and type. I love that you all come and sit with me while I work just to spend a bit of extra time with mummy!

And of course – thank you to all of my readers. You are the most important of all. Without you, I would be lost in the sea of words and unread books. You mean the world.

Mwah! xoxox

www.ingramcontent.com/pod-product-compliance
Lightning Source LLC
Chambersburg PA
CBHW051203120726
47905CB00004B/967